THE DEVIL'S ROPE

D0104784

NOVELS
by TIM WASHBURN

WESTERNS

The Rocking R Ranch

The Devil's Rope

THRILLERS

Cyber Attack

Cataclysm

Powerless

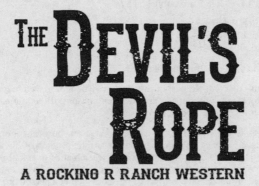

THE DEVIL'S ROPE

A ROCKING R RANCH WESTERN

TIM WASHBURN

PINNACLE BOOKS
Kensington Publishing Corp.
www.kensingtonbooks.com

PINNACLE BOOKS are published by

Kensington Publishing Corp.
119 West 40th Street
New York, NY 10018

All Kensington titles, imprints, and distributed lines are available at special quantity discounts for bulk purchases for sales promotions, premiums, fund-raising, educational, or institutional use. Special book excerpts or customized printings can also be created to fit specific needs. For details, write or phone the office of the Kensington sales manager: Kensington Publishing Corp., 119 West 40th Street, New York, NY 10018, attn: Sales Department; phone 1-800-221-2647.

PINNACLE BOOKS and the Pinnacle logo are Reg. U.S. Pat. & TM Off.

ISBN-13: 978-0-7860-4569-3
ISBN-10: 0-7860-4569-8

First printing: January 2021

10 9 8 7 6 5 4 3 2 1

Printed in the United States of America

Electronic edition:

ISBN-13: 978-0-7860-4570-9 (e-book)

ISBN-10: 0-7860-4570-1 (e-book)

To
Daniel & Nancy Washburn

CHAPTER
1

Under the light of a full moon, Percy Ridgeway repositioned his gun belt as he leaned against the trunk of a large oak tree, waiting. Using the deeper shadows created by the tree's enormous canopy to conceal his presence, it was now a little past midnight and he assumed they'd show up at some point after having done so the four previous nights. And Percy was determined to put a stop to the nefarious activity before things erupted into an all-out range war, something he didn't want but was preparing for anyway.

The spring and summer of 1883 had been as dry as the marriage chances for a seventy-year-old spinster, and water in sufficient quantities was scarce. That and a recent invention now spreading across the West had tempers flaring, turning longtime friends into bitter enemies. So, Percy was waiting, the time ticking down in his head and the sweat trickling down his back.

Along with the drought, the recent problems stemmed from the convergence of two things—one an act of Congress and the other the aforementioned invention. Passed by

Congress on May 20, 1862, the Homestead Act granted any adult citizen who had never taken up arms against the U.S. government the right to claim 160 acres of surveyed public land with the only stipulations that the owner file an application, make improvements, and occupy the land for five years. And now that the hostile Indians had been forced onto reservations, a great swath of land in the center of the country was up for grabs and homesteaders were crowding onto the open range, staking claims for their own pieces of paradise.

The second spark that threatened to ignite a range war was an unheralded invention that had been patented in December 1874 by a man named Joe Glidden on his farm a mile west of DeKalb, Illinois. And it wasn't just happening in Texas. Glidden's brainchild was now having major ramifications for ranchers all across the West. Using a short piece of wire and the guts from an old coffee grinder to create a small, sharp barb, Glidden had revolutionized the barbed wire fence. During the first year of production, Glidden's company produced 32 miles of wire. By the time 1880 rolled around, the factory in DeKalb was cranking out 236,000 miles of wire a year, enough to encircle the earth ten times over. Seeing the end of the open range rapidly approaching, Percy and the rest of the crew at the Rocking R Ranch were early adopters. And they weren't the only ones. Barbed wire fences were now going up all across Texas and some of the more unscrupulous ranchers had a bad tendency of throwing wire around land they didn't own. Roads had been fenced off and public buildings had been fenced in and it appeared that anywhere a man could string a strand of wire was fair game.

Hearing a twig snap, Percy stiffened as he was brought back to the present. He turned his head to see two shadowy figures approaching a section of fence that had already been repaired five times. When they were close enough to touch it, Percy lifted his Colt Single Action Army and cocked it, the four distinctive clicks loud in the stillness of the night. "Touch that wire and the next thing you'll feel is a bullet punching a hole in your forehead."

The two figures froze in place and Percy walked over for a close-up look at them. "You the same two that cut my fence the last four nights?"

"No sir," one of them said, a slight tremor in his voice. "We got stock that need water."

"Not my problem," Percy said, eyeing the two. They were a couple of pimple-faced boys who looked to be no older than thirteen or fourteen. He lifted his eyes and looked beyond them. "Boys, the moon is bright enough to read by and I ain't seeing any cattle or horses. They some special breed that makes them invisible?" Percy asked.

"We'll just be on our way, mister," the same boy said.

"Not just yet," Percy said. "What're your names?"

When neither of the boys offered their names, Percy said, "Either of you ever seen what a .45 caliber slug does to a man? I'll tell you it ain't real pretty. Now, answer my question."

The same boy said, "You ain't gonna shoot us, are ya?"

"Your name?" Percy said.

"I'm . . . Jimmy . . . Jimmy Martin and he's—"

"Shut up, Jimmy," the other boy said.

"Go ahead, Jimmy," Percy said.

"His name's Henry."

"Henry got a last name?" Percy asked.

When neither boy answered, Percy turned his pistol on Henry. "Well, Jimmy, I reckon you might get a chance to see what that big bullet'll do after all."

"Henry Parker," Jimmy blurted out.

"Henry Parker," Percy said. "Any kin to Ira Parker?"

"That's his pa," Jimmy said. "Please, mister, don't shoot 'im."

Percy slowly lowered his weapon. "Henry, did your father send you out here to cut my fence?"

"Look, mister—"

Percy held up a hand, cutting Jimmy off. "Henry's mouth was workin' just fine a minute ago." He turned to Henry. "You got lockjaw, Henry?"

"No," Henry said. "We's workin' for someone else."

"Who?" Percy asked.

Henry bristled at the question. "It don't matter. We ain't cuttin' your fences, are we?"

"No, but I reckon that has more to do with my pistol and not a sudden change of heart," Percy said. "Now, who are you working for?"

"Cal Northcutt," Henry said. "Can we go?"

Percy holstered his pistol and said, "If I ever see you within ten feet of one of my fences again, I'll shoot you on sight. Understand?"

The two young men nodded.

"One more thing," Percy said. "Tell Northcutt I'm comin'. Now git."

Jimmy and Henry turned and took off like a pack of wolves were nipping at their heels. Northcutt, like a half a dozen other men in the area, hadn't invested in fencing and hadn't toiled to string wire around their property because they had none. Him and others like him were open-range ranchers and now that fences were going up, they were being squeezed out. It used to be a man could put together a herd, brand it, and turn it out on the open range along with all the other cattle then cull them out at the next roundup. But that was all changing now, and water for the remaining open-range cattle was as scarce as a virgin in a whorehouse. As far as Percy was concerned, if they wanted access to water, they ought to fork over the money to buy some land just as he and his family had done. Walking down the fence line, he untied his horse, mounted, and rode for home.

It wasn't just the fence cutting and the drought that were weighing heavy on Percy's mind. Cattle rustling was a constant problem and, unfortunately, it was directly related to the Rocking R Ranch's location. Situated hard against the Red River in northwest Texas, a majority of the headaches were caused by the riffraff who hid out in the lawless lands of Indian Territory, just across the river. A den of sin and a refuge for killers, the Territory was home to outlaws of all stripes, most of whom had no legal claim to a single blade of grass in an area that stretched across seventy thousand square miles. Those lands were under the control of the United States government and occupied by another headache-inducing group of people the Indians. And there were thousands of them, all hailing from dozens of tribes who had spent an eternity stalking and killing one another. The only common trait they all shared was their hatred of the white man, and the ranch was only a stone's throw from some of the meanest, cruelest, and deadliest Indians to ever walk the planet—the Comanches and the Kiowas. They were only a few years removed from raping and killing whites all across Texas, and Percy had his own run-in with them after they kidnapped his niece Emma Turner and held her for over a year. It was just plain old bad luck, Percy thought, that they would all spend the rest of their days in such close proximity.

When he reached the barn, Percy quieted the noise in his head and climbed down from his horse. After unsaddling the mare and slipping off the bridle, he turned her loose in the corral and exited the barn. Exhausted, he knew he would be in for another long day tomorrow. Every day was a long day when you ran ten thousand head of cattle on a ranch that sprawled across sixty thousand acres. And, on top of that, he would need to carve out some time to have a chat with that asshole Cal Northcutt. Climbing the steps to the back porch of his house, Percy pushed off his boots and slipped inside.

CHAPTER
2

While Percy lurched tiredly toward his bed, his older son, Chauncy, was having difficulty just finding the room he had rented at a run-down boardinghouse in Fort Worth. After an evening of overindulgence, Chauncy was pinwheeling off the walls and jiggling door handles, not really sure if he was even in the right building. Then he remembered his cousin was staying with him for a few days, so he stopped, sagged against a wall, and began shouting his cousin's name.

A door down the hall cracked open and Seth Ferguson stepped out. "Hush, Chauncy," he said in an angry whisper. Seth walked down, took Chauncy by the elbow, and led him back to the room.

Although Fort Worth wasn't all that different from the other cow towns that had sprouted up across the frontier, there was one section of the growing city that was uniquely Texan. Residents of the city had several names for it but only one really hinted at the types of people who might inhabit that area—Hell's Half Acre. And the boardinghouse where Chauncy and Seth were staying was smack in the middle of it all.

The Acre, as most folks called it, was situated on the south side of town and had been the perfect resting stop for tired cowboys who were pushing cattle up the Chisholm Trail to the railheads in Kansas. But that eventually petered out and that portion of the cattle trail was replaced by a train depot for the Texas and Pacific Railway, funneling even more people into the rowdy red-light district. Home to a dense cluster of boardinghouses, hotels, bordellos, gambling parlors, saloons, and dope dens, the Acre also offered refuge to murderers, swindlers, crooks, outlaw gangs, and a slew of other unredeemable souls. And the "Half Acre" was a misnomer because the den of debauchery and deviant behavior now sprawled across two and a half acres. And with doors that never closed, the district operated like a well-oiled machine, where corrupt local lawmen would turn a blind eye after lining their pockets with bribes.

Once Seth had Chauncy safely inside their room, Seth climbed back in the single bed and left Chauncy to fend for himself. This wasn't the first time his cousin had returned to the room in a drunken stupor and Seth was getting tired of it. Chauncy floundered around and finally got his boots off before back-flipping onto the bed, crushing Seth.

"You're layin' on top of me," Seth hissed, trying to push Chauncy over to his side.

"Funny," Chauncy slurred, "I heard somethin' just like that not more'n a few minutes ago." Chauncy let loose with a loud laugh that rattled the headboard.

"Shh," Seth said, clamping a hand on Chauncy's mouth. "You're gonna get us kicked out of here." Although angry at his cousin, Seth was curious. He rolled up onto his side and said, "Who was it?"

Chauncy pulled Seth's hand away from his face. "Marcie Malone."

"Again?" Seth asked. Marcie was a parlor house girl, the cream of the crop when it came to sporting girls in the Acre.

"Yep."

"What did that cost you?"

"On the house."

"It was not."

"Was. Payback for runnin' off that guy who was pesterin' her this mornin'."

"I was there. Do I get a free one?"

"I reckon you'll have to ask her, if you got the moxie."

Chauncy had hit a nerve with that statement. Seth had been in town a few days and hadn't yet worked up enough courage to enter any of the sporting houses. "You ask, or did she offer?"

"Offered," Chauncy said.

Seth rolled onto his back. "Figures."

Tall at six-two, Chauncy was rangy and strong like his father and, with his long, dark hair and an obsessively groomed mustache, the women fell all over themselves to get at him. It was more than looks, though. Chauncy exuded confidence and he had an edginess to him that Seth found hard to explain. The best comparison Seth could come up with was that Chauncy was like a coiled rattlesnake—fine if left alone but deadly if disturbed. Whatever it was, the women lapped it up like a litter of puppies.

Unable to go back to sleep, Seth's mind wandered. A head shorter and thirty pounds lighter than Chauncy, women weren't tripping over themselves to earn his favor.

Although well educated after recently graduating from Washington and Lee University, Seth was finding that book learning wasn't a high priority among the female species along the frontier. Still young at twenty-two, he wasn't overly concerned about finding a mate and he was focusing most of his energy on launching his legal career after spending three years apprenticing with a large firm back East.

Seth startled when a series of gunshots erupted outside. He thought about getting up for a look, but this was the fourth night in a row he'd heard gunfire and he was ready to hightail it out of there. The only reason he had come was to talk to Chauncy about returning to the ranch or, if that failed, to convince him to leave this hellhole and go somewhere else—a place where a man didn't put his life in jeopardy every time he stepped outside.

CHAPTER
3

Waking from another nightmare, Emma Turner lay still as she listened for any subtle changes in the inner workings of her small three-room home, hoping the horror show had been in her head and not a premonition of things to come. Everything appeared normal inside, so she turned her attention to the open window above her bed. She was listening for any noises—a squeak of leather, a stamping horse, the whisper of footsteps on brittle grass—that might signal an enemy in their midst. After listening for several moments, she didn't hear anything unusual and she released the breath she had been holding. Of course, that didn't relieve all of her anxiety because she hadn't heard the Indians the last time, either. And that remembrance killed any hope of going back to sleep. She tossed back the sheet and climbed out of bed. After stripping off her sweat-soaked nightgown, she pulled on an old dress and wandered into the kitchen, pulled out a chair, and sat.

The nightmares weren't anything new and she had hoped they would have faded with time. But here it was a decade later and the nightmares were as realistic and vivid as the day they were imprinted into her memory. Held for over a year by the Comanches, she had seen things that no human should ever have to see and had endured hardships that no human should ever be forced to endure. But damn it, she wondered again for the hundredth time, was she going to be a captive to those things for the rest of her life? She knew it was an unanswerable question and she also knew the passage of time was the only variable that might eventually provide an answer.

Thirteen then and twenty-three today, any hope for a normal life had faded as quickly as the ranch buildings in the distance after the four savages had captured her one evening while she was picking blackberries along the river. The Indians had appeared seemingly out of nowhere and the heartache of watching her home growing smaller and smaller until it had finally disappeared was still palpable all these years later.

She tried to wall it off in her mind as she stood and walked over to the stove to grab a match. Striking it on the table, she lit the coal oil lamp that hung over the table and then walked over to light the lantern by the stove before dropping the match into the washtub. As the lanterns sputtered to life, she studied the stove for a moment and thought about starting a fire for coffee then decided against it, her fresh dress already damp with sweat. Instead, she grabbed a hand towel and stepped out the back door. The moon was still up, providing plenty of illumination as she walked over to the recently drilled water well the family shared. She engaged the pump on the windmill and waited for the cool, clear water to appear before dipping her head and taking a long drink. She wet the towel, squeezed out the excess, and wiped her face and arms.

After rinsing the towel, she draped the cool cloth around her neck and made her way around to the front porch and took a seat in one of the rocking chairs.

Leaning back, Emma looked up at the full moon and remembered the times when its appearance had struck fear in the hearts of Texans all across the frontier. Called a Comanche moon, the Indians had used the moon's light to raid, rape, and kill all across the state. But no more, Emma thought. The army had seen to that and the last of the hostile savages had been herded back onto the reservation years ago. Still, given her history and the two-legged vermin that roamed the lawless lands across the river, Emma never strayed more than a few steps from the house without cinching on her gun belt. And, as she thought about it now, she felt naked without a gun. Standing, she cracked the front door and reached up to grab the rifle that hung there. She eased the door closed and returned to her chair, propping the rifle against the side of the house. There was no need to check to see if the rifle was loaded—it stayed that way at all times.

Emma's home was the last in a line and the closest to the river, which left her feeling exposed at times. But of the six family homes, hers was the last to be built and it was either put it there by the river or on the other side, near the busy barn and the always-bustling bunkhouse. Lined out in a horseshoe pattern, the homes were originally configured that way to better ward off an Indian attack and now that that threat had been diminished, they constructed new homes using the old layout simply out of habit. Emma could have built elsewhere on the ranch, but she enjoyed sharing the large backyard with the rest of the family. Or that was the excuse she had used at the time, but her overriding concern had always been safety, not just for herself but mostly for her nine-year-old son, Simon, who was asleep inside.

Although Simon was conceived without Emma's consent and born on the last day of her captivity, there was still a good part of her in him and leaving him for the savages to raise had never entered her mind. She did have some concerns about Simon's paternity that still lingered all these years later. It could have been any of a half a dozen men who had repeatedly violated her and that included the evilest of her abductors, the one she'd named Scar, who had violently assaulted her on multiple occasions. She couldn't bear the thought that her sweet boy was the byproduct of one of those brutal encounters and it nagged her on occasion. She had tried to piece together what had happened and when, but she had lost all track of time, days, and dates during captivity. And to further complicate matters, the Indians had no concept of time and there were too many missing fragments to construct the exact sequence of events.

At the time of Simon's birth and her release, most of the male Indians had been away from camp for many months and she had no idea if any of her tormentors knew she had been pregnant much less that she had delivered a healthy baby boy. Despite that, she lived with the constant worry that the Indians might one day discover Simon's Comanche heritage. She knew kinship was strong among the Indians and she had no doubt they would try to lure Simon into their clutches if they were ever made aware of his existence.

Hearing the sound of approaching horses, Emma reached for the rifle, pulled it onto her lap, and cocked the hammer. A few seconds later a couple of riders rode by and she could tell from their silhouettes that it was a couple of ranch hands who were on their way to the bunkhouse. Emma eased the hammer down and leaned back in her chair.

Sometimes she felt as if she were cursed. Finally, after years of shying away from the touch of another man, she had found one who would have accepted her for who she was—a damaged and scarred Indian captive trying to find her way in the world. She had thought her life had taken a turn for the better when she ever so slowly warmed to a cowboy who had refused to take no for an answer. Joe Anglin, who had ridden for the Waggoner's Triple-D, had started a slow, gentle, months-long courtship with Emma, which finally led to her dropping her guard just enough to let him get close to her, to touch her, to kiss her. As they began to contemplate a future together, Emma's bad luck intervened again, and Joe had died after being thrown from his horse. Instead of planning a future, Emma found herself planning a funeral and, after that, turned her attention from men to horses in hopes of improving the ranch's equine bloodlines.

Tired of thinking and suddenly craving a cup of coffee, Emma stood and walked out far enough to get a glimpse of her grandmother's house and saw a lit lantern through the kitchen window. She walked back to grab her rifle and headed for her grandmother's.

Emma crossed the back porch and tapped lightly on the door before pushing it open. Her grandmother was sitting at the kitchen table while her cook, which she'd refused forever, puttered around in the kitchen. Her grandmother looked up and smiled when Emma entered. "Still totin' a gun, I see," Frances said as she pulled out a chair for Emma.

Emma propped her rifle against the wall and sat as the cook, a thin-framed, middle-aged Mexican woman named

Maria Garcia, placed a steaming mug of coffee in front of her. "*Gracias*, Maria," Emma said.

Maria rubbed Emma on the shoulder and said, "*De nada*," before returning to the stove.

Frances took a sip from her cup, swallowed, and said, "You look pale. Another nightmare?"

Emma lifted her cup and blew on it to cool it then took a tiny sip. "Yes. Will they ever stop?"

"They will when you die. Don't know much about between then and now, though. Have they tapered off over the years?"

"Some. I can go long spells without one, but then something'll trigger them to start up again."

"What's usually the trigger?" Frances asked. "Does just seein' an Indian bring it all back?"

"Not necessarily."

"Well, answer me this, then. Do you see the same images, say, faces, in your nightmares or is everything blurry?"

"Some of both, but definitely a face or two. The meanest one I called Scar, for sure, and the chief, of course."

"Have you thought about reporting their abuses to the Indian agent?"

"No," Emma said. "I'm not sure it would do any good after all this time. Besides, it'd just be my word against theirs."

Frances wanted to say there was living proof back at Emma's house, but she didn't. It wasn't Simon's fault that Emma had been abused, and everyone in the family loved the boy dearly. "I don't know. There're all types of people filing claims for Indian depredations back in the day.

Seems like you ought to be able to report a crime and have the government do something about it."

"I don't know that I want to relive all of that."

Frances turned and looked her granddaughter in the eye. "Why not? You're relivin' it just about every night as it is."

CHAPTER
4

Frances remained seated as she watched her granddaughter depart a while later, a wave of sadness and remorse washing over her. Emma, a beautiful, red-haired young woman in the prime of her life, had suffered enough grief and sadness to fill a half a dozen lifetimes. And it saddened Frances that Emma didn't have what other women her age had—a brood of babies and an adoring husband. Joe's death, after the many struggles Emma had endured to fit back into a normal life, had snuffed any remaining light in her granddaughter's eyes.

Back in those days the return of an Indian captive had been big news and Emma's return, especially with a child, had been splashed across the front pages of newspapers all across the country, despite the family's best attempts to shelter her. Because of that, Frances had tried to steer Emma and Simon away from the ranch many times, but to no avail. Her thinking had been that life would have been much easier for both of them if they could have escaped to somewhere their pasts couldn't follow—a place far removed from the constant reminder of the Comanches' continued existence just across the river. But Emma had refused all of Frances's offers of financial support and had planted her roots deeper into the sandy soil of the Rocking R, much to her grandmother's chagrin.

Frances sighed, pushed back her chair, and stood. After stepping over to the stove to top off her coffee, she asked Maria how long until breakfast then shuffled out to the front porch and sagged into one of the rocking chairs. The eastern sky was awash with the light of the coming dawn, painting the underside of the clouds a pink-purplish hue. At seventy-four, Frances didn't know how many sunrises were left in her future nor did she spend much time contemplating such things. A practical woman, she had always taken life as it came and her only regret was that her husband of forty years, Cyrus, wasn't there to greet a new day with her. Gone ten years now, Cyrus had died far from home during the long, fruitless search for the savages who had taken Emma. It was just one more reason she wanted to see the Comanches punished for what they'd done.

Her oldest son, Percy, now ran all the ranch operations, relegating Frances to the role of interested observer. Which was fine with her. Although still relatively healthy, she didn't want to be bothered by the day-to-day operation of a busy ranch that now stretched over ninety square miles. Percy had added to the ranch over the years until the homesteaders had crowded in all around them, severing any hope for expanding the ranch any further. The world was changing so quickly, Frances was having a hard time keeping up.

A train ride to the world was now as close as Wichita Falls, eight miles away. The Pony Express had come and gone as had the stage lines that had once ferried people across great swaths of the country on trips that had taken weeks to complete. Now there was no stopping to trade out tired horses, only to take on water or coal to keep the trains chugging along day and night. Frances had read somewhere that she could get on a train in New York City and step off in San Francisco only a few days later. That same trip, which would have taken most of a year only fifteen years ago, was now possible within a single week. It seemed unfathomable to Frances and, being a curious person, she wondered what else was coming down the pike. Not that she'd be there to see these things, and that depressed her some because there had more changes in the last ten years than at any point in her life. Frances drank her coffee and watched the sun rise for a few minutes before heading back inside to eat some breakfast.

Maria was at the table and already eating when Frances entered. She refreshed her coffee and grabbed a plate. Not particularly hungry, she opted for a single biscuit, two pieces of bacon, and a spoonful of scrambled eggs before taking a seat at the table. "Maria, you done much train travelin'?"

"Some," Maria said. "We took train to El Paso then another into Mexico to see *mi madre y padre*."

"How was it?"

"Is good."

"Much quicker than a horse or wagon, huh?"

"Sí. Mucho."

"How were the accommodations?"

Maria cocked her head to the side and said, *"¿Qué?"*

"Were you comfortable during your travels?"

Maria nodded. *"Sí.* You take train?"

Frances broke off a chunk of biscuit, put it in her mouth, and started chewing as she pondered that question. After a couple of moments, she swallowed and said, "Maybe."

Why not go? Take Emma and Simon to San Francisco to see another part of the world? Frances folded a piece of bacon into her mouth as those questions buzzed around her brain. She was still in good health and was mentally as sharp has she'd ever been. Plus, there was the added bonus that Emma might meet a suitor or come to the realization that living elsewhere might not be such a bad idea.

The more she thought about the trip the more she liked the idea. Percy might complain about the costs, but there hadn't been any major outlays since the rebuild after a monster twister had ripped through the ranch a few years ago. Besides, Frances thought, the family shared the profits equally and she had as much claim to the money as anyone did. The only sticking point Frances could foresee was if her two daughters, Abigail and Rachel, insisted on going. Not that she wouldn't want them along, but more people meant more expenses. However, the sharing of family finances allowed Rachel and Abigail to make their own decisions and if they wanted to travel along, they could. There would be headaches for sure—the hotels once there, the meals, the immense amount of baggage that would be required, and the inevitable family bickering—but nothing that wasn't insurmountable. Frances tore off another piece of biscuit, put it in her mouth, and chewed while she ruminated.

If a trip was in their future, it would need to be soon while she was still able. The time of the year was also going to be important. If they left too soon and traveled on the Southern Pacific rail line, they would roast on the train as it crossed the southern deserts into California. And if they left too late and chose a more northern route, they risked running into bad weather in the mountains. Of course, Frances had traveled neither route and all she was doing was speculating. Deciding the matter needed deeper study, she pushed back her chair and stood. "Thank you for breakfast, Maria."

"De nada," Maria said.

"Don't worry about fixing dinner for me. I'm going to ride over to Wichita Falls for the day."

"What you do there?" Maria asked.

"I'm gonna find out how to get to San Francisco on a train."

Maria cocked her head to the side again and with a confused look on her face, asked, "You go today?"

Frances chuckled. "No, but maybe soon."

After dressing in a skirt, shirt, and boots, Frances grabbed her Remington derringer off the fireplace mantel and dropped it into her pocket. She pulled a rifle down from a rack that contained a half a dozen other long guns, put on her stylish straw bolero, and turned to ask Maria if she needed anything from town.

"No," Maria said. "Be careful."

"I will," Frances said. "Don't worry about supper, either. In fact, take the rest of the day off, Maria."

"¿Pagada?" Maria asked.

"Sí, paid."

Maria smiled and Frances returned the smile before turning and exiting the house. Before delving too far into the details of the trip, she first needed to find out if Emma had any interest in going. Frances walked over to the barn and went inside, where she stowed the rifle in the smaller drop-front phaeton carriage and asked one of the hands, Morgan Anderson, to hitch up a horse, which he promptly agreed to do. She had contemplated saddling a horse, but her right hip was acting up again and she thought the carriage looked more comfortable. Frances said "Morning" to a few more ranch hands on her way out then turned toward Emma's house.

With the sun already up, a tardy ranch rooster crowed, momentarily startling her. Frances smiled as a chorus of other roosters announced their responses and she stopped at the communal chicken coop and opened the gate to let the chickens out for the day. A few eager hens were the first out, and they dispersed quickly in search of grubs or grit. Dottie, an older Plymouth Rock hen with black-and-white barred plumage, fell in behind Frances and followed along like a dog. Dottie's egg production had slowly declined over the last couple of years and she rightly belonged in someone's cookpot, but she was such a pet that no one on the ranch had the heart to kill her. Dottie was soon distracted by a grasshopper that fluttered up and she went chasing after it.

Although early, it was already blistering hot, and Frances's shirt was damp with sweat by the time she made it to Emma's house. She ascended the steps to the back porch and walked over to the door, knocking lightly before easing it open. Any expectation of privacy among family members had gone out the window long ago. Emma was sitting at the table thumbing through a mail-order catalog.

"What's wrong?" Emma asked, rising to her feet.

Frances waved a hand. "Nothing's wrong. Now sit."

"I don't remember the last time you came a-callin'."

Frances pulled out a chair and sat. "I know. Seems like everyone eventually ends up at my house."

"As it should be," Emma said. "Everybody likes to go to Grandma's house."

"Speakin' of goin' places, I was wonderin', now that train travel is so easy, if you and Simon would join me on a trip to San Francisco?"

Emma's eyes widened in surprise. "You're going to San Francisco?"

"Only if you'll come. Maybe leave sometime next month and spend a couple of weeks out there?"

"How long does it take to get there?" Emma asked.

"Don't know. I'm on my way into town and to have a talk with someone at the train station to get that all figured out. What do you think?"

Emma chewed on her bottom lip as she thought about it. "I don't have much money."

"I'll worry about the money."

Emma thought about it for another moment and then said, "In that case, we would love to go. I'll double-check with Simon when he gets in from milking, but I can't see him turning it down. It sounds too exciting. Are you sure you feel up to traveling?"

"I'm not dead, yet."

Emma leaned over and hugged her grandmother. "Thank you."

Frances patted Emma on the back and said, "It'll be a grand adventure."

CHAPTER
5

Percy paused by the front door long enough to strap on his gun belt and don his Stetson before stepping out of the house and into the dawning of a new day. Unfortunately, there was no dew on the grass and no hint of any moisture on the cloudless horizon. Percy didn't know how long the ranch's natural springs would hold out and he sure didn't want to find out. Due to decreased flow in the river, the salinity of the water had increased daily and was now unfit to drink. Although deeply concerned about the water issue, it was grass Percy was looking for this morning. And he thought he knew just the place to find some, if he could afford it. Thinking that thought, he turned and traced his steps back to the house and grabbed his rifle and a few extra boxes of ammunition. After all, he would be riding into Indian Territory—always a dicey proposition—after making a call on Cal Northcutt.

Percy exited the house again and headed toward the barn. A tall man at six-two, his long stride ate up the distance in a hurry. He looked over the hitched buggy sitting just outside the barn door and wondered who was going on a ride. That question was answered a moment later when he spotted his mother stepping out of the barn with a buggy whip in her hand.

"Where are you goin'?" Percy asked.

"Riding over to Wichita Falls."

Percy propped a foot on the spoke of one of the wheels. "Can't you send a ranch hand over to fetch what needs fetchin'?"

"I don't want to send a ranch hand. And I'm not fetchin' anything but information."

"On what?"

"Train travel," Frances said. She didn't really want to have this discussion with Percy until she had her facts all lined up.

"Where you goin'?"

"Don't know yet," Frances lied. "I want to learn how it all works. Switching trains and all that, you know."

Percy slipped his foot out and stood. He pushed his hat back on his head and looked at his mother. "Just seein' how it works, huh? Let me ask you a question, Ma. Was I born at night?"

"As a matter of fact, you were. At eleven-thirteen p.m."

"But it wasn't last night, was it?"

Frances frowned and said, "You're too funny. I'm just explorin' an idea, okay?"

Percy smiled. "I'm just joshin' you, Ma. If you want to travel, have at it, but I hope you're not thinkin' of doin' it alone."

"I'm not."

"Good. Just so you know, I might be gone for a day or two."

"Where are you going?" Frances asked.

"To see a man about some grass after I pay a call on a man in town. If you'll wait while I saddle my horse, I'll ride along with you."

"I'm not in any hurry. I'll wait."

Percy slipped inside the barn, propped his rifle against one of the horse stalls, grabbed a rope, and headed out to the corral on the other side. His favorite mare, Mouse, was still in the corral from yesterday afternoon. Hiding the rope behind his back and holding his left hand out, he approached her slowly, talking in a soft voice. She used to be harder than a rabbit to catch and she still had her moments, but she'd gotten better as she'd aged. Now about fourteen years old, Mouse allowed Percy to walk straight up to her and he slipped the rope over her neck and led her inside the barn.

After saddling Mouse and stowing his rifle, Percy led the horse outside and mounted up. Frances slapped the reins and clucked her tongue, putting her buggy in motion as Percy fell in beside her. They rode in companionable silence for a while, each busy with their own thoughts. And Percy had a lot on his mind. In addition to his upcoming confrontation with Cal Northcutt, he mulled over the lingering drought, the fence cutting, and the always-changing cattle industry. He steered Mouse closer to the buggy so he and his mother could talk. She knew the cattle business inside and out and had been an invaluable resource for Percy over the years.

"Ma, what do you think the future for cattle is?"

"I think the homesteaders are gonna eventually squeeze the smaller ranchers out of business. And that mess of the state givin' away a bunch of land out in the Panhandle to pay for a new capitol building in Austin is a disaster waitin' to happen. From what I hear, that outfit took a bunch of investment money from some folks in England and Scotland and they're likely a drought or a hard winter away from goin' belly-up before they even get started."

"You're probably right, but those folks out west aren't going to be squeezed as hard as we are, though. At least for the foreseeable future. Charlie Goodnight's got a big spread he's runnin' out of the Palo Duro Canyon, but it's bein' fronted by an Irish moneyman named John Adair. I hear they're still buyin' up land."

"More land, more cattle," Frances said. "And that would be fine if Mother Nature always played by the rules. What about you, Percy? You tired of punching cows yet? We could sell half the ranch and half the cattle and put our feet up and still have enough of a herd and enough land to maintain a very comfortable lifestyle."

"Pa didn't want the ranch broken up."

"Your pa's been dead ten years, Percy. He doesn't have a say in the matter anymore."

"Are you wantin' to sell some of the land?"

"Not necessarily. Financially we're still in good shape, aren't we?"

"Yes, for now."

"Don't you get tired of it all?"

"Don't know what else I'd do."

"You could find another woman and settle down. Maybe even travel together. See what the rest of the world looks like. Mary's been gone a long time, too."

Percy decided it was time to change the subject. "You all of a sudden get the travel bug or what?"

"If I still had to travel by horse and wagon, no. But traveling out west by train sounds doable. I don't have many years left on this here earth and I'd like to see a little more of it before then."

"West, huh? How far west you plannin' to go?"

As Frances debated about telling Percy her plans, she pulled on the left rein, steering the buggy around a washed-out area. Once clear, she gently pulled the right rein until the horse returned to the trail. She looked Percy over, reading his body language to get a sense of his current temperament. As his mother she was an expert and if he was upset about the thought of her taking a trip, it wasn't apparent. He wasn't all tensed up and was, instead, riding easy in the saddle. "I want to take Emma and Simon to San Francisco."

Percy nodded. "When are you thinking about going?"

"I don't know yet. Soon probably. I thought maybe we would stay out there a couple of weeks. Why?"

"I was trying to figure out the timeline of Emma's horse-breedin' duties. Doesn't sound like it's goin' to be a problem. The mares she bred in the spring won't start foaling until after the first of the year."

"Sounds like she's takin' the job serious."

"She is," Percy said. "She's smart as a whip. I just wish she'd devote a little less time to the horses and spend a little more time lookin' for a husband."

"She might not find one," Frances said.

"Why not?" Percy asked. "She and Joe were talkin' about tyin' the knot before he went and got killed. There's plenty of men out there that would be tickled to death to get a pretty gal like Emma."

"Whatever those savages did to her, scarred her bad. She's still havin' nightmares."

"There are some things you just can't fix. But a man and a passel of babies might make all the difference in the world. Get her so busy she don't have any time to think and all that stuff fades away."

"I've wondered if it would help her to confront some of those savages who had a hand in it. You know some of them have to be over there on the reservation."

"Might make things worse. Probably best to leave it lay."

"You aren't the one having nightmares. I wish I knew who they were. I'd ride over with my ten-gauge for a little payback."

"It's been a long time, Ma. No doubt, they did wrong by kidnappin' her, but by the time we found her, the Comanches had looked at Emma as part of their tribe."

"Making her a member of their tribe makes it sound so civilized when it was anything but. She certainly didn't choose to go live with those heathens. They tortured that girl. And they ought to be punished for it."

Percy was tired of the conversation and didn't respond. It was a problem with no answers. The bottom line, as Percy saw it, was that Emma needed to generate enough mental willpower to defeat the demons that still occupied her mind.

"Who are you goin' to see in town?" Frances asked.

"Cal Northcutt, a two-bit, part-time cowpuncher who runs one of the saloons in town."

"So, not a friendly meeting?" Frances asked.

Percy cut his eyes over to his mother. "The man paid a couple of boys to cut our fences. What do you think?"

"So, not friendly, I see."

"No. He's been running a bunch of cattle on the open range and now that everybody's stringing wire he don't have a place to put 'em or anyplace to water 'em. If he wants to run some cows, he needs to buy his own damn property like the rest of us."

Frances looked at her son and said, "Might be best if

you left that pistol of yours in a saddlebag during this here meetin'."

"I don't see it comin' to gunplay and you never know who else might be in the saloon. My pistol is fine right where it's at."

They rode in silence for the remainder of the trip, which wasn't far. With the ongoing drought, the Wichita River, which encircled the northern part of town, was little more than a trickle, and they crossed easily. As they entered, Frances turned left toward the train depot and Percy steered his horse toward the center of town.

Although this part of the country had been known as Wichita Falls for a few years, it had never been more than a wide spot on the river until the Fort Worth & Denver City Railroad extended their rail line from Fort Worth to Wichita Falls. The first train had arrived in September of 1882, the same day town lots were offered to the public. Percy had been there that day and the Ridgeway family were now the proud owners of a dozen town lots as a hedge against the crazy swings in the cattle market. The land had already appreciated a good deal, but Percy's goal was to lease the parcels and use the rental income as another source of ready cash. When he stopped Mouse in front of the Falls Saloon, he took a moment to clear his head. A man couldn't enter a possible confrontation with his head muddled by a bunch of nonsense. Climbing down, he checked to make sure his pistol was where he wanted it, and wrapped Mouse's reins around the hitching post.

Stepping up onto the boardwalk that fronted the saloon, he leaned against a porch post and spent a moment surveying the area. With advance warning, Percy wanted to make sure that Northcutt hadn't put together a welcoming party. The town was busy, with wagons and single riders jockeying for position along the hard-packed dirt street. Percy saw four other horses tied to the hitching post in front of the saloon and the only brand Percy recognized was the L on the left shoulder of a large, good-looking sorrel gelding. Why Sam Burnett, who owned the Four-Sixes ranch, branded his horses with an L was a mystery to Percy. But that was for another time. Refocusing on the reason for his visit, he turned, walked over to the saloon's entrance, and pushed through the swinging door.

He paused a moment to let his eyes adjust. When they did, he saw three cowboys standing at the bar and the bartender, a bald man nearly as wide as he was tall, was busy regaling the cowboys with a story. Sitting at a small table at the back of the room with a cup of coffee in front of him and a smirk on his face, was Cal Northcutt.

"Well, looky here, fellers," Northcutt said in a loud voice. "The famous Percy Ridgeway has blessed us by appearin' in my humble establishment. Ain't we lucky?"

Percy ignored Northcutt and quickly sized up the four men at the bar, making a mental note of their positions and who was armed and who wasn't. Two of the punchers were wearing gun belts and Percy assumed the barkeep had some type of weapon behind the bar. He turned and walked toward the back of the saloon.

"I heard you might be stoppin' by," Northcutt said loudly. "I reckon it's my lucky day."

Northcutt, who looked to be in his early forties, was a short, thin man with a beak for a nose and a face flush with hard edges—a pointy chin, sharp cheekbones, and a prominent brow. An ugly man, Percy thought as he walked up to the table and stopped. Northcutt wasn't wearing a gun, but Percy pegged him as the type of man to have one hidden somewhere on his person.

There had been several things Percy had learned during his time riding with the Texas Rangers that stayed with him today. He'd learned the best way to settle a dispute was not through idle threats, but through clear and decisive action.

"Have a seat if you want," Northcutt said, waving his hand at one of the vacant chairs.

"No, thanks. I won't be here long. Stand up."

"I ain't armed."

"I didn't ask if you were armed. I said, stand up."

When Northcutt made no effort to stand, Percy muttered, "I tried to do it the right way." He stepped around the table, balled his right hand into a fist, and, with a hard, straight punch to the face, knocked Northcutt off his chair. Percy sidestepped the chair, leaned down, grabbed a fistful of Northcutt's shirt, lifted him about a foot off the ground, and hit him with a haymaker right that crunched Northcutt's nose. As the blood streamed down Northcutt's cheeks, Percy looked the man in the eye and said, "Next time we meet, you better be reaching for a gun."

Percy released his grip and Northcutt's head bounced off the hardwood floor when he landed. Percy stood up straight, turned, and walked out of the saloon.

CHAPTER
6

Chauncy sat up in bed and cradled his head in his hands. It felt like a tiny person wielding a large hammer had wormed its way into his brain with the sole purpose to create as much misery as possible. He lifted his eyes from the floor and stopped when his gaze landed on Seth, who was sitting in the chair by the window, reading a book. "Whatcha readin'?"

Seth looked up. "*The Adventures of Tom Sawyer.*"

"Who's Tom Sawyer?"

"A fictional character. Do you remember anything from last night?"

Chauncy removed his hands and rocked his head side to side, trying to loosen the kinks in his neck. "Some of it."

"Marcie Malone?"

Chauncy threw his legs over the side of the bed and rubbed the sleep out of his eyes. "I ain't likely to forget her anytime soon." Having slept in his clothes, including his socks, Chauncy simply shoved his feet into his boots and stood.

"How many times have you been to see her?" Seth asked.

"A few. I could go for some breakfast."

Seth dog-eared the page in his book and stood, deciding not to prod his cousin further. Chauncy was busy strapping on his double-holster gun rig, the grips of his two Colt pistols pointing forward. "Have you had to use those pistols of yours?"

Chauncy paused for a moment and looked at Seth. "A time or two. Why? How come you ain't wearin' a gun?" Chauncy cinched the gun belt tight then began checking to see if the pistols were still loaded to his satisfaction. He glanced up when Seth didn't answer. "Huh? You always wanted to be a gunslinger, practicing all the time down at the river."

"I have a rifle when I'm riding, but I gave up any pretense of being a gunfighter long ago. I'll leave that to you."

Chauncy reseated his second pistol and slid the gun belt around until the buckle lined up with his belly button. "So, you walk around unarmed?"

"Well, yeah. I have a small derringer that I sometimes carry."

"All that'll do is make a man mad. Still, you might ought to bring it, just in case."

"I thought we were just going to breakfast?"

"Around here, everywhere a man goes could end up bein' an adventure. Ain't you learned that yet?"

"Why do you stay here, then?" Seth asked. "Do you get a thrill from the danger that seems to lurk around every corner?"

Chauncy shrugged. "I ain't decided what I want to do, yet. Thought I'd sow some wild oats as I puzzle over my choices. Grab that peashooter of yours."

"Surely, all the bloodthirsty outlaws are still asleep." Realizing his premise might be faulty, Seth reached into his bag, pulled out his derringer, and slipped it into his back pocket.

They exited the room and Chauncy locked the door before they walked down the stairs, which emptied into the dining room. Several bleary-eyed men were seated at the tables, drinking coffee or munching on food. Although breakfast was included in the price of the room, Chauncy thought the food was awful and refused to eat it. After stepping outside, the pair ducked down the alley to the back of the building, where each took a quick turn in the outhouse. It wasn't a place where a man wanted to linger, the odor so foul that it made Seth's eyes water. He stepped out and didn't' take a breath until they reached the front of the building, where the quality of the air was only marginally better. To tell the truth, a constant stench hung over the Acre. It was a mix of stale beer, vomit, rotting meat, and horse manure, all intermingled with the raw sewage that got tossed into the streets from upper-floor windows.

"Where are we going?" Seth asked, breathing through his mouth.

"El Paso Hotel," Chauncy said.

They turned and walked north on Main Street. The hotel was located on Main and Third, about seven blocks away, well removed from the befouled red-light district. They strolled past a row of shoddily built cribs that were one-room shanties where the whores on the lowest rung of the whoring ladder plied their trade. Several called out to them from within their lairs, like carnival barkers promising a peek at a miraculous two-headed turtle. Any man desperate enough to visit one of those soiled doves, Seth knew, would likely return home with much more than they bargained for, the clap and syphilis rampant among the crib workers.

Seth turned away from the squalor and glanced at Chauncy. "Going back to something I asked earlier, have you had to use those pistols of yours?"

"Sure, I've used 'em. That's why I wear 'em."

"Have you killed people?"

"Only the ones that needed it."

Seth wanted to ask how many but didn't. "Does your father know?"

Chauncy shrugged. "I ain't told him. Doesn't really matter now, does it? They're already dead."

"Have you been shot?" Seth asked.

"What do you think?"

"I've seen you shoot, so no. Any remorse?"

"Naw. When someone grabs for their gun, there ain't nothin' you can do but pull your own."

"Where do these incidents usually occur?" Seth asked, trying to think what he would do if someone pulled a gun on him.

"It usually involves a card table and a bottle of whiskey," Chauncy said. "Now, can we talk about somethin' else?"

"Sure."

But for the next two blocks neither said anything. The air quality improved significantly the farther they walked up Main. At the next corner, both paused and stared up at the second-floor windows of a large, beautiful, two-story mansion, both hoping for a glimpse of Marcie Malone through the glass. Those unfamiliar with the Acre would have no idea that the handsome home was a parlor house owned by a madam named Josie Belmont, who called her place The Belmont.

"You see anybody?" Seth asked.

"Naw. Probably still sleepin'. Ain't nobody sportin' this early in the mornin'."

They crossed the street and passed a ramshackle building that had been turned into a dope den, then two saloons, another boardinghouse, another grand parlor house, and, on the corner, a lumberyard, the northern boundary of Hell's Half Acre. Seth could feel some of the weight lift off his shoulders just knowing he was back in a more civilized world.

"How long are you planning on staying here?" Seth asked.

Chauncy shrugged. "I reckon until I get tired of it or they run me out."

"I'm headed back to the ranch at the end of the week. Why don't you come with me?"

"I might. If I do, I'm bringin' Marcie along."

Seth did a double take. "Do what?"

"I said—"

"I know what you said," Seth said, cutting Chauncy off. "Have you lost your damn mind?"

"You seen Marcie. She's a real beaut."

"I met her, briefly, when you ran off one of her . . . of her . . . customers that was pestering her. She's a parlor house girl, Chauncy."

Chauncy didn't respond and, instead, shot Seth an angry glare.

Seth thought he probably ought to leave it alone but couldn't. "How long has she been working at The Belmont?"

"Hell if I know. Why's that matter?"

Seth worked the math in his head. Even if she'd been

working for only a year or two, she had still slept with hundreds of men.

"Where's your woman?" Chauncy asked, a tinge of anger in his voice.

"I don't have one," Seth said.

"After all that travelin' back East and all them years at that fancy college and you still ain't got a woman?"

"I haven't asked anyone. Besides, this is not about me. Have you had this discussion with Marcie?"

"Not yet."

"How would you explain it to the family?"

"I don't reckon I gotta explain anythin'. Ain't nobody's business but mine."

Seth didn't have an answer for that. It really wasn't anyone's business, although he thought word of Marcie's previous profession would eventually reach the ranch. Just the sheer number of customers she had been with would eliminate any hope of keeping Marcie's livelihood a secret. And Seth could already imagine the awkward encounters that Chauncy and Marcie might face together and, when mixed with Chauncy's volatility, he could envision their lives being an unending cycle of violence and heartbreak.

Seth knew Chauncy was different from most folks and if he said he didn't care, then he probably didn't. For a long time, Seth had been aware of his cousin's lack of empathy and his disdain for what others thought, though that didn't make him a bad person. Seth knew it took all types to make a world and Chauncy appeared comfortable in his own skin. And he had been right, it was his life to live.

Seth was brought back to the present when Chauncy said, "I can see that ol' brain of yours is a-churnin'. You tryin' to figure a way of talkin' me out of it?"

"I do think it merits further discuss—"

"Hey, boy," someone bellowed from behind them.

Seth looked over his shoulder to see the same rough-looking scoundrel who had been pestering Marcie yesterday. A short, barrel-chested man, he was standing at the mouth of the alley, his right hand hovering over the butt of his gun. "Keep walking," Seth whispered.

Instead, Chauncy stopped and turned.

"I want a piece of you, boy," the man shouted.

Chauncy spoke out of the side of his mouth when he said: "Step away, Seth."

People on the street were scrambling to get out of the line of fire. "C'mon, Chauncy. I'm hungry. Let's go."

"Won't take but a second. Now step away fore you get hurt."

Seth took two big steps to the left and snugged up against the outside wall of a hardware store. He turned to look at Chauncy. His shoulders were relaxed and there wasn't an ounce of tenseness in his body. Both of his hands were resting comfortably on the buckle of his gun belt. He didn't shout or curse at his opponent. In fact, he didn't say anything at all.

Seth looked at the other man, who was about twenty feet away. A bead of perspiration had popped on his forehead and Seth could see his hands trembling.

Seth turned to look at Chauncy again. His gaze was sharply focused on the other man and Seth thought he could see a small smile forming on his cousin's lips.

Seth wanted to stop the madness but didn't know how without getting killed in the process. A moment later, Seth winced when he saw the other man reach for his gun. Seth's eyes darted back to Chauncy, who, in one fluid, controlled motion, pulled his pistol and fired. Smoke curled around his cousin's face as Seth turned to look at the other man, who teetered for a moment before falling face-first onto the dirt, his pistol still in the holster.

Chauncy opened the pistol's gate, ejected the spent shell from the cylinder, and inserted a fresh round before reholstering his pistol. He looked at Seth and said, "Let's eat."

"Is he dead?" Seth asked, still trembling from the shock of it all.

"Yeah, he's dead." Chauncy turned and started walking and Seth had to hurry to catch up.

CHAPTER
7

Frances came away from the train station an hour la_r, shaking her head. The vast assortment of timetables and route maps were enough to make her second-guess her decision. Traveling from Wichita Falls to San Francisco was doable, but there were many, many stops along the way, stretching the time of travel much longer than she had originally thought. She could, however, pay a higher fare to book them on an express train, which was obvious as far as she was concerned. Also obvious was the extra fare to book berths on a Pullman sleeping car. There was no way she was going to travel 1,700 miles without a bed to sleep in. Besides, Frances thought, it was just money, wasn't it? With time to kill now that she'd given Maria the day off, Frances made sure the brake was set on the buggy and took a walk down Seventh Street.

A trip would require luggage of some type and she hadn't priced a new trunk since she had moved to the ranch more than fifty years ago. And with the rapid changes in the way people were now traveling she was hoping there might be something new on the market. With that in mind, she turned into the mercantile on the next corner.

The store offered an assortment of cheap trunks and hideous carpetbags, and they were of such poor quality that Frances thought they'd all be busted open before they made it to Fort Worth. She quickly exited the store and continued down the street.

She visited two more stores and discovered they all offered the same selection of crappy goods. Deciding to try Dallas or maybe a mail-order catalog, Frances exited the store and paused on the boardwalk, thinking if she needed anything else in town. She couldn't come up with anything, then she hit upon the idea of having a chat with the town marshal. She knew Percy would think he had the fence cutting under control, but Frances thought it should be reported so there'd be a record of it if things really did spiral out of control. She continued on, turned at the next intersection, and headed for the marshal's office.

When she arrived, she paused at the door when she heard someone shouting inside. Not wanting to walk into a hornet's nest, she leaned against the building and waited her turn. The voices from inside were muffled and she couldn't make out what was being said, but it sure sounded like someone was hot under the collar. A moment later, the door swung open and an angry, short man with a blood-spattered shirt and a severely swollen nose charged out. He stopped, turned, and shouted back inside, "I'll handle it myself," before slamming the door and storming off.

Frances, slightly rattled from the man's outburst, opened the door and stepped inside. The marshal, John Wheeler, was seated behind his desk. "Who was that?" Frances asked.

Wheeler made an attempt to stand and said, "Mornin',

Mrs. Ridgeway," before sinking back into his chair. "That was Cal Northcutt."

"Oh," Frances said.

"Seems Percy walked into his saloon and punched him in the face."

He waved to a chair in front of his desk and said, "Have a seat, Mrs. Ridgeway."

Frances took him up on the offer and she settled into the chair. "He pressing charges?"

"I doubt it."

"Did Mr. Northcutt tell you why Percy was angry with him?"

"He left that part out, I suppose."

"He paid a couple of young boys to cut our fences. Percy caught them red-handed."

"Figured it was something like that. I wished to hell I'd never seen a spool of barbed wire."

"That bad?"

"Yep. I ain't got jurisdiction outside of town, but I'm hearin' about it just the same."

"I came by to report it so there'd be a record."

"I'll add your name to the list. I think everybody that's put up a fence has had 'em cut."

"Have you thought about wiring the Texas Rangers for some help?"

"Done did," Wheeler said. "Said they'd get here when they could, but it's happenin' all across the state. The drought's made it ten times worse than it was."

"Can we press charges against Northcutt?"

Wheeler raised his eyebrows. "That what Percy wants?"

"I doubt it. Just trying to explore all of our options."

"Well, I suppose you could, not that anything would

happen. Word is the governor is tryin' to make fence cuttin' a felony. Don't know if it's goin' to fly or not."

"What's the law now?" Frances asked.

"A misdemeanor. Willful destruction or something like that. It ain't much."

"How concerned should Percy be after Northcutt said he'd handle it himself?"

"Northcutt's a mean little bastard. You better tell Percy to watch his back."

"Anybody else in the family need to be worried?"

Wheeler thought that over for a moment. "I think his beef's with Percy."

Frances pushed to her feet. "If Northcutt is stupid enough to come after Percy, you best tell him to put his affairs in order. Good day, Marshal." Frances turned and exited the office.

CHAPTER
8

While Simon ate the eggs she had scrambled, Emma dressed, strapped on her gun belt, and slipped a sheathed bowie knife into her boot, now ready to take on the day. She had some important decisions to make regarding a couple of colts that had foaled in early spring. Both males, Emma had to decide whether to geld both or keep one for a stud horse.

Stallions were notoriously difficult to manage. Many were aggressive and, in the worst cases, impossible to train to a level where a rider wasn't risking his life every time he mounted up. But on a ranch, having stud horses was a necessary evil and choosing which colt to keep whole was a learning process and something Emma had focused her energies on for the last few years. She had learned a well-bred horse was a valuable commodity, often commanding prices that far surpassed what an average horse would bring. And to reward all of her efforts, the family allowed Emma to keep a generous portion of the proceeds for every horse she bred and sold.

Emma walked back into the kitchen and leaned over to kiss her son on the cheek. Simon grumbled and swiped the spot and Emma smiled. Nine going on twenty, Simon had the lean body, dark hair, and dark eyes of his Indian ancestors and her nose and mouth, which was often curled up into a smile, if he wasn't in a grumpy mood. Normally fun-loving and affectionate, his surly moods had increased in frequency of late and Emma chalked it up to another stage of his development.

She ruffled her son's hair. "I'm going to ride out and work with the horses a bit. You can come or stay here," Emma said. This time of the year, the ranch was a beehive of activity and there would be plenty of eyes on her son.

Simon forked the last of the eggs into his mouth, chewed, and said, "I'll stay. Me and Autumn got some stuff to do."

Emma wanted to ask what the "stuff" was though didn't. Autumn, a beautiful but bossy, red-headed girl the same age as Simon, was the daughter of Emma's aunt Rachel and her second husband, Leander Hays. If Simon was going to spend the day with Autumn then she didn't have to worry about him getting stung or bitten while searching for spiders, snakes, or lizards, because Autumn, like most girls, abhorred creepy-crawly things.

Emma ran a hand across his shoulders and said, "Be good. I might or might not be home for dinner, but I will be home in time to make a light supper."

"I ain't goin' to starve," Simon said.

"You ain't going to do anything because *ain't* isn't a word."

Simon groaned and Emma smiled. "See you in a little bit." Emma grabbed her rifle and donned her straw hat on the way out then made her way to the barn. The heat was intense, and she was sweating by the time she pushed the barn door back and stepped inside. She spotted her uncle Eli working with a horse in the corral and walked over.

"Mornin', Eli," Emma said.

Eli glanced over his shoulder and smiled. "Good morning to you, Emma." Working on the gait of one of Emma's two-year-old bay mares, Eli slacked the rope and the tired horse came to a stop. Eli turned and studied Emma a moment and said, "Off to war?"

Emma smiled. "Nope, just another day at the ranch."

"What's first on your to-do list?" One of the few men hailing from this area who attended college back in his day, her uncle's diction was always precise and grammatically correct.

"I'm going to ride out and watch those two male colts awhile."

"Trying to decide which one to geld?"

"Could be both of them. You have a favorite?"

"I'm partial to the bay, if you intend to save one from emasculation."

Emma chuckled at Eli's word choice. "Emasculation? What does that even mean?"

Eli pushed his hat back on his head, pulled a handkerchief from his pocket, and wiped his face, seemingly in no hurry to answer. As he began carefully refolding the handkerchief, he said, "In barbaric societies, emasculation refers to the removal of a male's . . . well . . . uh . . . basically it means castration." Once it was folded to his satisfaction, he put the handkerchief back in his pocket.

Emma chuckled again, then her cheeks flushed when she considered the subject matter.

Eli noticed and said, "I hope I didn't embarrass you."

"Maybe just a little."

"Damn Puritans," Eli said. "They are the scourge of society."

Emma took that as her cue to leave. If her uncle went off on one of his antireligious tirades she'd be stuck there all day. She told Eli good-bye then turned and reentered the barn.

Once she had her horse saddled, she tied on a couple of extra ropes, slipped her rifle into its scabbard, grabbed a canteen, and led the horse over to the windmill. She took a long drink from the pump, splashed some water on her face, and filled the canteen before mounting up.

When Emma reached the horse pasture a short time later, she climbed down, opened the gate, and led her horse through before closing it. The word *pasture* didn't really do the space justice. The horse enclosure sprawled across nearly ten thousand acres, or more than fifteen square miles. Emma didn't know the exact number of horses the ranch had, but she knew there were more than a thousand at last count—way too many, as far as Emma was concerned. Such a large number inhibited selective breeding and she would prefer to see the number pared significantly. With a majority of the ranch now fenced, there was no need to keep that many horses on hand. And the cattle driving days were over, something her uncle Percy was having a hard time accepting.

Emma remounted her horse and loosened the reins to let him set the pace. Although the Red River ran generally east to west, it had more bends and turns than a snake's trail in the sand. On this parcel of land, it acted as the pasture's eastern border, where the river meandered south for a few miles. With the water in the river unfit to drink because of the ongoing drought, they were lucky that they had a couple of spring-fed ponds, and Emma prayed they didn't dry up before they could get some rain.

The river was handy as a water source when it was flowing good, but it was a nightmare to fence. One of the ranch hands suggested it was like carrying water in a colander. When it rained there were washouts and, in the spring when it often flooded, debris mowed down long stretches of the fence. And it wasn't only Mother Nature that caused havoc—people crossing the river had no qualms about snipping a few strands of wire and riding on. Horses, being relatively smart animals, were quick to exploit any weakness, and the ranch hands spent almost as much time rounding up strays as they did fixing the fence. And if it had just been the Red to worry about it might have been manageable, but another river, the Wichita, meandered right through the heart of the ranch and it presented the same fencing difficulties.

Glancing at the ground, Emma spotted a trail of smaller hoof prints and adjusted her course. It didn't necessarily mean the trail was left by the two colts she was looking for though horses were sociable animals and almost always ran in herds.

As she rode along, Emma felt a tingling at the base of her neck, which grew stronger with each step of her horse. Turning, she looked behind her and found no one there and the gate was still closed. As she slowly turned back to the front her eyes probed the deep pockets of shade along the tree line. She didn't see anything there, either, but she couldn't shake the feeling she was being watched.

Riding over a small ridge, she spotted a group of forty or fifty horses in the distance that were grazing along the bank of the Wichita. Steering her horse left to intercept the herd, she continued to scan the area around her, trying to find the source of her uneasiness. She didn't have any enemies that she knew of, though, living where they lived, she knew trouble could arrive at any moment. And it didn't help that the banks of the river were heavily timbered, offering a multitude of hiding places.

As she drew closer to the horse herd, her gaze continually swept the tree line and she felt herself edging into full-blown panic mode.

"Stop it," Emma muttered out loud. "You're making yourself crazy."

Even that didn't help. If anything, the feelings grew stronger. The hair was now standing up at the nape of her neck and a rash of goose bumps had popped up on her arms. She knew deep in her soul that evil was lurking somewhere. Not trusting her trembling hands, she slowly reached down and slipped her rifle from the scabbard. After cocking the hammer, she took a deep breath, trying to slow her hammering heart.

Using her thighs, she steered her horse away from the trees and tapped him with her spurs to put him into a fast walk. She needed distance from whatever it might be—animal or human. When she turned back to the trees, she locked eyes with an Indian whose face was seared into her mind for all eternity—Scar!

The jolt of instant fear sucked the air from her lungs, and she froze up, as if paralyzed. The only thing still functioning was her brain, which was being assaulted by horrified images that pounded her like a fusillade of bullets. And then Scar smiled and a new wave of fear crushed down on her like a landslide. Her name for the vilest of her four abductors, Scar, whose face had been disfigured by what looked like a knife, had raped, beaten, and tortured her repeatedly during her year of captivity.

Move!

Even with her brain screaming at her, Emma felt as if she'd been trapped in a barrel of molasses. She slowly glanced down at the rifle in her hands and something new sparked inside of her—rage. When it reached full bloom, it quickly burned through the last remaining sluggishness, and Emma, fear and anger now coursing through her body, lifted the rifle and snapped off a shot before spurring her horse into a run. She knew she had missed and didn't care. What she needed most was time and distance so that she could formulate a plan. If he caught her and dragged her into the trees, he'd torture her until Emma begged to be killed. Of that she had no doubt.

She glanced over her shoulder to see how close he was and was dumbfounded to see him sitting easy on his horse, having made no attempt to follow. Rather than instill a sense of relief, his inaction launched a new fear—*Is Scar alone?* Emma slowed her horse to a walk as she swept her eyes from left to right. She was now out in the open with acres of prairie surrounding her, and it would be next to impossible for someone to approach without being seen. Not seeing anyone else, she pulled her horse to a stop and turned to face her mortal enemy. "What's your game, you sick bastard?" she muttered. He had a rifle slung over his bare shoulder but had made no move to reach for it.

Now about three hundred yards away, Emma levered a fresh round into the rifle's chamber. She hadn't seen hide nor hair of him in nearly ten years. *Why now? It's not like you didn't know where I lived because you and the others kidnapped me not two hundred yards from my own house.* Scar here now made no sense. Unless, Emma thought, he was letting her know that he hadn't forgotten about her and that he could get to her anytime he pleased. And not reaching for his weapon was a sign that Scar had no intention of killing her.

At least not with a gun.

That ember of anger in her gut flared red-hot. She'd be damned if she was going to spend the next forty years looking over her shoulder. Spurring her horse into a walk, Emma fed a new cartridge into her rifle to replace the one she had fired.

This was going to end right here, right now.

CHAPTER
9

Leander Hays rode out of the Rocking R barn—again—still on a mission. Although it was only late morning, he had already worn out one horse and was now on his second. His prize stallion, Sundancer, a dark, chestnut-colored palomino, had disappeared out of the west pasture sometime during the night. The fence, as usual, had been cut and Leander didn't know if the horse had escaped or if he had been stolen. Either way, he was determined to find him. After all, he had shelled out a thousand dollars for the stallion and he had never paid that much for a horse in his entire life.

In fact, he had never had a thousand dollars to spend on anything, much less a horse. Working as a Texas Rangers for a good part of his adult life, Leander rarely had two quarters to rub together. But that had all changed after bumping into Rachel Ferguson, the youngest of the Ridge-way siblings, while chasing after a couple of rustlers. Both instantly smitten, they'd had one major problem—Rachel's unhappy marriage to Amos, who, at that time, had been away on the search for Emma. In the end, Rachel and Leander began an illicit affair and when Rachel's mother, Frances, had found out she had threatened to shoot Leander on sight. Eventually, Frances had cooled down and, upon Amos's untimely death a few months later, Rachel and Leander had married and a child, Autumn, had arrived seven months later.

Riding along the west fence line, Leander studied the ground, searching for Sundancer's trail. The drought had sucked all of the moisture out of the ground and if the ranch hadn't been covered in a thick layer of sand from eons of river flooding, finding any trail would have been damn near impossible. Even with that, Leander was kicking himself for not corralling the horse at the barn. The only reason he hadn't was because the stallion was still young and needed to burn off some energy and the best way to do that without injury, was to give the horse plenty of room to roam. He should have known better, especially with the constant fence cutting, and Leander made a mental note to shoot the next man he saw with a pair of pliers in his hand. He was tired of it and he was going to put a stop to it one way or another.

Spotting something, he pulled his horse to a stop and climbed down. Yes, he was angry the horse was gone, though it wasn't just the thousand dollars he'd shelled out. He loved Rachel to death, but he knew she'd ride his ass for weeks if he didn't find that damn horse.

Like all marriages, he and Rachel had experienced the ups and downs every couple goes through. And he knew he wasn't a perfect man—none existed that he knew of—and Lord knew Rachel had her own faults, but every once in a great while, she'd get perturbed about something he had done and would nag him mercilessly, to the point that Leander would saddle his horse in the dark and not unsaddle it until the darkness returned. That would usually go on for a few days until they kissed and made up with a bounce on the marital bed. And that brief respite almost made the nagging bearable—almost.

Being a Ranger had made him a decent tracker, but there were two other men working on the ranch, Moses Wilcox and Winfield Wilson, that were in another class altogether. As he rode along, studying the tracks, he wondered if he should head back to the ranch to ask for help, then decided against it, having already burned up most of the morning. He rode another half mile west until the trail petered out when it merged with the road to town.

He brought his horse to a stop to mull over his choices. Why would somebody steal a horse and then parade it through town? It just didn't make sense. And he couldn't see the horse wandering away on its own when there were other ranch horses still grazing in the pasture. But, Leander thought, what would be the quickest way to get a stolen horse out of the country? He hit upon the answer a moment later—the train! He turned his horse toward town and spurred him into a lope. If the rustler decided to ship the horse somewhere by train, the odds of finding him again would be zero.

CHAPTER
10

Although Emma was determined to end whatever it was that Scar had in mind, she wasn't going to be foolish about it. Ideally, she would like to lure him out in the open and take her chances with the rifle. Although her body and mind had matured significantly since her last encounter with Scar, she knew she was no match for him and if he got his hands on her he would easily overpower her. She needed to draw him close enough for an accurate shot and no closer.

As she walked her horse forward, Scar still hadn't moved, and if his horse hadn't dropped his head to crop some grass, Emma would wonder if she was seeing things. But no, he was real and there he sat, watching, dressed only in a breechcloth. Her emotions swirled from anger to shame to fear before returning to anger again. Emma pulled her horse to a stop about seventy yards away. He still hadn't made any move to unsling his rifle though that was of little comfort. He was as deadly as a pit viper, even without a weapon. And that thought launched another flood of horrible memories of the many atrocities she had witnessed, including Scar's disembowelment of a man who had lived just long enough to see his own guts spilling onto the ground. Emma shuddered at the thought and shook her head, trying to clear her mind.

Emma locked eyes with Scar, lifted the rifle to her shoulder, and cocked the hammer. She adjusted her rifle until Scar's chest lined up in the gun's sights and that's when he made his move. His horse went from standing to running in an instant and he came charging out of the trees. Emma fired and missed. She levered another shell, aimed at a spot three feet in front of him, and pulled the trigger again. Another miss.

Scar was quickly closing the distance and her heart was drumming when she reined her horse around and buried her spurs in his ribs. The horse squatted for a millisecond before exploding forward, hitting full gallop in only two strides. Her horse, a gray gelding she had named Lightning, was an offspring of Percy's prized quarter horse, Mouse, and Emma didn't have any real worries about Scar catching her unless it turned into a long pursuit, something she planned to avoid. She glanced over her shoulder and was pleased to see the distance between them lengthening. Adjusting her course, she steered Lightning toward the large herd of horses grazing along the river, hoping to use them as a shield.

Glancing back again, she saw that Scar had fallen back even farther and her hopes soared. Turning back to the front, she pushed Lightning hard another few moments, then slowed him to a walk twenty yards from the grazing horses and eased him into the herd.

A few of the horses nickered and that helped to settle

her nerves. Emma reined her horse around and lifted the rifle to her shoulder. Scar had closed the distance significantly and was now only a hundred yards away and coming fast. Just as she got a bead on Scar, he slid over the side of his horse, out of sight. Adjusting her aim, she contemplated shooting his horse and then realized how futile that would be with hundreds of horses at hand. Lowering her rifle, she turned her horse and rode deeper into the herd, knowing she needed a better plan. Using the horses as a shield would work for only so long.

But even that simple plan went out the window moments later when she heard Scar shouting. She turned to see him waving his arms, trying to stampede the herd. If they bolted, she would be swept up in the melee and who knew how far the herd would run before tiring. In an effort to calm the horses around her, Emma began talking to them in a low, soothing voice. She didn't think that the horses, having been around cattle and people all of their lives, would spook easily. And so far, Scar wasn't having much luck and Emma wondered what his next move would be. She would be forced to leave the herd eventually if she wanted to go home at some point. And she didn't want to even contemplate being out after dark with Scar in the area.

Scar had been silent for the last few moments and Emma turned in her saddle to see him riding back toward the river. Rather than feeling elated, a wave of dread washed over her.

It would be madness to ride through the timber to go after Scar, but she sure didn't want to spend the rest of her life looking over her shoulder. She turned her horse to follow.

When she broke out into the clear, she lifted the rifle

to her shoulder, took aim at the center of Scar's back a hundred yards away, and fired. The bullet plowed into the dirt two feet behind Scar's horse, so she levered another round, took aim, and fired just as Scar kicked his horse into a gallop, the round falling well short. Emma lowered her weapon and spurred Lightning into a run.

Lightning was by far the quicker of the two horses and it didn't take long for Emma to close the gap. When she was thirty yards away, she pushed the rifle into its scabbard and pulled her pistol. Scar looked over his shoulder and laughed and Emma's anger flared red-hot. Now seething, Emma cocked the pistol at twenty yards and fired a second later. Blood erupted from Scar's left shoulder as she cocked the pistol again and took aim. Before pulling the trigger, she was struck with a sudden thought: *I'm too close!*

As soon as that thought registered, Scar wheeled his horse around, put him into an all-out run, and took direct aim at Lightning. Emma reined hard right and the horse immediately turned, but it was too late, and the two horses collided, launching Emma from the saddle and sending the pistol flying. A moment later, she slammed to the ground, the breath crushed from her lungs.

Scar was on her an instant later. As she gasped for breath, Scar pawed at her clothing and grunted, momentarily perplexed by the split skirt Emma was wearing. It was the one break she needed. As air began slowly filtering into her lungs and Scar continued yanking at her skirt, Emma arched to her right and reached into her boot. With the sheath sewn to the inside, the knife pulled free easily and, using all of her remaining strength, she plunged the knife into Scar's side.

Scar howled and snapped his head up, confusion washing across his face. He looked down at the knife handle protruding from the side of his chest before his eyes drifted up to Emma's face. He yanked her hands close to her body and pinned them to the ground with his knees, then reached up and clamped a hand around her throat. Working her right leg free, she began kicking at Scar, hoping to connect with the knife and did so on her third attempt. Scar grunted and his grip began to loosen then he fell over onto his right side.

Emma gulped air as she rolled over and pushed up to her hands and knees. When she had recovered enough to stand, she slowly pushed to her feet and stumbled toward her horse. Both horses appeared to be uninjured and when she reached Lightning's side, she reached for the saddle horn to steady herself. Once her breathing had evened out some, she looked down and discovered she was drenched with Scar's blood. Her first thought was to strip everything off, but she had more important matters to attend to.

Stepping around her horse, she slid the rifle out of the scabbard. She didn't know if Scar was dead yet, but she wasn't leaving anything to chance. Turning, she walked over to Scar and stared down at his face. A pink froth clung to his lips and his chest rose and fell slightly with each shallow breath. She had never imagined taking another person's life, but Scar was different. He had violently brutalized her and if any man deserved to die it was him. Locking eyes with Scar, she cocked the hammer on her rifle and lifted it to her shoulder. With zero remorse, she aimed at a spot where she thought his heart might be if he had one and pulled the trigger. She levered another shell and fired again. And again, and again, until her rifle emptied.

Leaning down, Emma pulled her knife out of his side and wiped the blood on Scar's bullet-riddled body before slipping the knife back into her boot. Standing, she turned and walked back to her horse, slid the rifle back into the scabbard, and went in search of her pistol, which she found in a clump of weeds. Now almost fully recovered, she strode back to her horse and led him over to Scar's body. She untied one of the ropes and looped one end around Scar's leg before mounting her horse. Frightened by the shooting and the scent of blood in the air, Lightning was rearing his head and stomping the ground. Emma talked to him softly as she looped the other end of the rope around her saddle horn.

Clucking her tongue, she put the horse into motion and dragged Scar's body into the trees. After freeing and re-coiling the rope, she tied it to her saddle and rode for home without a second look back.

CHAPTER
11

Having made his position on fence cutting crystal clear to Cal Northcutt, Percy was now heading north toward Indian Territory. He pulled off the glove on his right hand and looked at his swollen knuckles. Maybe he should have handled it differently, and he might have, if he hadn't spent half the night standing around in a pasture. He'd need to keep an eye out for Northcutt for the next few days, though it wasn't something that was going to keep him up at night.

A couple of miles later, Percy crossed the Red River and entered the Nations. That area of the country, between Texas and Kansas, had a half a dozen different names and Percy thought *the Nations* was probably most apt. The land had been carved into individual parcels for the different tribes and the Indians had been quick to name their parcels this nation or that nation, hoping to maintain some autonomy from the Great White Father and his government.

Percy got along with most of the Indians just fine and he and the others in the family had built solid relationships with a great many of them over the years. But he knew

most detested reservation life and he couldn't blame them
for that. Not only did the bureaucrats in Washington dic-
tate where the Indians must live, they also mandated who
their neighbors were going to be, even if they had spent the
last two centuries warring with one another. None of it
made much sense to Percy and he didn't know what the
solution was, but he didn't think turning Indians, who had
roamed the plains for thousands of years, into farmers was
a viable option. It was madness to expect people who had
never stayed in one place any longer than a few months
to settle onto a parcel of land and take up an occupation
that was as foreign to them as Paris would be to him. The
Indians weren't the reason the Territory had such a bad
reputation—it was all those other people who had no legal
right to be there—the cattle rustlers, bootleggers, killers,
outlaws, and other assorted vermin who used a gap in the
law to hide out among the Indians.

Although many of the tribes now had their own police
departments, they could arrest and render justice only to
their own citizens and had no jurisdiction over the other
outlaws who roamed freely throughout the Territory. Justice for them was meted out by federal district judge Isaac
Parker, who presided over the federal court for the
Western District of Arkansas in Fort Smith. Appointed
in 1875, Parker was the one man who was responsible
for delivering justice to all of Indian Territory, an area that
encompassed seventy-four thousand square miles. And it
hadn't taken Parker long to begin the cleanup, the judge
having hanged six murderers simultaneously only four
months into his first term. Percy didn't know the exact
number of men the judge had hanged since then, but he
thought the judge could probably hang ten times whatever

the number was and still not make a dent in the Territory's outlaw population.

While Parker was busy dispensing justice in Fort Smith, he deployed as many as two hundred deputy U.S. marshals across Indian Territory to hunt down the lawbreakers. It was a hazardous profession and Percy had met several men who had later died in the line of duty. The job was even more difficult than the one Percy had when he rode with the Texas Rangers years ago when the enemy—usually Indians—had been more well defined. Up in these parts, the next man you met might be a murderer, a cattle rustler, or simply a neighbor.

Two hundred deputy marshals sounded like a significant number until one factored in the enormous amount of territory they had to cover. Based on the number of unserved warrants issued in Fort Smith, Percy had heard the outlaws outnumbered the deputy marshals three hundred to one.

Mouse had worked up a lather by the time they came to West Cache Creek. He checked it for water and was surprised to see a couple of shallow pools. Mouse's ears pricked up when she caught the scent and he loosened the reins and the mare picked her way down the bank and dipped her muzzle in for a long drink. One would think the ongoing drought might dwindle the mosquito population, but that wasn't the case. They swarmed both horse and rider, probing for exposed flesh. Percy took off his hat and fanned it several times to little effect. When he'd had all he could stand, he spurred Mouse into motion and steered her up the far bank.

Thinking Quanah Parker might be the best person to talk to about leasing some Indian grass, all Percy had to do now was find him. Which sounded easy enough, but their reservation stretched across three million acres and, with the Indians moving whenever the whim struck them, it was an almost-impossible task. He was hoping someone at Fort Sill might know where the Comanche chief was camped, and that was his first destination.

However, that all changed a while later when he spotted a black man mounted on a large white horse about ten miles south of the fort. The way the man sat his horse was familiar, so Percy tapped Mouse with his spurs and put her into a trot. When he got close, he slowed the mare to a walk, not wanting to ride right up on the man and end up gut-shot. "Bass!" Percy shouted.

The man turned and pulled his pistol quicker than a startled snake could strike. Percy dropped the reins and reached for the sky. The man eyed him for a moment and then started laughing as he holstered his pistol. "Well, hell, Percy, I'd like to killed ya," Deputy U.S. Marshal Bass Reeves said.

Percy lowered his hands and grabbed the reins, nudging Mouse forward.

"What you doin' up this way?" Reeves asked.

"Lookin' for a man."

"Story o' my life," Reeves said, sticking his hand out.

Percy reached out and they shook. "You haven't been down to the ranch for a while."

"Busy chasin' outlaws. It's a never-endin' job."

"Who you huntin'?" Percy asked.

"A couple of horse thieves."

"Hell, Bass, you probably coulda caught you a couple of horse thieves a lot closer to home."

"Lookin' for two in particular."

The two men let their horses set the pace as they continued on. Bass Reeves was a tall, broad-shouldered black man who'd been riding a white or gray stallion as long as Percy could remember. Percy had learned the rest of Bass's story over a bottle of fine bourbon on a warm spring night while sitting on the back porch of Percy's house. Reeves was born into slavery on a farm in Arkansas, and Reeves's master, George Reeves, had moved his farming operation to north Texas when Bass had been a boy. At the outbreak of the war, Bass was forced to accompany the master's son, William, as he went off to fight for the Confederacy. Some-time shortly after that Percy had learned, Bass and William had gotten in an argument over a card game, and Bass had waylaid the son and had fled into Indian Territory, where he had lived with several of the Indian tribes until he was freed by the Thirteenth Amendment. Having learned their languages during his time with the Indians, he was now an invaluable asset for the U.S. Marshals Service.

Reeves looked over and said, "Say, you in a hurry to git somewhere?"

"No, not really. I'm tryin' to find a Comanche named Quanah Parker. You know him?"

"I do. Him and his kin are camped about six miles due west of the fort on Medicine Creek."

"Will I need to take the time to find an interpreter or does he speak English?"

"It's passable. Why are you lookin' for Quanah?"

"Trying to lease some Indian grass."

"Well, he ain't got no problems understandin' money, for sure. He's got a squaw or two that talk English pretty good. You'll do fine."

"Well, I reckon you just saved me several hours of lookin', so I got plenty of time now. What you got goin' on?"

"I was on my way to Sill to raise a posse so I could

arrest them two horse thieves. But I reckon you're about the only posse I need. And the less people stompin' round, the better."

"You know where they're holed up?"

Reeves nodded. "Ain't but about four, five miles, maybe. They's got a little hideout over in the Wichita Mountains. I just need you to back my play."

Percy pulled out his pocket watch and popped the lid to check the time. "Hell, it ain't even dinnertime yet. Lead the way."

Reeves and Percy turned their horses off the trail and took off for the Wichita Mountains. "Where's your wagon, cook, and sidekick?" Percy asked.

"Wagon broke down a ways back. Left the Indian to fix it. They'll be along shortly."

"They gonna be able to find us?"

"They'll find us. That Indian boy's like a bloodhound."

A spiffy dresser, Reeves had at least taken off his suit coat in the heat and was wearing a white, collared shirt and his suit vest. As usual, his black boots were polished to a high shine and on his head was the ever-present, flat-crowned, wide-brimmed, white hat he always wore.

"How's Miss Franny?" Reeves asked.

"She's good, Bass. Like all of us she's gettin' older every day. Told me this morning she wants to take a train trip out to San Francisco."

Reeves smiled. "Good for her. You gonna go?"

"Don't know. Gotta find some grass for the cattle before I do anythin'."

"Hell, Percy, the other cattle ranchers just push their cattle across the river like they owned the place. Same way up by Kansas. Damn cattle every which way you look and the Indians don't own any of 'em or get anythin' for the grass."

"I know," Percy said. "That's why I want a lease. So I can depend on it bein' there when I need it."

"The Indians oughta lease it all out if they ain't gonna use it."

"With all this good grazin' land, I don't know why they won't get some cattle herds started. By the look of things, I don't think the Indians are takin' to farmin' very well."

"Can't farm here, no ways. Too dry. And the government did buy some cattle for the Indians, but they had to end up killin' most of 'em just to eat. With the buffalo all but gone and the skimpy rations they get, most of 'em's right near starvin'."

It wasn't long before they were riding through the foothills of the Wichita Mountains, which Percy thought was a misnomer. One peak, Mount Scott, might top out at fifteen hundred feet and it towered over the surrounding landscape. But these and the Arbuckle Mountains to the east were the only tall land formations within five hundred miles, and he supposed they had to call them something. Percy looked over at Reeves and said, "Who're we after?"

"We're after a thievin' Cherokee by the name of Sam Starr."

"Never heard of him. Who's the other one?"

"His wife."

Percy eyed Reeves. "Huh. That's kinda unusual. Don't hear about many women gettin' arrested for horse theft. She got a name?"

Reeves looked over and grinned. "Myra Maybelle Shirley Reed Starr."

Percy repeated the name several times in his head. Something about it sounded familiar, but there were so many names it was confusing. On the fourth repetition it hit him, and he groaned. "Belle Starr? We're arresting Belle Starr? Didn't she run with the James and Younger gangs before they got shot all to hell?"

"She did. Word is she married one of them Younger boys for a spell. But that ain't none of my concern."

"From what I read in the papers, I thought they spent most of their time up in Cherokee country?"

"They do, but I chased 'em out of there. Been after 'em for right near a week."

"They got any other outlaws with 'em?"

"Not that I seen. Watched 'em some this mornin' and ain't seen nothin' but her and her old man."

"Unless the rest of the gang rode in after you left to gather a posse," Percy said.

Reeves shrugged. "Well, I reckon we're 'bout to find out."

CHAPTER
12

Leander, still in search of his lost stallion, crossed the river and rode into Wichita Falls. Wanting to check the train depot first, he turned his horse down Main Street. He checked the corral behind the building as he rode past and didn't see any sign of his prized stallion. When he reached the entrance to the depot, he climbed down from his horse, wrapped the reins around a hitching post, and stepped inside. The line at the ticket counter was five-deep and the man working behind it, dressed in a black suit, a string tie, and a round, short-billed wool conductor hat, was moving at turtle speed. Leander turned away and went in search of another railroad employee. He spotted an office at the back and hurried that way only to find it empty. He turned and walked back to the ticket counter. The line was now stacked seven-deep and the same woman was still at the front of the line, arguing with the ticket agent.

"Anybody else work here?" Leander shouted to the room.

The man behind the counter looked up and frowned. "You'll have to wait your turn."

"I ain't buyin' a ticket, for Christ's sake."

The man pointed over his shoulder and said, "Try the eating house."

Leander exited the building and walked around the corner to the railroad's eating house. Stepping inside, he waited for his eyes to adjust then scanned the crowd. He saw a man toward the back of the room who was wearing a black suit and a string tie with a name tag pinned to his chest, and he walked over. When Leander arrived at the table, he pulled out a chair and sat.

The man looked up from his coffee and frowned. "Yes?"

"You work for the railroad?" Leander asked.

"I'm on break," the man said, staring into his coffee cup.

"That so?" Leander asked. "I'm lookin' for a horse."

"Try the livery stable."

Leander thought about reaching across the table to grab the man by the throat, but he refrained. "Anybody load a horse on the train this morning?"

"Not that I seen," the man said.

"What time's the next train leave?"

"Ain't but one more. Five o'clock."

Leander pushed his chair back and stood. "The other man over at the depot is covered up and could probably use some help." When the man didn't respond, Leander said, "You know you can always get yourself another dog, if that's what's got you down."

The man looked up for the first time. "Ain't my dog. It's my wife."

"Can't say I blame her." Leander turned and headed for the door. At least he had a little time now. After exiting the eating house, he turned and walked back to his horse.

The next stop would be the livery stable. It didn't make sense for someone to steal a horse and then put it in a livery stable, but Leander had apprehended a large number of criminals and he guessed that seven out of every ten were dumber than a sack of rocks or so drunk they didn't know which end was up.

After a quick sweep through the livery stable with no luck, Leander made a ride through town, paying careful attention to the saloons, and came up empty again. Wondering if he'd been relying on a series of faulty assumptions, he decided it was time to rethink his strategy. His main concern had been an escape via the railroad, and he couldn't see a thief, even a dumb one, waiting around all day to ship the horse out on the evening train. He steered his horse toward a spot of shade and brought him to a stop as he contemplated the next steps.

Assuming the stallion had been taken sometime during the night, the thief could be miles away by now. And if the horse wasn't in town, then he needed to ride back to the ranch to convince Moses Wilcox to join him in the search. Wilcox was old and cranky, so Leander might have to sweeten the pot with something extra, but a return trip would also allow him a chance to grab a few extra supplies in case the search went longer than expected.

Leander turned his horse around and made another stop at the train depot. Miracle of miracles, there was no line in front of the ticketing agent and Leander hurried over. After passing along a description of the horse and his brand, Leander told the railroad man he would pay him a fifty-dollar reward if he recovered the stolen horse. The man's eyes lit up and Leander thought the man might actually keep an eye out for his stallion.

On the way out, he passed on the horse's description and the offer of a reward to a couple of other people and felt sure word would spread around town. Having done everything he could do in town, Leander mounted his horse and rode for the ranch.

CHAPTER
13

While Chauncy and Seth enjoyed breakfast at the El Paso Hotel, Marcie Malone was awakened by a sharp knock on her door. Having a good idea who it might be, she rolled over onto her back and stared at the ceiling, hoping she would go away. She was exhausted—physically and emotionally—and she wasn't up for the confrontation she knew was coming. There was another sharp knock and then the door swung open to reveal Josie Belmont, a hard-but-fair Irishwoman who was the proprietor and owner of The Belmont. She swept into the room and stopped, hovering over the bed, her hands on her hips.

"I heard a nasty rumor," Josie said. She was already dressed for the day in a fine bustle dress, and her long red hair had been parted in the middle and pulled into a bun on the top of her head.

Marcie rubbed the sleep out of her eyes, propped another pillow under her head, and turned to look at her boss. "Oh yeah? What's that?"

"That Mr. Ridgeway made another appearance without arranging payment with me."

"My last client was a no-show last night. I'll pay you your cut."

"That is not the point. This is a place of business and we don't give things away for free."

"It won't happen again."

Marcie used her elbows to push herself up against the headboard. After Chauncy had left, Marcie had stayed awake for most of the night, trying to find a way out of this life she had fallen into. She stared at the opposite wall for a moment, trying to corral her emotions before she either cried again or lashed out in anger. After a few moments, she felt composed enough to continue. "I'll pay what you're owed." Despite her best attempts, tears spilled out of the corners of her eyes.

Josie sighed and took a seat on the edge of the bed, the hard lines on her face softening. "What are you hoping for, Marcie? That Chauncy will come in here and sweep you off your feet? Maybe take you home to meet the family?"

Marcie angrily wiped the moisture off her cheeks with her palms. "What? Because I'm a whore, I can't dream?"

"Not if you're dreaming of fantasies."

"Chauncy's different."

"Honey, they're all different until they sober up and reality sets in again. You don't think every woman working in the Acre has the same dream? Even I had that dream when I was your age. The real world doesn't work that way. They love on us when it's dark and they're all liquored up but come sunup most of them act like we don't even exist. That is just the way it is."

"I can't do this much longer. Last night, one man pulled my hair so hard, I thought he was gonna pull it all out."

"Who was it?"

The tears had stopped, at least for the moment. "Does it matter? There's always gonna be a next one."

"I know some of them can be rough," Josie said. "I only see a few clients and I have one who likes some of the rough stuff, but he's never hurt me. All part of the job."

"Yeah? I'm tired of this job."

"What else would you do? Become a laundress? A seamstress? A cook? And you don't have the education to be a teacher. If you haven't noticed, there aren't many jobs for a woman that pay a living wage."

"I'd just like to be a wife. You were married once, right?"

"I was. It didn't last long. He turned out to be worse than any client I ever had."

"That don't mean it can't work for somebody else."

"No, it doesn't. And I'm not saying it's impossible. You're smart, pretty, and still young, so anything's possible. But be honest with yourself, Marcie. The odds are long." Josie reached over and patted Marcie's hand. "Take the afternoon off."

"Thank you."

Josie stood. "Start saving your money. If you stay away from the dope and the booze you might get your own place someday. That's where the real money is."

Josie turned and exited the room, closing the door softly behind her. Marcie didn't know how much stock to put in Josie's words. Marcie was one of the most popular girls in the house and a high earner, so Josie had a financial stake in every decision Marcie might make. She threw back the covers, stood, and walked around to the foot of her bed. Lifting the lid of the steamer trunk she used to house her personal items, Marcie reached way down to the very bottom and pulled her bankroll out of the old shoe where she hid it. Sitting on the edge of the bed, she counted the money.

She kept pretty close tabs on how much she earned, but even she was surprised to find she had forty dollars more than she had thought. But even with that extra forty, three hundred and thirteen dollars wasn't life-changing money. It was enough for her to survive on her own for a few months if she was frugal. But what then? She'd be right back at square one, a year older and a lot poorer. Going back home to Missouri wasn't an option. At least not while her step-father remained alive. And knowing her luck, the lecherous old bastard would outlive them all.

With that off the table, Marcie had few other options. She stretched out on the bed and stared at the same water spot on the ceiling that she often focused on when the men who paid for her services did their business. Although she tried to be engaging to enhance her prospects for a larger tip, there were times when she'd lose all interest and that's when her mind would drift, often focusing on the ugliness of her life. It could be a mood killer for sure, but she was an expert faker and had a knack for making the men who visited her feel like they were the most important thing in the world—at least for a few minutes.

Appearances were important, and most of her clients would be crushed to discover that, no, she didn't really enjoy their time together. Men and their egos, Marcie thought. They were as fragile as eggshells. She did have one or two regulars who flat out didn't give a damn if she enjoyed it or not. Their only interest was fulfilling their own needs and Marcie's body was simply a tool for their own use. And, if she was being honest, she'd almost prefer it that way. End all those emotional entanglements some men craved and get on with the job at hand—bing, bang, done.

However, it was hard to be in this business and not feel some emotional attachments at times. One of her regulars for a while, a cute older man who had lost his wife a couple of years ago, had no interest in sex and, instead, paid to spend a night spooning in her bed. There was no pawing or kissing, and most nights he was asleep within ten minutes of turning down the lantern. Marcie felt bad he had to pay for that privilege because she got something out of those nights, too—they almost made her feel human again.

What she felt on those nights was similar to what she felt when she spent time with Chauncy. And not just in the bedroom, either. Over the past couple of weeks, Chauncy had taken her on a few buggy rides and they had shared a few quiet suppers when time allowed. Through it all, Chauncy had shrugged off all the nasty stares from those that thought themselves morally superior.

"Doesn't it bother you?" Marcie had once asked while on one of their buggy rides.

"Why would it bother me?" Chauncy had asked. "I don't give a damn what they think. And neither should you."

"Yeah, you're just visiting. I have to live here," Marcie had said.

"Maybe you don't have to," Chauncy had said. Marcie's hopes had soared, but Chauncy hadn't said anything since, and she wondered for the thousandth time if she had misinterpreted his words.

A gunshot outside brought her back to the present. It happened so frequently she didn't even bother to stand for a look out the window. Instead, she looked down at the money and wondered how much money she would need to walk away from The Belmont and never return. Josie had been right. Marcie didn't know how to sew, and she couldn't see herself slaving away in a laundry for a dollar a week when she made fifty times that much or more, doing what she was doing. However, she also knew there was no longevity in this line of work, and she'd shoot herself in the head before she aged into being a crib girl, turning sixty or seventy tricks a week. No matter how much she analyzed her situation, she really had only two choices—keep whoring or find a husband.

CHAPTER
14

After riding for another half hour, Deputy U.S. Marshal Bass Reeves held his hand up and reined his horse to a stop. Percy followed suit and nudged Mouse closer so the two men could converse.

Reeves pointed and whispered, "They's camped just over that ridge yonder, 'long a little creek."

Percy pulled his rifle from the scabbard and took a moment to study the lay of the land. He pointed his rifle at a nearby ridge and whispered, "Can I see 'em from that ridge?"

"Yep. I reckon that might be a good spot for you, but we ought to see what we got first," Reeves whispered.

The two men climbed down from their mounts and tied the reins to the branch of a cedar tree. "What's the plan?" Percy asked as he quietly levered a shell into the chamber of his Winchester.

"To catch 'em," Reeves said as he loaded the empty cylinder on one of his pistols. No smart man rode around with the hammer of his gun resting on a live round.

"You want 'em alive, I expect?" Percy asked.

"Yeah. Ain't got nothin' on 'em other than horse thievin' at the moment, though I'm sure they done worse." Reeves reholstered that pistol and pulled the second one to load its empty cylinder. He wore a double-holster gun belt with the butts of the pistols pointing forward, the same way Percy wore his single gun rig. At one time Percy had worn two guns, but the times had changed and, as he'd gotten older, he didn't want to lug around the extra weight.

Reeves untied his suit coat from behind his saddle and slipped it on, running his hands along the lapels to smooth them down. Once satisfied he was properly attired, he grabbed two pairs of handcuffs from his saddlebags and slipped them into his coat pocket. "Let's go for a look-see."

They worked their way around the base of the ridge and into a thick stand of timber along a dry creek bed. As they advanced up the valley Reeves's movements reminded Percy of a big cat on the prowl. Percy's nostrils picked up a hint of woodsmoke, which meant they were close. An avid reader of any newspaper he could get his hands on, Percy knew Belle Starr's notoriety had grown after being linked to the bank robber Jesse James, who had been shot in the head by one of his own gang members.

As they approached a small clearing the trees began to thin out. Reeves held up a hand and they both stopped and squatted down behind a dead tree that had fallen over. As Percy feared, Mr. and Mrs. Starr were now entertaining company and there were six people lounging around in the shade of a large cottonwood tree. Instead of an easy husband-and-wife capture, they were now facing five well-armed outlaws and Belle Starr, who, rumor suggested, was a dead shot. Although outnumbered, Percy was only mildly concerned. He was confident in his own abilities and he'd

seen enough of Reeves in action to know that he was one
of the deadliest gunslingers to ever walk the earth. He put
all of those thoughts out of his mind and leaned over close
to Reeves and whispered, "How do you want to play it?"

Reeves stroked his long, bushy mustache with his right
hand as he studied the layout. He turned and glanced up at
the ridge, calculating angles and processing how things
might play out. After a few moments he turned to look at
Percy and whispered, "I don't like splittin' up. Gives 'em
too good a chance to get to cover fore we get 'em corralled.
Let's ease along the tree line a little further. We get lucky,
we get the drop on 'em."

Percy nodded and both men slowly stood. Reeves
turned and glided off into the trees and Percy followed
along, keeping a close eye out for downed limbs whose
snap underfoot could get them both shot to hell. Slow and
steady and with no sudden movements, they inched closer.
There wasn't a hint of a breeze in among the trees and the
sweat ran off Percy's forehead and into his eyes, stinging
them. Reeves had large sweat rings around the arms of his
suit coat and Percy thought he was crazy for having put it
on in the first place. When they were as close as they dared
go, Reeves held up his hand and they both stopped. Percy
took a deep breath as they studied the scene, pinpointing
the locations of the group's weapons. A couple of rifles
were propped up against the tree and two of the men had
their gun belts off, their pistols still within easy reach.

Reeves turned and looked at Percy and, using his hands,
signaled how it was going to go down. Percy interpreted it
to mean that he was to stay there while Bass moved to
flank them and, when the action started, the three on the
left were his responsibility.

Percy nodded.

Reeves pointed at his eye then his chest and Percy nodded again. Reeves moved off and Percy waited for him to get into position. His throat was dry as a powder house and he wished he'd brought his canteen. Reeves worked his way to a spot about fifteen feet away and stopped. Percy eased his rifle up, tucked the stock tight to his shoulder, and pulled the hammer back. He glanced over at Reeves to see him easing his pistol out. When he had it gripped tightly in his hand, he nodded and they both stepped into the clearing, shouting for the bad guys to put their hands up.

The one sitting closest to Percy reached for his pistol and Percy swung the barrel left and fired, putting a round through the fleshy part of the man's shoulder. The man fell back on the ground, squealing like a stuck hog. Percy ignored his screams and turned his focus to the rest of the group as he and Reeves walked forward. All the bandits now had their hands up as they closed in.

After disarming the group, Percy got his first real look at Belle Starr and wasn't very impressed. She looked like she'd been ridden hard and put away wet far more often than not. With a wide, hard face, deep-set, dark eyes, and short dark hair, Percy thought she looked more like a man, especially with that sneer on her face. And his low opinion of her really nosedived off the cliff when she opened her mouth. "Who the hell are you?" Belle Starr asked.

"Who I am ain't important," Percy said. He pointed at Reeves and said, "He's the one you need to be talkin' to."

She glanced at Reeves, curled her upper lip, and then turned and looked at Percy and said, "I don't talk to niggers."

"Probably music to his ears," Percy said, nodding toward Reeves. "I reckon he won't have to listen to you spew your nonsense on the long trip back to Fort Smith."

"I ain't goin' to Fort Smith. And I sure ain't goin' with no nig—"

"Oww," Starr yelped as Reeves ratcheted the handcuffs tight to her wrists.

Reeves smiled at her before moving on to cuff her husband. "Sam Starr and Belle Starr, you're under arrest for horse theft. I'm Deputy U.S. Marshal Bass Reeves representin' the federal court for the Western District of Arkansas and I'm takin' you to Fort Smith."

"We didn't steal no horses," Belle said.

Reeves shrugged. "That'll be up to the judge. I'm just hired to bring you in."

"I told you we didn't steal no damn horses, boy."

Reeves looked at her and smiled. "Ma'am, I been called about anythin' a man can be called, but I got to admit, hearin' it from a lady pains me a bit. But if it makes you feel better, you just keep it comin'."

Although Percy had disarmed the group, he hadn't done a thorough search for other weapons and he was wary about one of the outlaws having a boot gun or a hidden knife. A knife in the hands of a skilled man was as deadly as a gun and it killed just as quick.

"Percy," Reeves said, "I'd be obliged if you'd grab the warrants from my saddlebag."

"I'm on it," Percy said. "You want my rifle?"

"Nah. If I can't hit 'em with my six-shooter I probly ought to find a new line of work."

Percy turned and took off after the warrants. When he arrived at the spot where they had left the horses, Percy was surprised to see Reeves's Indian sidekick and old Mexican man he assumed was the cook sitting on the back of a buckboard wagon, swinging their legs like they were parked at a picnic.

"Been here long?" Percy asked, somewhat perturbed they hadn't offered their assistance.

Both men just looked up and shrugged.

Probably don't speak English, Percy thought before mumbling, "Thanks for the help." Thinking the gun battle over, Percy stepped over to his horse and stowed his rifle then turned to Reeves's big stallion and opened his saddlebag. He peeled off the two warrants for the lovely Mr. and Mrs. Starr and put the rest back, making sure not to get them out of order. Reeves was unable to read or write, and Percy knew that someone read the warrants to Reeves before he left town and he memorized the information and was careful to keep them in the same order they'd been read. Percy turned to look at the Indian on the wagon and waved him forward.

The Indian jumped down. "Is the shootin' over?"

"So you do speak English, huh?"

"Yeah, but I learned when there's lead flyin' it's best to stay out of Marshal Reeves's way. Should I drive the wagon?"

"Can't get through the trees. Be easier to walk 'em back over here. What's your name anyhow?"

"Sam Sixkiller. My pa's a lawman, too."

"I've heard of him. His name's Sam, too, right?"

Sixkiller nodded. "Makes things confusin' sometimes. Did you catch the horse thieves?"

"We did." Percy thought Sixkiller looked like he was twelve years old, but he knew he had to be older than that. "Your pa okay with you bein' out here trackin' down outlaws?"

"Only if I'm workin' for Marshal Reeves. Won't let me go with any of the others."

"Don't blame him." Percy shifted the papers to his left hand and stuck out his right. "Percy Ridgeway, Sam."

Sixkiller reached out and shook Percy's hand. "Heard of you, too. You were a Texas Ranger at one time, weren't you?"

"A long time ago. I'm a rancher now. Got a place on the other side of the Red River. Stop in if you're ever down that way."

"I will."

Rather than fight through the brush again, Percy led Sixkiller down into the dry creek bed and they arrived at the small clearing a few moments later. As they climbed up out of the wash, Percy saw that Reeves was turned slightly, interrogating one of the other men as the wounded man reached toward his boot. Percy shouted, "Bass!" Reeves went for his gun at the same time Percy reached for his.

In one fluid movement, Percy drew his pistol, cocked it on the way up, and fired almost simultaneously with Reeves.

The wounded man almost had the gun out of his boot when Percy's bullet punched a hole in the side of his head. Reeves's shot hit center mass and either shot would have gotten the job done. The dead man flopped down on his back as Percy ejected the spent shell and slid in a fresh round, the two shots still echoing off the canyon walls.

"Damn," Sixkiller said, "I ain't never seen any man as fast as Bass Reeves before."

Percy holstered his pistol and ignored Sixkiller's comment. He didn't like killing, but there were times when it couldn't be avoided. He and Sixkiller walked over to where Reeves was standing.

"Not bad for an old man," Reeves said.

"Who was he?" Percy asked.

Reeves looked down at Belle Starr. "Well?"

Starr spat into the dirt. "His name was George Lamb and he's got a whole passel of kinfolk that are gonna hunt both of you assholes down."

Reeves turned his head to look at Percy. "Hear that, Percy? They're gonna hunt us down."

"Yeah, I heard. Ain't the first time I've been threatened, and, as far as I can tell, I'm still upright and walkin'."

Reeves took the warrants out of Percy's hand and dropped one each onto the laps of Mr. and Mrs. Starr and said, "Read 'em or don't. Makes no difference to me."

Percy stepped up close to Reeves and said, "You recognize any of the new arrivals?"

"No. Tried to get names and got nowhere. No doubt they's guilty of somethin', but I ain't got nothin' on 'em other than associatin' with a couple of wanted criminals."

"How are we gettin' out of here without the others tryin' to follow us?" Percy asked.

"Done got that figured. This ain't my first go-round. We're gonna take their guns and horses with us, then leave 'em somewhere down the trail." Reeves turned and looked at Sixkiller. "Sam, Percy will grab the guns and you gather up their horses."

"What about the saddles?" Sixkiller asked.

"Leave 'em. I reckon they can come back after gettin' their horses."

"Now you wait a damn minute, Marshal," a short, portly man with a tobacco spit–stained shirt said. "We ain't done nothin'. You can't take them horses or them guns."

"I ain't takin' 'em. Just borrowin' 'em for a bit. Follow our wagon track. You'll find 'em. 'Sides, you're gonna be busy buryin' your friend over there."

"We ain't got nothin' to bury 'im with," the man whined.

"Not my problem," Reeves said. He turned back to the Starrs and said, "On your feet."

Sam Starr, who had the distinct features typical of a full-blood Indian, stood and helped his wife up. Through it all he hadn't said a word. Percy spotted a half-empty sack of beans and walked over and grabbed it. He tossed the pistols inside and gathered up the rifles, as Sixkiller bridled the horses. Reeves ordered the Starrs to walk, and Percy fell in behind them, with Sixkiller and the horses bringing up the rear.

"Hey, boy," Belle shouted, "what are you gonna do with *my* horse? Maybe I ought to turn your black ass in for horse stealin'."

Reeves didn't bother to respond and, after traveling back through the dry creek bed, they arrived at the wagon without incident, other than a stream of verbal abuse courtesy of Mrs. Starr. Percy, who had never laid a hand on a woman, figured that could change right quick if he had to spend any more time in her company. He walked up to the front of the wagon and put the sack of weapons and the rifles under the front seat and made a point to tell both Sixkiller and Reeves what he had done.

By the time the prisoners were loaded in the wagon and the horses were tied on at the back, the sun was high overhead, casting thin shadows across the rocky terrain. Reeves and Percy walked over to their horses and mounted up. "Bass," Percy said, "I'll hang here a little while to make sure those other three don't follow. You thinkin' of settin' up camp around Fort Sill?"

"Nope," Reeves said. "Too many people. I'm gonna try and put Mr. and Mrs. Starr in the stockade then make camp a little ways north on Beaver Creek."

"Okay. I'm gonna stop and have a chat with Quanah then I'll find you."

"Ride due south from here and you'll be close," Reeves said. "Wanna take Mrs. Starr with you?"

Percy chuckled. "I'll pass."

Reeves muttered something about it being a long trip before spurring his horse forward.

CHAPTER
15

While Percy was busy rounding up outlaws, Chauncy and Seth were killing time, lingering over a final cup of coffee at the El Paso Hotel. Seth glanced up to see a man with a badge pinned to his shirt standing at the entrance, his gaze sweeping the room. Seth kneed Chauncy under the table and nodded toward the door. Chauncy looked over at the same time the man's eyes landed on their table and he pulled off his hat and entered, making a beeline for their table.

"What are you gonna say?" Seth whispered to Chauncy.

Chauncy shrugged and said, "The truth."

His cousin didn't appear jumpy or nervous and Seth wondered if Chauncy might have had similar conversations before. They watched as the man threaded his way through the crowded room and, when he arrived, he placed his hat crown-down on the table, pulled out a chair, turned it around, and sat, propping his arms on the back. He gave Chauncy a long hard look before moving on to Seth.

His mouth, if he had one, was completely obscured by a salt-and-pepper mustache and long goatee.

Finally, he spoke, proving he did have a mouth. "I'm City Marshal Bill Rea. Which one of you boys killed one of my citizens?"

There was no hesitation in Chauncy. "I did. But only after he went for his gun."

Rea turned his head incrementally to glare at Chauncy and Chauncy matched him stare for stare. Seth couldn't believe how cool and composed his cousin was when he was as nervous as a cornered cat and he hadn't done much more than fart in public.

"You fancy yourself a gunslinger?" Rea asked.

"I don't fancy myself nothing," Chauncy said, his gaze still locked on the marshal's.

"What's your name, gunslinger?" Rea asked.

Seth didn't like the direction the conversation was going nor did he like the escalation in tension. "We'll pay for the man's funeral arrangements."

Rea's eyes slowly shifted over to Seth. "I already had that figured. How about you? You have a name?"

"My name is Seth Ferguson."

"I wish I could say it was nice to meet you, Mr. Ferguson, but it'd be a lie. I don't like people comin' into my town and shootin' my residents."

Seth had been watching Chauncy out of the corner of his eye and his cousin hadn't moved an inch, hadn't squirmed in his seat, and hadn't taken his eye off the marshal for a second. Seth took a deep breath and slowly raised his arms to show the marshal he wasn't wearing a gun. "As you can see, I haven't shot anyone."

"I didn't think you had," Rea said. "You don't look like the shootin' kind." Rea swiveled his gaze back to Chauncy.

"But this one, he's a different story, aren't you, gunslinger? I've seen about a hundred of your type parade through my town, only to piss their pants when they run up against a real man."

"Are you a real man, Marshal?" Chauncy asked, his eyes still locked on Rea.

Seth placed his hands on the table and leaned forward in his chair. "Look, I think maybe we got off on the wrong foot, here. We don't want any trouble, Marshal. Like I said, we'll pay for any burial expenses."

Chauncy remained as still as a statue when he said, "Well, Town Marshal Bill Rea, are you a real man?"

Seth saw the marshal lick his lips, the first hint of uncertainty by either of the men. Seth needed to find a way to unwind the situation before things spiraled completely out of control. In an effort to defuse the situation, he spouted off the first thing that came to mind. "Hey, Marshal, what'd you have for breakfast?"

The question didn't elicit the instant reaction that Seth had been hoping for, but after a brief pause, both Marshal Rea and Chauncy slowly turned their heads to look at him.

Rea's forehead was wrinkled in bewilderment. "Do what?"

"What'd you have for breakfast?" Seth asked.

"Nothin'," Rea said.

The question, though, had the desired effect and the tension at the table dropped from critical to manageable. Seth saw Chauncy take a deep breath, hold it, and then release it. It appeared to Seth that the gunfight at the El Paso Hotel had been avoided.

"My name's Chauncy Ridgeway," Chauncy said, his voice cool and calm.

Rea, with his gaze still centered on Seth said, "You part of the Ridgeway clan, too?"

Seth nodded. "My mother."

"Rachel or Abigail?" Rea asked.

Seth reared back in surprise. "Rachel. You know her?"

"I know all of the Ridgeways," Rea said as he turned to look at Chauncy. "Who's your Pa? Eli or Percy?"

"Percy," Chauncy said.

"He know you two are hanging out in the Acre?"

"I ain't told him. No reason," Chauncy said.

Rea stroked his long goatee for a few moments, thinking. About what, Seth didn't know, though he hoped the marshal wasn't contemplating Chauncy's arrest or they'd be right back where they started. Finally, Rea stopped grooming and said, "I want you boys out of town."

Chauncy leaned forward in his chair. "The man called me—"

Rea held up a hand, cutting him off. "I know what happened. Talked to a couple of witnesses. But the thing is, the man you killed, Dave Gibson, has a couple of crazy-ass brothers that are gonna come lookin' for you."

"I don't care," Chauncy said.

"Maybe not, but I do. I don't want no more killin' in my town. So, I'm asking nicely on account of your pa. You two can catch the afternoon train to Wichita Falls and be home by dark."

"And if we don't go?" Chauncy asked.

"Then I'm gonna lock you up and hold an inquest. I'd rather not have to do that, but those are your choices."

CHAPTER
16

Percy took Reeves's advice and rode south, looking for Quanah Parker's campsite somewhere along Medicine Creek. Although he had never met the Comanche chief and had only seen him at a distance, he was a little unsettled about the upcoming encounter. Because of Emma's kidnapping, their past histories had been briefly intertwined, and Percy wasn't sure what type of reception he might receive. Although he had never confirmed that Quanah had played a role in Emma's abduction, rumors at the time had suggested Emma had been held in Quanah's camp. Emma had been so traumatized by her ordeal she had refused, and continued to refuse, any discussions on what had actually occurred during her captivity.

As he rode, Percy contemplated how rapidly things had changed in such a short period of time. There hadn't been an Indian raid in eight years and the border of civilization had rolled westward, settlers and cattlemen staking claims to their own piece of the plains. With trains and telegraphs, a man could now travel from coast to coast or send a message to the nether regions of the country and get a response in minutes. But for all the progress, there apparently hadn't been many changes up in this part of the world. And nothing drove that point home more than the Indian lodges Percy spotted in the distance. The Indians were still camped along the rivers and streams, their lodges slowly decaying now that the buffalo had all but disappeared. A few had gone to the trouble of building intricate brush arbors to use during the more temperate months, but most of the Indians weren't any closer to putting down roots than the day they had arrived on the reservation, despite the offers of free lumber and help to build more permanent residences.

Percy didn't know what the answer was and, over time, thought maybe the Indians would change. After all, they really didn't have much choice, now that the ground they once roamed was being parceled out to eager pioneers. Despite how much some would like to return to the old way of life, those days were over forever. Maybe, Percy thought, two or three generations down the line, the Indians would find a way to better fit in with society.

As he approached Medicine Creek, the number of Indian lodges increased exponentially, and they lined both sides of the river. Yes, it was an ideal location with plenty of water and abundant shade, but Percy wondered why they were all congregated together when they had millions of acres at their disposal, including some of the best grazing land on the planet.

He was surprised a few of them hadn't carved out some space to raise some horses since that was one thing the Indians had coveted for centuries. The Choctaws and Chickasaws had settled on their reservations decades ago and they were now some of the sharpest cattlemen around and that included his old friend Montford T. Johnson, a full-blood Chickasaw, who owned a herd of carefully cross-bred cattle that numbered in the thousands. So maybe, Percy thought, there was some hope the relatively recent arrivals would eventually find their way—or not. In the end, the Indians controlled their own destiny, whatever it might be.

As Percy drew closer to the main body of lodges, he realized he had a problem. There were easily two hundred teepees in the area with no visual references to distinguish one from another. And it wasn't like the teepees had a fixed address—they were simply erected at the whims of their owners. Reeves had said Quanah was camped along Medicine Creek. What he had failed to mention was that there were hundreds of others also doing the same.

Percy pulled Mouse to a stop to study the situation. The last thing he wanted to do was ride into the midst of hundreds of Indians with no idea where he was going. Although the Kiowa and Comanche were now allegedly friendly, Percy didn't have any trouble recalling some of the things they'd done in the past. Seeing a man who had been gutted or a woman who had been violently brutalized were hard things to forget. And as Percy thought about that, he wondered, for the first time, if he'd made a mistake coming alone. Not that he wasn't confident in his abilities, but if something did happen, he didn't have enough bullets to shoot his way out.

He was on the verge of turning Mouse around when a young Indian girl with braided pigtails stepped out from behind a tree. She was as cute as a button and no more than seven or eight years old. Percy didn't see any weapons on her, so he assumed she wasn't looking to take his scalp. He held up his hand, palm forward, and said, "Hello."

The girl giggled and said, "I thought white men said, *How?*"

Percy chuckled. "I like to be a little different. I'm lookin' for Quanah. You know where he is?"

The girl nodded. "He's my papa."

"Well, I guess I came to the right place." Percy climbed down from his horse. "You mind takin' me to him?"

"Okay."

The girl turned and started walking and Percy fell in beside her, leading Mouse. "What's your name?" Percy asked.

The girl looked up at Percy and said, "Alice Parker."

"You go to school here, Alice?"

"I do when it's open, but it's summer now."

"That it is," Percy said.

As they approached the nearest grouping of Indian lodges, any hopes for further conversation with Alice were drowned out by a pack of braying dogs who swarmed out of camp, engulfing Alice, Percy, and Mouse. The mare showed her displeasure by flaring her nostrils and yanking her head up, nearly pulling the reins from Percy's hand. He pulled her close and ran a hand across her muzzle, trying to calm her. Both horse and man were relieved a moment later when Alice clapped her hands and shouted something in Comanche. Percy had no idea what she'd said, but it had an immediate effect on the hounds from hell. They turned and scampered away, their tails between their legs.

Although the setting was idyllic, there was nothing blissful about the foul odor that hung over the camp. The smell of rotting meat from discarded animal carcasses mixed with the fragrant aroma of human, dog, and horse feces was gag-inducing. How or why they lived among such filth was a mystery to Percy. Fear of offending his hosts was the only reason he didn't reach up and pull his neckerchief up over his nose and mouth. Instead he focused on breathing through his mouth and even that was of little relief. The stench was inescapable.

After walking for a few minutes, Alice gradually veered toward a cluster of five lodges that were set back from the creek and isolated somewhat from their neighbors. Four of the lodges, erected in a circle, were what Percy would call average size, but the fifth, positioned in the center, was enormous with a base diameter that was probably sixty feet or more, dwarfing the surrounding teepees. Looking at it in relation to the others, Percy was betting he'd found the man he was looking for.

When they neared, Alice stopped and said, "Stay here."

Percy nodded and then reached up and took off his hat, curious to see what type of reception he'd receive. And with that thought, he quickly switched his hat to his left hand, freeing his gun hand. He didn't expect any trouble, but if any came, he was going to be in a world of hurt, gun or no gun.

Alice, standing at the entrance to the large teepee, said something to someone inside and then stepped through the opening. Percy listened to the murmuring inside, hoping he didn't hear the chief levering a fresh round into his rifle. Alice reappeared a moment later, followed by an imposing-looking Indian man, who had to be the elusive chief Quanah.

Quanah studied Percy as he walked over. When he stopped, he looked Percy up and down, then smiled. "You Little Heap Big Guns."

Percy stuck out his hand. "And you must be Quanah."

"Me Quanah," he said as the two shook hands. "Where Heap Big Guns?"

"He's been gone a long time," Percy said, knowing he was asking about his father.

Quanah pointed at Percy and said, "Then you Heap. No more Little."

Percy chuckled and Quanah laughed and clapped him on the shoulder.

"Okay," Percy said. Their Indian names came from a specially designed wagon the family had bought nearly twenty years ago.

Quanah obviously knew who he was though the chief didn't seem the least bit apprehensive that Percy was paying him a visit. It made Percy wonder if he'd been wrong in his assumption that the chief had been involved in his niece's abduction.

Percy noticed that Quanah was eyeing his horse. The chief stepped past Percy and ran a hand along Mouse's neck. "Fine horse."

"Thank you," Percy said. "She's a quarter horse."

Quanah leaned over and ran his hand across Mouse's thick chest then looked up and said, "How much?"

"Not for sale."

"All for sale."

Well, at least Quanah had lived among the whites long enough to know how the world usually worked, Percy thought. The chief had also adopted the white man's way of dressing. He was wearing pants, a long-sleeve white shirt, and a suit vest, his long hair braided into pigtails, which he wore draped over the front of his powerful shoulders. "No, I can't sell her, Quanah."

The chief stood and clapped his hands. "Okay. Come Quanah lodge."

Percy began to wonder if he'd still have a horse when

he returned. With the hope and expectation that he would, he led Mouse over to a tree and tied the reins before following Quanah into his teepee. The bottom of his lodge had been rolled up for better airflow and it also allowed for plenty of light. Percy's nostrils picked up hints of wood-smoke, sage, and body odor, but it was much better inside than what he had expected. Quanah sat down on a bear rug and Percy took a seat to his left, as was customary.

The chief reached for his pipe and began filling the bowl with tobacco, giving Percy a chance to look around. On the other side of the teepee, hanging from a rope, was a beautiful eagle-feather headdress that was at least six feet long. The feathers on each side were all well spaced and secured in place with a thin piece of sinew and it was obvious someone had spent a long time crafting it. Buffalo robes were piled up on the ground and, by the way they were situated, it looked like the chief might share his lodge with three or four other people.

Once the pipe's bowl was filled and packed to the chief's liking, he lit it, took a puff, and passed it to Percy, who took a long draw before handing it back. Over the years, Percy had learned that customs varied among individual Indians when it came to the pipe. Some would get right down to business once everyone had a turn, while others insisted on finishing the tobacco before beginning. This being his first meeting with Quanah, Percy would need to follow his lead.

Quanah took another deep draw from the pipe and exhaled the smoke before saying, "You got a heap bunch cows."

"We do. That's part of the reason I came to see you."

Quanah turned to look at Percy. "You, Burnett, Waggoner, Armstrong. All want talk to Quanah."

Percy's hopes soured some with Quanah's mention of

the other big cattle ranchers in the area. "They payin' to push their cattle over onto your land? I'm willin' to sign a lease and pay for grazing rights."

Quanah took another hit from the pipe and put it aside. "Not Quanah's land. Land belong to all. Kiowa no want lease. Agent no want lease."

Percy looked Quanah in the eye. "What do you want?"

"People hungry. Quanah feed people."

"A grass lease would put some money in all of your pockets."

Quanah shrugged. "Quanah know."

Percy decided to try another approach. "You runnin' any cattle or horses up here?"

"Few horses."

"What brand do you put on 'em?"

"Why brand?"

"I'm thinkin' on somethin'."

Quanah studied Percy for a moment then picked up his knife and leaned forward to scratch something in the dirt and leaned back. Percy looked down at what he had drawn. It was a circle within a circle. The larger circle was about six inches around with the smaller one about half that.

As Percy studied what Quanah had drawn, he was thinking of options and wondering how much he could trust Quanah, whom the federal government had declared the principal chief for all Comanches. For eons, they had roamed the plains doing whatever they felt like doing as separate bands with no central hierarchy and no one person designated as chief. If someone had wanted to go on a raid, he rounded up some braves and took off. But all of that had changed once the Indians were settled on the reservation. With the government needing someone to represent the Comanches' interest, they had dictated that Quanah would be that person and Percy knew that hadn't set well with some members of his tribe. And it was a concern for him. If he made a deal with the chief and the others refused to cooperate simply to spite Quanah, then Percy would be in a pickle.

"Quanah, if you help me get a lease done, not only will you be helping your tribe, but I'll sweeten the pot by brandin' one hundred heifers with your brand this fall. And when they calve next year, I'll put your brand on those. We'll let 'em run with our herd until you're ready to get into the cattle business."

When Quanah didn't immediately respond, Percy wondered if he had gone too far. "You don't have to decide now. I need to visit with the Indian agent anyway. In fact, why don't you and your wife come to dinner at the ranch on Saturday?"

"All?" Quanah asked.

Percy wrinkled his brow in confusion. "All of what?"

"Wives."

"How many you got?"

Quanah held up his hand and splayed his fingers.

"Five?" Percy asked, the last note of his voice a little higher than the first.

Quanah nodded and smiled.

Well, hell, Percy thought. He didn't know if the wives all got along and he didn't want to end up in a family squabble, but Percy put those thoughts aside and said, "Sure, bring 'em all."

CHAPTER
17

Her clothes stiff with Scar's dried blood, Emma steered her horse up the road toward home. Her only goal now was to get inside without being seen. As she rode, she scanned the corrals and the area around the barn, hoping to catch a glimpse of Simon. She didn't want her son to see her covered in dried blood and be forced to explain what had happened. Knowing the Comanches' bloodlust for revenge after the killing of one of their own, it was a story that would need to be told, but not right now and certainly not to her son. She didn't see any sign of Simon though that didn't necessarily mean he was inside the house. There were dozens of places where he might be, and Emma knew he wasn't one to lie around the house when a world of new discoveries awaited outdoors.

Crossing her fingers, she rode up to her front porch and climbed down from the horse. After wrapping the reins around the hitching post, she tiptoed across porch and took a peek in the window. She didn't see any sign of Simon, so she pushed open the front door and stepped inside. Desperate to rid herself of Scar's blood, she began stripping out of her clothes the instant she was inside. She bundled up the clothes and tossed them out on the back porch before hurrying into the kitchen. Wetting a towel, she began wiping the dried blood from her skin.

With the trip to San Francisco quickly approaching, Frances was busy trying to nail down the timeline, and the train schedules for all the different railroads couldn't have been more confusing if they'd been written in Chinese. Deciding she needed some help, she stood, scooped up all of her paperwork, and exited through the back door. Emma was as smart as a whip and she would have it figured out in no time.

Frances made the short walk to Emma's place and, as she climbed the stairs to the back porch, she noticed a bundle of bloody rags or bloody something and she wondered what had happened. She tapped on the back door before pushing on through. When she saw her granddaughter covered with blood, she stopped in her tracks and her hands flew up to cover her mouth.

Startled, Emma dropped the rag and stood there as naked as the day she was born.

Overcoming her shock, Frances dropped her hands and rushed over. "Where are you hurt? Do I need to send for a doctor?"

"I'm fine," Emma said, trying to make herself as small as possible.

"You're not fine," Frances said as she took Emma by the elbow and turned her around. "You've got blood all over you."

"It's not my blood."

Frances froze and looked her granddaughter in the eye. "Whose is it?"

Emma bent down and picked up the rag. "Will you help get it off of me? I can't stand it any longer."

Frances took a deep breath and took the rag from Emma's hands. "I'll wait for you to explain, but please tell me all this blood came from an injured animal or something."

"It didn't," Emma said.

Frances's knees sagged and Emma grabbed her by the arm, afraid she might fall. "Maybe you better sit down." Emma said.

Frances nodded and she let Emma guide her over to a kitchen chair and she sat down. Emma, embarrassed, hurried down the hall to her bedroom and slipped on an old shirt before returning to the kitchen. She took the rag from her grandmother, rinsed it, took a seat at the table, and handed Frances the rag. "Please wipe it off my face."

Frances nodded, leaned forward, and began cleaning her granddaughter's face. "You're trembling."

Emma nodded.

"And your cheek is all scraped up."

"Consider me lucky, then," Emma said.

"What happened?"

"I went out to the horse pasture and . . . and . . ."

"Shh," Frances said. "You need some time to recover, but I need to know if trouble's heading our way."

Emma shook her head. "Not right now."

What did that mean? Frances wondered. A delayed attack? Emma was traumatized and Frances knew she needed to give her some time, but if someone was coming after her family, she needed to know right now. "You sure no one's coming?"

"I'm sure."

Frances nodded. She stood, walked over to the stove to grab the pail of water, and returned. After rinsing the rag, she continued cleaning. "I can't do much to get the blood out of your hair. We'll have to go out to the well to rinse it out when I'm through."

"Okay," Emma said.

Frances couldn't believe how much blood there was. It was like Emma had stood under a hog that was being bled out after slaughter.

"This happened when you were out at the horse pasture?"

"Yes."

"Indian or white?" Frances asked.

"Indian," Emma said.

Now we're getting somewhere, Frances thought. "Was it one of those involved in your kidnappin'?"

Emma nodded. "The worst of the bunch."

"The one you called Scar?"

"Yes."

"Is he dead or do I need to send someone after him?"

"He's dead. I made damn sure of that."

"Pull your shirt down and turn around so I can clean your back."

Emma slipped her arms out of the shirt and let it fall to her waist. She heard her grandmother gasp when Emma turned.

"Oh Lordy, child, what did those savages do to you?" Frances whispered.

It was a question Emma didn't want to answer. She knew she had scars back there from the burns, from the whippings, and from other things the Indians had done, but she had made it a point to never look at it in the mirror. That was the past, and nothing was going to change it.

"Who did this to you?" Frances asked.

"Squaws mostly. It tapered off after a while."

No wonder the poor child had nightmares, Frances thought. And she was seeing only the scars on the outside. It was Emma's inside scars that troubled Frances more. Physical wounds healed with time. It was the emotional scars that took forever to heal, if at all. "How did you get all this blood on you? Was it a surprise attack?"

"No. I saw him. He knocked me off my horse and I had to stab him with my knife."

"Why didn't you just shoot him?" Frances asked.

"I tried. I put one bullet in him before I ended up on the ground. I had my split skirt on and it probably saved my life."

"How so?"

"It confused him. Gave me time to get to my knife."

Frances didn't want to ask but knew she needed to. "Did he get your skirt off?"

"No. I stabbed him before he could."

Frances exhaled the breath she had been holding. "I've done all I can do with the rag. Go slip on an old dress and we'll go out to the well to rinse your hair."

Emma nodded, pulled up the shirt, then stood and walked down the hall to her bedroom. When she returned, Emma grabbed a towel from the kitchen, and they walked out to the well, where they rinsed Emma's hair until the water ran clear. As Emma was wrapping the towel around her head, she spotted Eli on his back porch, his nose buried in a book.

"We need to tell Uncle Eli what happened," Emma said.

"You feel up to it?"

Emma shrugged. "His body is going to be found at some point."

They walked over and Emma slumped into one of rocking chairs, emotionally and physically exhausted.

"What happened to your cheek?" Eli asked.

"It's all part of what I need to tell you."

Eli dog-eared a page and closed the book. "I'm listening."

"Well, I went out to look at those colts like I told you I was going to do and . . . well . . ." Emma paused as her eyes watered and a fresh tear fell onto her right cheek.

Eli reached out and covered her hand with his. "Take your time."

Frances wanted to jump in and tell her son what had happened, but she knew this was Emma's story to tell.

When Emma had regained a small measure of composure she continued. "Like I was sayin', I went out to look at the two colts and spotted an Indian hiding in the trees."

"Not all that unusual around here," Eli said.

"You're right, except I knew this one. And not in a good way."

Eli raised an eyebrow. "One of your abductors?"

"The worst of the lot. He did things to me that . . . that I'm too ashamed to talk about."

"No need for details, Emma," Eli said. "Please continue."

"Anyway, there he was, just sittin' on his horse." Emma continued with the rest of the story, including the collision of horses and her stabbing of Scar. She did not tell her uncle about riddling his body with rifle bullets.

"But I'm worried some of his kinfolk might come looking for revenge. I've seen what the Comanches do when one of theirs is killed. They once spent three days skinning a man alive after he killed one of their braves."

Eli looked at Frances and said, "Your thoughts, Mother?" He pulled his pipe and tobacco from his shirt pocket and began filling the bowl.

"I'd have been terrified if this had happened back when they were raidin' all across the state, but I don't know now. I'm hoping they've been tamed some."

Eli struck a match and lit his pipe. He took a deep draw and the smoke danced around his mouth when he said, "I agree. We've advanced as a society and the days of Indian war parties are over. However, that doesn't imply the Indians aren't capable of inflicting damage." He looked at Emma and said, "Where's the body?"

"I drug it into the trees. Did I do the right thing?" Emma asked.

"Doesn't matter. The Indians will have a difficult, if not impossible, task linking anyone on the ranch to this killing."

"Even if they find his body on our land?" Emma asked.

"Doesn't make any difference where the body is found. We own and operate a large cattle ranch and are unable to monitor the traveling habits of those who choose to cross our property."

"Okay, I can see that."

"If the Indians come, we'll deal with it then. How are you emotionally?"

Emma thought about it for a moment. "Are you asking if I regret what happened?"

"I suppose."

"Not for a second."

CHAPTER
18

With their options limited to leaving town or Chauncy going to jail, Seth and his cousin made the decision to depart Fort Worth as soon as possible, preferably on the afternoon train. However, Chauncy had a loose end or two to tie up before leaving and one of those, despite a heated argument with Seth, involved Marcie Malone.

Now standing at the corner of Tenth and Rusk streets, and thirty feet from the red front door of The Belmont, the argument between the cousins reignited.

"Have you really thought this through?" Seth asked.

"Ain't nothin' to think about," Chauncy replied.

Having witnessed his cousin coolly and calmly kill a man in a gunfight earlier this morning, Seth was wary about pushing Chauncy too hard. "I just think you're askin' for a lifetime of heartache. You gonna kill every man who recognizes her and says somethin' about it?"

"Well, no. Unless they need killin'. What's the big deal? She likes me and I like her. Ain't that how that works?"

"What if she's using—never mind." Seth stopped, thinking that might be the one question that might put Chauncy over the edge.

He gave Seth a hard look and said in a low, menacing voice, "Go ahead and ask it if you reckon you need to."

"I don't. Why don't you think about it for a few more days? You can always catch a train down here anytime you want."

"I done thought about it. And right now, I'm tired of talkin' about it." Chauncy turned and walked over to the door. He stopped with his hand on the knob and turned to look at Seth. "You comin'?"

Seth, against the idea from the very start, wasn't too keen on getting involved. "You want me to come?" Seth asked.

"Better'n standin' out in the sun, ain't it?"

Seth sighed and joined Chauncy as he opened the door and held it, allowing Seth to pass through first. This was Seth's first time inside and he looked around in amazement at all the finery. He knew the purpose of the house was to lend a refined atmosphere to the business that went on upstairs, but the furnishings, carpets, and draperies rivaled any of the fine homes he'd visited back East. It was immediately obvious to Seth that running a parlor house was big business.

An attractive, red-haired woman wearing a beautifully cut dress, stepped through a doorway and approached. "Good morning, gents."

"Mornin', Mrs. Belmont," Chauncy said.

"I hope you slept well, Mr. Ridgeway." She turned to Seth and stuck out her hand. "I don't believe we've met. I'm Josie Belmont."

Seth took her hand, which was as soft as a ball of cotton. "Seth Ferguson, Mrs. Belmont."

"Nice to meet you, Mr. Ferguson." She gave his hand a playful squeeze before releasing her grip. "Are you and Mr. Ridgeway friends?"

"Cousins."

Mrs. Belmont studied Seth's face for a moment, then turned and looked at Chauncy before turning back. "I can see the family resemblance. Do you work on the cattle ranch, Mr. Ferguson?"

"I did when I was younger. I've recently returned after graduating college and plan to either join a law practice or begin my own."

"Oh, that's marvelous," Mrs. Belmont said. "Is it your intention to practice here in Fort Worth?"

"No, ma'am. Dallas."

"A pity. I'm always looking for a good lawyer."

"How did you know we had a cattle ranch?" Chauncy asked.

"Why, Mr. Ridgeway, everyone around here knows about the Rocking R Ranch. What I don't know is which one is your father. Percy or Eli?"

"Percy, ma'am. You know him?"

"We've met. What can I help you two handsome gents with? Unfortunately, we haven't yet opened for the day."

Seth thought it odd that Mrs. Belmont went to the trouble of asking Chauncy about his father then immediately changed the subject. Most people would have asked a follow-up question or two, maybe asking about a person's well-being or how someone was getting along. Mrs. Belmont had done neither and Seth thought it strange. But maybe she was just pressed for time. After all, time was money, especially in her business.

"Is Marcie around?" Chauncy asked.

"I believe she is unless she stepped out for a moment. Would you like to speak to her?"

"Yes," Chauncy said.

"I'll tell her you're here. We have coffee in the kitchen if either of you gentleman would like a cup. Mr. Ridgeway, I believe you know where the kitchen is."

"I do, ma'am, thank you."

Mrs. Belmont turned with a swirl of her skirt and headed up the stairs. When she was out of earshot, Seth whispered, "Does she . . . huh . . . huh . . . oh, never mind."

Chauncy chuckled then whispered, "You want some of that? You ought to see the other girls."

"I can only imagine. But that doesn't mean I want to mar—"

Seth snapped his mouth shut, cutting off the rest of his sentence. A moment later they heard someone padding downstairs, and they looked up to see Marcie descending. Dressed in a long, flowing robe and her feet bare, Seth couldn't deny she was stunningly beautiful, even at this time of the day after having probably worked most of the night. With long blond hair and blue eyes, she was everything a man could hope for—if she'd been a schoolteacher.

"Mornin', Chauncy. Mornin', Seth," Marcie said.

"Morning, Marcie," Seth said.

"Let's sit." She took Chauncy by the hand and led him over to a long, dark green sofa, and Seth followed. He took a seat at the far end to give them a bit of privacy, although he could clearly hear every word they uttered. He quickly discovered that Chauncy wasn't one for dabbling in small talk.

"How long is it goin' to take you to pack?" Chauncy asked.

"Pack what?" Marcie asked, obviously confused. "A picnic basket? An overnight bag?"

"Well, no," Chauncy said. "I meant to pack all your stuff."

"I don't understand. Did Josie kick me out for givin' you a freebie and didn't tell me?"

Seth cringed. He felt bad for his cousin. Chauncy might be slicker than most with a gun, but he was absolutely clueless when it came to romancing a woman.

"No, Josie ain't kicked you out. I want you to come with me."

"Where?" Marcie asked. "I'm sorry, Chauncy, but I don't understand."

Chauncy sighed. "I want to take you to the ranch."

"And I would love to see it. But I have to work."

"No, you don't," Chauncy said.

"I do if I want to eat. I might could talk Josie into givin' me the night off and I guess I could take the train back tomorrow."

Chauncy turned and looked at Seth with a *please help me* look on his face.

Seth shrugged and smiled. That bought him an angry glare.

Chauncy turned back to Marcie. "I . . . I . . . I want to marry ya."

"What did you say?" Marcie asked.

"I want us to get married."

Marcie jumped to her feet and her hands flew up to cover her mouth as tears shimmered in her eyes. As she stared down at Chauncy, the tears began spilling out, running down her cheeks and dripping onto her bosom.

After a few moments she dropped her hands and said, "What did you say?"

Chauncy pushed to his feet. "I want you to be my wife."

She stepped forward, wrapped her arms around Chauncy's neck, and kissed him hard on the mouth. "You . . . you mean it?"

Chauncy reached up and brushed a strand of hair from her face. "I do. If you'll have me."

Marcie kissed him again. "Yes. A thousand times, yes."

Seth thought that if she was acting it had to be one of the best performances he'd ever seen. Maybe he had been wrong about her, but he knew time would tell the true tale. He stepped over and wrapped his arms around both of them. "Congratulations, you two. I hate to break up your joyful moment, but if we're going to make the afternoon train, we need to get packing." Seth stepped back and Marcie and Chauncy untangled themselves.

Marcie wiped the tears from her face and nodded. "It won't take me long."

"Good," Seth said, "While you're doing that, I'm going to buy your fiancé a beer and then we'll go pack our stuff." Seth pulled out his pocket watch and clicked the lid open. "The train leaves at three o'clock. We'll be back here at one-thirty to carry your stuff to the station."

Marcie nodded, stepped over, gave Seth a hug, and kissed him on the cheek. "I'll be ready."

CHAPTER
19

Marcie, over the moon, charged back up the stairs to pack her belongings. Although she and Chauncy didn't know each other all that well, she made a promise to herself to do anything and everything she could to make it work. It was the chance she had been praying for and she'd leave disease-free and having never been pregnant. Not that there hadn't been a close call or two, and she'd had to resort to the use of Madame Restell's Preventive Powders if she missed her time of the month, but that was just part of the business. All the girls she knew had done the same and the powder, when it worked, was much preferable and much safer than the alternative.

About as handsome as any man she'd been with, Chauncy had it all, the looks, the charm, and most important, the will to look beyond Marcie's shortcomings. She did have concerns about Chauncy's family discovering her previous occupation though she felt certain she could win them over if she had a chance to start with a clean slate. After all, she'd had to rely on her charm every night just to survive. Stepping over to the wardrobe, Marcie opened the door and began sorting through her dresses.

In her profession, appearances mattered, and Josie had always insisted that everyone who worked in her parlor house wear only the finest garments. Of course, each woman was responsible for buying their own clothing and that was going to make it difficult for Marcie to leave any of her things behind. At the present time, she had six dresses that had been purchased via mail catalogs from several high-end stores back East. One or two had bad memories attached and these she would either give to the other girls or leave behind for them to fight over. Although friendly with the other women who worked at The Belmont, real friendships within the house were difficult to maintain because of the constant competition. If Marcie didn't work, she didn't get paid and, other than a handful of regulars who visited her, any man who walked through the door was fair game. And the competition could be fierce if it had been a slow couple of days. She had to pay Josie twenty dollars a week for room and board and Josie also took a cut from everything she and the other women earned. Add in the expenses for clothing and other needed accessories and Marcie was doling out a significant amount of cash every month. That was definitely something she wouldn't miss.

Marcie pushed all thoughts of the past from her mind. All of that was over and done with and day one of her new life began today. And it would be a life where anything was possible, and she would be able to dream the same dreams she'd had as a child.

She jumped when there was a knock on her door and all thoughts of her future were put on hold. Now would come the difficult matter of separating herself from Josie, who had always treated her well, considering. "Come in," Marcie shouted.

Josie pushed open the door and stepped inside. "So, you're leavin' me, huh?"

Marcie stopped what she was doing and turned to look at her. "I'm really sorry I didn't give you much notice."

Josie waved a hand in the air. "Don't worry about it. I've got more girls than places to put them. Though I'm sure most aren't as sweet and intelligent as you."

Marcie's cheeks reddened. "Thank you." She turned back to the wardrobe, pulled out two dresses, and spread them out side by side on the bed. "Which one should I wear to meet his family?"

Josie stepped over to the bed for a closer look. She rubbed her fingers across the embroidered sleeve of a beautifully finished red dress and said, "This one is perfect." Josie looked at Marcie and said, "But, right now, you need to think a bit beyond your attire. You're going to face some difficult questions ahead that you need to be prepared for."

Marcie pushed the dresses to the foot of her bed and she and Josie sat down. "I was hopin' questions about my past wouldn't come up."

"They may not, at least for a while," Josie said. "People out here usually don't care much about where you're from or what you did in a previous life. That's because some people have very little curiosity and others are too busy or too ignorant to think much beyond their own little world. Neither applies to the Ridgeway family. I don't know what you envision, but you won't be riding to a ranch managed by a bunch of cowpunchers fresh off the trail. There's a reason they've been in business as long as they have."

"How do you know so much about them?" Marcie asked.

"I know . . . huh . . . well, I just do. Let's just leave it at that, shall we?"

"Sure. What do I tell them if they ask where I'm from?"

"Tell them you grew up on a farm in Missouri. Which is in fact, true, right?"

Marcie nodded. "What do I say if they ask where me and Chauncy met?"

"That's something you two will have to work out. Maybe you ran into each other at a mercantile store or on a train or somewhere like that. Keep it simple and if you have to, try to give vague answers and try not to lie. Or, if you want to be honest and frank, you can just tell them the truth."

"The truth?"

"It's not as crazy as it sounds. As far as I know there are no perfect people and we've all done things we wish we hadn't. It's called forgiveness. However, I would suggest you try to avoid the subject until they've had an opportunity to really get to know you. If things get too dicey you need to remember you aren't marrying the entire family, only one member of it. And I'd suggest you do that sooner rather than later."

"Marry, you mean?"

"Yes. I don't know Chauncy enough to know if he's the impulsive type though he doesn't strike me as someone who goes around half-cocked. He appears self-assured and comfortable in his own skin. And he seems smitten with you although we both know how quickly those whims can change. I'm not suggesting you run down to the justice of the peace and get married this afternoon. There's time. What you don't want to do is wake up one morning and realize it's been six months and you two still haven't tied the knot."

Josie stood as did Marcie and the two women embraced. "I'm very happy for you," Josie said. "I hope all goes well for you and Chauncy."

"Thank you for not hatin' me for leavin'," Marcie said.

They separated and Josie said, "I'm proud of you. There aren't very many girls in this business who get a chance to leave this life." Josie reached up and brushed a strand of hair out of Marcie's eyes. "Make the most of your opportunity."

"I will," Marcie said.

Josie turned and exited the room, pulling the door closed behind her. As she descended the stairs, she wondered if she should have been more forthcoming about what she knew about the Ridgeway family. By the time she reached the bottom of the stairs, she had decided not to say anything more. Discretion was one of the cornerstones of her business and betraying someone's trust would get her run out of town in a hurry.

CHAPTER
20

As Percy rode away from Quanah's camp, he wondered if he had made a mistake inviting the chief and his family to dinner. It wasn't that he disliked the chief or had any strong feelings one way or the other on the issue of polygamy. Any man who thought he needed more than one wife was welcome to it, along with all the misery and bickering that came along with it. No, what Percy hadn't considered, was Emma's possible reaction to seeing the chief again. However, rescinding the invitation now would be an affront, so he had to hope that Quanah's appearance at the ranch wouldn't send Emma into a tailspin. A few moments later he thought of a better idea. He could offer Emma and Simon an all-expenses-paid weekend in Fort Worth or Dallas to lure them away from the ranch. It might hurt his pocketbook some, but it would solve what could be a sticky situation.

The more Percy thought about that, the more he liked it. And he could send his mother along. Knowing her, she would be just as likely to stab or shoot Quanah as she was to offer a hello. She had complained for years that the Indians who had kidnapped Emma should be punished. How would she react if one showed up at her door? Percy didn't want to know what the answer might be and the best way to avoid it was to send them away for the weekend.

After riding for the better part of an hour, Percy turned Mouse onto the main road into Fort Sill. He had always found it strange that, unlike other army posts he had visited, Fort Sill wasn't surrounded by a stockade fence or a wall or anything else that might slow a raider's advance. It was wide open, with people coming and going at will. Other than that, Fort Sill was laid out with the same military precision evident at forts all across the frontier, with the main buildings configured in a large square with an open parade ground at the center. The inhabitants were a mix of Indians, traders, and soldiers, mostly from the 9th and 10th Cavalry regiments, whose ranks were filled with black enlisted men. Better known as the Buffalo Soldiers, they had called Fort Sill home for years and Percy, who had interacted with the troops many times over the years, thought they were some of the finest soldiers in the army.

Percy knew the constant rifle fire echoing across the river valley was part of the training program the current post commander, Major Guy Henry, had implemented upon his arrival two years ago. Major Henry, a stickler for details, drilled his troops relentlessly, required 100 percent participation in the marksmanship training, and strongly opposed cursing, gambling, and the consumption of alcoholic beverages. Percy could tolerate him in small doses, but the major was the polar opposite of Percy's dear friend Lieutenant Colonel John W. Davidson, who had been the previous post commander. Davidson could smoke, drink, cuss, and play cards with the best of them and he and Percy had spent several long nights doing just that.

Percy pulled Mouse to a stop in front of the Sherman House, the post's headquarters, and climbed down from his horse. Although he and Major Henry had an uneasy friendship, Percy made a habit of stopping by when he was in the neighborhood. It was never a bad idea to curry favor with the army, because no one knew what the future might hold. Wrapping Mouse's reins around the hitching post, he stepped up on the porch, took off his hat, and pushed through the door.

Stepping inside, he paused a moment to let his eyes adjust then approached the sentry who was manning a desk near the entrance. He was a young, handsome, black soldier with yellow corporal stripes sewn onto the sleeve of his dress uniform. Percy felt for him, dressed in all that wool, because it was hotter than hell. "Afternoon, Corporal," Percy said.

"Afternoon, sir. Can I help you?"

"Percy Ridgeway to see Major Henry."

"The major was on the range, earlier, but I'll check to see if he's back."

Percy nodded and the soldier stood, turned on his heel with military precision, and disappeared into the bowels of the building. Percy would usually share a meal or a game of cards with the post commander then rack out in the officers' quarters. But he didn't know if he could stomach an entire evening with the major and he was leaning toward returning to Reeves's camp for the night. It meant sleeping outdoors, but the company would be a damn sight better.

The corporal returned a moment later and ushered

Percy down a hall and into the commander's office. Henry rose from his chair and stepped around the desk. Like most cavalry men, Henry was small in stature and probably didn't weigh more than 130 pounds. The first thing one noticed when first meeting the major was the scar below his right eye, which Percy knew came from a Sioux bullet. Henry stuck out his hand and said, "Hello, Percy."

Percy shook and said, "Good to see you again, Major." Henry had stopped by the ranch a few times over the last three years and, as best as Percy could recall, had never stayed more than an hour or two.

Henry waved to a chair in front of his desk and said, "Have a seat."

Percy sunk down in the chair while Henry walked back behind his desk and sat. It was really hard to look at Henry without staring at the wound and Percy had to force himself to look elsewhere.

Henry leaned back in his chair and crossed one leg over the other. "What brings you up this way?"

So much for the small talk, Percy thought. "Well, Major, I need some grazin' land."

"You and every other rancher within three hundred miles."

"Has anyone offered to lease some of the Indian land? I'm willin' to pay."

"They have, as a matter of fact. But the bureaucrats in Washington aren't interested in leasing any land. Believe me, I've tried. Common sense says the Indians could use the money, but that's one thing in short supply on Capitol Hill.

"How does the Indian agent feel about the idea?"

"From what I gather he wouldn't be opposed to it. His

major problem is getting all the different tribes to agree. And most of the time they can't even agree on what day of the week it is. There might come a day when they'll wake up in Washington though I don't see it happening anytime soon."

"What about the other outfits that let their cattle drift over onto the reservation? How do they get away with it?"

"Lack of manpower, mainly. I've had orders to clear the Territory of all non-Indian cattle before and we've done it a few times, but it never works. The cattle either drift back or are driven back within days."

Percy paused a moment to organize his thoughts. He needed grass or they were going to be in a world of hurt.

"I know what you're thinking, Percy," the major said. "There's not much I can do to stop you from pushing your cattle across the river. But who's going to manage the herd? Maybe pull out a calf that gets bogged down in a creek? Need I remind you that the only people allowed on the reservations are the government employees and their families and the Indians themselves?"

Percy didn't care for the major's haughty tone—all that "need I remind you" bullshit. He gave the major a hard look and said, "Maybe I'll marry me a squaw."

Henry uncrossed his legs and leaned forward in his chair, propping his elbows on his desk. "And leave that fine ranch of yours to your Indian wife when you die? I do believe that Texas is a common-property state, meaning your legal wife will get half of your estate upon your death."

Percy glared at Henry and said, "Point made, Major." The tension in the room was now palpable.

Henry leaned back in his chair and sighed. "Look, Percy,

I know you're in a bind with the drought. Maybe you could work out a deal with the Indian agent to sell a few thousand cattle to the government for the Indian rations. If you could do that, you'd probably be allowed to hold the herd on the reservation until they were dispersed to the various tribes. Would that take some of the pressure off?"

"A little. Do you know if they already have a contract for winter delivery?"

"That I don't know. Probably worth a trip to Anadarko to find out."

Percy stood. "I agree."

Henry stood and walked around the desk. "Anything else I can help you with?"

"No, but you and your wife are welcome to dinner at the ranch anytime." The two men shook hands and Percy turned toward the door. About halfway there, he remembered something he wanted to ask, and he stopped and turned around. "Major, any word about where my good friend John Davidson is currently posted?"

Henry frowned and crossed his hands behind his back. "He died two years ago, Percy."

Percy's eyes widened in surprise. "Died? He wasn't much older than me. What happened to him?"

"Freak accident. His horse slipped on the ice and fell on top of him. He lingered a few days after, but there wasn't anything the doctors could do."

Percy shook his head. "I'll be damned. After all the battles he fought, and he dies like that. Beats all I ever seen."

"We never know when we're going to be called home," Henry said.

"I guess not." Percy turned and walked out of the office.

Outside, Percy took a moment to digest the information.

Davidson had been in an untold number of scrapes over his forty-year army career. And to survive all that and then get killed after a horse fell on him was almost as bizarre as Percy's brother-in-law Amos Ferguson dying by hitting his head on a wagon on a dark, dark night, long ago. Percy didn't put much stock in that "being called home" nonsense, but it did make him reflect a bit on his own mortality as he untied Mouse's reins and mounted up.

CHAPTER
21

With Moses Wilcox's services secured, Leander Hays was back on the hunt for his prized horse. Wilcox, a tall, thin, bowlegged man, was squatted down, studying the tracks that Leander had found earlier in the day. He stood, spit a long stream of tobacco juice into the dirt, and remounted his horse.

"Is it the stallion?" Leander asked.

"Yep, though it's a wonder how you found it." Wilcox put the spurs to his horse and steered toward the road.

A few choice words popped into Leander's mind, but he held his tongue. Back at the ranch, he had packed enough supplies for a couple of days, knowing anything longer would be futile. There were just too many places where a thief could hide a horse. As they rode in silence, Leander was wishing he'd asked someone else to ride along for the company. Wilcox didn't talk much, and like most trackers, he usually left at first light and wouldn't show back up again until he found something, or it got too dark to see.

Leander noticed that Wilcox wasn't spending much time studying the ground. "Are we on the stallion's trail?"

Wilcox looked up, spit another mouthful of tobacco juice, and said, "Yep."

"So, you think he was headed for town?"

"Didn't say that. Just hide and watch."

Leander gave up on starting a conversation. When he'd first met Wilcox many years ago, he had been a story-telling fool, laughing and joshing with the men around the campfire. But that had been twenty years ago, and Wilcox hadn't been a young man back then. If Leander had to guess, he'd bet Wilcox was now in his late sixties and he knew every one of those years had been hard living. It could be Wilcox was just worn out, Leander thought. He still got around good and didn't seem to have any trouble getting on or off a horse though Leander knew the man had to have some aches and pains because he sure did, and he was twenty years younger.

When they reached the ranch's western property line, Wilcox pulled his horse to a stop and focused his gaze on the ground. Leander let him work without bothering him. He had sweated through his shirt hours ago and what little breeze there was only stirred the heat around.

Wilcox turned his horse and rode north along the fence line and stopped about three hundred yards away. Leander groaned when Wilcox waved him forward. Riding north into Indian Territory rarely turned out well. He spurred his horse forward and rode out to meet Wilcox.

"Town never did make no sense," Wilcox said when Leander arrived. He pointed at the land across the river and said, "I reckon there's more horse thieves yonder than flies on a fresh cow patty. I figured we was headed that way from the get-go."

Leander sighed. "Ain't ever easy, is it?"

"Nope."

"How many men we looking for?" Leander asked.

"Three. I sure hope you brought plenty of ammo." Turning his horse, Wilcox spurred his horse forward and Leander fell in beside him.

They followed a wide game trail down into the river bottom and they splashed through a thin ribbon of water that wasn't more than a foot wide and rode up the far bank, entering Indian Territory.

"I hate this country," Wilcox said.

"You and me both," Leander said. "How many times you reckon you traveled up this way?"

Wilcox spat out his chaw of tobacco and spat a couple more times to clear his mouth before saying, "Too damn many. I reckon I'm on borrowed time up in these parts." A little farther on, Wilcox said, "Hold your horse so I can parse out the trail."

Leander pulled his horse to a stop as Wilcox rode a large circle, his eyes scanning the ground. Finding a trail after a river crossing could be a bit dicey if the party you were following was up to no good. The Indians were masters at it, often riding along the river for miles before exiting onto a patch of rocky ground. He didn't think a horse thief in a hurry would take the time to mask his trail and that thought proved correct a moment later when Wilcox waved him forward, the trail only a few yards downstream from where they'd crossed.

Leander put his horse in motion and joined Wilcox as they rode deeper into enemy territory. Grazing cattle dotted the landscape and from what Leander could see, it was a mixture of brands. He spotted cattle from the Waggoners' Triple-D, the Burnetts' Four-Sixes, and even a good number from the Rocking R. Technically, it was illegal for those cattle to be grazing there and Leander was a bit surprised to see the Rocking R brand because Percy was usually a stickler for things like that. But as dry as it had been, the cattle would search for grass wherever they could find it and they didn't much care who the land belonged to.

Wilcox didn't seem to have any trouble following the rustlers' trail through the thousands of cattle milling about. They crossed a couple of dry creeks and soon spotted an Indian encampment along East Cache Creek. Leander estimated there were well over twenty-five lodges and a half a dozen brush arbors where the Indians mingled during the hotter months. Apparently, the rustlers had no interest in rubbing shoulders with the Indians, and neither did they as they followed the thieves' trail as it cut a wide berth around the Indian camp. An hour later, they crossed Beaver Creek and entered the Chickasaw Nation.

An original member of the Five Civilized Tribes, along with the Cherokee, Choctaw, Creek, and Seminole, the Chickasaws had been settled on their reservation a full two decades before the Comanches gave up their weapons and surrendered to the army. Leander didn't know how the Chickasaws and those other tribes picked up the name *civilized* because at one time, they all had been every bit as wild as the Comanches and Kiowas had been before being forced onto the reservation.

Wilcox and Leander continued following the rustlers' trail east. They crossed the aptly named Dry Creek and the land opened up to a wide, windswept plain of low, rolling hills dotted with an occasional elm or oak. With views that stretched on for miles, it was obvious at first glance that the area was uninhabited and there was no sign of Sundancer.

After another hour, Leander rode up close to Wilcox and said, "Do you get a sense where the trail may be headed?"

"Nope. Won't know till we get where we's goin'. But I got a feelin' we might be gettin' close."

Leander surveyed the empty landscape. "How do you figure?"

Wilcox shrugged. "A hunch." He pointed at the ground and said, "Them tracks ain't more than a couple of hours old."

Leander looked down at the trail and couldn't see any discernable difference from what they had been looking at all along. But if Wilcox said they were made two hours ago, then they were made two hours ago.

After traveling another half hour, the trail led them down to a small spring-fed creek and they allowed their horses a chance to drink. It was the first water they'd found since leaving the ranch and both men climbed down for a few minutes to stretch their legs and to refill their canteens. Wilcox reloaded his cheek with a fresh plug of tobacco. Once he had it tucked in where he liked it, he pointed at the creek and said, "Be a good place to hide out with that there spring a-flowin'. Ain't nobody else round, neither." He handed his horse's reins to Leander. "I'm a-gonna walk up the far bank for a look-see."

As he walked away, Leander noticed that Wilcox was limping. And he understood why. Straddle a horse every day of your life where each step the horse took radiated up your spine and everyone limped a little when they got off. That was just part of it. And as Leander watched, Wilcox's limp got a little better with each step forward.

Wilcox climbed up to the top of the bank and disappeared. His limp was mostly gone by the time he returned.

"Well?" Leander asked.

"There's three half-ass sod houses dug into the hillside 'bout a hundred yards or so from where we's at now. They's got a little corral a little ways east of the last 'un."

"Any horses in the corral?"

Wilcox nodded. "Yep. One."

Leander felt like he was pulling teeth. "Is it my stallion?"

Another nod from Wilcox. "Yep."

Leander and Wilcox pulled their rifles from their scabbards, tied the horses to a cottonwood sapling, and went for a closer look.

CHAPTER
22

Seth and Chauncy were seated at a table nursing a couple of beers and killing time inside the Alamo saloon. Both had estimated that packing their things wouldn't take more than ten minutes, but neither really had a particular taste for beer this early in the day, either. Especially after swilling too much who-hit-John the night before. How long it would take Marcie to pack was one topic of their conversation. Chauncy had estimated an hour, and Seth two, which would be pushing his one-thirty deadline.

Seth pushed his beer away. "When are you two going to get hitched?" If Chauncy was having second thoughts, he was keeping it to himself.

Chauncy shrugged. "I reckon whenever she wants."

"So, what's the plan after that?"

"Whadda you mean?"

"Well, where are you two going to live?"

"The ranch for a while."

"I figured, but where specifically? Your pa's house? Might be awkward for a newly married couple."

"I reckon we can use the guesthouse for a while. Ain't nobody stayin' in it, is there?"

"There wasn't when I left for here."

They fell into silence for a few moments and Seth studied the table's wood grain as his mind churned for a way to talk Chauncy out of marrying Marcie. Seth knew he was going to face an onslaught of family questions about Marcie and he had no ready answers. And he was a terrible liar. It was almost enough to make him think about hopping on a train to somewhere else—anywhere but the ranch. Having run out of arguments against Marcie, Seth took one final stab at it. He looked at Chauncy and said, "It's not too late to change your mind."

"Why would I want to do that?"

"Just saying."

Chauncy gave Seth a long, hard look and said, "And I'm tired of hearin' it."

"I won't say another word about it."

"Good. You's the same age as me. Maybe you ought to worry about your own self."

"You're right," Seth said, now desperate to change the subject. "Probably ought to go pay the undertaker before the remaining Gibson boys find out you killed their brother."

Chauncy curled his upper lip into a snarl. "I ain't afraid of the Gibson brothers."

Seth stood. "I know you're not, but Marshal Rea said he didn't want any more killing. You have enough money to pay for the burial?"

Chauncy pushed his glass to the center of the table and

stood. "I've got money. Chaps my ass that I have to pay after he's the one to call me out."

"I know it does," Seth said, "but sometimes it's easier to go along to get along."

"Don't make it right."

The cousins exited the saloon and took a left on Fifteenth Street. It being a weekend, the streets were jammed with horses, people, and wagons of all types. And there was no method to the madness, people and wagons going every which way with an abundance of starts, stops, and turns to avoid colliding with an oncoming traveler. And the sidewalks weren't much better and really went downhill when they made a left turn onto Main. A horse-drawn trolley ran through the center of the street, shuttling passengers between the business district and the train station.

Seth didn't know if the city fathers had done any planning about what went where, but it was a little disconcerting to see a meat market next door to the undertaker's office, which was situated in the middle of the block. A bell over the door dinged when they entered and a few moments later, a tall, thin, balding man with a pasty complexion stepped through a curtain that separated the front office from the rest of the building. He was wearing an apron covered with fresh wood shavings and, from the distinct aroma, Seth thought it most likely pine.

"Can I help you?" the man asked.

A waist-height glass counter ran nearly the width of the room and inside were wooden samples of various furniture parts, such as carved finials and turned spindles.

Chauncy reached into his front pocket and pulled out a ten-dollar gold eagle. "Need to pay for a burial. How much?"

The man's eyes lit up at the sight of the gold coin. "Well," the man said, "it depends."

"On what?" Chauncy asked.

"Things like the quality of the casket, graveside services, et cetera. Some like it fancy. I assume we're discussing this morning's arrival?"

"That's him. And I don't give a damn about fancy. Just put him in the ground." Chauncy slapped the coin on the counter. "I reckon that'll cover it. If it don't, do it without a casket." Chauncy turned and walked out of the office, Seth following behind.

"Now what?" Chauncy asked.

Seth pulled his watch from his pocket and popped the lid. They had about two hours to kill. "Let's walk down to the train station to buy the tickets then we can catch the trolley to the shooting gallery so you can give me some pointers."

They turned and started walking toward the train station. "With that derringer of yours? Ain't no pointers but aim, shoot, and pray."

"I was hoping you'd let me use one of your Colts."

"Ain't nobody handles my pistols but me. They got guns you can rent."

"Those rental guns don't even shoot straight. Why won't you let me use one of yours?"

Chauncy shrugged. "Never have let nobody use my guns. You want a Colt, we'll stop in the store and you can buy one."

"I bet you'd let Marcie shoot your pistols."

"No, sirree. What part of not handlin' my guns you not gettin'? *Nobody* means *nobody.*"

They walked in silence for a while, crossed the next street, and continued on.

"Maybe we should just—" Seth turned to look at Chauncy, but he wasn't there. Seth turned his head some more and saw him leaning against the side of a building, his gaze riveted on something down the street. Seth walked back. "What are you doing?"

"Look around. Don't see many people waving guns, do you?"

Seth surveyed the crowd and his cousin was right. "Where?" Seth asked.

"A couple of hundred yards south and coming this way. Looks a little like that feller from this morning, don't he?"

Seth looked at the man in the distance, but he was too far away to say for sure. "Maybe. How would he know who to look for?"

"How many other two-gun rigs you seen since you been here?"

"None."

"That's right. And there was a bunch of people seen us this mornin'. Duck into the store behind you."

"Why don't you come with me before he sees you?"

"I'd rather face it head-on instead of worrying about him bushwhacking me later. The marshal said there was two brothers, right?"

"Yes."

"See if the other one's around."

Seth scanned the busy street then let his eyes drift up to the top of the nearby buildings and didn't see anything that looked suspicious. He turned back to Chauncy. "Don't see the other one. But if it is one of the Gibsons how would he know to find you here?"

"Easy," Chauncy said, his gaze still centered on the man with the rifle. "This is the busiest street in town. He's playin' the odds."

Seth was eager to avoid another gunfight. "Let's go into the store and you can help me pick out a new pistol."

"You go look first and narrow it down some."

Looking at the jammed street and thinking how quickly the situation could go sideways, Seth's stomach did a couple of flips. "Okay. Think about it. If you shoot and miss and kill somebody else there's going to be hell to pay."

For the first time since locking eyes on the rider, Chauncy cut his eyes over to look at Seth. "I don't miss. Ever."

"What if he does and kills someone in the process?"

"He ain't never gonna get that chance. Now move away, Seth."

Seth glanced back at the rider who was inching up the street. It didn't appear that the man had spotted Chauncy yet, but Seth knew it would be only a matter of time. Chauncy was a head taller than most of the people scurrying about and he would be hard to miss. "If he spots you, maybe we could draw him down an alley and away from all these people."

"I told you I got it handled. Quit worryin' and scatter."

Seth sighed and took about three steps to his right, to the edge of the wooden boardwalk. Any farther and he risked being run over by a wagon. All he could do now was watch. Chauncy might be supremely confident in his shooting abilities, but the man hunting him was armed with a rifle and would be able to shoot more accurately from a distance. With that thought in mind, he turned to look at Chauncy and said, "What happens if he's out of range when he spots you and decides to shoot?"

"Not gonna happen. He's already in range."

Seth turned, found the man in question, and estimated his present distance. "He's more than a hundred yards out right now." Chauncy might be good, Seth thought as he turned to look at his cousin again, but it was hard to believe he could shoot that distance with any accuracy.

"So?" Chauncy said. "I can group ten shots inside six inches at a hundred yards. And he looks to be a tad bigger than that." Chauncy pushed off the wall with his shoulder and stood up tall. He shuffled his feet to widen his stance, his gaze still riveted on the man riding up the street.

Seth turned to watch the approaching rider. A moment later he saw recognition register on the man's face when his jaw clenched and his eyes narrowed. He dropped the reins and was in the process of raising the rifle to his shoulder when Chauncy's pistol roared, making Seth jump. Blood erupted from the man's chest and within a half a second, Chauncy's pistol roared again, and the second bullet punched another hole in the man's chest, an inch to the right of the first one.

As the man slumped over and began sliding off his horse, Seth turned to see Chauncy calmly reloading his weapon. When he finished, he jammed the pistol back in the holster, turned, and started walking.

"Where are you going?" Seth asked.

Without breaking stride, Chauncy said, "To pay the undertaker."

CHAPTER
23

Marcie had packed most everything she wanted to take and was surprised to find it had all fit into her one moderately sized trunk. However, there were a few items she remained undecided on and she took a seat on the edge of the bed to look over the things strewn across the duvet. Some were hard to look at and others brought back a flood of unpleasant memories. But they were all essential tools of her trade and, despite the promise of a new life, she was having a hard time deciding what she might need in a normal world.

Most of her apprehension was rooted in uncertainty. She could foresee a rocky beginning to their relationship as they learned each other's tics, but there were other concerns as well, chiefly among them, Chauncy's thoughts on starting a family. And most of the devices laid out on the bed were designed specifically to prevent such occurrences. The last thing either of them needed was for Marcie to get pregnant before she and Chauncy had a chance to firm up their partnership.

Marcie picked up a box of Madame Restell's Preventive Powders, which promised 100 percent satisfaction, and read the list of ingredients. It contained things like pennyroyal, savin, tansy tea, cedar oil, ergot of rye, mallow, and motherwort, all as foreign to Marcie as someone speaking French. She tossed the box in the trash, knowing she wouldn't have the heart to end something she and Chauncy had created. She did the same with the vaginal syringes, other powders and pills, and was left staring at a collection of womb veils she had used over the years.

Terminating a pregnancy was much different from preventing one. Although none offered the guarantees of some of the other products, Marcie had learned from experience that, if used correctly, they could be relatively effective. Making a snap decision, Marcie leaned forward and snatched a stocking from her trunk. She put one of the womb veils inside, folded the stocking over, and stood, stuffing it into the bottom of her belongings. Better to have it and not need it, than to need it and not have it, she thought. She did want children of her own, but she didn't know if her used and abused body would be capable of pushing out five, six, seven babies and survive.

Decision made, Marcie closed the lid on her trunk. It was now time to get ready for her debut to the Ridgeway family. Nervous and not knowing what to expect, Marcie encountered her first problem before putting on her undergarments. One thing Josie had always insisted her girls do was to shave their legs, armpits, and private parts. According to her, this was not a torture the women had to endure for beauty reasons but was done for more practical purposes that were directly related to their profession and the high turnover in questionable clientele—and that was to inhibit the spread of lice. Marcie hadn't seen any evidence that the practice did indeed stop the spread of lice though it did a fair job of keeping the nasty critters from taking up residence in her nether regions.

She would soon be married and would no longer have to worry about lice, right? Or did a proper society lady denude her body of hair for her husband's pleasure? It was a question she couldn't answer. She knew for sure that her mother never shaved her body, but she wasn't known for taking baths, either. Probably why she was already on her third husband, Marcie thought. She leaned down and ran her hands across her calves then across her pubic region and decided she could afford to slide by for a few days, or at least until she had an opportunity to ask Chauncy his preference.

Thinking of the heat, she decided to forgo the heavy, burdensome dress Josie had selected and opted for a hand-embroidered, heather-gray, silk skirt and a tailed bodice with black satin trimming. It fit her like a glove, and it wasn't so pretentious to be off-putting. She slipped on a pair of lightweight cotton bloomers and a camisole and was interrupted by a knock on her door.

"Come in," Marcie said.

The door opened and in walked Brandy Bordeaux, her best friend if such things existed inside a parlor house. It was a name she had created from two different types of alcohol they often served their clients. Brandy walked over and wrapped her arms around Marcie. "You really leavin'?"

Marcie was hoping to escape without a round of tearful good-byes, but that was now out the window.

"I am."

Brandy broke the embrace and flopped down on Marcie's bed. "Gettin' married, too?"

Marcie nodded and sat down beside her friend.

"Who's the lucky fella?"

"Chauncy."

"I knew it. I should have snatched that boy up the minute he walked through the door." Brandy dropped her head. "I'm never gettin' out of this life."

"You can't say that," Marcie said. "If it can happen for me it can happen for you."

"I'll be a whore until I catch one of them diseases and die or somebody kills me."

"What about that guy who owns a store that's always comin' to see you?"

"He's married."

"Of course he is." Marcie stood. She wasn't in the mood for a pity party and they'd already had this conversation more times than Marcie could remember. "Somebody'll come along."

Brandy wiped away the moisture that had formed in the corners of her eyes. "Guess all I can do is hope. I'm sorry."

"For what?"

"For spoiling your day."

"Nonsense," Marcie lied. She began dressing again, as she thought of ways to get Brandy out of her room without being rude. She liked Brandy fine, but her envy was seeping through her pores and Marcie didn't want to ride a guilt trip all the way to the ranch. Especially for something she had wanted for so long. Then she was struck with another thought. She stopped what she was doing and took a long look at Brandy. She was very attractive—one had to be to work at The Belmont—with long, curly, dark hair, large blue eyes, a thin, delicate nose, and curves in all the right places, especially when it came to filling out the top half of her dress.

"What're you lookin' at?" Brandy asked.

"You. I'm thinkin'," Marcie replied.

"About what?"

Marcie's only hesitation was that Brandy had a wild streak that grew in magnitude with the introduction of alcohol. But away from The Belmont and the Acre, how much drinking was there going to be? "Tell you what," Marcie said. "You go doll yourself up, put on your best dress, and come find me when you're done."

"Why?" Brandy asked.

"There's someone I want you to meet."

"A man?"

"Yes."

Brandy jumped to her feet, gave Marcie a hug, and hurried from the room.

Marcie had no idea if Seth was drawn to a specific type, or if he'd be willing to take up with a woman like her or Brandy, but it wouldn't cost anything to find out.

CHAPTER
24

It took Percy a while, but he finally found Reeves's camp along Beaver Creek, about four miles north of Fort Sill. Although it was still fairly early, Percy didn't think he had enough daylight left to make it to Anadarko or home, whichever he ended up deciding on. And if Indian Territory was dangerous during daylight hours, it could be a real kill zone after dark once the outlawed liquor began flowing. When Percy drew closer to the camp, he pulled his horse to a stop and called out to Reeves, not taking any chances on catching a bullet for riding in unannounced. After receiving the okay, Percy nudged his horse forward and immediately wished he'd made other arrangements for his overnight stay.

Belle Starr was not in the stockade as was suggested and was, instead, cuffed to a long chain that was bolted to the wagon bed. He debated his options and it was a tough choice. He didn't think he could stomach whiling away the rest of the day in the company of Major Henry, either, so he sighed and climbed down from his horse.

Bass walked over as Percy stripped the saddle from Mouse's sweaty back. He nodded in Starr's direction and said, "No room in the stockade?"

"Not for no woman," Reeves said. "Jailer took her husband and thought she'd be too much trouble with all the men they got in there. Looked like Major Henry's been busy dolin' out the punishment."

"It don't take much to get him riled up. He's a persnickety feller, for sure. She been mouthy?"

"Some. But I'll take mouthy over somebody tryin' to escape any day."

Percy slipped off the bridle and Mouse opened her mouth to spit out the bit before moseying over to a half-dead patch of grass. "How many more outlaws you lookin' for on this trip?"

"Many as I can get. I usually head on back when I get me a dozen or so. Don't you worry, Mrs. Starr'll be as gentle as a kitten by then. Find Quanah?"

"I did," Percy said, "though it didn't help much. Much like everythin' else the government gets involved in, nothin's simple. The Comanche and Kiowas are lettin' all the grazin' land lie fallow or it's bein' used by ranchers for nothin' when they could be makin' money off it."

"You said it, Percy. White folks been cheatin' the Indians since they got to this here country. And it ain't gonna change. Supper'll be ready soon." Bass turned and walked back to the fire, where his cook was busy stirring a pot of something.

Mouse was trained not to wander off, but up around these parts, horse thieves were as thick as ants on a dropped piece of penny candy. So, he could either let Mouse graze for a while and take his chances or hook her up to Reeves's picket line. Knowing how persnickety the mare could be to other people, he'd almost dare someone to try and take her. With that in mind, he decided to let her be and would wait until dark to tie her up. He pulled his rifle free and lugged his saddle and all of his gear closer to the wagon and took a seat on the ground. Belle Starr was leaned up against one of the wagon wheels, picking her teeth with a stick.

She looked over at Percy and gave him a long hard look. "You a lawman?"

"Used to be," Percy said.

"I ain't got no use for lawmen."

"Most criminals don't."

Starr stopped picking her teeth a moment and barked out a harsh laugh then said, "I look like a criminal to you?"

"Hard to say. I've found that outlaws come in all shapes and sizes. And you're probably lucky they only got you on horse theft."

"How do you figure?"

"The company you keep. Word is you spent a lot of time running with the James and Younger boys before half of 'em got killed and the other half got sent to prison."

Starr curled her upper lip into a snarl. "You don't know nothin' about me. And for your information, Jesse James would have mopped the floor with you."

The cook shouted that supper was on, and Percy slapped his knees and stood. "Guess we'll never know since one of his own gang members shot him in the head. And you're right, I don't know much about you. But I know your type. You'll do a stretch in prison for horse rustlin' and then get out and fall back into your old ways until you get crosswise with somebody else who'll end up putting a bullet in you." Percy walked over to the fire, grabbed a plate, and filled it before walking over to take a seat next to Bass, who had chosen a spot in the shade and away from the hot fire.

Sam Sixkiller came in carrying a load of wood as the two men ate in silence. Back in 1878, the Kiowa and Comanche Indian agency had been combined with that of the Cheyenne and Arapahos and had moved from Fort Sill, thirty-five miles north to Anadarko. Percy was wondering if a trip up there would accomplish anything. From what Henry had said, any decisions on Indian leases would be made by the bureaucrats in Washington. He did wonder if his voice would carry any additional weight on the outcome of the decision, knowing that Sam Burnett and Dan Waggoner were already applying immense pressure to open the Indian lands to leasing. Percy put another spoonful of beans into his mouth and chewed as he thought that over.

Another thirty-five miles north meant he'd have to ride seventy miles on the return to the ranch, eating up another day or possibly two. And for what? To be told what he already knew? Of course, there was the idea of selling some cattle to the various Indian agents like the major had suggested though Percy knew those contracts were usually booked at least a year in advance. Even if the agents had been looking to buy some cattle, the market was now flooded with beef and he couldn't imagine they hadn't already filled those orders. Besides, Percy wasn't eager to sell two or three thousand steers at prices that were about half of what they were last fall.

His thoughts were interrupted when Bass leaned over and said, "You leavin' out of here at first light?"

"Just what I was thinking about. I don't think there's anythin' to be gained by talking to the Indian agent, so most likely."

"Hell, Percy, them other cowpunchers don't care if their cattle drift into the Nations. Don't know why you reckon you got to have a piece of paper givin' you the okay. Worst the agent can do is tell you to get 'em off or ask the army to drive 'em off."

Percy turned to look at Bass. "Is that the lawman talkin'?"

Reeves smiled. "Ain't got no jurisdiction over cattle, lessen somebody stole some."

"I suppose you're right. At least until we get a little rain. Why'd you ask when I was leavin'?"

"I might need you in the mornin'."

"More outlaws to round up?" Percy asked.

"Always. Got word yesterday that a nasty-mean whiskey peddler I been after for months might be holed up around Marlow, about six, seven miles due east of here."

"What makes this one particularly mean?"

Bass smiled and Percy hated when he did that before giving him all the details. "Well, I'll tell you straight up, Percy, this one's a cold-blooded killer. I ain't got no warrant for murder, but I do have one for whiskey peddlin'. He's a no-account squaw man—"

Bass was interrupted when a man rode up and hailed the camp. Reeves squinted across the distance and then waved the man forward.

"You know him?" Percy asked.

"Yeah. Name's Bill Doolin. He's a cowboy on Oscar Halsell's big spread up on the Cimarron." Reeves scraped the last of his beans from his plate and spooned them into his mouth. After chewing and swallowing, he said, "Word is Doolin and some of the Dalton boys got a side bidness rustlin' cattle, but ain't nobody caught 'em at it yet."

"I thought a couple of them Dalton boys were lawmen?"

"I reckon it depends on the day of the week. Word is they work both ends."

"And you let Doolin ride into your camp?"

"You bet. Never know when he might let somethin' slip."

"Always workin' the angles, huh?" Percy asked.

"All part of the job."

Doolin climbed down from his horse, took off his hat, and stepped over to shake Bass's hand.

Reeves set his plate aside and stood, taking Doolin's hand. "How you doin', Bill?"

"Just gettin' by, Marshal."

Ever the perfect host, and never revealing any hints of his suspicions, Reeves took Doolin by the elbow, turned him, and said, "Bill, meet an old friend of mine, Percy Ridgeway."

Percy stood and grasped his hand. "Nice to meet you, Bill."

"Likewise." Doolin released Percy's hand and stepped back. "You the man that owns that big spread south of the river?"

Percy nodded. "It's a family-owned outfit, but, yeah, I end up doin' most of the ramroddin'." He eyed young Doolin. The man was almost as tall as he was and had a scraggly mustache, dark, curly hair, and a lazy left eye that was a tad off center. He wore a one-gun rig that rode low on his hips, gunslinger style. If he was a rustler, he wasn't showing any signs of nervousness being in the company of a deputy marshal. "What brings you down this way, Bill?"

"On my way down to the Triple-D to pick up a stud horse for the boss. Didn't think I could make it all the way down there before dark and thought I'd throw in with y'all for the night."

"Go fix you a plate, Bill," Reeves said.

"Thank you, Marshal." Doolin put his hat back on and headed over to the fire as Bass and Percy sat back down.

"So, back to what I was sayin'," Reeves said. "This whiskey peddler I'm talkin' about can smell a posse from a mile away. But I reckon if it's just me and you we got a chance."

Percy looked up to see Doolin talking to Belle Starr. He nudged Reeves with his knee and Bass turned to look.

"Think he's plannin' on springin' your captive?" Percy asked.

Reeves turned back. "Nah. He ain't got the moxie for it." He reached down and wiped the dust off his boots before continuing. "So, you up for bein' my one-man posse again?"

"On one condition," Percy said.

"What's that?"

"If we're goin' to a gunfight, you're gonna have to loan me some oil so I can clean my pistol."

Reeves smiled and stood. "Be right back."

Reeves returned and handed Percy a small can of gun oil and a rag.

"How far away did you say this whiskey runner was?" Percy asked.

"Probably close to seven miles from here."

"We got plenty of daylight left. Wanna go round him up now?"

"You itchin' for a fight?"

"Not really, but I probably ought to head home at first light. Got to get the cattle situation squared away."

Reeves spent a moment thinking then said, "Well, I reckon we can go now. 'Sides, he's liable to be gone by mornin' anyhow."

"Give me ten minutes to clean my pistol and we'll roll out. We takin' the wagon?"

"Might as well," Reeves said. "Never know. Might get lucky and have somebody to chain up."

CHAPTER
25

   While Percy was busy cleaning his gun for another outlaw roundup, his brother-in-law Leander Hays and Moses Wilcox were tucked up under the lip of a creek bank, watching for any activity around the three soddies and the corral. Before they could make a move, they needed to know how many men they might be up against. So far, they'd seen zip. From their lair to the first domicile was about a hundred yards of wide-open space, meaning they would be easy pickings even for the greenest of greenhorn shooters. And it was twice that distance or more to reach the corral and the object of their search—Sundancer.

   Leander's stallion in the corral suggested someone was around, but where was a mystery. With little to no breeze and a late-afternoon sun that was still broiling, neither man thought it likely anyone would be holed up in one of the dirt houses. However, that hypothesis was shattered a moment later when the sheet covering the doorway on the first house billowed out to reveal a young girl with a bucket in her hand. She turned toward the creek and started walking.

"Hell," Leander muttered. "We got to hide."

Wilcox and Leander scrambled down the bank and hurried over to untie the horses. There was much cover up top, so they led their horses farther down the creek and around a bend, taking cover behind a thick stand of brush.

"She'll see our tracks," Wilcox whispered.

"She can't be more than ten years old," Leander whispered. "Not everyone is a world-class tracker like you."

"Still, you never know."

Leander rolled his eyes. He handed his reins to Wilcox and climbed up the bank for another look. The young girl was about thirty yards from the creek when she stopped and turned to her left. An instant later, Leander heard a flurry of hoofbeats, and four men rode into the yard. They bypassed the houses and rode directly for the corral. He looked down at Wilcox and held up four fingers.

Wilcox kicked the dirt with the toe of his boot and nodded. What had looked easy a moment ago had become much more complicated.

Leander watched the girl disappear down into the creek and then slid partway down the bank so he and Wilcox could talk. Wilcox leaned in and Leander whispered, "Looks like they might be tryin' to sell the stallion to some sucker."

"What do you wanna do?"

"I'm thinkin'." After a few moments, Leander whispered, "This actually might be good news. If the guy buys the horse, we'll follow him and take the stallion back anytime we want."

"You got you a bill o' sale on that there horse?"

"I do. And I brought it, too."

"Still, that guy ain't gonna be happy with us takin' a horse he just paid good money to get."

"I don't give a damn if he's happy or not. It's my damn horse. And I might be of a mind to ride back and hang them bastards that took him, too."

"Might be best to let a marshal handle them."

"Where am I gonna find a marshal? You know where one's at?"

"Well, no."

"Exactly. At the very least I gotta come back and see if I can get their names."

"They probably ain't gonna come out and tell ya."

"I don't expect they would. Probably gonna take some persuadin'."

"I'm a little long in the tooth to be gettin' mixed up in a gunfight."

"I ain't askin' you. You're gonna be in charge of gettin' the horse back to the ranch."

Wilcox ran his fingers through his long, gray beard and said, "I can do that."

Leander climbed back to the top of the creek bank and Wilcox followed, taking a spot next to him. The young girl had filled her water bucket and she was struggling mightily with it. A couple of the men in the corral looked over at the girl but made no move to relieve her of the burden. "I hate horse thieves," Leander muttered.

The four men were doing a lot of standing and jawing and Leander wondered if he had misinterpreted the situation. He assumed they were haggling over a price but hadn't yet seen any money change hands. If the buyer balked, he was going to have to come up with a new plan.

The girl was about halfway to the house when she stopped, set the bucket down, and rubbed her right shoulder. He turned his attention away from the girl and back to the men in the corral.

At two hundred yards it was difficult to discern much about them, other than their sizes in relation to one another. Three were of average height and were as skinny as rails. Leander pegged them as the owners of the three soddies. The fourth man was almost a head taller and he was better fed, his gut lapping over the top of his britches. Something was vaguely familiar about the man, but Leander couldn't quite put his thumb on what it was.

The man in question, the prospective buyer, had to be a man of means. Even if the thieves gave the man a rustler's discount on the stallion, he would still be forced to fork over a good amount of cash. In addition, the man buying the horse would have to know the stallion was being acquired under dubious circumstances with a medium-to-high probability of losing his investment or even his life if caught with a stolen horse.

Leander pondered those thoughts and more. The man had to be assured he had a market for the horse or was planning on moving the horse so far out of the area that recovery would be impossible. Either scenario was plausible, but what the man probably hadn't considered, Leander thought, was the fact that the real owner of the stallion—a former Texas Ranger who had an impeccable record of rounding up outlaws of all stripes—would be on his trail.

Wilcox looked at Leander and said, "What's takin' so long?"

"Hagglin', I expect."

"I take it that tall feller is the buyer."

"That's the way I read it," Leander said.

"I seen him somewhere before."

"You can see that far?"

"I'm old but I ain't dead and my damn eyes still work jus' fine. Looks like he's the only one packin' iron."

"Even I can see that. So, who is he?"

"I ain't got that figured yet."

"So, your eyes work just fine, but maybe that noggin of yours is runnin' a little slow?"

Wilcox shot Leander an angry glare. "You just wait till you get to be my age." Wilcox studied the men in the corral for a few moments, then said, "Figured it out. He come by the ranch might near two months ago lookin' for some breedin' horses."

"That's where I saw him," Leander said. "And he didn't buy none, neither, did he?"

"Nope. But I recall him takin' a fancy to that stallion o' yours."

"The bastard. You recall his name?"

"Don't reckon I ever heard it."

"Don't matter anyway," Leander said. "A thief's a thief."

Turning back to the proceedings in the corral, it appeared to Leander, based on body language, that they were close to wrapping up a deal. The four were standing relaxed and laughing at something that was said. A moment later, just as it looked like the tall man might be reaching for his bankroll, Leander was shocked to see a pistol in the man's hand instead. Calmly and coolly, the man thumbed back the hammer and shot the man farthest to his left before turning the pistol on the next man. Again, he cocked and fired, and the second man dropped like a bag of sand. As for the third man, he had turned and was trying to run for cover when the tall man's bullet slammed into the back of his head, launching a spray of blood and brain matter into the air.

It had happened so fast that neither Leander nor Wilcox had time to react.

"What the hell was that?" Wilcox asked.

"Murder," Leander said. "Although I ain't got nothin' against hangin' a horse thief, it's another thing to sit here and watch 'em get gunned down like a flock of turkeys."

Wilcox looked at Leander. "We can't let him get at that little girl."

Leander nodded toward the killer. "Looks like he's only got an interest in my horse."

They watched as the man unhurriedly mounted his horse, unfurled a rope, and rode over to slip a lasso over the stallion's head. Without seemingly a care in the world, he spurred his horse into a trot and rode out of the corral, the stallion trailing behind.

Leander turned to climb down the bank and Wilcox reached out a hand to stop him.

"Let 'im put a li'l distance tween us," Wilcox said. "I reckon he'll get real comfortable after a couple miles of ridin'."

"What happens if we lose his trail?"

Wilcox, deeming the question undeserving of an answer, slid down the bank and stood.

CHAPTER
26

There had been no shooting gallery, no new Colt Peacemaker for Seth, and no shooting tips from Chauncy. Both had made a beeline from the undertaker's to Chauncy's boardinghouse room, hoping to avoid another run-in with City Marshal Bill Rea. Not that Chauncy had done anything illegal, but two dead bodies in a single day and the potential for a third, in the person of Gibson's last surviving brother, was just too much.

Seth, rattled from the day's violence, had never seen a single man get gunned down, much less two, and his brain was having trouble processing it all. What he needed was a few moments away from Chauncy to clear his head. Seth stood and said, "You stay and clean your guns or whatever you need to do, and I'll go buy the train tickets."

"Sounds good. Pick up a bottle of whiskey on your way back."

The last thing they needed was to get all liquored up, but Seth didn't want to start another argument, either, so he simply ignored his cousin's request. Seth tucked his derringer into his back pocket, put on his new Stetson hat, and slipped out of the room. After descending the stairs, Seth took a long look through the front window and, seeing nothing amiss, exited out onto the boardwalk.

The traffic had abated some now that the afternoon heat had settled in though there were still enough horses and wagons about to kick up a heavy cloud of dust. As he walked toward the train station, he kept an eye out for the third Gibson brother. He didn't think the man could connect him to Chauncy unless he'd been somewhere in the vicinity of the other two shootings. Even then, Seth thought there was a good chance the man would have focused all of his attention on Chauncy and not the bystanders. Still, there was safety in numbers and Seth felt comfortable shuffling along with the rest of the crowd and arrived at the train station unmolested.

The station was a cramped, two-room structure that had been built with little planning or thought about the needs of the traveling public. Seth fell in at the back of the line that was six-deep, all awaiting the services of the lone ticket agent. It was sweltering inside, and the poor agent's sweat-stained uniform looked as if he had walked to work in a downpour. Seth had some sympathy for his plight, but he appeared to be the only one, as tempers flared at the smallest of slights.

The man at the head of the line took issue with something the man behind him had done, and he turned and shoved the second man backward, forcing everyone in line to take a step back. In the process, Seth accidentally tangled feet with a short, stocky man in front of him and both almost went down. The man, wearing a black bowler hat, turned and glared at Seth. He didn't know who the man was, but his look sent a tingle of dread racing down

Seth's spine. He couldn't say why, but he had the same butterflies in his stomach that he'd had when Chauncy was squaring off with the two Gibson bothers.

"I'm sorry." Seth said, eyeing the pistol on the man's right hip. Eager to defuse the situation quickly, Seth said, "To what fine city are you traveling?"

The question had the desired effect and the man visibly relaxed. "Austin, if I can ever get a damn ticket. You?"

"Wichita Falls. My family owns a ranch near there."

The man stuck out his hand and said, "Ben Thompson."

There was a slight tremor in Seth's hand when he reached out to shake. "Seth Ferguson. Nice to meet you, Mr. Thompson." Ben Thompson's only rival as the deadliest gunslinger in Texas was the notorious John Wesley Hardin, who was now serving a twenty-five-year sentence for murder at the Texas State Penitentiary at Huntsville. "Austin's home for you, isn't it?"

"It is. Even served as city marshal for a while."

"I'd heard that," Seth said. Being next to Thompson was like standing next to a deadly pit viper whose fangs, though momentarily retracted, could strike a fatal blow in the blink of an eye.

The angry man at the front of the line left and they shuffled forward a few steps as Seth debated leaving and coming back later. But that would only delay the process, so he decided to stay, despite the fact that he was shoulder to shoulder with a known killer who had been acquitted of his own murder charge last year, in a sensational trial Seth had followed closely in the newspapers. Although acquitted, the trial had ended Thompson's run as city marshal.

Thompson turned and asked, "That ranch of yours got a name?"

Seth hesitated before answering as he wrangled with

how much to say. He wasn't keen on Thompson knowing much about him, but he'd already told him about Wichita Falls. "It does. The Rocking R."

Thompson smiled. "How's ol' Percy?"

Seth was only mildly surprised that Thompson knew Percy, who had his own reputation. "Percy is doing well."

The next man at the counter left and they shuffled forward again.

"What's he to you?" Thompson asked.

"He's my uncle."

"Which one's your ma, Rachel or Abigail?"

So much for limiting personal details, Seth thought. "Rachel."

"She took up with Leander Hays a few years back, didn't she?"

Again, Seth was only mildly surprised that Thompson knew his stepfather, who had served as a Texas Ranger for years. "Yes, they've been married almost ten years now."

The next two people in line left together and that left Thompson the next man up. As he stepped to the counter Seth heaved a sigh of relief. Thompson was nice enough, and him knowing Percy and Leander was a help, but Seth sensed that it wouldn't take much of a spark for him to spring into action.

Seth slipped his wallet out of his back pocket, ready to make his purchase and clear out. A river of sweat had cut a course through his shoulder blades and now his ass was wet. The front door had been propped open and all that did was allow a swarm of flies to enter, adding to the misery. How the ticket agent hadn't passed out was a wonderment.

Thompson paid for his ticket, turned, and shook hands with Seth again before departing. Seth stepped up, requested three tickets to Wichita Falls, and paid the fares.

With his mind still swirling about his encounter with the notorious gunslinger Ben Thompson, Seth exited the building and was waiting to cross the street when he felt the touch of cold steel on the back of his neck.

"Where's your friend?" a voice said from behind him.

"What friend?" Seth asked, raising his hands.

"Put your damn hands down," the man said, jamming the pistol barrel against the base of Seth's skull.

Seth dropped his hands and quickly scanned his surroundings, hoping to see his new friend. He thought he caught a glimpse of Thompson's hat as it weaved through the crowded sidewalk—but he was gone and would be of no help.

The man cocked the pistol and Seth had to squeeze his thighs together to keep from pissing his pants.

"I ain't askin' again," the man said.

"I don't know who you think I am, mister, but I just came down here to buy a train ticket."

"Why'd you buy three of 'em? I seen ya."

Good question, Seth thought. "The other two are for my parents."

The man lowered the pistol and jammed it against Seth's spine. "Bullshit. Walk and keep your hands where I can see 'em."

"I'm unarmed," Seth said as he began walking.

"Don't mean a damn thing to me."

As Seth made his way down the sidewalk, his brain worked furiously to find a way out of the predicament without him or Chauncy getting killed.

CHAPTER
27

Leander and Wilcox had checked on the young girl before leaving. Although distraught about the death of her father, the girl had assured them that her mother would return soon. They had sat with her long enough to get her calmed down and she had assured them she would stay in the house until her mother arrived. Now they were trailing a good distance behind the murdering horse thief, hoping to get a clue of the man's final destination before confronting him. Yes, they ran the risk that the man might soon meet up with a band of cohorts though Leander was willing to take the risk, at least for now. Riding a southeasterly course, it appeared the thief was heading toward the river and into Texas.

Leander, still seething about the murders, no longer thought the train was in play because the closest train station to their current position was in the other direction in Wichita Falls. While that didn't completely rule out the possibility the thief was eager to ship the horse off to parts unknown, it just wasn't logical, based on his current heading. That meant the thief was either headed home or he was on the way to another rendezvous where he planned to sell the stallion to a third party.

Wilcox nudged his horse closer to Leander and said, "We seen him shoot three unarmed men dead. Save a lot of time if you was to pull out your rifle and plink 'im so we can get on home."

"Don't you want to know where he's goin'?"

"I know where he's a-goin'—the river. Best to finish it fore he gets a chance to cross."

"I agree. But it could be he's got a place on this side. Be nice to know and we got a little time to let it play out. Plus, I ain't no bushwhacker." Leander nodded toward the rider in the distance and said, "That man's a cold-blooded killer and I'm goin' to look him in the eye when I kill him, so's he knows it's comin'."

"Dead's dead, seems like to me. Don't matter how he got that way."

"Well, it matters to me. How long you reckon before we hit the river?"

"Hour, maybe."

"About what I figured. Far as I can recall, there ain't nobody livin' in this part of the country. You know different?"

"Ain't nobody here and ain't never been that I know of."

"Let's close the distance a bit."

"Ain't seen you shoot. How good a gunhand are ya?"

"Good enough, I expect."

"Good as Percy?"

"Don't know. We ain't had no call to go at one another."

"Well, I seen Percy. Fastest man I ever seen draw a pistol. That man might could shoot wings off a fly, to boot."

Leander was a little perturbed Wilcox was questioning

his skills. "Well, I reckon you're gonna have to hide and watch."

Wilcox reached down and patted the stock of his sheathed rifle. "Me and ol' Bessie'll be standin' by just in case."

Leander scowled then spurred his horse into a canter and Wilcox matched him. After a few minutes of riding, the thief came into view just as he was disappearing down into a creek, and they slowed their horses to a walk as they talked strategy.

"I'd like to come in on him from the front. Less chance of the stallion gettin' hit," Leander said.

"We start runnin' the horses he's gonna hear it." Wilcox pointed to his right. "If I remember rightly, there's another little dry creek a few hundred yards beyond this 'un with a heavy stand o' timber twixt 'em. I expect that'll tamp down the noise some."

They steered their horses to the right, crossed the creek, then picked up a game trail that angled back to the east through the trees. They spurred their horses into a lope and rode hard until the trees began to thin out then slowed their horses to a walk again.

"We're gonna have about fifty yards of open ground till we hit that other little dry creek," Wilcox said. "We get across that, then drift south 'long the tree line and we might catch 'im comin' out."

Leander gently rubbed his nose where a tree limb had slapped him in the face then checked his fingers for blood. There was no blood, but his eyes were still watering from the blow. "Works for me. We go nice and easy across that open ground and maybe he won't spot us."

"And if he does?" Wilcox asked.

"We'll have to run 'im down, I reckon."

"Iffen he switches onto that stallion o' yours, we ain't gonna catch him."

"Unless he's the best damn bronc rider in Texas, I can guaran-damn-tee you he ain't gettin' on that stallion."

Wilcox chuckled. "You ain't broke 'im yet?"

"Hell no. And I ain't goin' to, neither. I aim to hire it done."

"One of them young hands round the ranch could probably break him."

"Then I'd have to pay their doctor bills."

They stayed in the trees for as long as possible and let the horses set their own pace across the open ground, before riding down into the next creek. After riding up the other side, they drifted south, using the brush for cover. As they rode, Leander pulled out his pistol and inserted a .45 caliber cartridge into the empty chamber and reholstered the gun. He took a deep breath, released it, and did it again. A dose of adrenaline dumped into his system, accelerating his heart rate. Even so, there was no fear and no apprehension, Leander confident in his own abilities. The ease the thief had displayed in dispatching his latest victims suggested that hadn't been his first go-around and Leander would bet the killer had a list of victims as long as his arm. He was aiming to make those three dead men the last names ever added to that list.

Scanning the timber to his left, Leander was hoping for a flash of color that might pinpoint the man's location. He didn't see anything, and he wasn't all that surprised, his vision not what it once was. He looked over at Wilcox and whispered, "See him?"

"I seen 'im," Wilcox whispered. "He'll be ridin' out of the trees 'bout thirty yards ahead."

Leander shook his head. Wilcox might be old, but his

eyesight was as sharp as ever. "Hang back a bit. I got it from here."

Wilcox nodded and slowed his horse.

When the thief broke into the clear, Leander put a smile on his face, stood in his stirrups, and waved his hand, shouting, "Hey, pardner, I see you found my horse."

The man's head whipped around like he'd heard a gunshot as Leander walked his horse closer. He wanted to crowd the man so he couldn't make a break for it.

"Do what?" the man asked.

"I been lookin' for that stallion all damn day. I'm grateful to you for finding him." Leander stopped when his horse was almost nose to nose with the murderer's.

The man squirmed in his saddle then held up the stallion's lead rope and said, "This here's my horse. Bought and paid for."

"You been had, mister. That there's stallion's mine."

"You're wrong, stranger."

Leander quickly assessed the situation. The man's gun was on his right hip, meaning he would be forced to drop the rope before going for it. Leander held up his left hand and splayed his fingers to show the man he was empty-handed. "I'm gonna reach into my back pocket for somethin'."

"What is it?"

"You'll see." Leander slowly reached behind him and pulled the bill of sale from his pocket. With a flick of the wrist, he unfurled the paper and held it up for the man to see. "This here's a bill of sale for my stallion."

"I told you," the man said, "the horse was bought and paid for."

"That's where you're wrong, friend. Not only are you a liar, you're also a murderer."

Leander saw the rope fall, and, in one controlled motion, he drew his pistol, cocked the hammer, and fired, punching a hole in the man's forehead. Startled, the stallion reared up and took off at a dead run. "Wilcox," Leander shouted.

"I got 'im," Wilcox shouted, spurring his horse into a sprint, as the man's body slid off his horse and thumped to the ground.

Leander was a little surprised to see the man's pistol still holstered as he climbed down from his horse. Curious about the man's identity, Leander leaned down, rolled the body over, and searched through his pockets. They were empty as were the man's saddlebags, other than some jerky and a small package of coffee. *You were a cold-hearted bastard,* Leander thought as he looked at the corpse one final time. With no money on him, it was obvious the man was planning to kill those men from the start. Leander stripped the saddle and bridle off the man's horse and slapped him on the rump before climbing back in the saddle. He turned his horse and took off after Wilcox.

CHAPTER
28

Seth Ferguson was trying to slow-walk his way back to the boardinghouse as a slew of scenarios bounced around inside his brain. If anyone noticed he was being propelled down the sidewalk by a man with a gun, they were doing a good job of staying hidden. Even a simple shout might be enough to turn the tables, Seth thought. Then he felt the barrel of the gun pressed against his spine and an image of himself crutching around with a pair of dead legs popped into his mind. He shuddered at the thought and knew he needed a better plan.

As he walked, Seth swept his gaze from side to side, hoping to spot a friendly face. Ideally that friend would be Ben Thompson, who had disappeared somewhere up the sidewalk. He'd settle for Chauncy, too, though he didn't think Chauncy would be out and about after the day's earlier activities. Whatever plan he came up with it needed to be now, because they were only a block from the boarding-house. And contemplating being in the middle of a gunfight in the close confines of their room was making him nauseous.

Then he had a sudden thought.

His kidnapper had no idea where Seth was taking him, and he wondered if he could lead the man all the way to the courthouse or maybe even to the marshal's office. How far could he go before the man became suspicious, or angry—possibly angry enough to shoot him and call that revenge? It was an unanswerable question. And Seth didn't know how far he could push it without getting paralyzed, or worse, killed.

As they drew closer to the boardinghouse, Seth's heart rate kicked up another notch. Then he thought of something else. The window in their room—the one that looked out over Main Street—had been open when he left. Praying, he let his eyes drift up the building and was relieved to see the window still open.

But how was he going to alert Chauncy without getting shot in the process? He scanned the busy sidewalk in front of him and hit upon another idea. If it played out like he thought, there would be some blowback and that might have caused him to hesitate if he didn't know he would be leaving town in an hour. Besides, he was now officially out of options.

He had noticed the matronly woman in front of him earlier but hadn't paid her any mind, his brain occupied with other, more pressing, matters. The woman, dressed in all her finery with the latest in handbag fashions draped around her wrist, was walking just ahead of Seth, her chin up, her stride determined. With his movements screened by his own body, Seth watched the bedroom window and when they were about six feet away, he reached out, grabbed a handful of the woman's butt, and squeezed.

As expected, her reaction was instantaneous. She swung her handbag around like she was going to rip Seth's head off and screamed at the top of her lungs. Luckily, Seth avoided permanent damage by ducking low enough to avoid the bag as the man behind stumbled back, momentarily startled. As Seth had hoped, that was all it took. He glanced up to see Chauncy leaning out the window, the harbinger of death gripped firmly in his hand.

"Drop it," Chauncy shouted as Seth took a couple of steps to the left.

The last Gibson brother was raising his pistol when Chauncy fired, the blood blooming in the center of the man's chest as the shot echoed down the street.

The woman, startled by the blast, paused only briefly before ripping into Seth again. She swung her bag and missed again and that only infuriated her. She crowded in on Seth and began kicking him in the shins with her pointy boots, her face so red he was afraid she was going to have a heart attack. He mumbled a quick apology, turned, and raced down the alley. Skidding to a stop at the back door, he yanked it open and charged up the stairs, nearly colliding with Chauncy, who was stepping out into the hall, his bag in his hand.

"Where are you goin'?" Seth asked.

Chauncy put on his hat and said, "To pay the undertaker. I'm glad there weren't but three of 'em or I'd be busted. Pack your stuff and I'll meet you over at Marcie's place."

CHAPTER
29

While Chauncy made his third trip to the undertaker's in as many hours, his father, Percy, was on the hunt for a murdering whiskey peddler with Deputy U.S. Marshal Bass Reeves.

"This man we're after have a name?" Percy asked.

"Probably a dozen different ones, but I know 'im as Bose Copley. He married a full-blood Chickasaw gal a while back, though he don't have much to do with her no more. Probably a good thing for her."

Having left the fugitive Belle Starr behind under the watchful gaze of Sam Sixkiller, Reeves and Percy had chosen to drive the wagon in hopes of capturing their prey. It and the accompanying chain made subduing a prisoner much easier than trying to put him or her on a horse.

"Whiskey peddlin' a big problem up this way?" Percy asked.

"Lordy, yes. I always got a stack of warrants for whiskey runners. Probably seven out of ten o' my arrests is for whiskey peddlin'. And they's hard cases to make, too."

"What kind of sentences does Judge Parker dole out for sellin' whiskey to the Indians?"

"Judge Parker don't got no sympathy for whiskey runners, I'll tell you that. It all depends on how much liquor they got when I catch 'em. Most ain't more than a few pints. That'll usually buy a man a few months in jail in Fort Smith. Somebody caught with a bunch of whiskey'll be shipped up to the big house in Detroit for several years."

"Detroit, Michigan?" Percy asked, his voice taking on an incredulous tone.

"Yep. All the convicts go there if they's doin' hard time."

"Seems like it'd be more trouble to ship 'em up there. Ain't they got any prisons in Arkansas?"

"Course they do. Don't know why they ship 'em up north. My job is just to catch 'em. Where they go after ain't up to me."

They rode in silence for a while. Percy reached into his back pocket, pulled out a handkerchief, and mopped the sweat from his face and the back of his neck. When he finished, he wrapped the kerchief loosely around his throat and knotted the end, hoping it would absorb some of the sweat running down his back. Percy couldn't tear his eyes away from all the dead grass, and his mind returned to the reason why he'd started up this way to begin with. If they didn't get any rain soon, finding forage for the cattle would go from critical to unsustainable and Percy didn't want to think what that might mean.

"Still frettin' about your cattle?" Reeves asked.

Percy nodded. "It's a hell of a mess."

"Next thing you know, you'll be gripin' about too much rain."

"Don't reckon I'll complain about too much rain ever again. How much further, you reckon?"

"We're close." Reeves looked over at Percy and said, "You need to clear your head 'cause Copley is a stone-cold killer."

"I'll be ready. He campin' or holed up in a house?"

"A house, if you can call it that."

"Figures. Can't ever be easy, can it? Can we get close without being spotted?"

Reeves pointed to a line of trees in the distance. "We get to that timber we'll be pretty close."

A few minutes later, Reeves steered the wagon up to the tree line and set the brake. The two men climbed down and Reeves tied one of the reins around the trunk of a young oak tree before both men proceeded farther on foot. After fifty yards, the trees began to thin out, revealing a log structure of questionable integrity. Both men squatted down to study the area for a few moments.

Reeves was right, it wasn't much of a house and it was obvious the builder had no use for a steel square or any type of plan. The front-left corner sagged and the roof, a mixture of sticks and sod, had more holes than a thirty-acre prairie dog town. Someone had nailed an old, stained sheet over what, on any other house, would have been the front door.

"You know what Copley looks like?" Percy whispered.

"Seen him once when he got hauled into jail for horse theft a few years ago."

"He know who you are?"

"I don't reckon he does. Gives me an idea, though. Let's walk back to the wagon."

Percy wondered what Reeves was up to this time.

One of the cleverest men Percy had ever known, Reeves didn't rely only on bravado or his gun when apprehending criminals and often used various disguises to get the drop on unsuspecting outlaws.

When they reached the wagon, Reeves's transformation began. He unbuttoned his suit vest and laid it on the folded jacket under the seat. After unbuckling his gun belt, Reeves pulled out his shirttails, unbuttoned the shirt almost to his navel, and rolled up the sleeves. He took off his hat and placed it on the wagon seat then leaned over and stuffed his pant legs into his boots. For a man known as a nifty dresser, his metamorphosis was remarkable. Reeves unholstered one of his pistols and tucked it into his pants at the small of his back and draped the shirttail over it. He shook his arms out, loosened his shoulders, and then assumed a stooped posture. "What do ya think?"

"Even knowing you as well as I do, I'd do a double take. What's your story?"

"I done and gone lost my hoss," Reeves said, layering on a heavy Southern accent. He walked over and picked out a long stick from a pile of brush, and using it as a cane, limped back to Percy. "My ol' knee's shot and I'm plum wore out lookin' for that dern horse of mine."

Percy chuckled. "You'd fool me for sure. And all you need is a look inside." Percy reached under the seat and pulled out his rifle. "I'll cover you."

Reeves nodded and said in his normal voice, "If it goes as planned, won't be any gunplay."

"What if Copley's not there?"

Reeves switched back into character. "Then I's gonna keep on lookin' for my hoss."

His ability to turn it on and off was uncanny. "You

gonna work your way through the trees and come out east of the house?"

"Yep."

Reeves took off at a brisk walk as Percy worked his way into position, selecting a spot that would provide some cover and give him a wide field of fire. He kneeled down behind a tree and waited. A few moments later, he watched as Reeves came limping out of the trees. Although the sun was now on its downward slide, sweat stung Percy's eyes and he wiped his forehead with his sleeve. Refocusing, he ignored Reeves as he limped forward, and kept his gaze centered on the house and the immediate area around it.

Whoever had built the structure hadn't bothered with a front porch, meaning Reeves wouldn't have a post to hide behind if gunfire erupted from inside. Percy cut his eyes over to check Reeves's progress. He was now only twenty yards away and his labored approach was so deliberate that Percy almost felt sorry for him. He took a deep breath to clear his head and braced the stock of the rifle tight to his shoulder.

Reeves made it all the way to the door unchallenged. He rapped on the side of the house with his stick and waited. With the sheet covering the opening and no windows on this side, there was no way for Reeves to get a look inside. A few seconds later, a silver-haired, stout woman wearing an apron pulled back the sheet and looked at Reeves. Percy wasn't close enough to hear what was being said, but he did see Reeves take a long look inside. The next few seconds were a blur as Reeves dropped the stick, pulled his gun, and sidestepped the woman, entering the house. Percy stood and, with the rifle tight to his shoulder, raced for the left corner of the house. When he reached it, he heard

Reeves shouting inside as he turned his body and drew a bead on the entry, using the edge of the house for cover.

A few moments later, Reeves shouted, "Percy!"

"I'm here, Bass," Percy shouted.

"Prisoner comin' out."

"Okay!" Percy held his position as a short older man with a bald head stepped out, his hands raised. "Come to me," Percy shouted.

The man turned and walked toward Percy as Reeves backed out of the house, his pistol still aimed at something inside.

When the prisoner was five feet away and within can't-miss range, Percy ordered him to stop.

Reeves backpedaled toward Percy, his pistol out and leveled at the entryway. When he reached the corner of the house, Reeves whispered, "Two inside plus the woman. I didn't like the looks of one of them fellers. Cover me and the prisoner and I'll do the same once we get to the trees."

Percy nodded.

Reeves waved his gun toward the trees and ordered Copley to walk and he complied. The distance from the house to the trees was close to forty yards and Percy glanced that way every few seconds to check their progress. He disliked not being able to see what was happening on the other side of the house. From where he was, he could see two small windows on that side of the building and assumed there were two on the opposite side to take advantage of the breeze. What he didn't know was whether there was a back door. With Copley having slipped through his hands before, Reeves hadn't wanted to do much moving around and they hadn't spent much time casing the house and grounds. Percy regretted that now. The windows would be a tight squeeze for anything larger than a child, but the idea of a back door gnawed at him. With that in mind, Percy began slowly backpedaling away from the house for a wider look at the overall scene.

He had gone only a few steps when his heel caught on something and he went down hard, knocking the breath out of him and sending his rifle skittering across the dirt. Momentarily stunned, he looked back toward the house and was horrified to see a rifle barrel inching out from behind the sheet. He turned his head to shout at Bass, but with no air, he couldn't manage anything more than a whisper.

Reeves, unaware of Percy's mishap, had his back turned and was still walking toward the trees. Desperate, Percy yanked his pistol out and snapped off two quick shots that splintered the wood near the door just as the rifle boomed, launching a tongue of flame and smoke that billowed out from the opening.

Percy snapped off another shot and was afraid to turn and look, knowing that whoever was in the house was shooting a Sharps big-bore buffalo killer. Hearing two other quick pistol shots in reply, Percy finally turned to see Reeves and his prisoner tucked safely behind a large oak tree that was now scarred by a .50 caliber slug that had hit about a foot above Reeves's head. With his lungs filling with air again, Percy scrambled to his feet, scooped up his rifle, and hurried toward the trees, as Reeves plunked the house with pistol rounds.

As Percy slid to the ground, the big rifle boomed again, and Percy's hat was ripped from his head as he slid behind a tree. He didn't know if a limb had snagged his hat or what but worrying about it in the middle of a gun battle was a good way to get killed.

"We're not staying to fight, are we?" Percy asked Reeves.

"No, sir. We got what we came for," Reeves said as he ejected the empties from his pistol and reloaded. "Think you can keep 'im pinned down long enough for me to get the prisoner squared away?"

"I can. While you're doin' that, sweet-talk that horse of yours, so he'll be ready to run like hell."

Bass smiled. "Cover me."

Percy began pumping rifle rounds, peppering the area around the entryway as Bass and his prisoner stood and moved off. With the woman in mind, Percy was careful about placing his shots and avoided shooting directly into the house. He paused, glanced over his shoulder, and saw Reeves disappear over a ridge. He pulled shells from his cartridge belt and fed them into the rifle then took a moment to reload his pistol.

The Sharps roared again and the bullet plowed into the tree he was using for cover. He eased around the right side of the tree, launched another fusillade at the house, then stood and hightailed it out of there.

Reeves already had the wagon in motion when Percy cleared the trees at a dead run. He adjusted his course, ran along the side, and used the wagon seat to pull himself aboard. Reeves snapped the reins, urging the horse into a run. As the wagon picked up speed, Reeves reached under the seat and pulled out Percy's hat. "Found this," Reeves said, passing it across. "Damn lucky your head wasn't still in it."

Percy looked down to see a gaping hole through the crown, about two inches above where his head would have been. He looked at Reeves and said, "Pretty close, huh?"

"I'd say."

CHAPTER
30

His bag in hand, Seth took off his hat, opened the door to The Belmont, and stepped inside. The parlor room was vacant, and the house was quiet, leading him to wonder if whores were like bats and only operated at night. He placed his bag on the floor, put his hat on top, and took a seat on one of the four sofas that were arranged around the perimeter of the room. He assumed the large open space in the center was used for dancing or mingling, depending on the mood.

Thinking that Chauncy should have already arrived, Seth began to worry his cousin had fallen into the clutches of Marshal Rea. The marshal had been angry after Chauncy's first shootout and Seth couldn't imagine what his reaction would be now that there were three fresh bodies piled up at the undertaker's. Seth fished his watch out of his pocket and popped the lid. They had blown well past his arbitrary deadline and they now had a little more than an hour before the train departed.

Hearing footsteps, Seth turned to see Marcie and another woman descending the stairs. Marcie, her hair in a bun, was wearing very handsome outfit that, Seth thought, had probably cost a fortune. The other woman was dressed just as stylishly, in a long, flowing, blue dress. Her long dark hair had been brushed to a high sheen and was parted in the middle and worn forward over both shoulders. Seth stood to greet them.

Marcie put a hand on his arm and leaned forward to kiss him on the cheek. "Seth, I would like to introduce you to my friend Brandy Bordeaux."

Seth, unsure if he should stick out his hand, instead turned and offered a small bow. "Nice to meet you, Miss Bordeaux."

Brandy smiled and said, "You, as well."

Brandy wasn't quite at Marcie's level in the looks department, however she was very attractive with large blue eyes, a button nose, and full, luscious lips. It was hard to judge her figure buried under the yards of fabric, but if her bottom half closely resembled her curvy, well-developed top half, then she was a stunner.

"Seth," Marcie said, interrupting his examination of Brandy.

He turned to Marcie. "Yes?"

"Where's Chauncy?"

There was worry in her voice and Seth wondered if she thought Chauncy had skipped town. "He had to run an errand. He should be along any minute." He saw her chest heave as she exhaled her breath.

"In that case, I'll leave you two alone for a moment," Marcie said.

As she disappeared down a hallway, Brandy put a hand on his forearm and said, "May we sit?"

"Of course." He waited for her to sit, then sat down, leaving a couple of feet of empty space between them. But that gap closed quickly when Brandy scooted over close to him and slipped her arm under his.

"Are you married, Seth?" Brandy asked.

"No," Seth replied.

"I can't believe some woman hasn't snapped up a handsome fellow like you."

Seth shrugged. "I guess I haven't found the right woman." Seth's eyes roamed around the room, trying to avoid looking into Brandy's beautiful, deep blue eyes.

"What's your idea of the right woman?"

"Don't know, really."

"Well, is it an instant-attraction thing for you?"

"I don't know," Seth said. "Maybe."

"Do you find me attractive?"

Seth turned to look at her and, as he feared, he was drawn into those deep pools of blue. "Yes. You're very pretty. And, I have to say, you have the most beautiful eyes I've ever seen."

She batted her eyelashes and laughed. "Are my eyes the only thing you find appealing?"

"Well, no," Seth said as a bead of perspiration popped on his upper lip.

She intertwined her fingers with his. "What else do you see that you like?"

"Well . . . uh . . . well . . . you're certainly easy on the eyes."

She gave his hand a squeeze and said, "You aren't so bad yourself." After a pause, she asked, "You live around here, Seth?"

"No, we have a ranch up near Wichita Falls."

"A ranch, huh? Does that make you a cowboy?"

Seth knew she was trying to draw him into her web, but

his little head—the one below his navel—was doing most of the thinking now. "Do you like cowboys?"

"Depends on how well they ride, I suppose." She unlaced her fingers and her hand dropped onto Seth's thigh and she gave it a squeeze. "I bet you're an expert rider, aren't you?"

"I wouldn't say *expert*. Let's go with *capable*."

Brandy laughed and Seth thought her even more beautiful and she had a mischievous glint in her eye. "Capable, huh? At least you're honest."

"I try to be," Seth said, chuckling.

Brandy scooted out to the edge of the sofa and turned her body to face him as her hand drifted farther up his thigh. "Speaking of being honest, I know you are pressed for time, Seth. I'm not normally so forward and I don't like doing things this way, but would you like to come upstairs?"

"Well . . ." Seth stammered. "I . . . I don't think we . . . don't think we have time."

Brandy leaned forward and her breath was hot when she whispered in his ear, "I promise you'll like what you'll find."

She pulled back and looked him in the eyes, as her hand inched upward. If she got any closer, she was going to find out what he really thought. He took a deep breath, held it for a second, and blew it out, hoping she didn't discover the bulge in—

"Oh my, someone seems interested," she whispered.

Seth groaned and squirmed in his seat.

She leaned forward and whispered in his ear again. "Now would you like to go upstairs?"

Seth pushed her hand aside and jumped to his feet. "Yes."

Brandy laughed as she stood. She took him by the hand and led him up the stairs, all thoughts of the train disappearing from Seth's mind.

When they reached her room, she opened the door and pulled Seth inside before nudging it closed. She turned, tiptoed up, and began kissing him, probing his mouth with her tongue. Seth was momentarily shocked. From his limited experience with prostitutes he knew they rarely kissed their clients. But that thought barely registered before it was whisked away.

Brandy stopped kissing him long enough to turn around. "Unbutton my dress, Seth."

Seth, his hands shaking with excitement, was having trouble with the buttons, and Brandy reached back to help him. When the dress was unbuttoned, Brandy turned around and looked him in the eye. "Take it off, Seth."

Seth reached out, lifted the dress over her head, and let it fall to the floor as his eyes devoured her beautiful body.

"Your turn," Brandy said.

Seth, always self-conscious about the brand on his butt, shucked off his pants in world-record time, all thoughts of the scar obliterated from his mind.

Brandy stepped forward, put her arms around his neck, and kissed him deeply as she gently pulled him toward the bed. When her knees hit, she lay back on the bed and said, "I'm yours."

After it was over, Brandy rolled over onto his chest and straddled his hips. She pushed herself up on her hands and looked down at him, her long, dark hair spilling all around them. "What did I tell you downstairs?"

Seth, still breathing hard, said. "That . . . that . . . I'd . . . like what . . . I found."

Brandy leaned down and kissed him on the lips. "And did you?"

"Yes. Oh Lord, yes."

Brandy laughed and kissed him again before sliding off. She stood and pulled on a robe. "I think you have a train to catch, mister."

Seth stood and dressed quickly although not nearly as swiftly as he had gotten undressed.

Once he was ready, Brandy walked over and opened the door and let her hand rest on the knob. "Safe travels."

He walked across the room, leaned down, and kissed her a final time before stepping into the hall.

Brandy closed the door softly and leaned her back against it. She had done all she could do.

The rest would be up to him.

CHAPTER
31

Stepping lightly down the hall with his mind swirling with pleasant thoughts of what had just happened, Seth was startled when heard Chauncy say, "In here."

Seth's cheeks reddened when he turned to see Marcie and his cousin sitting on the bed in the room next to Brandy's. Both were smiling. "You two been up here long?" Seth asked, dreading the answer.

Chauncy laughed as he stood. "Long enough, I expect, to hear most of it."

Seth's face turned a deeper shade of red. Desperate to change the subject, he said, "Shouldn't we be on our way to the train station?"

"It's why we're up here," Chauncy said. He pointed to Marcie's trunk. "Grab the other end."

Seth obliged and they carried the heavy trunk down the stairs, paused to grab their bags and other items, and ventured out onto the boardwalk. Seth glanced up at the upstairs windows and Brandy leaned out and blew him a kiss. Loaded down, all Seth could do was nod. He was going to need some time to digest whatever that was. The encounter was unlike anything he had ever experienced with a woman and it felt much more intimate than a simple business transaction, even if it had been a hurried freebie. But what he knew about women wouldn't fill a thimble, so he was going to need to talk it through with someone and he immediately thought of his uncle Eli.

The intense afternoon heat had driven most people off the streets and sidewalks, and the three of them made it to the train station with plenty of time to spare. When they entered the small depot on their way to board, Seth immediately noticed that every eye, both male and female, was drawn to Marcie.

As he scanned some of the faces of the men boarding, he thought they were mostly working-class men, well outside the social circle of the men who visited Marcie and Brandy. Seth knew that the parlor house girls serviced the bankers, lawyers, and other monied men who could afford to drop twenty-five dollars or more for an evening of their company once the bar and food tabs were tallied. He didn't spot anyone who fell into that category and he was relieved there would be no awkward encounters.

They left Marcie's trunk with a baggage handler and boarded. Marcie selected a bench seat toward the back of the car and slid over next to an open window. Chauncy sat next and Seth claimed the aisle seat as they settled in for the one-hundred-mile, four-hour journey to Wichita Falls. Although the steam locomotive could run at higher speeds, Seth knew the hastily cobbled-together tracks limited the train's speed to about thirty-five miles per hour. And when you added in all the stops along the way, time slowly piled up.

After a few stifling moments, the engineer finally blew

the whistle and the Fort Worth & Denver City Railroad locomotive chugged away from the depot. The three rode in silence for a while, each with their own thoughts. Seth tried to put Brandy out of his mind and turned his focus to Marcie and her upcoming introduction to the rest of the family. Taken at face value, Marcie was a beautiful young woman who would be a prize catch for any man. Seth expected most of the family would accept Marcie as she was without too much concern about her past. That said, he anticipated there might be a few sticky situations ahead, especially if his mother and his aunt Abigail started nosing around. But, in the end, the only two opinions that mattered were those of the potential bride and groom.

Despite Seth's best attempts, thoughts of Brandy began seeping into his mind again, launching a new flood of emotions. He had dated some over the last few years though none had led to any long-term relationships. One reason for that had been his desire to return to Texas, something that hadn't interested the few women he *had* dated. Another reason he hadn't clicked with any of those women was that Seth had never felt that spark or whatever it was, and he had almost convinced himself that such things didn't exist—until today. What he had experienced with Brandy wasn't a spark, but a full-on bonfire.

He hadn't been with a woman in a long time and he began to wonder if that somehow magnified the encounter with Brandy. After all, Brandy was a professional, right? Well practiced at treating men as if they were the center of her universe? He leaned close to Chauncy and said, "Trade places with me, please."

Chauncy nodded and stood, and Seth slid over next to Marcie. She looked over at him and smiled. "Did you like spending some time with Brandy?"

Seth nodded. "I did." They were talking quietly, trying to avoid being overheard.

"So why does your face look like your best horse just died?"

"Confusion, mainly."

"Or maybe you're overthinkin' it?"

Seth watched his cousin walk toward the front of the car, stretching his legs, before turning to look at Marcie again. "How long has Brandy been workin' at The Belmont?"

"Does it matter? You tryin' to add up the number of men she mighta been with?"

"No, not necessarily," Seth said, surprised at Marcie's sudden anger. "Just trying to get a sense of her as a person."

"What you see is what you get with Brandy. She's as down-to-earth as anybody I know."

Seth mulled that over as he watched the passing terrain. Could he convince himself that her past didn't really matter? After a few moments, he felt Marcie put her hand on his forearm and he turned to look at her.

"If you've got more questions, ask them," Marcie said, "because once this train rolls into the station I'm done talkin' about it. Forever."

Seth nodded. "I understand. This is a delicate subject, but does . . . Brandy . . . uh . . . have any . . . diseases?"

Marcie gave Seth a hard stare. "It's a little late to be askin' that question, isn't it?"

Seth's cheeks reddened, but he didn't look away. The topic was too important.

It was Marcie's turn to look out the window and she did so for a few long moments. Seth didn't want to pressure her on such a sensitive topic so he waited. Eventually she turned to look at him and said, "Not that I know of.

The men that visited us wouldn't have tolerated that. Couldn't have them takin' it back to their wives."

"Thank you," Seth said.

"Look," Marcie said, lowering her voice. "Just 'cause you and Brandy did a little headboard bangin', it doesn't mean you two have to get married. Believe me, working in that place that's something you learn on day one. But if she kindled your interest, then take the train back down there in a few days and take her to dinner, or on a carriage ride, or anywhere away from Josie's place. That'll give you a better sense of her as a real person."

"Good idea," Seth said. "I might just do that."

Seth began to scoot back to his seat, but Marcie reached out and grabbed his arm. "Listen, Seth, I know you been to college and you're a really smart man, hoping to be a lawyer and all, but sometimes you need to shut down that big brain of yours and listen to your heart. I don't have any idea if you and Brandy are a fit. You have to remember that jobs for women out this way are scarce and Brandy and me did what we had to do to get by. That doesn't make us bad people."

Seth turned to look Marcie in the eye. "No, it doesn't. Thank you for your honesty. I think you'll fit nicely into our family."

"I sure hope so. I don't have anywhere else to go."

"Where's your family?"

"Don't have one as long as my ma stays married to her third husband."

Seth didn't want to wade into that mess. "I'm sorry."

"Don't be. My real pa's been dead a long time."

"Any brothers or sisters?" Seth asked.

"Had two older brothers and a younger sister but they're all dead, I guess. I haven't seen my brothers since they left home years ago. My sister died of something that was goin' around about a year before I pulled up stakes. Probably a good thing for her, considering who my ma married."

What a hard life, Seth thought. If anybody deserved a break, it was Marcie. He slid back over, and Chauncy returned to his seat. As Seth's thoughts returned to Brandy, he realized she probably deserved another chance, too. To hell with what anyone thought.

CHAPTER
32

The sun was well into its descent by the time Leander Hays caught up to Moses Wilcox back at the ranch. Wilcox was sitting on Leander's back porch, sipping a cup of something—most likely whiskey—as Leander rode up and climbed down.

"Where's the stallion?"

Wilcox pointed his cup at the barn. "In the corral."

"Good. Thanks for catching him."

"Didn't catch 'im," Wilcox said. "One of the hands done put him in the corral when I rode up. Just about rode my horse to death, too. Ask me, that dern horse is more trouble than he's worth."

Leander chuckled. "You just wait and see them colts he's goin' to sire."

"If they ain't any gentler than their daddy, ain't nobody goin' to be able to ride 'em."

"You'll see," Leander said. He turned and led his horse over to the barn and began to unsaddle him. Once the saddle and bridle were off, he grabbed a handful of straw and wiped the horse down. He hadn't pushed the gelding much on the return journey, yet the horse had still sweated through the saddle blanket.

Leander stepped over and opened the gate to the corral and shooed the horse inside. By the time he made it back to his porch, Wilcox was gone. Leander opened the front door and stepped inside. Rachel was sitting on the sofa in the living room, thumbing through another of her mail-order catalogs. She looked up and asked, "You catch that ornery horse?"

Leander took off his hat and hung it on a peg by the door and did the same with his gun belt. "In a roundabout way, yeah." Leander walked across the hardwood floors and leaned down to kiss his wife. "Had to kill a man to do it."

Rachel closed the catalog and tossed it aside. "Who was it?"

"Don't know his name. But I watched him gun down three unarmed men."

"Wouldn't it have better if you'd killed him before that?"

"Happened too sudden. Nothin' we could do about it."

Rachel stood and wrapped her arms around her husband. "Who did he shoot?"

"The men who stole the stallion."

Rachel leaned her head back and looked up at her husband. "Well, then, sounds like everybody got what they deserved. I guess it's a good thing you don't notch your pistol grips, or you would have run out of room long ago."

Over the years, Leander had been in his fair share of shooting scrapes. "That's for amateurs." He stepped back, breaking the embrace. "Too hot to be all cuddled up."

Rachel gave him a mischievous smile. "That's not something I hear from you very often."

He smiled. "Ain't that the truth?" What had begun as an illicit affair was now a solid, loving marriage that had lasted a decade and was still going strong. "Where's Autumn?" Autumn was their nine-year-old daughter.

"She and Simon are off somewhere. Doing what, I don't know. Those two are thick as thieves."

"Sounds like we got us a tomboy."

"Bite your tongue, Mr. Hays."

"Y'all had supper?" Leander asked.

"Had a late dinner and nobody was hungry for supper, so I sent Consuelo home early. There's leftover beans, bacon, and biscuits warming on top of the stove."

Leander fixed a plate, poured a good dose of Old Grand-Dad bourbon into an enamel cup, and carried everything out to the back porch, where he settled into a rocking chair. Having missed dinner, Leander was hungry, and it wasn't long before he was mopping up the last of the beans with a chunk of biscuit. He set the plate aside and reached for the cup of whiskey. Taking a sip, the liquid burned the back of his throat and left a trail of heat that stretched all the way to his stomach.

It was about fifteen degrees cooler outside than inside, but it was still miserably hot. He reached back and pulled a red paisley handkerchief from his back pocket and mopped his face. A mosquito whined in his ear and he swatted at it and missed. It returned a few seconds later and Leander did his best to ignore it. He didn't understand why those damn bugs even existed.

Rachel opened the back door, stuck her head out, and said, "Skeeters ain't carried you off yet?"

"They're workin' awful hard at it."

"So, you're sayin' I ought to stay inside?"

"No, come on out. Maybe you can draw 'em away from me."

Rachel chuckled and said, "I'll pass," before closing the door.

Leander smiled. He took a quick peek at the position of the sun and figured they had an hour or so until sunset—the witching hour when the mosquitoes would arrive in droves. He looked out over the shared backyard and saw Eli threading his way through a pack of pecking chickens on a direct line to their house. Leander groaned. He liked Eli just fine, but conversations with him could be exhausting.

Eli stopped at the edge of the back porch and said, "Good evening, Leander. May I have a word with you?"

Leander reluctantly waved him forward. "Come have a seat, Eli."

Eli removed his hat, climbed the steps, and walked across the porch, settling into a rocking chair next to Leander. "I see you recovered your stallion."

"It took some doin'," Leander said.

"He's rather high-spirited, isn't he?"

"He's about half-crazy, for sure. Hope I didn't waste my money on him."

"He's young. He'll settle down eventually."

"I hope you're right."

Leander lifted his cup. "Whiskey?"

"Yes, please, if you don't mind sharing."

"Not at all." Leander pushed to his feet, wondering how bad the news could be. He couldn't remember the last time his brother-in-law had accepted an offer of whiskey. He stepped inside and returned a moment later, passing the cup to Eli before retaking his seat.

"That bad, huh?" Leander asked.

"Not necessarily." Eli took a sip of the whiskey and waited for it to blaze a trail to his stomach before continuing. "Though you will need to hone your observation skills."

"Why's that?"

"Emma had an encounter that could have implications for all of us."

Leander felt like banging his head against the side of the house. "What happened?"

"While out with the horse herd this afternoon, Emma was confronted by one of her Comanche abductors. After a series of parries and thrusts, a scuffle ensued that resulted in the death of the Indian."

Leander emitted a low whistle. "Damn, that girl's got some moxie, ain't she?"

"Yes, she is incredibly brave. There are, however, some concerns about a Comanche response. Are you aware of their customs when one of their loved ones is killed?"

Leander nodded. "I've seen it and it ain't pretty. They'll be out for blood."

"Precisely." Eli took another sip of whiskey. "I don't doubt that reservation life has moderately quenched the Indians' thirst for blood, but revenge is another matter entirely."

"Where's the body?"

"Emma dragged the corpse into the trees along the Wichita."

"Maybe we ought to bury it."

"I've given the matter considerable thought. As of now, there are no eyewitnesses nor any way to connect Emma to the killing. However, if someone observed us burying the body, then we would lose any claims of deniability. If we leave matters as they are, we can deny any knowledge of the Indian's death."

"Even if his body is found on ranch land?"

"Yes. People, including the Indians, are constantly trespassing across ranch property, creating a vast pool of potential suspects."

Leander drained his cup and spent a moment thinking, looking for weaknesses in Eli's logic. "And if a witness comes forward?"

"Then we'll readdress the situation."

"Only hiccup I see is the fact that there's a bunch of Comanches across the river that know Emma was a captive. That's a mighty strong motive."

"Motive does not equal guilt."

"I know it don't. But I got a feelin' the Comanches ain't goin' to care about motive or witnesses or any of that other stuff if they get it in their heads that we had somethin' to do with killin' their kin."

CHAPTER
33

By the time Reeves and Percy made it back to camp with their newly acquired prisoner, Percy had about decided he was done with rounding up outlaws. If he had any doubts, the hole through the crown of his hat was a visual reminder. He decided that the first thing he was going to do when he got back to the ranch, was to bury or burn the hat and forget it ever existed. Not that he hadn't had close calls before, but a pistol, or even a rifle round, was small when compared to the finger-long cartridge fired from a Sharps sporting rifle. Too embarrassed to put the hat back on, Percy leaned over and stuffed it under the wagon seat.

Reeves pulled the wagon to a stop and set the brake and both men climbed down. Sam Sixkiller came over and began unhitching the horse.

"Any trouble?" Reeves asked Sixkiller.

"Nope. But I'm about tired of listenin' to that Starr lady. Seems she's got her own ideas about everythin'."

"No surprise there," Reeves muttered. He looked up at Percy's bare head. "Where's yer hat?"

"Funny," Percy said.

Reeves chuckled. "I reckon you can afford a new one. You better not let Miss Franny see that hat. She's liable to ride up here and skin me alive."

"I already got plans for that hat, thank you."

This time Reeves burst out laughing and bent over and put his hands on his knees until he could stop. He was still chuckling when he walked to the back of the wagon and ordered Copley out. When the prisoner was standing, Reeves unhooked him from the chain and took him by the elbow and steered him over to a spot by Belle Star and said, "Sit."

Percy wasn't all that surprised when Copley looked at Starr and said, "How ya doin', Belle?"

"About the same as you, looks like. What'd they get you on, Bose?"

"Says I was peddlin' whiskey, but I ain't done it."

Percy ignored the rest of their conversation. He pulled a cup from his saddlebag and joined Reeves by the coffee-pot. Reeves filled Percy's cup, then his own.

"All these outlaws know one another?" Percy asked.

Reeves took a sip from his cup and then said, "Seems like. Starr probably knows more than anybody. She's been ridin' through this territory a long time."

"How come the army don't run all the white folks out?"

Reeves took a sip from his coffee cup. "The army's got their hands full with the Indians. Hell, Percy, they's two hundred deputy marshals workin' this country and we can just barely keep our head above water. You'd need ten or twenty times that number and you still ain't gonna notice no difference. The thieves and outlaws is as thick as a litter of ticks all over this country."

"Tell me somethin' I don't know. We get more than our fair share of 'em when they drift across the river. Can't hardly go to the outhouse without takin' a gun with you 'cause you never know who's goin' to show up."

"I hear you got other troubles down that way," Reeves said. "You done fenced your place?"

"We've got most of it fenced." Percy paused to take a sip from his cup. "Problem is keepin' it that way. Had a visit with a man on that very topic before riding up this way. He'd hired a couple of kids to cut our fences."

"How'd you know he hired 'em?"

"I caught 'em red-handed. After a little persuadin' they told me his name."

"What's he got against your fences? It's your land, ain't it?"

"It is. He's been runnin' a bunch of cattle on the open range and is gettin' squeezed out with all the fencin' everybody's doin'."

"Ain't your problem, is it?" Reeves asked.

"No, but he's tryin' to make it my problem. I think I got him set straight for now."

"What'd you do?"

"Walked into his saloon and punched him in the nose."

"Best watch your back trail."

"Oh, I will. He's a mean li'l bastard." Percy turned and scanned the area around the camp. "Speakin' of that, where do you reckon that Doolin kid got off to?"

"Don't know. Probably payin' a visit to the whorehouse."

"There's a whorehouse up in these parts?"

"Course they is. Ain't never seen a army post that ain't had a whorehouse or a hog ranch somewhere close."

"Huh," Percy said. "I bet they got some special gals in there."

"Don't you know it. Boy'll be lucky if he don't come away from there with a little somethin' extra." Reeves dumped out the rest of his coffee, walked over, and dropped the cup into the washtub, and went to talk to the cook.

Having no desire for another conversation with Belle Starr and deciding it was too hot for coffee, Percy poured out the rest and walked over to his belongings. After stuffing the cup into his saddlebag, he picked up his rope and went in search of Mouse. It took some doing, but he finally found her grazing down in a creek bottom, taking advantage of what little green grass was left. Percy talked softly to her as he slipped the rope around her neck and led her up the bank and back toward camp. As he approached, Percy heard a man shouting and then watched as both Reeves and Sixkiller raised their hands.

Not knowing if there was a single intruder or a dozen, Percy tied the other end of the rope around a small bush and eased toward a line of cedar trees that ran east of the camp. Once his movements were screened by the trees, he sped up his advance. As he drew closer, he heard a man telling Reeves to free their most recently captured prisoner.

"I ain't gonna do it," Reeves said. "I got a warrant for his arrest."

"I don't care what you got," the man said. "I said, cut 'im loose."

As quietly as possible, Percy worked his way around the cedars and when he had had a good view of what was happening, he squatted down to study the situation. From what he could see, there was only the one man and he was kneeling behind a giant cottonwood tree, a Sharps rifle held tightly to his shoulder. Even though a clock was ticking down in his head, Percy took a moment to thoroughly scan the surrounding area.

When he was satisfied the man was alone, Percy stood and pulled his pistol. From his current position, he was behind the man, so he stepped out from the cedars and lifted his pistol. "Drop the rifle," Percy ordered.

Percy saw the man's shoulders tense up an instant before he began to turn. He saw Reeves reaching for his pistol out of the corner of his eye as he pulled the trigger. Reeves's gun roared an instant later and the rifle slipped from the man's hands.

Percy cocked his pistol again and walked forward as the man slumped to the ground. When Reeves reached the body, Percy lowered the hammer and holstered his pistol. Reeves kicked the rifle out of reach and nudged the man in the ribs with his boot. When there was no reaction, Reeves holstered his pistol and was rolling the man over when Percy arrived.

"Know him?" Percy asked.

Reeves stood and looked down at the dead man's face. "Yeah, I knew 'im. He was one of 'em in the house when I rousted Copley out of there. He's another no-account whiskey peddler, went by the name of Lucky Davis."

Percy looked down at the body and said, "Well, looks like his luck's finally run out."

CHAPTER
34

After finally arriving in Wichita Falls, Seth and Marcie had elected to stay with the trunk and bags while Chauncy ventured over to the livery stable to hire a buggy and driver to take them to the ranch. Now sitting on a bench in front of the train depot, Marcie was looking the small town over. "Not a very big place, is it?"

"Well, it depends on your perspective," Seth said. "It's not a bad start considering this part of the country was still ruled by the Comanches only ten years ago. Back then you'd have been lucky to have ridden through here and still be alive to tell about it."

Marcie unfurled her fan and began fanning herself. "How'd your family survive? Didn't you say the ranch wasn't far from here?"

"It's just a ways east of here. And they, I guess we, survived through ingenuity. Ask Chauncy to show you the war wagon."

"What's that?"

"A verbal description wouldn't do it justice. You have to see it to believe it."

Before their conversation could continue, Chauncy arrived in an old spring wagon with a pimply faced kid on the reins.

"They didn't have no buggies," Chauncy said as he climbed down. "This is the best I could do."

Seth eyed the wagon and the two large draft horses and knew they were in for a slow, hot, dusty drive. He was curious to see how Marcie would hold up.

After loading their bags and the trunk, the three sat at the back of the wagon, their legs dangling over the edge as it rolled out. The driver worked his way through town and picked up the road to the ranch. Although well traveled, it was jaw-jarring bumpy, and Marcie was forced to link arms with the men to keep from being tossed from the bed.

"How far did you . . . say . . . it was?" Marcie asked.

"Not far," Chauncy said.

Marcie frowned, but didn't say anything.

The horses and wagon kicked up a cloud of dust that hung in the still air, coating their sweaty faces with a layer of grime. The large horses, bred for brute strength, weren't exactly fleet of foot, and the trip took a full two hours. By the time the wagon turned up the lane to the houses, all three had sworn off wagon travel for the foreseeable future. To her credit, Marcie never once complained.

Chauncy directed the driver to his father's house and he and Seth unloaded the trunk and carried it inside. After retrieving the bags, Chauncy sent the driver on his way and the three spent an awkward moment talking before Seth took his leave.

Marcie stood in the front yard and took a moment to

orient herself. Marcie pointed at the large house in the middle and asked, "Who lives there?"

"My grandma," Chauncy said.

Marcie nodded. With the sun now hovering on the horizon, lanterns had been lit in most of the homes, casting a golden glow over the entire scene. Marcie felt a sense of warmth or contentment or something she couldn't quite put her finger on. Then she hit on the word—*home*. Tears spilled down her cheeks as she stood and took it all in.

"Why you cryin'?" Chauncy asked as he wrapped an arm around her waist.

Marcie looked up at Chauncy. "Is this real?"

"Well, I reckon so. It's where I grew up."

Marcie dabbed at the corners of her eyes with the back of her gloved hands. "And you're sure you still want me here?"

Chauncy gave her a squeeze. "Of course. I wouldn'ta asked you if I didn't."

Marcie whispered, "Thank you."

"You're welcome. I'm beat. How about we save the family meetin' till tomorrow?"

"Okay." She nodded at the dark house before them. "Is your pa inside?"

"Don't look like it. We'll move to the guesthouse in a couple of days if nobody's usin' it."

"You have a guesthouse?"

"Sure. They's people comin' through here all the time lookin' to buy horses or cattle. It ain't much but it'll do us for a while."

Talking about where to live brought Marcie back to the here and now. "I don't care where we live. But I do have a question."

"What's that?"

"How are we goin' to make money?"

Chauncy shrugged. "I ain't worried about it. We'll make do."

For Marcie, who accounted for every penny she earned, his answer was disconcerting. She wasn't going to make an issue of it now, but she saw the faint beginnings of storm clouds building on the horizon.

"You worried about it?"

"Some. I've got enough to see us through for a while."

"I reckon I've got a few cattle and horses we could sell if we get desperate."

"What's a few?"

Chauncy shrugged again. "Probably eight hundred head of cattle and maybe a couple dozen horses."

Marcie sighed with relief. She had no idea how much a cow was worth, but at least they weren't destitute. "Can we go in now?"

"Sure." Chauncy took Marcie by the hand and led her across the porch and through the front door of his father's house.

Unable to sleep because of the grass situation, Percy had risen well before daybreak for an early start toward home. The full moon had provided more than enough illumination and as the sun broke on the horizon he was on the north bank of the Red River, preparing to cross. His mind consumed by ranch matters, he was jerked back to the present when a rifle shot rang out and a geyser of dirt erupted a foot in front of Mouse's right leg. Percy slid off Mouse's back, pulled his rifle, and whacked her on the rump and she took off for the barn at a dead run.

Before Percy could take stock of the situation, another

rifle shot sounded and this time the round hit a little closer to the mark when the bullet hit him in the left arm and spun him around. He dived for the ground, his arm feeling like someone had clubbed him with a red-hot poker. Belly-crawling, he headed toward a tree line thirty yards away. He still had no idea where the shooter was, but right now he was more concerned about surviving. Hopefully when Mouse showed up at the barn someone would come looking, if they weren't already on the way. All Percy needed to do was to buy some time.

Another shot echoed across the river bottom and the bullet plowed into the dirt three feet in front of him. Unfortunately, he was crawling through a stand of tall, dead grass and there was no way to mask his movements. He lifted his rifle and levered off three quick shots. He didn't have a prayer of hitting anything, but he hoped it might force whoever was shooting to take cover.

Taking advantage of the momentary lapse, he dug his elbows into the ground, trying to propel himself faster. He angled left, adjusting his course to make his position less predictable. If he could get into the trees, he liked his chances. Blood soaked his shirtsleeve and he didn't yet know how serious the wound was. Although it hurt like hell, he was still able to move his arm and he took that as a good sign.

Finally, mercifully, he made it into the timber and rose to his knees behind a large oak tree.

"Percy!" someone shouted from across the river. He thought it sounded like Jesse Simpson, the ranch foreman, but he didn't know for sure. What he did know was that it was a friendly voice and it boosted his confidence.

Not wanting to give away his current position, Percy

didn't respond to Jesse's call. He rolled up his left sleeve and was relieved to see the bullet had only creased his biceps. Although bleeding profusely, he would live to see another day. He pulled his handkerchief from his back pocket and used his other hand and his teeth to cinch it around the wound. Once he had stemmed the flow, he turned his focus back to finding the shooter as his mind clicked through a list of possible suspects. At the top of that list was Cal Northcutt. Percy had no doubt the slimy little bastard was the type to bushwhack a man though he knew proving it would be difficult unless he could put a bullet in him. But first he had to find him, and the shooter hadn't fired another round since the last miss. His eyes constantly scanning, Percy still hadn't picked up any hint of movement.

A few moments later, Percy heard a twig snap behind him, and he swung his rifle around. Jesse shot his hands up so quick they were a blur and Percy lowered the hammer.

Jesse dropped his hands and walked over, squatting down beside Percy. "Who you shootin' at?"

"It's the other way around. Someone tried to dry-gulch me as I was about to cross the river."

Jesse looked off in the distance and said, "Where's he at?"

"Don't know. Probably gone by now. You see anybody ridin' away from this area?"

"Nope, but they's a dozen different ways a man could go." Jesse looked at Percy's bloody sleeve. "How bad shot are ya?"

"It's nothin'," Percy said as he pushed to his feet.

"You got any idear who was shootin' at ya?"

"Maybe," Percy said. He walked to the edge of the tree

line and paused, hoping he was right that the gunman was gone.

Jesse walked over and said, "He put that hole in yer hat, too?"

Percy had forgotten he had put the hat back on. "No. That was somebody else."

"I swear, Percy, how many men you got shootin' at ya?"

"Hopefully none, now. You see anything?"

"No, but my ol' eyes ain't what they once was."

Percy took two steps out of the trees and paused again. If the shooter was still around, he was missing the perfect opportunity. When no more shots sounded, Percy waved Jesse out and the two men stepped across a trickle of salty water and climbed the far bank.

"Before I forget," Percy said, "start pushing the cattle across the river this morning."

"You get a lease?"

"Nope. Don't need one, I reckon. Somebody put my horse up?"

"Yep. That mean ol' mare come near to bitin' me, too."

Percy chuckled. "Probably why you never got married."

Jesse scowled.

"Any more fence cuttin'?" Percy asked.

"Ain't heard yet. I'm bettin' there was. And I'm a-gettin' tired of it."

"You and me both. It'll probably take a couple of them fence cutters gettin' shot to tamp it down."

The two men split up and went their separate ways. Little did Percy know that the morning's surprises weren't over yet. He stepped up on his back porch, tossed his hat on one of the rocking chairs, pushed through the back door, and came to an abrupt stop when he saw the woman sitting at the kitchen table.

He looked at her and she looked at him and both of their jaws dropped open.

Marcie's eyes were as big as dinner plates when she said, "You're Chauncy's pa?"

Percy, too stunned to speak, simply nodded. He finally found his voice a moment later. "What are you doin' here, Marcie?"

"Well . . . it's . . . kind of . . . a long story," Marcie stammered.

Percy looked around for Chauncy before pulling out a chair and sitting. He ran a hand across his face and said, "Does Josie know you're here?"

Marcie nodded. Although she had seen Percy plenty of times when he came to visit Josie, she didn't know much about him other than his first name. And now she was having the most awkward of awkward moments, something she couldn't have predicted in a thousand years. "Chauncy asked me to marry him."

"Where did you meet him?"

"Where do you think?" Marcie asked.

"Boy, oh, boy," Percy said. He looked at Marcie and said, "And you said yes?"

Marcie nodded again. "You want me to leave?"

Before Percy could answer, Chauncy came shuffling into the kitchen. "I see you two met." Chauncy pulled a cup from a shelf overhead and poured himself a cup of coffee. He looked back at his father. "Pa, you want coffee?"

"Sure," Percy said, his mind still spinning.

Chauncy brought Percy his coffee and took a seat next to Marcie.

Percy took a sip and scalded his upper lip.

Chauncy nodded at his father's bloody sleeve. "What happened to you?"

When Percy didn't immediately reply, Chauncy said, "Pa?"

Percy refocused his gaze on his son. "What?"

"I said, what happened to your arm?"

Percy looked down at his bloody sleeve as if seeing it for the first time. "Oh. Someone took a couple of potshots at me."

"I heard someone firing a rifle and thought it was just target practice," Chauncy said.

"Yeah, I was the target he was practicing on."

"Well, who was it?" Chauncy made no mention of the three men he had killed yesterday.

"Don't know yet."

"Okay," Chauncy said. "Who do you think done it?"

"Could have been a man I braced for cuttin' our fences."

"He got a name?" Chauncy asked.

Unable to wrap his mind around any of it, Percy stood. "I need to unsaddle my horse." He picked up his coffee, walked over to the back door, and went out.

Chauncy looked at Marcie and said, "He ain't normally so scatterbrained. Don't know what's goin' on with him."

"Maybe gettin' shot at had somethin' to do with it," Marcie said.

Chauncy thought about that for a moment and then said, "Could be right."

CHAPTER
35

By the time Saturday rolled around, Percy was a bit more accepting of Marcie's presence at the ranch. He came to the realization that whether he liked it or not, there wasn't a hell of a lot he could do about it. It was Chauncy's life and he had to live it his way. As far as he knew, Marcie's former occupation remained secret and the family had welcomed her with open arms. But that didn't mean he didn't have a bone to pick with Josie Belmont and that was number two on his list of things to do. Item one on that list was a chat with Cal Northcutt, and Percy was hoping to scratch that off sometime today. He thought he could make the trip to town and still be back in time to put the finishing touches on preparations for tonight's dinner with Quanah and his wives.

That he might not return from his encounter with Northcutt never entered his mind.

Despite his best efforts, Emma and his mother had declined his offer of an all-expenses-paid trip to Dallas, so Frances would attend the dinner and act as host. To cook, Percy had hired Maria and Consuelo and had ordered a steer slaughtered. Most Indians he had met wouldn't touch a piece of pork so after a consultation with his mother, it was decided that steaks would be the featured menu item.

As for beverages, Percy wanted to steer clear of alcohol because you never knew what you were going to get when an Indian started drinking. And with multiple wives coming to the dinner and unaware of how Quanah's family dynamics worked, Percy thought including alcohol with dinner would be begging for trouble. He took a final swallow from his cup and pushed back his chair.

Chauncy and Marcie had moved over to the guesthouse, which had suited Percy just fine. It was awkward enough seeing her around the property and downright uncomfortable sharing a house with her. He was just damn glad he had never acted on his impulses to spend some time with the woman who might now be his daughter-in-law. It had been the age difference that Percy couldn't get past, so he relied on Josie's services exclusively. Not that she couldn't get mischievous at times by inviting a third into the room, but, thankfully, none of those had been Marcie. Percy stood, dropped his cup in the washtub, and went outside. His first stop of the day would be his mother's house.

Percy crossed the porch and slipped inside. After saying good morning to Maria, who was puttering around in the kitchen, he took a seat next to his mother, who polishing off the last of her breakfast.

"There's one thing about tonight we ain't thought about," Percy said as Maria set a steaming mug of coffee down in front of him. He looked at her and said, *"Gracias."*

"De nada," Maria answered.

"What is it we haven't thought about?" Frances asked.

Percy hated to bring it up, already knowing what his mother's response would be. "Well, it'd be long ride home for them after supper."

Frances gave her son a hard look. "They aren't stayin' here."

Percy sighed. "You ain't being very hospitable."

"Quit saying *ain't*. I raised you better than that."

Percy instantly regretted riling her up with an entire day stretching out before them.

She pushed her plate aside. "Put them in the guesthouse. It's bad enough having them in my house for dinner."

"We've had dinner with a countless number of Indians."

"None of them were kidnappers, as far as I know."

Percy let that comment slide. "Can't put 'em in the guesthouse because Chauncy and Marcie are using it."

"Then they can stay with you. Why a man thinks he needs more than one wife is madness. And now that I think about it, I don't like the idea of them stayin' with you, either. They're liable to get in a quarrel and wind up slittin' your throat in the melee."

"Nobody's throat is gettin' slit," Percy said, exasperated. "We may be arguing over nothin', but I reckon they can stay at my place. Might seem a little odd that we're shuffling them off to another house, though."

"Too bad," Frances said. "And while we're talking about Chauncy, are he and Marcie goin' to continue livin' in sin or are they plannin' to get married?"

Percy groaned. "I didn't think we were talkin' about them."

"Well, we are now."

"It's complicated. Why does it matter? I never took you to be a prude."

"I'm not. If they want to shack up, then let 'em as long as they do it elsewhere. It sets a bad example. Besides, he isn't doin' right by her."

If you only knew, Percy thought.

"Where's Marcie from anyway? I can't see her mother being any too happy about havin' her daughter shacked up with my grandson."

"I don't know where she's from." Percy pushed back his chair and stood, eager to put an end to the conversation.

"You gonna talk to Chauncy or not?" Frances asked.

"I'll talk to him," Percy said, though he had no intentions of doing so.

"Where you goin'?" Frances asked in a more friendly tone. "It's Saturday. You don't have to work every day of the week."

No, I don't, Percy thought. But working sure beat sitting there talking about something he had no desire to talk about. "I've got a couple of things I gotta get done." He said, "Adios" to Maria, exited through the back door, and felt a sense of relief to have escaped his mother's sharp tongue. However, his relief was short-lived when he returned home to find Marcie sitting at his kitchen table, nursing a cup of coffee.

"Where's Chauncy?" Percy asked.

"Over at the guesthouse. We had a fight."

Well, that's promising, Percy thought. Maybe his son was having a change of heart. "About what?"

"He wants to ride over to Wichita Falls and have the justice of the peace marry us."

Okay, maybe not. "I thought that's what you wanted."

"I'm only goin' to get married once and I'd like for it to be a little nicer than standing in someone's dusty office."

Percy almost rolled his eyes but stopped himself in time. "What did you have in mind?"

Marcie shrugged. "I don't know. I know I don't have a right to ask, but could we have a little ceremony here and have a cake and maybe a nice supper? I know you don't much like the idea of Chauncy marrying someone like me, but people can change, can't they? Or do I have to carry that stain with me the rest of my life?"

"Of course people can change. And I don't think poorly of you for doin' what you had to do. But why Chauncy?" Percy pulled out a chair and sat.

"'Cause he asked me, that's why. And not to be mean, but you visited Josie on a regular-like basis. Do you think less of her for what she does for a living?"

"Well, no, but . . ." Percy left the rest unsaid.

"But what?" Marcie asked, her voice laced with anger. "You wouldn't marry her? It's okay to use her body for your own pleasure and then deny you even know her to your friends and family?"

"This is not about me and Josie," Percy said, his cheeks turning a deep shade of red.

"Sure, it is. You ever take Josie out to dinner?"

"As a matter of fact, I have on multiple occasions. But again, this is not about me and her."

"Good for you. The mayor used to show up every Saturday night like clockwork and then he'd go to church with his family the next morning and start spouting off about cleaning up the town. I don't much like people like that."

"I'm not like that. Of course, I don't go around tellin'

everybody I meet that me and Josie meet up on occasion. That's private business."

"That it is," Marcie said. "Let me ask you this. If you didn't know what I'd done in the past, how would you feel about me? Say me and Chauncy met on a train instead of at The Belmont?"

Percy shrugged. "It's hard for me to get past."

"I understand that, but how do we move forward? Or am I always gonna be a whore in your eyes?"

Percy shrugged. "I guess not."

"Well, that's reassuring." Marcie sighed and took a sip from her cup. "Look, I get it. I'm damaged goods. But I didn't have an opportunity to grow up on a big fancy ranch. We were dirt poor and when my ma married a man who had more interest in me, I left home and had to fight and scratch just to get by. So, please, don't condemn me for doing what I had to do simply to survive." She took another sip of coffee and said, "Do I seem like a nice person?"

Percy took a particular interest in the table's wood grain. "Well, yeah, I guess."

"Do you think it's possible for people to change?"

Percy shifted in his chair. "Yes."

"Do people deserve second chances?"

"Ain't nobody perfect, so yes."

"Then why is it not possible for me?"

Percy let that roll around in his mind for a bit and then finally lifted his head and looked Marcie in the eye. "Pick a date. We'll have us a nice ceremony."

Marcie nodded. "Thank you. The only thing I can say for certain is that I will never do anything to make you regret my being here."

Percy nodded and stood. "You and Chauncy ought to patch things up if we're goin' to have a weddin'."

Marcie smiled for the first time and stood. "Oh, we will. Neither one of us can hold a grudge."

"That's a good start. Marriages are hard enough as it is."

After Marcie exited out the back door, Percy ducked into the living room and strapped on his gun belt—it was time to pay Northcutt a visit.

CHAPTER
36

Try as hard as he might, Seth couldn't get Brandy Bordeaux off his mind for more than a few minutes at a time. He disliked the name immensely and assumed she was using an alias. Every time he thought about her name an image of a table littered with empty liquor bottles popped up in his mind. Although he was curious, he was also a little apprehensive about seeking even a minor truth, fearing such knowledge would only make her seem more real. If he thought of her only as Brandy, the occasional tryst partner, then he wouldn't have to confront all the other emotions that were swirling through his mind.

The problem, though, was that now that he had finished school and returned home, the number of matrimonial prospects in Texas was sparse when compared to the larger cities back East. He assumed the field of potential candidates would widen once he began work in Dallas or wherever it might be, but he knew there were no guarantees. And Seth wasn't the best of sweet-talkers and often found it difficult to initiate a conversation with members of the opposite sex. His thoughts were interrupted when their cook, Consuelo Ruiz, handed him a plate of scrambled eggs and two piping-hot biscuits.

Seth thanked her as pulled one of the biscuits apart and slathered on some butter. He forked some eggs into his mouth and took a bite from the biscuit as his mind drifted back to the quandary that Brandy presented. Was he really going to ignore all of the advice he'd doled out to Chauncy? If they had all been valid points then, why not now? Realizing he needed some clear-eyed advice from someone who didn't have a stake in the outcome, he decided to pay a visit to Uncle Eli. He finished off the eggs, mopped his plate with a piece of biscuit, popped it in his mouth, and stood. Chewing, he carried his plate over to the washtub and dropped it in.

After draining the last of the coffee from his cup, he dropped it in the tub and slipped out the back door. Although the sun hadn't yet cleared the horizon, Seth's shirt was damp with sweat by the time he arrived at Eli's house. His uncle was on the back porch, his pipe dangling from the corner of his mouth.

Seth paused before mounting the steps and said, "Uncle Eli, do you have a minute?"

Eli pulled out the pipe and said, "Certainly, Seth."

Seth climbed the stairs and crossed the wooden deck, taking a seat next to his uncle.

"What's on your mind?" Eli asked.

"Well, I'm in a quandary and don't know what to do about it."

Eli took a draw from his pipe and said, "I'm listening."

"It's kind of a touchy subject and I don't even know where to start."

"I've found it best to start at the beginning."

"Okay. What are your thoughts on women who might . . . well . . . might work . . . as a . . . no, in a . . . in a . . ."

"Brothel?" Eli asked.

Seth nodded.

"Prostitution is as old as mankind. And it will exist long after we are gone despite all the righteous indignation to banish it from our society. Many women are forced into it out of desperation and once there, find it extremely difficult to escape. Jobs for women are few and those that do exist offer such a measly wage they aren't worth having. I can't fault a woman for selling access to the one thing she has in her possession men crave."

"I get all of that, but how would you feel if a man was to marry one?"

Eli tapped the tip of the pipe against his chin. "Are you referring to yourself?"

"Maybe."

"Interesting." Eli took a long draw from his pipe and blew out a long stream of smoke. Then he did it a couple more times before pulling the pipe from his mouth. "Before things proceed further, you should request that she undergo a doctor's examination to confirm she is disease-free."

With that statement, all the color drained from Seth's face.

And Eli noticed it. "Too late for that, I assume?"

"Yes."

"How well do you know this young lady?"

"Not too well," Seth said.

"Yet, you're contemplating a marriage proposal?"

Usually unflappable, Seth was surprised by the incredulous tone in Eli's voice. "I know it seems kind of strange.

Shoot, it even sounds odd to my own ears now that I said it out loud."

"What's driving this compulsion?"

Seth shrugged. "Just something about her."

"You do realize that this young lady is a practicing professional whose sole occupation is to entice men into paying for her services?"

"Well, yeah, I guess so. It sounds bad the way you put it, though."

"Have you had an opportunity to spend any time with this young woman outside of her place of employment?"

"No."

"I would advise you to start there. We each have our own lives to live and it would be presumptuous of me to suggest who you may or may not marry. However, that said, I do think you need to be careful here. I assume there are no time constraints in play, so I recommend you take your time and do your due diligence. Of utmost importance is the doctor's examination and if she receives a clean bill of health, she will need to curtail her occupational activities going forward."

"Should I ask her to stop now?"

"Are you willing to cover her revenue shortfall?"

"For a while, sure. Though I don't know how much we're talking about."

"You'll have to ask her. Also keep in mind, she may be unwilling to suspend her activities without some assurances on your part. I would advise you to suppress the urge to overpromise anything at this point. You also need to understand that if she isn't producing, she'll be forced to find other living arrangements. Are you willing to foot that bill as well?"

"I hadn't thought about that."

"From my perspective, there are a number of items you haven't given due consideration, Seth. That said, I do have some final advice, if I may?"

"Of course."

"Sexual attraction is a powerful stimulant and you would do yourself well to make all of your decisions while fully clothed. And also remember this, from an old Egyptian proverb: 'For every joy there is a price to be paid.'"

CHAPTER
37

Now that Saturday had arrived, Emma regretted her decision not to take Percy up on his offer of a weekend in Dallas. She didn't know if she could stomach seeing Quanah again, especially so closely on the heels of Scar's reappearance and subsequent killing. But it wasn't just herself she was worried about. Quanah was very charismatic, and he drew people to him like bees to a hive and she could easily recall the heady days of being in his orbit. She had no doubt that Simon, her half-Comanche son, would feel that same pull and that was something she wanted to avoid at all costs.

Emma drained the last of the coffee from her cup and stood. She ruffled Simon's long, dark hair as she walked by on her way to drop the cup in the washtub. "What are you doing today?" Emma asked.

Simon finished chewing the piece of bacon in his mouth and said, "I don't know. Ain't got nothin' planned."

"Well, I want you home well before suppertime."

"Why?"

"Because I said so. And quit sayin' *ain't*. The word

doesn't exist in any dictionary I've seen." Although her education had been interrupted during that lost year, Emma had resumed her studies with a vengeance as she nursed her son through infancy.

"Everybody else around here says it," Simon said.

"You aren't everyone else. You're my son and I expect you to use proper grammar."

Simon groaned.

Simon and Autumn were the only remaining children of school age around the ranch and it no longer made fiscal sense to hire a teacher just for them. Instead, both Emma and Rachel took turns schooling the two children, but that would change in the fall with both children enrolled in the newly built school in town. It was going to be a struggle to get them there and back every day, but both mothers thought the hardship would be worth the effort.

Emma watched as Simon wolfed down the last of his breakfast, pushed his chair back, and stood. He was turning for the door when Emma said, "Excuse me, sir."

Simon turned. "What?"

Emma pointed at his plate left on the table. "Are you expecting that plate to walk to the washtub by itself?"

Simon whined, but he heeded his mother's words then left out the back door. A few moments later, as Emma was putting on a pot of beans for dinner, Simon burst through the front door, out of breath. "Ma," he shouted, "there's a . . . whole passel . . . of Indians over at . . . Uncle Eli's house."

Emma's breath caught. Had Scar's body been found? Momentarily frozen in place, Emma's mind spun through possible scenarios—none of them good. The only way to know was to go have a look for herself. Hurrying down the hall to her bedroom, she slipped off her dress and pulled on a pair of trousers she wore when working with the horses. To cover the top half, she put on a long-sleeve, well-worn, bib-front shirt that had once belonged to her father and topped that off with a leather vest that was large enough to conceal her breasts. She didn't know who was out there, but if they were Comanches there was a fair chance she might be recognized.

Sweat was already trickling down her back by the time she returned to the living room.

Simon gave her a funny look. "What are you doin'? If it weren't for your long hair, you'd look like a man."

"Good, that's what I was aimin' for." She walked over to the door and paused. After gathering her hair, she gave it a couple of twists and then piled it onto the top of her head and covered it with the widest-brimmed hat she owned, an old, moth-eaten, straw sombrero that was almost as old as she was. The last thing she did before stepping outside was to pull her gun rig down from a peg by the door and buckle it on. She didn't need to check if it was loaded, because it remained so at all times.

She turned to look at Simon. "Please stay here."

"And miss all the action?"

She knew he would slip out of the house as soon as she was gone, so she laid down a few ground rules. "You can go in the back door of Grandma Frances's house and work your way to the parlor. You'll be able to see out the windows. But if I catch you outside, I'm taking away your horse and rifle for a month. Understand?"

Simon looked down at his shoes. "I understand."

Emma's heart was racing as she opened the front door and stepped outside. Eli's house was on the other side of the horseshoe-shaped line of homes. As she edged around the front of her grandmother's house, Emma's worst fears were realized when she saw a blanket-covered body tied to one of the Indian ponies. Emma eyed the horse and was fairly certain it was the one Scar had been riding. As for the rest of the group, it consisted of a dozen warriors who sat their horses while Eli, unarmed, spoke to them from his front porch. Her uncle, who had an uncanny knack for learning languages, was conversing with the Indians in a mix of their own tongue and sign language.

Her ruse hadn't fooled Eli in the slightest and he nonchalantly held up a hand in her direction, suggesting she should stop. Emma eased into the shade created by her grandmother's house, her hand never far from the butt of her pistol. When one of the Indians turned to look in her direction, Emma nearly sagged to her knees. It was another of her abductors, the one she had named Big Nose. Although he had been the nicest of her four kidnappers, he, too, had used and abused her, and it took all of Emma's willpower not to pull her pistol and blast him off his horse. She searched his face for signs of recognition and didn't see any. Although he was older, the image of his face would be seared deep into Emma's mind until the day she died.

From their tone, she could tell the well-armed Indians were angry and Emma thought the situation might spiral out of control at any moment, although Eli's manner was relaxed and his words measured.

Apparently, Emma wasn't alone in her thinking, because she heard a high-pitched squeal and looked up to see the two doors high up on the barn's face swinging open. Emma knew what was inside, but she doubted the Indians did. A couple of the Indians glanced up at the noise but quickly dismissed it when nothing else happened. They had no inkling that they could all be slaughtered in a matter of seconds. Emma saw Jesse appear out of the darkness of the opened doorway, and it was clear he was closely watching the action taking place below.

Rebuilt after the massive twister had destroyed every structure on the ranch, inside those open doors was a specially designed platform built by the Peter Schuttler Wagon Works Company out of Chicago. Constructed for easy deployment, the platform was built on a set of rails and could be pushed out the open doorway to cantilever over the side of the barn in a matter of seconds. However, it wasn't the platform itself that would strike fear in the Indians' hearts. It was what was mounted on said platform—a Model 1881 six-barrel Gatling gun, capable of firing four hundred .45-70 caliber rounds per minute. Each shell, packed with seventy grains of black powder and capped by a heavy lead bullet, could chew through man or beast at ranges that extended out to hundreds of yards. And as close as Jesse was, if he was forced to deploy the gun, they'd be walking over tiny pieces of Indian and horse flesh for weeks to come.

Emma assumed Eli and Jesse didn't want to tip their hands unless they absolutely had to. The Indian doing most of the talking was an older man with a face creased by years of exposure to the elements. Emma had never seen him before, but his body language suggested he was a man whose voice was rarely ignored.

A few of the ranch hands had spilled out of the barn and bunkhouse, probably waiting, Emma thought, to see if Jesse was going to have to crank up the Gatling gun. After a few more minutes of discussion, Eli pointed at Luis Garcia, a short, compact Mexican, and waved him over. Emma wasn't close enough to hear their conversation, but he turned, hurried back to the barn, and rode out on his horse a moment later.

Eli said something else to the Indians in their native tongue and whatever he said had an effect on the Indians as some of the tenseness went out of their shoulders and they visibly relaxed. After a few long minutes, Luis returned, driving a herd of steers out in front of him. The Indians put their horses in motion and picked up the cattle as they passed, and Luis reined his horse toward the barn.

Once the Indians disappeared down the riverbank, Emma walked over to talk to Eli. "Did they think we had something to do with the killing?" she asked.

Eli nodded. "In the beginning, yes. However, I believe I dissuaded them of that notion. I don't think we'll have any further trouble. Did you recognize any of them?"

"Yes. The one on the black-and-white pinto was one of them that kidnapped me."

"I know you would like nothing better than to exact your revenge, but I suggest you refrain for now. It would be difficult for us to explain if two of your abductors suddenly showed up dead in the same week."

"I think I'm done with exacting my revenge," Emma said.

"Probably smart," Eli said. "There's an ancient proverb whose origins are somewhat muddled. Some suggest it originated with the Jews, others say the Arabs. Nevertheless, it's pertinent to this situation. The old proverb says: 'If you live to seek revenge, dig a grave for two.'"

CHAPTER
38

Percy parked Mouse two blocks south of Northcutt's saloon and wrapped the reins around the hitching post. After adjusting his holster to his liking, he set off down the boardwalk. The downtown area covered only six square blocks with plenty of vacant parcels still available for development. It was a mix of hotels, dry goods stores, saloons, and, for Sunday-morning repentance, a slew of churches featuring various denominations. He didn't know the difference between a Presbyterian and a Baptist although he understood they were all trying to get to the same place in the end. Why they all had to go about it in different ways was a mystery to Percy, who hadn't been inside a church in more than forty years. He didn't put much stock in any of their nonsense and figured a man could get more religion from riding the land than sitting in a specific building at a specific time and on a specific day.

As he neared Northcutt's saloon, he cleared his mind of all extraneous matters and turned his focus to the upcoming confrontation. He didn't know how it would play out, but ideally it would end with Northcutt gasping for his last breath while lying in a pool of his own blood. Although he couldn't prove Northcutt was the man who tried to bush-whack him, Percy was convinced he was the culprit and he aimed to put a stop to it before Northcutt had a chance to try again.

Percy crossed the street and paused a moment to survey the scene. Plenty of people were out and about and, despite the early hour, several horses were tied to the hitching posts that fronted the drinking establishment. Easing up close to the window, Percy took a peek inside. Three men were standing at the bar and Northcutt was playing cards with two men at the same table in the back where he'd been sitting before. All five of the visitors were armed with six-shooters and, after marking their locations, Percy pulled back and spent a moment strategizing. Pulling his pistol, he slid a forty-five cartridge into the one empty chamber and reholstered his weapon. Northcutt had claimed to be unarmed during their last confrontation, but Percy had a plan for that if he tried to use that excuse again. After taking a deep breath, he slowly exhaled as he walked over to the door and pushed through.

He paused a moment to allow his eyes to adjust. The three men at the bar turned to look at him then went back to their beers. The bartender, who was wiping down the counter, glanced up at Percy and continued cleaning. Northcutt was jawing with one of the men at the table and hadn't yet looked up to see who had entered. Once he could see everything clearly, Percy began walking, his spurs jangling with each step. Northcutt's nose was still swollen, and he had black rings under his eyes. Northcutt finally looked up and stopped in midsentence when he saw Percy approaching. The other two men, who had their backs to the door, turned to find the reason for Northcutt's sudden silence. They glanced at Percy and, not sensing anything amiss, turned back around. Their presence might be problematic, but Percy wouldn't know that until the action started.

Percy stepped up to the table, reached down and relieved the man to his left of his pistol, and tossed it on the table. That sent the two men scurrying, leaving Percy alone with Northcutt. Percy took a step to his left and turned slightly so he could see the rest of the room.

With his arms relaxed at his sides, Percy nodded at the pistol and said, "Pick it up."

Northcutt licked his lips and looked around, as if searching for help.

Out of the corner of his eye, Percy saw the men shuffling toward the other side of the saloon, out of the line of fire.

"Pick it up," Percy said again, his eyes now locked on Northcutt.

Northcutt's hands were on the table, only inches from the butt of the gun. "What's this about?" Northcutt asked.

"If you're goin' to ambush a man, you ought to learn to shoot a little better."

"What makes you think it was me?" Northcutt's hand inched a little closer to the pistol.

"'Cause you're a gutless, yellow-bellied back-shooter. The best part of you ran down your daddy's leg."

Northcutt licked his lips again as his gaze darted around the room, before landing on the pistol again. "My hand ain't but inches away from it," Northcutt said while still looking at the gun. "I heard you was fast but ain't no way you's that fast."

"I reckon we're about to find out."

Northcutt looked up and locked eyes with Percy. "I should have killed—"

And that's when he went for the gun. He had it in his hand and was in the process of cocking it when Percy's bullet pierced his forehead and blew out the back half of his skull.

Percy spun around, his pistol still smoking. "Anybody else?"

All the remaining men reached for the sky. Percy reholstered his pistol and walked out of the saloon.

CHAPTER
39

Despite the seeds of doubt sown into his mind by his uncle, Seth couldn't help himself. After dressing, he stuck his derringer into his back pocket and headed to the barn to saddle a horse. He had considered quizzing Marcie for more in-depth information on Brandy, but decided he'd ask the questions to Brandy herself. Relationship building was how he thought of it.

As for the big dinner tonight, he had no desire to spend an evening with some old Indian chief. Growing up on the ranch, Indian sightings were as common as ants at a picnic and any novelty for the once-wild savages had worn off long ago.

Once he had the horse saddled, he led the roan gelding out of the barn and paused, wondering if he should strap on his father's old gun belt. Then he recalled how effort-lessly Chauncy had dispatched those three men and he knew he was no match for someone like his cousin. He also knew the Acre was populated by dozens of men who had similar talents. He tied his bag on behind the saddle and led his horse over to the house, where he stuck his head inside to tell his mother he might be gone a couple of days. Then he mounted his horse and headed for town.

When he arrived, he stabled his horse at the livery, walked to the bank to withdraw some money from his account, and headed to the train station, where he purchased a one-way ticket to Fort Worth. He was thinking his stay might last anywhere from a few hours to a few days, depending on how things went and whether he could ever overcome his distaste for what Brandy did for a living. When the train arrived, he boarded, settled onto a bench seat by a window, and pulled the Mark Twain novel from his bag.

Cracking the book open as the train pulled out, he soon found it difficult to concentrate on the words, the pros and cons of a relationship with Brandy bouncing around inside his mind. He closed the book and set it on the bench. His mind drifted back to the few relationships he'd had before. None had ever lasted more than a few weeks and he didn't know if it was something to do with him or if he'd merely made bad choices. He was self-aware enough to know he wasn't the handsomest of men, but he also knew he wasn't an ugly duckling, either. And what he lacked in looks he more than made it up with his intelligence and determination. Yes, his sandy blond hair had thinned some, but he had years to go before worrying about going bald. His father, Amos, had lost most of his hair by the time he was thirty-five and Seth assumed the same would be true for him although it didn't really matter when it might happen because there wasn't anything he could do about it. As far as he was concerned, if a woman was so shallow to be offended by his receding hairline then she probably wasn't the one for him.

So, looks aside, there had to be a reason that Seth hadn't clicked with a woman yet. He thought it probably had something to do with the X branded on his butt. At the age of twelve, Seth had ignored all his parents' warnings and had ventured across the river into Indian Territory for the first time in his life. Angry at being left behind after a group from the ranch left to pursue rustlers, Seth had saddled a horse and followed a short while later. After a series of unfortunate events, he was abducted by three men who had slapped him around and branded him with a red-hot iron. Rescued by his uncle Eli and ranch hand Winfield Wilson, the three men had not lived to tell the tale, but Seth would wear their mark on his butt for the rest of his life.

Even though he had been held captive for only a few hours, the encounter had scarred him deeply. The shame, the humiliation, the feelings of helplessness had shattered any confidence he might have had at the time. Knowing he wasn't perfect, he realized he couldn't expect Brandy to be perfect either and that thought slowed some of the buzzing going on in his head.

As the train chugged onward, Seth tried to force his mind to think of other matters. He had reached out to a couple of lawyers in Dallas and had a job—if he wanted it. That meant he'd need to look for a place to live soon and he needed to spend a few days in Dallas to get a better feel for the city before making that decision. Although he'd been there numerous times, there really wasn't a reason to go beyond Fort Worth anymore because just about anything a person might need was available in that city, including the offerings found in Hell's Half Acre.

Seth stood to stretch his legs. The rocking, swaying, and jerking forced him to grab on to the back of the bench to keep from falling. The tracks between the two cities had been thrown together and, although convenient, the ride was like being in an iron-wheeled wagon on a badly potted road. Eventually, Seth gave up and sat back down.

Looking around the passenger car, he thought it lightly populated for a Saturday. He blamed it on the long-simmering heat wave that had sucked the life out of both man and beast. The window beside him was open, but it offered little relief. Sweat ran down his back like a river and his shirt was soaked through.

It was early afternoon when he disembarked the train in Fort Worth. Opting for a room at the El Paso Hotel, he walked past the boardinghouse where he and Chauncy had stayed and continued on. The hotel offered amenities the boardinghouse couldn't match. The El Paso had its own restaurant, saloon, and billiards room. It was farther away from The Belmont, but Seth didn't see that as necessarily a bad thing. As he walked, he kept an eye out for the woman he had pinched on the butt. He still had nightmares of being decapitated by her handbag and the last thing he wanted to do was run into her again.

He had worked up a lather by the time he reached the hotel. After signing for a room and getting the key from the manager, he carried his bag upstairs and took a few moments to freshen up. After stripping off his shirt, he poured some of the furnished water from the pitcher into the washbasin and wet a towel to wash the accumulated dust and soot from his face and upper torso. With that task completed, he pulled a fresh, bright blue shirt from his bag and slipped it on. Feeling human again, he exited the room, locked the door, and descended the stairs to the lobby. He walked into the hotel's saloon for a little liquid encouragement before heading over to see Brandy.

After ordering a beer, Seth walked to the end of the bar and picked up yesterday's copy of the *Fort Worth Daily Gazette* before taking a seat. His beer arrived and he took a sip as he read through the paper. One article, about a recent lynching in nearby Terrell, grabbed his attention. Seth wasn't all that surprised to read that the person lynched was a negro man who had been accused of accosting a white woman. His perspective on race had aged with time and he believed everyone deserved the same rights, regardless of the color of their skin or what equipment they had between their legs. Equal meant equal in his mind, period. Disgusted, he folded the paper and put it aside. He drained his beer and signaled the bartender for another.

He sipped his second beer more slowly, killing time. He watched the traffic in the lobby for a while, using the mirror behind the bar. When he got bored with that, he paid his tab and stepped outside. Standing in the shade cast by the three-story hotel, he pondered his next steps. He fished his watch from his front pocket and popped the lid to check the time. It was late for dinner and early for supper, but he was hungry anyway. With his uncle's advice playing in his mind, he headed toward The Belmont to see if Brandy was interested in going somewhere to eat.

By the time he arrived at Josie's place, his fresh shirt was no longer fresh, and he had big sweat stains under his arms. He paused before entering, still unsure of his intentions. He could hear the piano and laughter from inside and that's when he realized his first mistake. It was Saturday, the busiest day and night for every parlor house in town. That knocked some of the wind out of his sails, but he took a deep breath, took off his hat, opened the door, and stepped inside. When his eyes adjusted, he could see a half a dozen men lounging around the parlor, sipping whiskey and smoking cigars while listening as the piano man banged out a version of "Blue Tail Fly." Seth didn't see Brandy and assumed she was busy working, a thought that turned his stomach.

Josie stood, walked over, and stuck out her hand. "Mr. Ferguson, nice to see you again."

"You as well," Seth said, pumping her hand.

She released her grip and placed her hand delicately upon his forearm and used it to steer him deeper into the room. "I take it Marcie's well?"

"Yes, she is."

"Would you like a cocktail or perhaps a glass of champagne?" Josie asked.

"I'm fine for now, thank you. Is Brandy around?"

"She is. Would you like to book an appointment?"

Appointment? What the hell. "Well . . . yeah . . . I guess so."

"Let's see what we have available," Josie said, leading him over to a small desk tucked away in one of the corners of the room. On top was a black ledger book that she opened and then ran a finger down a list of what looked like a bunch of initials. "Brandy's next available is nine o'clock this evening. Would you like to book it?"

Seth was disgusted with the entire mess and wanted to leave, but instead said, "Yes, and for the rest of the evening, too."

Josie looked up from her ledger. "Are you sure? It might get expensive."

"How so?"

"Saturday nights are our busiest. It all depends on the number of guests who come in requesting Brandy's services."

Seth was close to walking out the door forever but took

another stab at it for Brandy's sake. "Can't you offer me a flat rate?"

"Well, I suppose I could. Why don't you go have a seat while I look through the records for the last few Saturday nights so I can come up with a reasonable fee for both of us?"

Seth sighed. "Okay." He shuffled over to a sofa well away from the other men and took a seat. A few moments later, he heard someone laugh and looked at the stairs to see Brandy and a man descending, the two holding hands. When they reached the bottom, the man pecked her on the cheek then walked over to Josie, presumably to pay. Brandy walked over to one of the other men, took a seat on his lap facing him, and pulled the cigar from his mouth and took a puff before putting it back. The man said something, and Brandy tossed her head back in laughter.

Seth wanted to puke. What the hell had he been thinking? He stood, put his hat on, and turned for the door. As he was pulling the door open, someone grabbed him by the elbow. Thinking it was Josie, he was trying to think of an excuse when he turned to see Brandy. She pushed him through the open door and followed him out, closing the door behind her.

"You came back," Brandy said. She tiptoed up and kissed him on the lips.

Seth had to work hard to keep from gagging. He took a step back and leaned against one of the four large pillars that fronted the two-story house. "I did. My mistake."

Brandy frowned. She stepped over, linked arms with him, and titled her head up to look him in the eyes. "Why do you think it was a mistake?"

Seth shrugged.

"You know where I live and what I do, right?"

Seth nodded. "It's one thing to know and another to see it."

"Do you think I enjoy it?" Brandy asked, her voice edging toward incredulity.

"Sure looked like it to me."

"What would you have me do, Seth? Sit by myself and wait until one of 'em decides to drag me upstairs? It doesn't work that way, unless you'd rather I went to work in a crib. Those men come in here expectin' to be entertained, Seth."

Seth blew out a long breath. "I know it."

"Then don't judge me."

"I'm not judgin' you."

"Yeah, you are." Brandy pulled her arm free and took a step back. "Go back to your fancy ranch and"—she gave him the once-over as tears welled up in her eyes—"your fancy clothes and be glad you don't have to work just to scrape by." She wiped her eyes, turned, opened the door, and went back inside.

What Seth should have done was gone straight back to the train station.

But he didn't.

CHAPTER
40

Back at the ranch, the dinner preparations were complete, and they were just waiting for the arrival of their guests. Now sitting on the front porch of the main house and waiting were Percy and his mother along with Eli and his wife, Clara, Abigail, Isaac, Rachel, and Leander. A few ranch hands had also been invited, but they'd all had a bellyful of Comanches after years of warring with them. Emma, Chauncy, and Marcie had begged off as did any of the other children around.

Leander looked over at Percy and said, "You get the chief a gift?"

"Why would I?" Percy asked. "We're givin' 'em a free dinner."

"Well, you better come up with one 'cause he'll be expectin' it," Leander said.

"Like what?" Percy asked.

"Maybe a horse or two or one of your guns," Leander said.

"We aren't givin' that heathen a gun," Frances said,

offering her two cents on the matter. "I don't see why we gotta give him anything."

"I'm just sayin'," Leander said. "I ain't yet had a parley with an Indian where they didn't expect some kinda gift. I guess we can blame the government for that."

"Well, hell," Percy said. He pushed out of his chair, walked across the porch, descended the stairs, and disappeared around the side of the house, grumbling the entire time. He returned a few minutes later and retook his seat.

"What did you come up with?" Leander asked.

"Luis is gonna go cut out a nice horse for him."

"Just one?" Leander asked.

Percy gave Leander a hard look. "Yes, damn it, just one."

"Don't get all riled up at me," Leander said.

"I ain't riled up," Percy said.

"What did I tell you about sayin' *ain't*?" Frances asked.

Percy just shook his head. A few minutes later, Quanah and only three of his five wives turned up the lane toward the house. They were mounted on four beautiful paint horses, and Percy muttered a curse word or two. They were far better animals than any horse Luis would probably cut out of the ranch's herd.

Percy looked over at Isaac, Abigail's husband and Emma's father, to watch his reaction to the chief as they rode up the lane. After what they'd done to Emma, Isaac hated the Comanches with a passion. He'd been with Percy when they had found Emma and it was like his soul had been crushed when he saw that his daughter was pregnant and in labor. His hatred of the Indians had just about ruined his marriage and had strained the relationship between him and his daughter. He had mellowed slightly since then and Percy knew that Isaac cared deeply for his grandson, Simon, though he was somewhat surprised that Isaac would be attending the dinner. Still, Percy didn't want anything happening to the Comanche chief on his watch. "Isaac," Percy said, "you didn't bring any weapons, did you?"

"I damn sure thought about it, but no, no weapons, unfortunately," Isaac said.

"Good," Percy said. "Are you gonna be okay at the dinner?"

Isaac shot an angry look at Abby and said, "I'll manage."

"We've got too much riding on this, so no offending our guests, okay?"

"I'm not goin' to offend them," Isaac said. "If I get to the point I can't stand it anymore, I'll leave."

"That's all we can ask for," Percy said.

As the Comanches drew closer the family stood to greet them.

Eli nodded at the four riders and said to Percy, "How many people do you think Quanah has killed during his lifetime?"

"I don't wanna know," Percy said.

One of Quanah's wives was as big as a barrel, but the other two were lithe and lean and very pretty. Percy found it difficult to accurately judge an Indian's age, but he guessed the larger of the three was somewhere in her midthirties and the other two, who appeared much younger, maybe early twenties.

They rode up to the house and dismounted as Percy stepped down from the porch. The older wife took charge of Quanah's horse as he and Percy shook hands. Quanah was dressed in a dark gray suit with matching derby hat and his long hair was braided into pigtails and worn over the front of his shoulders. His three wives were dressed more traditionally, outfitted in beautifully beaded, knee-length buckskin dresses and high-top moccasins that hit them about midcalf.

With the aid of one of his younger wives who spoke good English, introductions were made, and they entered the house, where Frances took charge of the seating arrangements.

Emma was sitting on her front porch rereading Alcott's *Little Women* when she glanced up to see Quanah and three of his wives riding up the road. That she didn't have an immediate visceral reaction surprised her somewhat. Although she had been abused and held against her will by members of the chief's tribe, not every moment of her stay had been misery and despair. There had been a few good times sprinkled throughout and most of those, as she thought about that now, involved Quanah in some capacity. He was charismatic and fun-loving most of the time, and what she remembered most was Quanah's laughter, which had never been in short supply.

Her thoughts were interrupted when Simon stepped out onto the porch. He looked at the approaching riders and said, "Who's that?"

"I don't know," Emma lied. "Probably someone comin' to see Uncle Percy."

"Is that man in a suit an Indian, too?" Simon asked.

"Looks like it," Emma said, hoping Simon wouldn't ask any more questions. Simon knew that he looked different from the other members of the family, but he hadn't yet reached the age where he might begin to question those differences. Which was just fine, as far as Emma was concerned.

Simon shrugged and went back inside.

"Well, that was easy enough," Emma muttered. After all of her worries, it seemed almost anticlimactic. She had been afraid Quanah would show up in full Indian regalia with his long, flowing, feathered headdress and his weapons of war—something that would have surely sparked the imagination of a nine-year-old boy. Quanah in white man's clothes might look unusual to Emma, but it wasn't anything Simon hadn't seen a hundred times before. And for that she was grateful.

Emma studied the faces of the women. The older one looked like a squaw Emma had nicknamed Big Hands, but it had been almost ten years since she'd seen her and wasn't certain. She didn't recognize the two younger women although she thought them much closer to her own age. And not recognizing them wasn't all that unusual. The Indians were strict about who married whom, having some sense about bloodlines and knowing that to survive they needed to select mates from different branches of the tribe, or even different tribes altogether.

Due to the unusual layout of the homes, the Indians soon disappeared from view as they drew closer to the main house. Emma returned to her book and read another chapter before finding the story difficult to follow. Her mind kept returning to Quanah. She hadn't laid eyes on him for almost ten years and he didn't appear to have aged at all.

The chief had given her the name Taabe Piahp, which she later learned translated to "Sun Hair." And thinking about it, now, made her smile. Emma's red hair and constant sunburns had been a source of fascination to the Indians.

They couldn't quite comprehend why her skin didn't darken to the nut-brown hue of their own skin. Instead, Emma's skin would burn and peel and she had suffered through many nights where her blistered skin made it impossible to sleep. But she could no more change her makeup than the Indians could change theirs.

Emma turned down a corner of the page and closed the book. She sat and listened to the cicadas humming for a long while. There were so many emotions swirling through her mind she couldn't make much sense of any of them. Not all of her memories of Quanah were pleasant, but would seeing him now bring some type of closure? Maybe allow her to see him as he was, now that he wouldn't be surrounded by a pack of wild savages?

She knew Simon was nose-deep into a serialized story called *Treasure Island* that had run in *Young Folks* magazine, and she thought she could slip out for a few moments without his noticing. Quanah meeting Simon was out of the question. Period. The end.

Should she, or shouldn't she? Emma thought about it a little longer then stood and went inside. As expected, Simon was sprawled on the sofa, reading.

"How's the story?"

Without looking up, Simon said, "Good."

Yep, he's hooked now, Emma thought. And the good news was the story had been spread across several issues, which Emma had accumulated over the past couple of years. With Simon unlikely to run out of reading material anytime soon, Emma drifted down the hall to her bedroom. She quickly changed into one of her nicer dresses, brushed her hair, and slipped out the back door. Crossing over to her grandmother's house, Emma climbed up to the porch and paused at the back door. Did she really want to do this?

Before she could change her mind, she pulled the door open and stepped inside. Maria and Consuelo, who were doing all the cooking, looked frazzled and they paid her no mind. Emma walked through the kitchen and tiptoed down the hallway that led to the dining room and paused again. She could hear Quanah's voice though she couldn't make out what he was saying. Whatever it was, it made her family laugh. When it died down, Emma heard a chair scrape and then footsteps. Still unsure, she turned and scurried back to the kitchen, and her grandmother entered a moment later.

She walked over to Emma and wrapped her arms around her. "Do you want to do this?" her grandmother whispered.

"I don't know," Emma said. "What do you think?"

Frances broke the embrace, stepped back, and took a long look at her granddaughter. They talked for a few moments in hushed tones and Frances finished with a question: "Did you get any funny feelings when you saw him riding up?"

Emma shook her head.

"Then I don't suppose it'll hurt anything to go tell him hello. Might even help."

Frances asked Maria to bring out the next course and then took Emma by the hand and led her down the hall and into the dining room. Quanah's face lit up when he saw her. He shouted her Comanche name and jumped up from his chair as Emma walked around the table. Emma glanced at her mother to see a horrified look on her face. Emma mouthed, "It's okay," and her mother nodded. She glanced at her father and she could tell he was miserable, yet she was proud of him for hanging in there.

When she reached him, Quanah put a hand on her shoulder and just stared at her face for a long time and Emma didn't think it unpleasant at all. In fact, she beamed. While Quanah looked at her, she looked at him. His face was smooth and unlined and he still had the same piercing gaze that felt like he could look deep into your soul. It was a bit disconcerting to see him in white man's clothes because she remembered him as a fierce Indian warrior wearing only a breechcloth.

"Oh," Quanah said, "It good see Taabe Piahp again. It been many moons. You are, how you say, beaut . . . beau . . ."

"Beautiful?" Frances asked as she retook her seat.

"That," Quanah said, and laughed, his eyes alight. He took Emma by the hand and offered a small bow then turned and introduced the three wives, using their Comanche names.

Emma began using some of the sign language she had learned to extend her best wishes to the three women when one of the younger wives giggled and said, "We speak English."

Emma was horrified but their exchange elicited another round of hearty laughter from everyone in the room. When it finally died down, Emma said, "My apologies. It's very nice to meet all of you. Enjoy the rest of your evening."

Quanah frowned and said, "You not stay?"

"I'm sorry, but I made other plans." There was no way she was going to tell Quanah about her nine-year-old half-Comanche son at home just across the yard.

"You come see Quanah."

Emma smiled. "We'll see."

Quanah gave her hand a final squeeze and smiled one more big smile before he released her hand. Emma turned and made her leave. If her mind had been a swirl of emotions before, it was now a whirlwind as she walked through the kitchen and exited out the back door. It was going to take her a while to sort it all, but she was glad she had done it. Maybe she would sleep a little easier tonight.

As she walked back to her house she was hit with a sudden, unpleasant thought: What would Quanah's reaction be if he discovered she had killed a Comanche warrior? One who had ridden with him back when they had been the Lords of the Plains?

Emma shivered at the thought and sent a silent prayer heavenward in hopes that Quanah never found out.

CHAPTER
41

Seth had spent the afternoon and early evening wallowing in self-doubt. He tried to look for clarity through the bottom of a whiskey bottle and found all that did was make him sick.

However, that had been hours ago and, now, as he made his way through the streets of Fort Worth, he was as sober as a church deacon reading scripture at a Sunday-morning church service.

He pushed through the doors of The Belmont at a quarter to nine and wasn't all that surprised to find the place hopping. Four men and two of Brandy's apparent coworkers were bunched around the piano, singing along with the piano man as he played "Old Dan Tucker." The parlor was thick with cigar smoke and it was clear from the revelers that the whiskey tap had been open for a while.

Josie stepped out of an adjoining hallway, looking as fresh and composed as she had hours earlier. She smiled and placed a hand on his arm. "Good evening, Mr. Ferguson."

"Same to you, Mrs. Belmont," Seth said.

"Josie, please. May I offer you a cocktail or perhaps a glass of wine or champagne?"

"No, thank you, ma'am. Looks busy."

"Another Saturday night," Josie said. "Please, make yourself comfortable and Brandy will be with you shortly."

"Thank you. Did you come up with a number for me to . . . well . . . huh . . . pay for the rest of Brandy's evening?"

"I did, but I like you, Mr. Ferguson. Enjoy your evening and we'll discuss it later."

"Thank you." Seth worked his way to a spot as far from the piano as he could get and took a seat on the end of one of the sofas that allowed him a good view of the parlor and the stairway. There were a few magazines scattered about, but the coal oil lamps had been turned down low, making it impossible to read. Seth crossed one leg over the other and waited, watching the four drunken fools as they slobbered over the two women.

The men were well attired in fancy suits and it appeared they were men of means. What astounded Seth was how brazen the men were. They didn't seem to be the least bit concerned that each knew the other's purpose for being there and it was obvious they had no worries that someone might call them out for visiting a house of ill repute. Seth would have thought their behavior would have been the exact opposite—slip in, slip out, and hope no one saw you entering or leaving. But apparently that wasn't true, at least in this town.

It wasn't long before the women led two of the men upstairs and Seth fished his watch out of his pocket to check the time. It was well after nine o'clock and there was still no sign of Brandy. Still somewhat apprehensive about even being there, he decided to give her another few minutes before he said adios to The Belmont forever.

While he waited, his brain churned with indecision. Was it just sex that had him so enraptured? If so, how important was that in the overall scheme of things? Unfortunately, he had limited experience in that department, having been with only two other women, both prostitutes. But even then, those other two encounters had been cold and lifeless affairs, a world away from his encounter with Brandy.

He checked the time again and promised himself he'd stay for only ten more minutes. Then he began to replay in his mind some of the arguments he'd had with Chauncy on this very issue. *Am I too dense to take my own advice?* Chauncy certainly didn't seem to have any hang-ups about what Marcie had been doing for a living. However, there was no doubt that Chauncy was a different breed of cat, but they both had that same Ridgeway blood flowing through their veins, didn't they? *Why was it so easy for him and so agonizing for me? Or am I overthinking the entire issue?*

Before he could formulate any answers, he saw Brandy at the top of the stairs. She was wearing a beautiful silk robe, her bare feet just visible beneath the hem as she descended. Her long dark hair was parted in the middle and appeared to be damp, as if she'd just come from a bath. Seth stood, picked up his small bag, and walked over to the bottom of the stairs as if in a trance. As she drew closer, he saw that her face was devoid of makeup, and her bright blue eyes were beaming.

Brandy stopped on the last step, took his hand, and looked him in the eye. In a soft voice she said, "*This* is me."

All Seth could do was nod. He thought her more beautiful without all the face paint.

Brandy turned and led him up the stairs. When they entered her room, Brandy closed the door softly behind them and led him over to a small table that was flanked by two chairs. On top were two covered dishes and a bottle of wine accompanied by two long-stemmed glasses. "I took the liberty of having dinner sent up. I hope that's okay?"

"Of course," Seth said, pulling out the chair for Brandy.

Once she was seated, he stepped around to his chair and sat, overwhelmed by it all. It was the total opposite of their first encounter. "You smell wonderful."

"Thank you. Sorry I was late. I decided to take a bath before seeing you."

"You didn't have to," Seth said as he worked to free the cork, which had been partially opened by someone in the kitchen.

"I know I didn't. I wanted to."

Seth looked at the label on the bottle. It was a Bordeaux, and he chuckled as he poured. "Was that intentional?"

Brandy smiled. "Maybe.

He recorked the bottle and put it back on the table. Brandy lifted her glass and Seth did the same. "What are we toasting to?" Seth asked.

"To possibilities," Brandy said. They clinked glasses and each took a sip.

Whatever was plated beneath the metal covers smelled delicious, but Seth wasn't quite ready to dig in yet. "Before we begin," Seth said, "let's clear something up."

Brandy cocked her head to the side and said, "What's that?"

"Brandy Bordeaux is not your real name, is it?"

Brandy hesitated, and he could tell she was trying to decide if she wanted to reveal the truth or not.

"I came back," Seth said, urging her on.

"Yes, you did." She stuck out her hand as if they were meeting for the first time.

Seth laughed and grasped her hand.

"Mr. Ferguson, so very nice to meet you. I'm Grace Cunningham."

"Likewise, Mrs. Cunningham."

Grace giggled and pulled her hand free. "Can we eat now?"

"One more question," Seth said.

Grace sighed and said, "I'm kind of hungry, here, Mr. Ferguson. Okay, go ahead."

"Can I call you Gracie?"

Grace smiled and said, "I'd like that."

They both lifted the covers to see a big juicy steak, scalloped potatoes, and hot buttered corn and they both dived in. As they ate, they had a normal conversation about current events with no mention of their location or what went on there. Seth wanted to ask Grace how she ended up at The Belmont, but didn't, deciding it was none of his business. If he hadn't been born into a wealthy family, who knew where he would have ended up. He would like to think he'd be the same man he was today though he also knew a bad decision here or there could have vastly altered his life course. Obviously, Grace had faced some type of adversity, which had forced her to sell her body to make ends meet. And she had been right when she had accused

him of being judgmental. He had been and he made a
silent vow to do better.

Their conversation was interrupted by an occasional
odd noise, much like a hotel, although they did a good job
masking it with their own laughter. Seth regaled her with
funny stories of his time in college and Grace told him
some of the town gossip. She was witty and charming, and
it was clear to Seth that she'd had some schooling somewhere along the way.

"What was it like growing up on a ranch?" Grace asked.

"It was good," Seth said. "Plenty of hard work, but we
had plenty of fun, too. Where did you grow up?"

Her demeanor instantly changed. "In Missouri. It was
pretty grim and got worse after my pa died."

"How old were you when that happened?"

"I was eight." She fell silent and after a few moments,
looked up and said, "I don't much like talkin' about any
of it."

"That's fine. You don't have to."

"Thank you."

She smiled and seemed to shake off her melancholy. It
wasn't long until she was back to laughing again, her
bright blue eyes alight with merriment. Seth refilled their
glasses with the last of the wine as Grace gathered up
their dirty plates and placed them on the floor just outside
her door.

"Do I need to take them back to the kitchen?" Seth
asked.

"No, the housekeeper will pick them up."

"Is it common to eat in your room?"

"Only on special occasions."

"And this qualifies?"

Grace laughed. "I suppose it does, now that you know

my real name." She returned to her chair, picked up her wineglass, and took a sip. She looked at Seth over the rim of her glass and said, "Would you be terribly disappointed if we didn't do the deed tonight?"

"No, I don't suppose so. What would you rather do?"

"I would love to snuggle with you and fall asleep in your arms. Are you okay with that?"

"I don't see why not." He stood and walked over to his bag he'd left by the door. "Let me change into my night-shirt."

"You don't need your nightshirt," Grace said.

"Well, I certainly don't want to sleep in my clothes."

"You're not."

"What am I going sleep in, then?"

"Nothing."

"Huh," Seth said. "Are you going to be wearing the same thing?"

Grace laughed and drained the last of her wine. "Soon as you shuck those clothes off, I'll turn out the lamp."

"You want me to take them off, here?"

For an answer, Grace stood and took off her robe. "There. Your turn."

Seth found it difficult to pull his gaze away from her beautiful nude body.

Grace put her hands on her hips. "Your clothes, Mr. Ferguson."

Seth slipped off his clothes and felt extremely uncomfortable in his nakedness.

"Don't be so shy," Grace said. She twirled her finger. "I want to see it all."

Seth, self-conscious about the brand on his butt, hesitated.

"What's wrong?" Grace asked. "Too shy?"

"Well . . . uh . . . uh . . ."

"What is it?" Grace asked.

"I have an ugly scar . . . on . . . my . . . well . . . butt."

"Show me."

Seth slowly turned around. He heard Grace approach and he flinched when she began tracing the *X* with her fingers.

"How old were you when this happened?"

"Twelve. I don't like talking about it much."

"You don't have to." Grace put a hand on his shoulder and slowly turned him around. She leaned in and kissed him gently on the lips. "We both have scars." Taking him by the hand, she led him over to her bed, turned down the lamp, and they slipped beneath the covers.

Grace snuggled up next to him and he could see her face in the moonlight and the dampness on her cheeks. He brushed a strand of hair out of her eyes. "Why are you crying?" he asked in a hoarse whisper.

"These are good tears." Grace gave a contented sigh and snuggled closer, wrapping an arm around his chest. A few minutes later, Grace's breathing evened out as she drifted off to sleep. Seth, lying on his back, stared at the ceiling as his mind spun.

It was time to make some decisions.

CHAPTER
42

Percy thought the dinner had gone remarkably well and Quanah's two younger wives, Tonarcy and Toe-pay, had done a good job bridging the language barrier. During the evening, it was discovered that Quanah had a brood of nearly two dozen children, some of whom he had adopted. Percy had no idea how the chief managed it all. Just keeping that many mouths fed had to be a chore, but it did give Percy some leverage to use with Quanah.

After dinner, Percy pulled Quanah aside and asked Toe-pay to act as an interpreter so there would be no misunderstandings. "We started pushing some of our cattle across the river and onto Comanche land a few days ago," Percy said. "If you can convince the Indian agent to sign a formal lease, I will gladly pay a fair price for grazing rights."

Percy waited while Toe-pay translated. Quanah began nodding and Percy took that as a good sign.

When Toe-pay finished, Percy continued, "In the meantime, I'll give your family five steers a month and I'll put your brand on those one hundred heifers I mentioned during our last meeting and I'll put your brands on their calves, too."

Toe-pay translated, and Quanah looked at Percy and said, "What for Quanah's people?"

Percy was ready for the question. "If you can persuade them to leave our cattle alone, I'll give them ten steers a month."

Apparently, Quanah didn't need a translation of that. He said, "Twenty."

"Fifteen," Percy countered.

Quanah stuck out his hand. "Deal."

Percy shook and breathed a sigh of relief.

"You have present for Quanah?" he asked.

"I do," Percy said. "Let's step outside." Percy had his fingers crossed, hoping Luis had picked out a good horse. When he and the chief stepped out on the front porch Percy was relieved to see one of Mouse's offspring tied to the hitching rail. Fifteen hands tall, the light gray, two-year-old stallion was one of the finest and fastest horses on the ranch. Emma had handled the breeding, which seemed appropriate, given her reconnection with Quanah this evening. She had named the horse Ghost.

Quanah smiled, stepped off the porch, and ran his hands across the horse's back. "Strong horse," Quanah said.

"He's a quarter horse," Percy said.

"What that?" Quanah asked as he leaned down to feel Ghost's heavily muscled chest.

"It means he's fast." Percy was glad to see Luis had slipped on a halter and attached a lead rope.

Quanah moved to the horse's head, parted Ghost's lips, and took a look. He turned to look at Percy. "Young."

Percy held up two fingers and Quanah nodded. "Put

him in with some of your mares," Percy said, "and you'll have some dandy horses."

"Heap good horse," Quanah said. "Thank you."

"You're welcome. Just don't eat him."

Quanah laughed loudly. "Quanah no eat." Quanah walked over and shook Percy's hand. "You good friend."

"You, too," Percy said. He looked up at the sky. "Be dark soon. Sure you don't want to stay here tonight?"

"No. Quanah go camp with his people. You bring steer to Quanah or Quanah take?"

Good question, Percy thought. As much as the Indians moved around, it would be a chore just to find him. But if Quanah culled his own steers there was no way to know if he was taking more than the five every month for himself or the fifteen for the rest of the tribe. For Percy, it all came down to a matter of trust. "You can cut out your own steers for you and the other members of your tribe."

"Quanah only take what we shake on."

"I trust you. We'll run your branded cattle in with the ranch herd. You can come and get 'em anytime you want."

"Quanah wait many moons. Make heap big herd."

"Probably be best," Percy said as the dinner attendees spilled out onto the porch. Quanah called his wives over to show them his new horse. The women oohed and aahed over the generous gift and Quanah stood a little taller, his chest swelling with pride. Looking over at Leander, who had come up beside him, Percy whispered, "Good idea."

"Emma's probably not gonna be very happy with you," Leander whispered back. He nodded at the stallion and said, "That's one of her favorites."

"I think she'll be okay with it, considering who he's goin' home with," Percy said.

After a round of good-byes and promises to do it again,

the four Indians took their leave. Once they were out of earshot, Percy turned to his mother and said, "That wasn't so bad, was it?"

"Better than I expected," Frances said, "but he's still a kidnapper."

Percy chuckled. "You're never gonna let it go, are you?"

"Probably not," Frances said.

As the others dispersed to return to their homes, Percy and Frances took a seat on a couple of rockers and continued their conversation.

"Oh, I forgot to tell you," Percy said, "Bass Reeves said to tell you hello."

"Where did you run into him?" Frances asked.

"Up around Fort Sill." Percy made no mention about the gun battles they had been involved in. There were just some things a mother didn't need to know.

"I worry about him. Seems like I read in the paper every other week about another marshal gettin' gunned down up in that godforsaken country."

"Bass is about the slickest operator I've ever been around. You can probably quit worryin'."

"Well, I can't. The Dallas paper says Indian Territory's the most dangerous place in all of America."

"Don't think you need to read a paper to know that." There was a momentary lull in the conversation. After a moment or two, Percy said, "I paid Maria and Consuelo extra to clean up, so let 'em do their job."

"I will," Frances said. "I'm too tired to mess with it."

"Are you feelin' poorly?" Percy asked.

"I'm fine. I said I'm tired. I didn't say I was dying."

Percy smiled at her spunk. "Still up for your trip to San Franny?"

"Yes, and I wish you'd go with us."

"Can't. Too much to do. When're you leavin'?"

"Three weeks."

"And you'll be gone how long?"

"Depends on how long it takes us to get there. I'm just hopin' the weather's cooler out that way."

Percy stood and leaned down to kiss his mother on the cheek. "I'd best go tell Chauncy and Marcie to get a move on with their weddin' plans."

"Afraid I'm not gonna make it back?" Frances asked.

A pained look washed across Percy's face and Frances immediately regretted the question. Cyrus, her husband and the father to their four children, had died on the trail during the search for Emma, and Percy had been the one who had to bury him. Frances stood and gently placed a hand on her son's cheek and looked him in the eye. "I'm coming back, Percy."

Percy took a deep breath and held it a moment before exhaling. "I know you are." Percy smiled and said, "Besides, you're the one worried about them livin' in sin."

"I didn't say I was worried, but it isn't proper." With images of her own husband now playing through her mind, Frances said, "Gettin' married is one of life's milestones. We need to do it up nice for Chauncy and Marcie."

"We will. Good night, Ma."

"Good night, son."

Percy stepped off the porch and made his way over to the guesthouse. Hearing the sound of laughter from inside, Percy paused before knocking on the door. It had been a long time since he'd heard his son's laugh. Losing a mother at the age of twelve would do that to a boy. Maybe, Percy thought, Marcie was just what Chauncy needed. When the laughter died down, he gave the door a light tap.

Marcie, wearing a beautiful scarlet robe, was still chuckling when she opened the door.

"I hope I'm not interrupting," Percy said, automatically reaching up to remove the hat that wasn't there. He let his hand drop, hoping Marcie hadn't noticed. He was angry that he got so flustered around her.

"Of course not," Marcie said. "Come on in."

Percy stepped inside, and Marcie closed the door behind them. Chauncy, dressed in his nightshirt, was sprawled on the bed. "Pull up a chair, Pa." Chauncy said, pushing himself up against the headboard.

"I don't want to disturb your evenin', so I won't be long."

Marcie slipped around Percy, took a seat on the bed, and leaned back against Chauncy's broad chest. "How was the dinner?" Marcie asked.

"Long, but good. It's hard to believe it's only been a few years since that man sitting at our dinner table tonight and us were mortal enemies. Back then, neither of us would have given a second thought about killing the other. So that part was strange."

"You ever square off against Quanah?" Chauncy asked.

"Tried to but couldn't never find him. Had plenty of scrapes with the Comanches and a bunch of other tribes. Anyhow, I didn't stop by for a history lesson. A big chunk of the family will be leaving for San Francisco in three weeks. I was hoping we could have your wedding ceremony before then. That okay with you two?"

"Sure," Marcie said, turning her head to look at Chauncy for confirmation.

"Sounds good," Chauncy said. "Since this is a Saturday, let's shoot for two weeks from today. That okay, Marcie?"

"Perfect," Marcie said.

"Great. I'll spread the word," Percy said. "Good night, you two."

"Good night," Chauncy and Marcie said in unison.

Percy turned, opened the door, and stepped outside, closing the door behind him. He hadn't taken more than a few steps before the laughter inside started up again. Percy thought it a pleasant sound and he smiled as turned for home.

CHAPTER
43

Seth must have fallen asleep at some point during the night because Grace awakened him the next morning with a kiss.

"I've been doing some thinking," Seth said, "and I—"

She silenced him with a finger on his lips. She rolled over on top and guided him inside of her. If heaven existed, this was it, Seth thought as Grace leaned down and kissed him, her dark hair spilling all around them. Their lovemaking was tender and unhurried, and both peppered the other with kisses wherever their lips might land. It was unlike anything Seth had ever experienced, and he wanted it to last forever and knew it wouldn't.

When they were both spent, Grace flopped down on Seth's chest, their bodies coated in a sheen of sweat. "Wow," Grace said as she ran her hand along his arm. "You've got goose bumps."

"I'm not surprised. I've never experienced anything even remotely close to that."

Grace giggled and turned her head to look at him. "Me, neither."

"What do you mean?"

"I've never felt that . . . that . . . intense explosion of . . . of . . . pleasure, I guess."

"Really?"

"Really." Grace slid off him and snuggled up against his side, throwing her arm across his chest and her leg across his thigh. "I thought I was havin' a heart attack. Not that it was unpleasant by any means. In fact, I enjoyed it very much." She tilted her head up to look at Seth. "Can we do it again?

Seth chuckled. "Might have to wait a bit."

Grace laughed and played with what little chest hair he had. "What were you sayin' before I interrupted you?"

"And a nice interruption it was, too." If Seth had any reservations about moving forward, they had just evaporated. "Have you ever thought about leaving this place?" Seth asked as he threaded his fingers through her long, dark hair.

"Only about a million times. But there's no way I could find a job that paid anywhere close to what I'm makin' now."

"That's not exactly what I meant."

"What exactly did you *mean*, then?"

Seth hesitated for several long moments as his brain churned. If he went forward with what he was thinking, it might very well end any hope of being a lawyer anywhere in the vicinity. Even Dallas might not be far enough. However, out of sight was out of mind and if Grace quit now, she would eventually be forgotten, especially if she went back to using her given name.

"Your eyes are open, so I know you didn't fall asleep," Grace said.

"No, I'm not sleeping, just thinking."

Grace scooted up the bed until their heads were even. "Wanna talk about it?"

Seth rolled over onto his side so he could look into her beautiful blue eyes. "I really like you."

"Same here. I know we've only been together a couple of times, but it feels different to me."

"Are you just sayin' that?"

"Do you know how many men I've let sleep in my bed an entire night?"

"I don't have any idea."

"One. And he's a really sweet sixty-five-year-old man who has never done anything more than give me a hug. And before you ask, yes, we were properly clothed."

"Why'd you do that?"

"His wife had recently died, and he had just wanted to sleep with someone in the bed next to him again."

"How often did this happen?"

Grace shrugged. "Two or three times."

Seth walked his fingers up her rib cage. "And he never tried to feel you up?"

Grace squirmed and laughed as she grabbed his hand. "Not once. Like I said, he was as sweet as he could be. He died about a month ago."

"I'm sorry," Seth said.

"Him and his wife had been married for something like forty years. I think he died of heartbreak."

"Is that what you envision?" Seth asked.

"What's that?"

"Being married for forty years?"

"Me?" She pointed at the door to her room. "Have you forgotten where we are?"

"No, I haven't forgotten."

"How good do you think my prospects for marriage are? Me workin' here?"

Seth kissed her. "It happened for Marcie."

"That was a one-in-a-million chance."

"I'd say the odds for you are much better than that."

"What are you sayin', Seth? You want some type of exclusive arrangement? Where every Saturday night is yours? Something like that?"

"No. I want every night to be mine."

"I don't understand. That's gonna cost you—"

Seth silenced her by placing a finger on her lips. "Grace Cunningham, will you marry me?"

Grace sat up suddenly and twisted to look at Seth. "Really?"

"Is that a yes?"

She pushed him over on his back, climbed on top of him, and began covering his face with kisses. She paused momentarily, stiffened her arms against his chest, and locked eyes with him. "Really?"

Seth laughed. "Really."

"Are you sure? Have you thought this whole thing through?"

Seth reached up, gently cupped the back of her head, and pulled it down until they were nose to nose. "I've thought of nothing else since I last saw you."

Tears welled up in her eyes and ran down her cheeks, dripping onto Seth's face. She wrapped her arms around his neck and collapsed onto his chest, weeping.

Seth gently stroked her back as she cried. "I hope those are tears of joy."

Grace nodded and squeezed him tighter. "When are . . . we . . . leaving?" she asked, her breath hot on his chest.

"Today?" Seth asked.

She nodded again. Eventually, the weeping subsided, and she wiped the moisture off her cheeks with her palms and pushed herself up to look at him. "I'll love you, I'll bear our children, and, yes, forty years sounds perfect to me." She kissed him deeply one more time then slid off him and stood. "What time does that train leave?"

Seth sat up and turned to put his feet on the floor, any shame about his nakedness now gone. "Three o'clock."

"Let's get dressed and go downstairs for breakfast. I need a cup of coffee before I talk to Josie."

"Is she going to be angry?" Seth asked.

"I might have to give her some of my stash to cover any appointments she's already booked for me, but, no, she won't be angry."

"I'll cover your expenses."

"No, you won't. I can pay my own way. At least for a while, that is."

Seth stood and began dressing. "You're now my fiancée. I'm payin'."

Grace slipped on her robe and said, "Say that again."

Seth looked up and said, "What? That I'm payin'?"

"No, the other part."

"You're my fiancée?"

"That's it." Grace walked over and wrapped her arms around him.

They stood, hugging each other, for a long time. Eventually, Grace loosened her arms and stepped back, tears, once again, shimmering in her eyes.

"You gonna cry every time you look at me?"

Grace chuckled as she wiped the accumulated moisture out of the corners of her eyes. "Maybe."

After Seth finished dressing, they walked downstairs and entered the kitchen. Josie, already dressed for the day, was sitting at the table with a cup of coffee as she perused the morning paper. "Good morning," Josie said. "I hope you both slept well."

"We did," Seth said.

Grace sidestepped the cook slaving over the stove and poured coffee for herself and Seth and they joined Josie at the table.

"Are you heading home today, Mr. Ferguson?"

"It's Seth. And yes, I am." He searched for Grace's hand under the table and when he found it, gave it a tiny squeeze for encouragement.

"Josie," Grace said, "I'm . . . I'm . . ."

Josie looked up from her paper and said, "Going with him?"

Grace nodded. "How did you know?"

"I'm not blind, dear," Josie said. "I could tell by the way you two looked at each other."

"Are you mad?" Grace asked.

"Of course not, Grace. I assume you shared your real name with Seth?"

"I did. I'll pay you for any future appointments you've already booked for me."

"No," Josie said, "you will not." She turned to look at Seth and said, "How many more Ridgeway boys are there?"

Seth laughed. "I'm the last that wasn't spoken for."

"That's a relief," Josie said, smiling. "Your family has about put me out of business."

All three laughed. "Will you have trouble finding others to take Grace's place?" Seth asked.

"It might take me a while to find one that I believe is compatible, but, no, it won't be an issue. I've already found a replacement for Marcie. Really, I'm very happy for both of you." Josie took a sip of coffee and said, "Where will you live?"

"At the ranch for now," Seth said. "I'm still hoping to move to Dallas at some point to start my law practice."

Josie thought about that for a moment and then said, "A word of advice, if I may?"

"Of course," Seth said.

"You might expand your horizons to include other cities. Let's be honest, this business and what we do generates tremendous scorn."

Seth looked at Grace and said, "What percentage of your business came from Dallas?"

Grace shrugged. "Never wasted much time askin'."

"About thirty percent," Josie said.

When Seth didn't say anything for a while, Grace frowned and said, "Are you having second thoughts?"

"Not at all," Seth said. "We'll make it work. Someone is eventually going to need to take over the ranch when my uncle gets tired of it." Out of the corner of his eye, he saw Josie flinch at that statement, and he wondered what that was about.

Josie folded the newspaper and stood. "I have errands to run. You two fix a plate and enjoy your breakfast."

"Will you be back before I leave?" Grace asked.

"I should be. But you better stand up and give me a hug in case I don't make it back in time."

Grace stood and walked into Josie's outstretched arms. They hugged for a long time and Seth heard them whispering to each other, but he couldn't hear what was said. Not that it was any of his business. Josie gave Grace a kiss on the cheek and the two finally parted. Both had tears in their eyes when Seth stood to shake Josie's hand. She bypassed his outstretched hand and wrapped her arms around him.

"I'm glad you have the courage to see her as a person," Josie whispered in his ear. "Most people don't. So, thank you for that. I wish the very best for both of you. Take good care of her, Seth."

"I will," Seth said.

Josie broke the embrace and was dabbing at her eyes with a handkerchief as she exited the kitchen.

Seth watched her go and said, "That's one hell of a woman."

"I know," Grace said, wiping her cheeks dry—again. "Let's eat."

CHAPTER
44

After saddling his horse, Percy led him outside and mounted up. It was time to have a talk with Josie. He had selected a bay gelding named Cinnamon for his trip to town. Mouse, his favorite mare, could be somewhat persnickety and often didn't play well with others, especially in the tight confines of a livery stable. Cinnamon was as gentle as a kitten and he didn't much care where he was at any time.

The sun had been up for only an hour and it was already blazing hot. He wasn't looking forward to the train ride to Fort Worth. It being Sunday, he was guessing the passenger coach would be stuffed with people heading into town for the day. Being a terminal town for the railroad, there were no tracks that extended beyond Wichita Falls and if anybody wanted to go anywhere, they had to go to Fort Worth first. And with no trains going elsewhere to relieve some of the pressure, everyone had to cram aboard the one train, no matter the weather.

As he rode, he couldn't help but lament the sparseness of edible grass. If it didn't rain soon there would be no way for it to recover before winter set in. He had purchased a couple of the new-fangled Whiteley's Champion hay mowers and two horse-drawn hay rakes a couple of years ago that were now sitting idle in the barn. They might get one cutting if it rained in the next week or so but anything beyond that was iffy. And Percy didn't want to contemplate the problems a winter with no hay presented.

When he reached town, he rode to the livery stable and climbed down from his horse. The man that ran the place, Gordon Baker, was in his late forties and he was almost as tall as Percy and so thin he barely cast a shadow. He stepped outside, wiping his hands with a rag.

"How ya doin', Percy?" Gordon asked.

"I'm good. Headed to Fort Worth for a day or two." Percy handed him the reins to his horse. "Just put it on my account, Gordo."

"I'll do it. Want me to put your nephew down, too?"

"Which nephew?" Percy asked.

"Seth. Left yesterday for Fort Worth. Ain't never seen a family that travels as much as yours."

"Yeah, put it on my account." Percy thought it strange that Seth had gone back to Fort Worth so soon after coming home with Chauncy and Marcie only a few days ago. "Did he say why he was goin'?"

"Nope. Ain't none of my business."

"I'll see you tomorrow, Gordo."

Percy made his way over to the train depot and after standing in line for twenty minutes, he was told by the ticket agent that he had purchased the last available ticket. Percy muttered a curse word or two as he turned and threaded his way through the crowd, trying to get back outside. It wouldn't be much cooler out there, but Percy thought it would smell a whole lot better. The odor emanating from a mass of unwashed bodies pressed inside a small building with the temperatures approaching a hundred degrees was as foul as a hotel outhouse. He finally made his way to the exit and pushed outside, taking his first deep breath since entering. It would be a little better on the train with the windows open, but only marginally.

With forty minutes to kill and deciding to wait until the last possible moment to board and still get a window seat, he walked down the street to the Rusty Spur Saloon, stepped inside, and bellied up to the bar.

The bartender, a tall man wearing a white apron, walked over. "What'll ya have?"

"Is your beer the same temperature as this room?" Percy asked. It was stifling hot, even with the doors open.

"I try to keep it cool with some water, sawdust, and gunny sacks, but it don't help much."

"At least you're honest," Percy said. "Give me a shot of your best bourbon, instead."

"Coming right up," the bartender said. He reached beneath the counter and pulled out a bottle of bourbon and filled a shot glass. As he carried it back to Percy he said, "Don't think I've seen you in here before."

"I do most of my drinkin' at home. Keeps me out of trouble." Percy downed the whiskey and placed the glass back on the counter. If that was the best they had, Percy doubted he'd be seeing the bartender again anytime soon.

"Want another?"

"No, thank you. What do I owe ya?"

"Four bits."

Although Percy thought a half-dollar for a shot of rotgut was steep, he paid the man and turned for the door just as another man entered. He was a tall, lanky man no older than twenty-five and he was wearing a two-gun rig like he was some kind of badass. A badge was pinned to his vest and he had a toothpick stuck in the corner of his mouth.

Percy took a quick glance at his gun to make sure it was where he wanted it to be as the man approached, stopping about four feet away.

"You Percy Ridgeway?" the man asked.

"Depends on who's askin'," Percy said.

"Name's Jake Willis, deputy town marshal."

"You new?" Percy asked.

"Hired on last month, not that it's any of your bidness. Want to talk to you about a killin' yesterday."

"Talk," Percy said. "I have a train to catch."

"You might not make the train," Willis said. "All depends on how much cooperatin' I get out of ya."

"Was there a question in there I missed?" Percy asked.

"Don't get smart with me."

"Where's the marshal?"

"Busy. Don't need him anyhow."

"I want him here to be a witness to your killin' if you don't wise up," Percy said. "Now get the hell out of my way." Percy sidestepped Willis and headed for the door.

"I ain't done with you," Willis said.

Percy stopped and turned around. "Yesterday's killin' was self-defense. There were four or five witnesses inside when it happened, including the bartender. If that's not good enough for you, I'm standing right here." Percy waited, his arms relaxed at his sides.

Out of the corner of his eye, Percy saw the bartender pull a double-barreled shotgun from under the bar. When he cocked both hammers it was loud in the stillness. "Ain't gonna be no killin' in here. Willis, get on down the street. Mr. Ridgeway is a man of his word."

Willis turned and looked at the bartender. "I ain't gonna forget this."

"Keep actin' like that and I won't have to worry for long before somebody punches your ticket. Now, git," the bartender said.

Willis pulled his hat down and slunk out of the saloon.

"Thanks. I didn't want to have to kill him," Percy said. "But I think you and me just made us an enemy."

The bartender dropped the hammers on the double-barrel and laid it on the bar. "His type is about a dime a dozen. He ain't gonna be walkin' the earth long. Probably be best if you watch your back till then, Mr. Ridgeway."

Percy walked over to the bar and stuck out his hand. "It's Percy."

The bartender shook and said, "Name's Art Bradley. Nice to meet you, Percy."

"Same here." Percy pulled his hand back and said, "I'll keep an eye out." Percy patted the top of the bar, stopped at the door for a cursory look in both directions, and walked out of the saloon.

When he returned to the depot, the train was boarding. He fell in at the back of the line, hoping he wasn't too late to snag a window seat. People were still spilling out of the depot and he thought his chances good though he wasn't so concerned about it that he didn't keep an eye out for the deputy marshal. He didn't think the kid would make another run at him today though Northcutt's recent attempt to dry-gulch him was still fresh in his mind.

He eventually made it onto the train and took the last window seat as people piled in around him. A large, rotund woman with sweat rolling off her face took the seat next to him. She had dabbed on so much sweet-smelling perfume that he was finding it difficult to breathe. Finally—

mercifully—the train began to move and slowly picked up speed. Percy greedily gulped in the fresh air as he settled in for the trip.

The only redeeming thing about having passengers packed together tight as teeth was the fact that they wouldn't have to stop to take on more at the other stations along the route, shaving time off their expected arrival. They did have to stop briefly at Gainesville to let three riders off and three on before rolling on again.

At one point during the journey, the fat woman sitting next to Percy glanced down at his pistol and sneered. "Must you carry that on the Sabbath?" she asked.

Percy thought about pulling his pistol to order the woman to the other side of the train just to alleviate the stink, but he didn't. Instead he said, "My gun, my business." Needless to say, that was the beginning and the end to their conversation during the entire trip. And he couldn't get away from her fast enough when the train braked to a stop in Fort Worth at half past noon. Carrying his small overnight bag, which contained a fresh change of clothes, Percy struck out for The Belmont.

Bypassing the front entrance, Percy worked his way around the side of the house and entered through the back door, which opened into the kitchen. He pulled off his hat and paused a moment, waiting for his eyes to adjust. When they did, he saw one of Josie's girls standing by the stove, loading food onto a couple of plates. He hung his hat on the back of a chair and walked over to see what was heating on the stove. "Afternoon, Brandy," Percy said.

The young woman turned her head and smiled. "Hi, Percy. Josie said she had some errands to run, but she should be back soon."

"I'm not in any hurry." Percy lifted the lid on one of the

pots and peeked inside to see a delicious-looking pot roast along with potatoes and carrots. "Guess what?" Brandy said.

Percy looked up to see her bright blue eyes gleaming. "I give. What?"

"I'm engaged to be married," Brandy said.

Percy had no idea where it came from, but a tingle of apprehension started at the base of his neck and raced down his spine. "Who's the lucky fella?"

"I'll introduce you to him after lunch. I think you're really gonna like him."

"I'm sure I will. Congratulations."

"Thank you. I'm over the moon." With the two plates in hand, Brandy exited the kitchen and a moment later Percy heard her climbing the stairs. Two of Jessie's girls getting engaged within days of each other seemed strange. Rare was the woman who escaped the profession via marriage and the odds of it happening twice in the same parlor house had to be off the charts. Although Chauncy seemed to be at peace with Marcie's past life, Percy also realized his son had been cut from a different bolt of cloth. His firstborn didn't have the same wants and wishes others strived for, so he was curious to meet Brandy's new suitor. He took a seat at the table and picked up the newspaper.

A little while later, the back door opened, and Josie stepped inside, the top half of her dress wet with sweat. "Percy," she said, smiling. "This is a pleasant, though expected, surprise." Percy stood to greet her, and she walked over and pecked him on the lips.

"Want to take a nice cool bath with me?" Percy asked.

Josie laughed and wrapped an arm around his waist. "In due time. I need to bid Brandy a fond farewell first."

"She told me she was engaged, but I've yet to meet her suitor."

"Oh," Josie said, taking a step back. "She didn't tell you?"

"Tell me what?" Percy asked, confused.

"Well . . . uh . . . I'm so hot I can't think." She spun around and said, "Would you please unbutton my dress?"

"Of course," Percy said as he began unbuttoning the heavy dress. "You were saying?"

"Let me change first. Then we'll talk about all of it."

"Okay." Percy was struggling, his large hands no match for the tiny buttons. He muttered a curse word or two and finally got the dress unbuttoned enough that Josie would be able to shimmy out of it. She disappeared down the hallway and returned a moment later wearing a beautiful silk robe and Percy realized it was one he had bought for her last year.

Before they could exit the hot kitchen, a door slammed overhead, and they heard laughter as feet pounded down the stairs. He saw Josie's shoulders stiffen and wondered what that was about.

Brandy, still laughing, came flying around the corner, the now-empty plates in her hands. "Hi, Josie. Hi, Percy," she said as she breezed by.

Percy turned toward the door where Brandy had entered and froze when Seth came around the corner.

Seth pulled up short, his eyes widening in surprise.

"Seth?" Percy said.

"Uncle Percy?" Seth said.

Brandy circled back, a confused look on her face. "You two are related?"

Seth slowly turned his head to look at Brandy. "Chauncy *is* my cousin," Seth said.

"Well, that doesn't tell me much," Brandy said.

Seth turned back to his uncle. "What are you—"

Josie held up both hands and said, "Everyone stop. It's too hot in the kitchen so let's go somewhere else and we'll discuss this like adults."

Josie led them into a side parlor where four wing-back chairs were arranged in a circle with a coffee table in the center. "Sit," Josie ordered. Once everyone was situated, Josie said, "Now, who would like to begin?" When no one responded, Josie said, "Grace, as you've already discovered, Percy is Seth's uncle. Seth's mother and Percy are brother and sister."

"Grace? Brandy's real name is Grace?" Percy asked, looking at Josie.

"Yes," Grace said. "Where does Chauncy fit in all this?"

"I'm Chauncy's father," Percy said.

"Oh," Grace said, looking at Percy. "Oh my. I guess you're a bit overwhelmed by it all, huh? I mean, me with Seth and Chauncy with Marcie?"

Percy rubbed the stubble on his chin. "Gonna take me a while to wrap my head round it, that's for sure."

Josie looked at Seth and said, "As for Percy being here, he and I have had a relationship since the death of his wife years ago."

Seth nodded. He glanced at Grace before turning to look at Josie. "You and Percy have an exclusive relationship?"

Percy winced at his question. It was the one thing he'd want to know if he were in Seth's shoes. "Yes, Seth," Percy said. "At least exclusive on my end, I can't speak for Josie."

Josie left the question unanswered. "There's nothing wrong with two people spending time together if they both enjoy it. I don't know about him, but I treasure my time with Percy."

"Me, too," Percy said. What he left unsaid, and what he desperately wanted to explain to both Seth and Chauncy, was that you didn't have to buy the cow to get the milk. But he bit his tongue, knowing whatever he said wouldn't result in anything but hurt feelings. After all, they were each consenting adults, free to make their own decisions.

"Josie, does anyone else from the ranch visit your establishment?" Seth asked.

"Not that I know of," Josie said. "I don't know everyone that comes through here. Some of our clients are out-of-towners or people passing through on their way to somewhere else. In the end, it doesn't really matter who comes in because the key to surviving in this business can be traced to one thing—discretion. I drill that into anyone who works here."

"That's reassuring," Seth said. He reached for Grace's hand as he looked at Percy and said, "Can I count on your discretion?"

"Absolutely, and that works both ways," Percy said. Sensing the inevitable, he stood and walked over to the bar on the other side of the room. He grabbed a bottle of Hennessy brandy and four glasses and carried them back to the small table in the center. After pouring two fingers into each glass, he passed them around then lofted his glass and said, "To Grace and Seth."

The four clinked glasses and downed the whiskey.

CHAPTER
45

Another two weeks of hot and dry weather had rolled past and people were beginning to wonder if it would ever rain again. It had now been almost two months since the last shower and the grass had gone dormant. Most of the ponds were bone dry and, worse yet, most of the springs had dried up and Percy was praying the few that remained could hold out until it rained again. With little to no forage, the cattle were dropping weight at an alarming rate and with everyone selling, the cattle market had collapsed. Every water-well driller within two hundred miles was so swamped they were telling Percy it might be next summer before they could fit him in. But it was critical they have water, so Percy had telegraphed every water-well driller in six states and finally found one in eastern Missouri who was now on his way after Percy agreed to a price that made his gut churn.

Financially, they were okay—for now. The family trip his mother had arranged would put a dent in the ranch's finances, but it was just as much their money, too, and Percy didn't have the heart to ask them to postpone it. Besides, it wasn't their fault it hadn't rained. In the beginning stages of the trip planning, Percy had given some consideration to joining them, but that was now out the window.

Percy pushed his half-eaten plate of food away and leaned back in his chair. The large dining room at the main house was packed with people as they dined in celebration. The entire family was there as were the ranch hands and their wives, if they had one, and a smattering of guests who had all just watched Chauncy and Marcie and Seth and Grace tie the knot. Percy had made good on his promise to Marcie, and a preacher from town had come to the ranch to perform the double ceremony.

Both couples appeared to be happy and, as far as Percy knew, the young women's previous lives remained cloaked in secrecy. There had been some rumblings about the lack of bridal family members present, but it wasn't all that unusual with travel still being so burdensome. Percy had really taken a liking to Marcie and the changes in Chauncy's demeanor were remarkable. Usually morose and distant, Chauncy had laughed and smiled more over the last few weeks than at any point in his life.

Percy wished his wife had been there to see it, but Mary had been gone a long time. He missed having a companion, someone to talk to, someone to laugh and cry with. He did enjoy spending time with Josie though neither of them was interested in a long-term relationship or anything beyond the provider-client partnership that currently existed. Josie had her business and Percy assumed she had other men she spent time with. He stood and made his way to the front porch.

The sun had reached its zenith a couple of hours ago

and was now making a slow descent toward the horizon, casting the front of the house in shadow. After taking a seat in one of the rockers, he pulled his pipe from his shirt pocket and began filling the bowl with tobacco. Once he had it packed to his liking, he struck a match on the sole of his boot and lit up, the smoke curling out his nostrils as he slowly exhaled. That first draw was always the best and he savored it as he leaned back in his chair.

Hearing footsteps, he turned to see his mother coming through the door. She grimaced as she slowly lowered herself into a rocking chair next to her son.

Percy pulled the pipe from his mouth. "Your back stiff?"

"Live long enough and everythin' gets stiff." Frances looked around at the empty porch and said, "You sittin' out here with all your friends?"

"Too hot inside." Percy took another long draw from his pipe, tried to blow a smoke ring, and failed.

"You're out here brooding, that's what you're doin'. You're going to worry yourself sick. It'll rain again and you can take that to the bank." Frances leaned back in her chair, unfurled a hand fan, and began fanning herself.

Percy didn't have anything to add to what she'd said and remained silent.

"How much you think land is selling for around here?" Frances asked.

Percy shrugged and pulled the pipe from his mouth. "Maybe twenty-five dollars an acre. I'd buy more but Burnett and Waggoner are buying up every section of land that comes up for sale."

"More land would just mean more headaches," Frances said. "If my math is correct the land we now own is worth more than a million dollars. And that's just for the land.

Let that sink in for a moment, son. No one in the family would ever have to work again."

Percy turned to look at his mother "What do you think the land'll be worth ten or twenty years from now? Double or triple that? And what would the rest of the family do? Sit around and spend the money until it was all gone? Then what? The ranch ain . . . isn't for sale."

"Maybe we could invest the money," Frances said.

"In what? All the railroads went belly-up taking most of the banks along with 'em. Besides, we are invested."

"In cattle and horses. I was thinking of something more permanent. Like a bank, maybe."

"What do we know about banking other than they're a bunch of crooks? I know cattle prices fluctuate but if we can get Emma's horse-breedin' business off the ground, there's real money in that. Look at what Leander paid for that stallion of his. Sell a couple of hundred well-bred horses a year and you're lookin' at real money. And, don't forget, we've invested in several town lots in both Fort Worth and Wichita Falls and those two places are now growin' like a weed."

Frances flicked her wrist. "I'm done arguin'. Let's talk about somethin' else."

"Suits me," Percy said. Tired of the pipe, he dumped out the ashes, scraped out the inside with his pocketknife, and put it back in his pocket. "Not much of a breeze," Percy ventured.

"We're not talkin' about the weather, either," Frances snapped.

"Okay, you pick the topic."

"What do you think of Marcie and Grace?" Frances asked.

Great, Percy thought. He'd much prefer talking about the weather. "I'd be more interested to hear your take."

"I like both of them, but they're a little too forward for my tastes."

Percy cringed as his mind searched for a different angle. "Marcie's been good for Chauncy. And Seth and Grace seem to get along well. They're stayin' at your house. You ever hear them argue?"

"No, it's almost too much the other direction. Can't keep their hands off one another."

Percy chuckled. "I bet you and Pa was the same way when you started out."

Frances smiled. "Maybe. But you weren't around then, were you?"

"They can stay at my house if they're botherin' you."

"No, I like havin' them there. Gives me someone to talk to and it makes the house feel alive again. I am a tad bit concerned about Seth's plans to move to Dallas."

"Why's that?" Percy asked.

"He hasn't said much about it lately."

"Probably has other things on his mind. Having a woman around will do that."

Frances reached out and put her hand on Percy's arm and said, "Since we're talking about that . . ."

"We're not. I was just sayin' they get along well."

"Do you think you'll ever remarry, Percy?"

Percy shrugged. "It takes a man *and* a woman, and I haven't found anyone that sparks my interest."

"That's because you're not lookin'."

"I've raised my kids and I'm not lookin' to raise any more now that Franklin's finally off to college."

They were interrupted when Percy's daughter, Amanda,

stuck her head out the door and said, "They're cuttin' the cakes." Now that Amanda was twenty-six and had three children of her own, Percy didn't get to see her or the grandchildren very often because her husband, Joe Williams, had moved the family out to the Texas Panhandle to take a job with Charles Goodnight, who was running the JA Ranch. With the railroads finally expanding toward Amarillo, Percy was hoping he'd get to see them more often once that line was completed in the next few years.

"We're comin'," Percy said, pushing to his feet. He offered a hand to help his mother up and she slapped it away. Percy chuckled and said, "You're as stubborn as a mule."

His mother scowled and Percy followed her into the house, still chuckling. If it was ninety-five degrees outside, it was well above that inside. Every window and door had been opened but it offered little respite, the trees along the river as still as statues in the afternoon heat. To add to their misery, the flies inside the house were as thick as raindrops in a thunderstorm. A few years ago, Percy had hired a man to fit screens over all the windows and build screen doors for all the houses, but with all the comings and goings today, the screen doors were useless. He watched them cut the cakes then stepped over to the bar and poured three fingers of brandy into a glass and carried it back outside, where he was soon joined by his brother, Eli.

Eli dropped into a rocking chair next to Percy and immediately pulled out his pipe and began filling the bowl. Although Percy didn't smoke his pipe often, it was rare to see Eli without his. He struck a match, lit the tobacco, and took a deep draw as he settled into his chair.

Eli exhaled a long stream of smoke and said, "That went rather well."

Percy took a sip of brandy and said, "I suppose."

Eli glanced at his brother. "Not in a celebratory mood?"

Percy shrugged. "It's too damn hot to do much celebratin'. They ought to cancel the barn dance they want to have this evenin'."

Eli took another draw from his pipe. "I would imagine the chances of that happening range somewhere between slim and none. A marriage should be celebrated, considering how difficult they are to maintain if one wants them to succeed for any length of time."

"You and Clara have done all right."

"Indeed, we have. However, I believe the foundation of our successful partnership was constructed during our lengthy courtship."

Percy turned to look at his brother. "You sayin' Chauncy and Seth are doomed to failure?"

"Not necessarily," Eli said. "Grace and Marcie are much more refined than I had anticipated and they both have a unique incentive to assemble and maintain a healthy, loving relationship with their spouses."

"So, you knew?" Percy asked.

"I did," Eli said. "Judge not, lest ye be judged."

"My brother is quotin' scripture?" Percy asked, his eyes widening in surprise. "I'd say watch out for a lightning strike if we didn't need rain so bad."

"It's good for an occasional quote if nothing else."

"So, you think Marcie and Grace are gonna stick?"

"I do. Right now, Marcie and Grace have no other alternatives. And that might be a good thing. They will strive hard to form a viable relationship because it is in their best interests to do so. The added bonus is that both couples appear to be enamored with their spouses."

"I hope you're right," Percy said.

Eli took a long draw from his pipe and the smoke danced around his mouth when he said, "I traveled into town yesterday and while perusing several items in the hardware store overheard murmurings about a confrontation involving you and another man which resulted in gunfire recently."

Percy nodded. "I confronted the man, Cal Northcutt, about cuttin' our fences and he tried to bushwhack me a couple of days later as I was crossin' the river. So, I paid him another visit."

"Northcutt attempted to ambush you after a single verbal altercation?"

"It was a little more complicated than that," Percy said.

"Oh, I see. Would you care to enlighten me?"

"I walked into his saloon, punched him in the face, and ended up breaking his nose."

Eli nodded. "A typical Percy response to a slight. And this last meeting?"

"He went for his gun and I shot him." His brother didn't need to know all the details.

"I assume it was justified?"

"Yes. There were three or four witnesses inside when it happened," Percy said. "And you know what? We haven't had any more fences cut since then, neither."

Eli pulled the pipe from his mouth and said, "May I ask you a question, Percy?"

"Well, I guess so."

"How many men do you estimate you have killed?"

"You asked me the same thing about Quanah. Why does it matter?"

"Just curious. Humor me," Eli said.

Percy thought about it for a moment. "Don't know the exact number. But I didn't kill anybody that didn't have it comin'."

"More than a dozen?" Eli asked.

There was no hesitation this time when Percy said, "Yeah, I reckon so."

CHAPTER
46

Grace Ferguson sat next to Marcie Ridgeway as they ate their cake and surveyed their new family members. Both had pinched themselves multiple times over the past two weeks to make sure it was all real. Never in their wildest dreams would they have thought both would get married on the same day much less into the same family. It really was a fairy-tale beginning to their new lives.

There hadn't been a cross word between Marcie—her real name—and Chauncy since they had moved to the ranch. If anything, their relationship had deepened and her thoughts on intimacy had been turned upside down. Marcie had been fearful those interactions would feel too similar to her previous experiences, but the emotional attachment she had with Chauncy had opened an entirely new world. And she knew Grace felt the same way. They were women. They talked.

Both couples had decided to forgo a honeymoon, not that Marcie and Grace wouldn't have liked to go somewhere nice. Their decision wasn't based on a lack of funds, either, because their wedding guests had been very generous with their gifting. No, it was simply a traveling issue.

To go anywhere by train, they would have been forced to go to Fort Worth first and neither couple had any desire to visit that town again anytime soon.

Sitting at the main table, Grace surreptitiously pointed her fork at the younger woman who had arrived yesterday with three young children and leaned in to whisper in Marcie's ear. "Who's that again?"

"Amanda," Marcie whispered. "Chauncy's sister."

"Got it," Grace said. "Her children are adorable."

Marcie gave her a funny look and whispered, "Never expected those words to come out of your mouth."

Grace chuckled. "Yeah, me, neither." In their previous lives, pregnancies were taboo. "I'm going to go say hello." Grace stood and ran her hands across Seth's shoulders as she made her way around the table and took a seat on the couch next to Amanda.

"Welcome to the family," Amanda said.

"Thank you. Everyone's been so welcoming."

"That's who we are," Amanda said, offering Grace a smile. "I know it's not like that in every family. Shoot, half the people in my husband's family won't talk to one another over some minor slight. Beats all I ever seen."

"Well, everyone has been wonderful to me," Grace said. "Your children are adorable."

"Thank you." Amanda called them over to introduce them. The first was seven-year-old Mary, who was named after Amanda's mother. Mary had blue eyes and dark curly hair. She shook Grace's hand then ran off to play.

"This," Amanda said, putting her arm around a small boy, "is five-year-old Cyrus, who was named after my grandpa."

Grace thought the boy was the spitting image of *his* grandfather Percy. He walked up to Grace, buried his head in her stomach, and hugged her.

"He's gonna be my lover boy, I'm afraid," Amanda said.

Grace nodded, tears shimmering in her eyes. She leaned down and kissed Cyrus on the cheek. "Nice to meet you, Cyrus." He turned and darted off and Grace said, "He's a beautiful little boy."

"Thank you," Amanda said. She pulled her youngest daughter close and said, "This is three-year-old Margaret. We call her Maggie."

Grace leaned down and pulled the girl onto her lap. "Hello, Maggie." She had big blue eyes and curly red hair and she reminded Grace of Frances. Tears were leaking out of the corners of Grace's eyes as Maggie looked up at her and smiled.

"Why you cryin'?" Maggie asked.

"She's never met a stranger," Amanda said, a gleam in her eye.

"I'm just being silly," Grace said. She kissed Maggie's cheek and Maggie wiggled out of her arms and went chasing after her siblings. Grace looked at Amanda and said, "All of your children are beautiful."

"Thank you. I'm kinda partial to 'em. Do you want children?" Amanda asked.

It was a question Grace had never considered until Seth came into her life. "Absolutely," Grace said.

"I can tell." Amanda placed her hand on top of Grace's and said, "You're going to be a great mother."

With that comment, Grace's tear ducts opened full bore and, rather than sit and sob in front of her new family, Grace nodded, stood, and hurried toward the back door.

Marcie, watching from afar, excused herself from the table and hurried after her friend, angry about Grace's lack of self-control. She stepped through the back door and crossed the wood decking to the other side of the porch where Grace was sitting on the steps. Marcie gathered her skirt and sat down next to her, glad to see her sobbing had slowed.

"What was that about?" Marcie asked.

"I don't know," Grace said. "It just hit me. I mean, we worked so long and so hard to avoid becoming—"

"Stop," Marcie hissed as she grabbed Grace by the elbow. She looked around to see if anyone had overheard and was relieved to find they were the only ones on the porch. Marcie turned back to Grace and said in a low voice, "You can't do stuff like that."

"Do what?" Grace asked, a tinge of resentment in her voice. "Cry?"

Marcie released Grace's elbow and sighed. "I'm sorry for snapping at you. But you need to understand that things like your overreaction to Amanda's children might lead to questions we don't want asked." Marcie took Grace's hand and interlaced her fingers. "You have to push the past from your mind forever. As of now, none of that, what we did, ever happened. You are now Mrs. Grace Ferguson and your mind should be focused only on the future. Do you think you can do that?"

Grace nodded and squeezed Marcie's hand. "I'm sorry. It's just been such a huge adjustment, you know."

"I do know. But we were given a second chance and we're done with that other life. We won't talk about it or think about it ever again. Agreed?"

"Agreed," Grace said.

"Then let's get back to our husbands, shall we?" Marcie stood and pulled Grace to her feet. "How many of those little critters do you plan on havin'?"

Grace laughed and said, "As many as I can."

CHAPTER
47

The long-planned-for and long-talked-about trip to San Francisco would begin this morning, a week after the weddings, which, according to everyone, had been a smashing success. Up before daybreak, Percy was now busy organizing the loading of the wagons, trying to get the travelers into town for the morning train. And it wasn't an easy task with four adult women among the traveling party. There were trunks and bags piled up in the backyard and Percy still wasn't sure that it would all fit in the two spring wagons he'd asked the ranch hands to hitch up.

Percy pulled his watch from his pocket to check the time. They were going to be pushing it. The eight miles to town didn't sound like much until one factored in the relative speed of a wagon and team that might make three or four miles an hour if they didn't want to kill the horses. So, allotting two hours for the trip to town, Percy needed everyone loaded up and ready to roll within the next thirty minutes, a nearly impossible task.

It took a lot of hard work, but they finally had the

wagons loaded. Percy climbed up to the driver's seat of one of the two buggies that had been hitched and waited for his passengers to arrive. In addition to his mother, others going on the trip were Abigail, Rachel and her daughter Autumn, Clara, Eli's wife, and Emma and her son, Simon. Percy had tried to convince Eli to go along so there would be a man among the group, but he had declined, saying he'd rather pull out every single hair on his head with a pair of tweezers than go on a trip with a group of women who had a tendency to argue among themselves.

Emma was running through a mental checklist of the items she had already packed as she scurried through the house. After grabbing her hairbrush from the bedroom, she finally thought she had everything that would be needed. Thinking her normal gun rig would be unlady-like, Emma walked over to the front door and lifted her skirt. Her dress boots were too tight to slip in her bowie knife, so she leaned over and strapped the scabbard to her left calf. On her right thigh, she buckled on the custom-designed holster a local saddlemaker had made and seated her pistol. With her regular Colt revolver too large to wear comfortably, Emma had opted for a compact, five-shot Webley revolver known as the British Bulldog. Although the nickeled, ivory-gripped pistol was small compared to the Colt, the Bulldog did have a lethal bite.

"We're not goin' to war, Ma," Simon said from his perch on the couch.

"I know that, but it's always better to be prepared." Emma smoothed out her skirt and added two boxes of pistol ammo to her handbag. She turned and looked at Simon. "Ready?"

Simon stood. "I was ready an hour ago."

Once everyone was loaded up, Percy slapped the reins and put the wagon train in motion. Eli was driving the other buggy and Leander and Isaac were manning the wagons. Percy was hoping to fill the wagons with lumber on the return trip so they could get started on a house for Chauncy and Marcie. Seth and Grace were still plotting their future and they would move into the guesthouse for a while, once the house was finished.

It had now been three long months since the last rain and Percy was trying hard not to think about the dead grass he was seeing as he steered the buggy onto the road to town. He didn't have a clue how they were going to make it through the winter or any idea of how many cattle they'd have left come spring. Pushing most of the cattle across the river had been a big help, but the cattle would have most of that grass nipped down by winter.

Percy tried to put it out of his mind as he turned to look at his mother, who was riding next to him. "When are you comin' back?"

"I haven't booked the return trip yet," Frances said, "but I'm thinking three weeks from today if all goes according to plan."

"Which never happens," Percy said.

"If it's nice and cool out there like the newspapers say, we might stay longer," Frances said. "I've had it with this heat, so we'll just play it by ear."

"Simon and Autumn are going to miss the start of school," Percy said.

"They'll get a better education on the trip than they would in any old schoolhouse. There's a lot of world out there."

"I suppose you're right. How are you set for money?" Percy asked.

"Fine for now. If we get short, you may have to wire us some."

"I can do that. When will you get to San Francisco?"

"Don't know, exactly. But I booked express trains for most of the trip. And we have our own Pullman car, too."

"Look at you. A month ago, I bet you didn't even know what an express train was."

"Well, I'm educated now," Frances said.

They pulled into town an hour before departure. At the depot, they unloaded all the trunks and bags and hit their first snag. They wouldn't board their Pullman car until they arrived in Fort Worth and there was a question of who was going to be responsible for making sure all the luggage made it onto the other train. They did catch a break when they learned the luggage would be checked through to their final destination and they wouldn't have to worry about keeping up with it once they left Fort Worth. However, no one had really planned on being separated from their luggage for the duration of the trip, so the trunks were thrown open and items retrieved, and Percy was about to pull his hair out.

Finally, it was decided Emma would oversee the transfer and would hold all receipts when the luggage was checked in. Once everything was loaded into the baggage car, everyone said their good-byes and the four men, all drenched with sweat, returned to their wagons and buggies and headed toward the lumberyard.

Once there, Percy placed his order and they left the two

wagons to be loaded as they struck out to find some grub. Leander insisted the Windsor Hotel had the best food in town, so they made a right on Seventh Street for the three-block walk to the hotel.

Percy didn't know if he was born with it or had acquired it during his time riding with the Rangers, but he had an uncanny ability to sense danger, and the back of his neck was now tingling. He glanced over his shoulder to see that two men had fallen in behind them. Both were gunned up and something about them seemed familiar, but he couldn't put his finger on what it was. Turning back to the front, he took a quick inventory of who was armed and wasn't all that surprised to find that only he and Leander had strapped on their gun belts this morning.

He turned to Leander, who was walking beside him, and said in a low voice, "Don't look now but trouble's a-brewin'."

Leander never broke stride when he asked, "Where?"

"Behind us."

"How many?"

"Two."

"Know 'em?"

"Nope," Percy said.

"Nothing we can't handle, then," Leander said confidently.

"Sure would be nice to come to town sometime and not have to kill anyone."

"Wishful thinkin'," Leander said.

The four men were grouped close enough that everyone was now aware of the danger lurking behind them. "When we come to the next street," Percy said, "Eli, you and Isaac turn left and cross over to the other side, so you'll be out of the line of fire."

"Why do you believe these two men are a threat?" Eli asked.

"Remember askin' me for a number?" Percy asked.

"I do," Eli said.

"That's why," Percy said.

When they reached the next intersection, Eli and Isaac peeled off to the left and Percy and Leander spun around to confront the two men. "Can we help you with somethin'?" Percy asked.

"Maybe," the one on the right said. They continued their pace a few more steps then stopped when they were about ten feet away. "Been lookin' for ya," the same man said.

"Must not have been tryin' too hard," Percy said. "I'm an easy man to find."

"Well," the man said, "to tell you the truth we ain't been in town long." He looked at Leander and said, "We ain't got no beef with you."

"You do now," Leander said.

The man turned back to Percy and said, "The name Northcutt mean anything to you?"

Bingo, Percy thought. "Both of you got the same ugly mug. You his brothers?"

The man nodded. "And you killed him."

With his gaze still centered on the two men before them, Percy said, "Leander, the man's right. This ain't your fight."

"Hell, I got nonthin' better to do. I'll stick," Leander said.

"Suit yourself. Left or right?" Percy asked.

"I'm partial to the one on the left," Leander said. "I can tell he thinks he's a real gunhand."

"How many more brothers are there?" Percy asked.

"Why's that matter?" the Northcutt on the right asked.

"Just tryin' to get an idea of how many more men I'm gonna have to kill."

"We ain't dead yet," the other Northcutt said, finally joining the conversation.

"Well, fellas," Leander said, "I sure hope you two said good-bye to your momma fore you left."

"You're a cocky bastard, ain't you?" the Northcutt on the left said.

"No, I ain't real cocky at all," Leander said. "What you two fellas don't understand is that Percy here doesn't even need my help. I could stand here with my arms crossed and you two would still be dead 'cause I promise you, you ain't never seen nobody like Percy."

The man on the right dry-swallowed, his Adam's apple bobbing up and down. The other Northcutt shuffled his feet and quickly wiped the sweat from his forehead.

"We're not gonna stand here and jaw with you all day," Percy said. "If you want to try your hand then get after it or get the hell out of here."

Both Leander and Percy stood easy, their arms hanging loosely at their sides. The brother on the right glanced over at the people spilling out of the businesses on the other side of the street, then turned back to look at Percy.

Percy, sensing the brothers were looking for a way out with some honor still intact, said, "Not too late for you to turn around and go back home. We'll just call this a little misunderstandin'."

Instead of turning, the brother on the right went for his gun.

The roar from Leander's gun was about a half a second behind Percy's and, as the shots echoed down the street, the Northcutt brothers crumpled to the ground. Both excellent marksmen, there was no need for Percy and Leander to walk over to see if the brothers were dead.

Percy opened the gate on his pistol and ejected the spent shell and inserted another round. He turned to Leander, who was doing the same thing. "Go on to the hotel. I'll go pay the undertaker."

"Sounds like a plan," Leander said.

Percy holstered his pistol, turned to ask a man on the opposite sidewalk where the undertaker was, and started walking when he had the answer.

CHAPTER
48

Doubt began to creep into Frances's mind before the crowded train even made it to Fort Worth. Although she had considered the weather while planning the trip, it was one thing to think of it and another to be living it. Even with all the windows open, it was miserably hot. She turned to her daughter Rachel, who was sitting next to her, and said, "Think it'll be this hot on the entire trip?"

"Probably hotter when we get into the deserts down south," Rachel said.

"You really know how to cheer a gal up, huh?"

"It'll be better when we get on the Pullman. We'll be able to shuck some of these clothes."

"You gonna ride around naked?"

Rachel unfurled a fan and began fanning herself. "Maybe. If I had the option right now, I might take it."

Frances chuckled. "Glad to see I'm not the only one sufferin'."

"No, we're all sufferin'. Is it so bad you want to go back home?" Rachel asked.

"Not yet," Frances said. "I guess we're gonna have to go through hell to get to paradise."

"Why did you pick San Francisco?" Rachel asked. "Why not Boston or New York City?"

"Too hot back East," Frances said, "and I want to see the Pacific and all the newspaper articles I've read about San Francisco piqued my interest."

"You think the Pacific is any different than the Atlantic?"

"Won't know until I see it. A magazine article I read a while back said the coastline along California was some of the prettiest scenery in the world."

Abigail, who was seated farther down the row, leaned forward and said, "Ma, will there be a dining car on the train?"

Frances nodded. "There is and I hear the food is delicious."

"I'm just glad someone else is going to be doin' the cookin'," Abby said before leaning back.

When they reached Fort Worth, the transfer of the luggage went more smoothly than anyone had anticipated.

However, no one in the traveling party took notice of the ten men, bristling with guns, who were waiting to board the mail and express cars. If they had, they might have wondered why so many armed men were needed or what precious cargo they might be guarding.

With some time to kill, Emma took Simon by the hand and they walked forward to get a look at the locomotive. From the moment her grandmother had mentioned the trip, Emma had read everything she could find about trains and how they worked. She had hit a gold mine at her uncle Eli's house when she stumbled over a stack of printed pamphlets entitled the *Railroad Gazette*. Published annually, the pamphlets were packed with information that included railroad earnings, accidents, expansions, the latest happenings, and her favorite—detailed drawings of locomotives, train cars, bridges, or anything else that might be railroad related.

Simon's jaw fell open when they reached the massive, huffing beast. Gray smoke belched out of the smokestack, water dripped from various outlets, and steam hissed from too many locations to count. Heat radiated off the massive boiler and it was extremely loud, forcing Emma to shout to be heard. "It's a 2-8-0 Consolidated built by the Baldwin Locomotive Works."

Simon shrugged. "What does that mean?"

Emma pointed at the wheels. "There are two smaller wheels at the front and that's where the first number comes from. Behind those are the eight driving wheels, four on each side. The last number is a zero because there are no wheels behind those giant drivers."

"Can we look inside?" Simon shouted.

"We can ask." She grabbed Simon's hand and led him over to the steps that ran up to the cab. She put her foot on the bottom rung and pulled herself up so she could see inside. The fireman, covered in a layer of grime and soot, was shoveling coal into the glowing red firebox. He glanced up and Emma asked if they could come inside and he nodded. Emma reached down and took Simon's hand and they climbed up into the cab.

What Emma quickly realized was that running a steam locomotive was a dirty job. In addition to the fireman there was an engineer, who occupied a spot on the other side. A short, broad-shouldered man, his clothing was spotted with grease and oil stains, but he had a friendly smile on his face.

Emma hadn't known what to expect and she was now

confronted with a dizzying array of valves, levers, handles, and gauges, which looked like a nightmare to operate. A tad quieter inside, Emma introduced herself and Simon and found out the engineer's name was Gus Teague.

"How far can you travel between water stops?" Emma asked.

"Depends on the area. This run down to El Paso, we'll have to stop about every hundred miles or so." Using his thumb, Teague pointed over his shoulder and said, "Got plenty of coal in the tender. Won't need to take on any more till about the halfway point."

"How fast does the train go?" Simon asked.

"Well, on a good set of tracks we can get her up to forty-five, fifty miles an hour. Problem is, there ain't many good ones," Teague said. "We'll be lucky to make thirty or thirty-five for most of this here trip."

"Which puts us into El Paso when?" Emma asked.

"El Paso is might near six hundred miles. If we get out of here on time, we'll be in El Paso tomorrow somewhere around midmornin' if we don't hit any snags."

"How often does that happen?" Emma asked.

Teague shrugged. "It happens. Ain't much we can do about it."

"One more question then we'll get out of your hair," Emma said. She pointed at the vast array of equipment in front of them and said, "How long did it take you to learn how to drive this thing?"

Teague smiled. "A long time to do it right without blowin' nothin' up. Sure beats the hell out of shovelin' coal, though."

Emma and Simon shook hands with Teague and climbed down from the cab.

Simon looked up at his mother, his eyes bright. "Mom, you think I can be a train driver?"

"I don't see why not. Be a fun way to see the country."

They worked their way back along the tracks and eventually found their Pullman sleeper car and were greeted by a friendly black porter as they boarded. Emma and Simon stepped inside the train car, built by the Pullman Palace Car Company, and stopped abruptly, marveling over the furnishings. Well, they got the name right, Emma thought, as her gaze roamed around the interior. It did look like a palace with heavy drapery, fine woodwork, and overstuffed chairs upholstered in bright, brocaded fabrics.

His eyes wide, Simon said, "We're riding in this?"

"I guess," Emma said. "It's somethin', huh?"

"I'd say. You think there's a bathroom?" Simon asked.

"Don't know. Never been on one before. Maybe you should go do a little explorin'."

Simon waved Autumn out of her chair and they went off to explore as Emma took off her hat and sat down next to her grandmother. She hated wearing the fancy hats, but her mother had insisted it wasn't proper for a young woman to travel across the country without being appropriately attired. Emma tossed her hat onto an empty chair and spotted her mother and Rachel seated in the corner. Judging by their hand movements, they appeared to be arguing about something. Not a good start, Emma thought.

Emma turned to her grandmother and said, "How much did a ticket on this thing cost?"

"You'd be surprised, considerin' how fancy it is. It didn't add a whole lot to the overall cost, but I did pay extra to have this car to ourselves. Where have you been?"

"Once the luggage was squared away, Simon and I went

up to look over the locomotive. Now he wants to be a train engineer."

"Not a bad way to make a livin'," Frances said. "It's nice to be able to spread out, huh?"

"It is," Emma said as her gaze roamed around the interior. "It feels a bit cooler, too."

"It feels cooler because we're not packed in here like a tin of sardines," Frances said.

It wasn't too much longer before the engineer blew the whistle and the train chugged out of the station, slowly picking up speed. The porter scurried about, tidying up, putting away shoes, bags, and other loose material. Emma, really noticing him for the first time, pointed to a chair and asked him to sit.

"I'm not supposed to, ma'am," the porter replied.

"Just for a moment, please," Emma said. "We'd like to get to know you since we'll be traveling in such close company."

"Yes, ma'am," the porter said. He reluctantly sat and Emma could tell he was nervous about it.

"What's your name?" Emma asked. He was a tall, thin, black man with a bushy mustache and an endearing smile.

"Benjamin Gaines, ma'am."

"Nice to meet you, Mr. Gaines," Emma said. She went on to introduce herself and the rest of the family who were scattered around the coach.

"How long have you been workin' on the railroad?"

"Almost ten years, ma'am."

Emma touched Frances's arm and said, "Ma'am is my grandmother, here. I'm Emma."

Gaines smiled and said, "Yes, ma'am."

Emma chuckled. "I bet you've seen a lot of the country during your travels."

"I have, ma'am."

"Do you have a favorite place?"

"I do. Home. Don't get back that way too much."

"Where's home?" Frances asked.

"Beulah, Mississippi, ma'am."

"Does it get this hot in Beulah, Mississippi?" Frances asked as she unfurled a hand fan and began fanning herself.

Gaines smiled. "Hotter, ma'am."

"Lordy," Frances said.

"Well, thank you for everything, Mr. Gaines," Emma said. "If you need anything from us, just ask."

"Thank you," Gaines said. He stood, turned to leave, then stopped and turned back. "Ma'am, you're the first to ask my name in a long while. I 'preciate you puttin' in the effort."

"You're welcome, Mr. Gaines. I hope you'll find that we're not like most people."

"I done had that figured, ma'am." Gaines offered another brilliant smile then turned and walked off.

As she expected, no one scolded Emma for speaking to the porter. She was proud that her family had always been welcoming, regardless of the color of one's skin. Emma reached up and unbuttoned the first few buttons of her dress, hoping for trickle of air. When that didn't offer any relief, Emma decided more drastic measures were needed. She leaned over to her grandmother and said, "Would it be scandalous if we put on a lightweight summer dress or maybe even a nightdress?"

"Who cares?" Frances said. "Sounds like heaven to me." Emma and Frances stood up and Frances told the others what they were doing, and it wasn't long before everyone had changed into lightweight cotton garments.

A short time later Simon and Autumn returned from exploring. "Ma," Simon said, "they do have a bathroom. It's kinda like our outhouse, but everything just falls onto the tracks. But the black man said we can't use it when the train's parked at the station."

"That's good to know," Emma said. "The black man has a name and it's Mr. Gaines. And I expect you to address him as such."

"Yes, ma'am," Simon said. He pulled a deck of cards from his back pocket and he and Autumn moved over to one of the small tables to play cards.

As the locomotive chugged onward, the family settled in for the long ride ahead. Emma spent most of her time staring out the window, watching the world go by. The last time she'd been this far west she'd been tied to an Indian pony—not the ideal situation for soaking up the scenery. Her only goals back then had been to escape and, if that failed, to survive. And survive she had, though she was kicking herself now for even thinking about it. Talking to Quanah had quieted the nightmares some, but she was a little concerned that traveling across this part of the country again might trigger new ones. And as she thought about that, her hand drifted down to the pistol strapped to her thigh. Never again would she rely on someone else to come to her aid in a time of need.

Her grandmother leaned over and said, "What are you thinkin' about?"

"Nothin'," Emma said. "Why?"

"Your facial expressions say otherwise."

Frances was the most perceptive person Emma had ever

met. She noticed the tiniest of things whether it be body language, facial expressions, or a small tic that suggested something was off. "I'm okay," Emma said.

"Yes, you are, and it'd be best if you remembered that." Her grandmother reached out and covered Emma's hand with her own as the train rolled onward.

CHAPTER
49

Although the shooting with the Northcutt brothers had been a matter of self-defense, Percy and Leander had no desire to linger around town. Each took a buggy and headed for the ranch, leaving Eli and Isaac to drive the wagons home once they were loaded with lumber. Percy had no idea if other Northcutt family members might come gunning for him though he didn't spend much time worrying about it. One had to take life as it came and spending time worrying about what might or might not happen was a waste of energy. Just like the weather. It would either rain or it wouldn't and there was nothing Percy could do to change the outcome.

Neither man wanted to eat dust all the way home, so the buggies were lined up, side to side, as they traveled down the road. Percy looked over at Leander and said, "How many men you reckon you killed?"

Leander shrugged. "Ain't never counted them up. Why?"

"It was a question Eli asked me a while back. Got me to thinkin'."

"Any of 'em you regret?" Leander asked.

Percy mulled that over for a moment or two then said, "No, I don't reckon there is. You?"

Leander shook his head. "I sleep pretty good most nights. Most of 'em happened so quick I didn't have time to do much thinkin' beforehand."

"Same here," Percy said. "Except for Northcutt. I goaded him into goin' for his gun after he tried to bushwhack me. Only time I recall startin' a gunfight."

"I don't think it makes much difference who starts 'em," Leander said, "as long as you're the one still standin' at the end. Ever have any close calls?"

"Not straight up man to man, but I've been shot at plenty. Took a bullet in my side once and had several that creased the skin in different places. Had a hole shot through my hat a while back when I was helpin' Bass Reeves capture an outlaw."

"Hell, you got off lucky."

"How's that?"

"I been shot four times. Once in each leg, once in the side, and once through the left shoulder. That was the worst one. Didn't think it was ever gonna heal up. Still bothers me some on a cold mornin'. How is ol' Bass? I ain't seen him in a long time."

"He's still marshalin'. Don't know why, though. Looks like a thankless job to me. Not to mention it's dangerous as hell."

"Bass is gonna outlive all of us," Leander said. "I've seen his gun work and there ain't many better than 'im. You're about the closest I ever seen. I'd say it'd be a toss-up if you two ever had a fallin'-out."

"Ain't happenin'," Percy said. "Bass is about as good a friend as a man could want. He'd come at the drop of a hat if I needed him and I'd do the same for him. Ain't a whole lot of people I can say that about."

Spotting a wagon coming from the other direction, Percy slowed his horse and steered the buggy in behind Leander's. Although they weren't traveling fast, the dust was thick, and Percy pulled his neckerchief up to cover his nose and mouth. As soon as the other wagon passed, Percy clucked his tongue and slapped the reins to speed up the horse, steering the buggy up next to Leander again. He reached up and pulled the neckerchief back down. Percy looked up at the sky, something he found himself doing about a hundred times a day and, just like every other day, there was no rain anywhere in sight.

The lack of rain didn't appear to have any adverse effects on the grasshopper and locust populations. The buzzing from the thousands of locusts perched in the trees along the river was loud enough in the afternoon heat to induce a headache. Hoppers by the hundreds flittered this way and that with every clop of the horses' hooves, the flutter of their flights adding to the din.

"You have any worries about them makin' the trip out to Californy?" Leander asked.

"I worry every time someone I know loads onto a train. Run into somethin' in a wagon or on a horse and the likelihood of dyin' is about zilch. Them trains are rolling death traps. Seems like I read a newspaper story every week about another train wreck. So, yeah, I'm worried."

"Well, hell," Leander said, "I ain't even thought about that. Thanks for puttin' that idea in my head."

"What are you worried about, then?"

"I was thinkin' more about all the evils lurkin' out there in the world. Tried to get Rachel to take a pistol along, but she wouldn't."

"Emma will be packin' a pistol and probably that knife of hers."

"What makes you think Emma took a gun with her?"

"She won't go nowhere without one after the kidnappin'."

"She know how to use it?" Leander asked.

"Damn right, she does. She ain't real quick but she hits what she's aimin' at nine times out of ten."

"Still, that ain't a lot of firepower if somethin' was to happen."

"Times a-changin', Leander. I bet three quarters of the men I seen today weren't packin' iron."

"It ain't them I'm worried about. The army's still tryin' to round up Geronimo and his band and they'll be rollin' through the heart of that country in a day or two.

"What would Apaches want with a train?"

Leander shrugged. "It ain't just the Apaches, neither. There's always some kind of skirmish goin' on down there on the border."

"Well, if you was so worried, why didn't you go along with 'em?"

"I did all the travelin' I wanted when I was rangerin'. 'Sides, there ain't no tellin' when they're gonna get back. I'm kinda partial to my bed."

Percy chuckled. "Can't blame you there. I reckon they'll be just fine."

"I sure hope you're right."

CHAPTER
50

The family had redressed and were now having supper in the dining car. The terrain outside the window had slowly transitioned and Emma knew they were now traveling across the Llano Estacado, an immense expanse of nothingness. She knew it wasn't possible, but she could swear her skin was tingling as she recalled the severe sunburn she'd suffered during her first few days in captivity. Her Indian abductors had stripped off all of her clothing within minutes of taking her and, for a young red-headed girl keen on keeping the sun off her skin as much as possible, her entire body had blistered terribly The pain had been intense—almost as intense as the pain the Indians had inflicted upon her during their many assaults—

Stop it! That's over and done with!

Emma's hand trembled when she reached for her wineglass. She took a long sip of the red wine as she worked to regain her composure. The topography was bleak, an unbroken sameness that continued mile after mile. Emma could remember how small she had felt among that vastness and the endless riding, day after day, seemingly going nowhere. With no landmarks to speak of—no large grouping of trees or craggy mountain peaks in the distance—navigating that expanse was almost impossible for anyone but the Indians who had roamed those plains for thousands of years.

Emma set her wineglass on the table and took up her fork again. Her grandmother had been right. The food in the dining car was delicious and, according to Rachel, who had done more traveling than all the other family members combined, it was as good or better than many of the big-city restaurants where she had dined.

Later, once everyone had eaten their fill, the group made their way back to the Pullman car, which had been transformed into sleeping quarters.

"My word, Mr. Gaines," Frances said, taking it all in, "You've been busy."

"Yes, ma'am," Gaines said. "All part of my job."

Sleeping berths had been pulled down from the ceiling and the hinged chairs had been flattened into beds and were outfitted with pristine sheets and luxurious-looking pillows. "Thank you, Mr. Gaines," Frances said. Having read about George Pullman and his desire to hire former slaves as his porters, she wanted to ask Gaines about his journey to the railroad, but she didn't, knowing it wasn't any of her business.

With everyone exhausted from the traveling and the infernal heat, they changed into their nightclothes, washed up, and made their bed selections before settling in for the night. As expected, Autumn and Simon opted for the upper bunks and they chattered and giggled among themselves until both eventually fell silent.

Gaines had arranged the curtains in a way to allow the adults a small measure of privacy. Emma sat down on her bed and was glad to finally be free of the holster and pistol strapped to her right thigh. After shoving it under her pillow, she unstrapped the knife and sheath from her left calf and tucked it under the seat cushion that was serving as part of the mattress. She lay her head on the pillow, pulled the sheet up over her, and was soon fast asleep.

As the others began to nod off, Frances was fighting to quell the nausea that arose every time she attempted to lie down. Although the railroad tracks appeared to be straight and true, they were far from it, and the constant swaying and dipping and bouncing had her stomach doing flips. Yes, she had traveled by train before, but this was the first time she'd been on an overnight train. As the skies deepened to full dark and the horizon disappeared, she lost her point of reference and she felt like she was floating in limbo.

Frances tried to focus on one of the hanging lamps that had been turned down low, and that only made the nausea worse. Sighing, she tossed the sheet off and sat up, deciding to wait for moonrise before trying again. She made her way to the chairs at the front of the coach and took a seat by the window.

Frances knew that towns or homes or any hints of humanity were nonexistent in this part of the world and the only thing she could see out the window was her own reflection that was being cast by the low-burning lamp. If she hadn't been certain she was in a railroad coach that ran on rails that had been affixed to the earth, she'd think she was adrift in the middle of one of the world's oceans. She craned her neck and could see lights still on in the dining car ahead, but what feeble light escaped beyond the windows was swallowed up by the immense darkness beyond.

It had been a long time since Frances had been this far from civilization and she finally had a better understanding of how Amos, her son-in-law and Rachel's first husband, had tripped over something in the dark and ended up dead after his head collided with a wagon. She glanced up, looking for stars, and realized that cloud cover had moved in sometime during the evening. "Maybe it'll finally rain," she mumbled as she squirmed in the chair, searching for a more comfortable position. She eventually found it and her chin soon dropped onto her chest.

Sometime during the night, Emma awoke to screams as the sleeping car began to jerk violently from side to side. Before she could register what was happening, the entire car tilted to the right and slammed to the ground. Coal oil lamps exploded against the side of the car as Emma was ejected from the bed, her body tumbling toward the ceiling as the screams and the sounds of shrieking metal shattered the night. Emma's head slammed into something that was hard and unyielding and she slumped, the cries of pain and anguish slowly fading to silence.

CHAPTER
51

Startled by a thunderous explosion, Percy sat straight up in bed. His heart hammering in his chest, his first thought was the ranch was under attack. "What the hell was that?" he mumbled. It sounded like someone had fired off a cannon right outside his bedroom window.

The answer came a moment later when lightning struck nearby, the white-hot flash lighting the interior of his bedroom like a million lanterns. His pupils momentarily seared, Percy jerked his head away and dropped back onto his pillow as thunder, sounding like the roar of a thousand cannons firing simultaneously, rolled across the landscape. Percy smiled as the storm unleashed a torrent of water, pounding the roof above him. Feeling like the weight of the world had been lifted from his shoulders, Percy snuggled down against his pillow and dozed off as the storm raged on.

When Percy awoke the second time, the aroma of fresh-brewed coffee permeated the house, which was strange because he lived alone now that Franklin had gone off to college. He pushed off the sheet and sat up, pleased to see the rain still falling though the intensity had lessened. He pulled on his pants, slipped on his shirt, and moseyed into the kitchen barefoot to find Chauncy sitting at the table and Marcie busy making biscuits. "Good mornin'," Percy said as he pulled a cup from a shelf and poured himself some coffee. "It's not my birthday, is it?" Percy asked as he leaned against the counter and took a sip from his cup.

Marcie, her fingers thick with biscuit dough, smiled and said, "We're celebratin' the rain."

Percy looked at Marcie and said, "Your idea?" He knew making breakfasts—or much of anything else for that matter—for someone else wasn't usually in his son's wheel-house. That wasn't a knock on him, that's just the way Chauncy functioned.

Marcie shrugged. "We talked about it."

Percy smiled. "Can I help?"

"I may not be much of a cook," Marcie said, "but even I can manage bacon and biscuits. Now, go sit down."

Percy obliged, taking a seat across from his son at the table. "We got two wagonloads of lumber to start a house for you and Marcie."

"I saw it," Chauncy said. "Thank you."

Percy was momentarily taken aback. He didn't know those words were in his son's vocabulary, either. "You're welcome. We'll get Leander to lay it out for us."

"Okay," Chauncy said. "I don't know a whole lot about building, but I can swing a hammer. Heard you and Leander got in a scrape over in town yesterday."

Percy nodded. "Couldn't be helped."

"That happens," Chauncy said before taking a sip from his cup.

Percy wanted to ask how Chauncy knew that, but he

refrained from asking. There was a reason Chauncy wore a double-gun rig and the less Percy knew, the better. Marcie slipped the biscuits in the oven, cleaned off her fingers, and carried a plate of bacon over and took a seat.

"Do we have to build it here where everyone else is?"

Percy thought about it for a moment. The reason they had originally laid out all the houses in a shape like a horseshoe was to defend against an Indian attack. But with the Indians now settled on the reservation, the likelihood of another attack was almost nonexistent. Of course, the Indians could stage an uprising at any time though Percy didn't think that very likely. "You have a spot in mind?" he asked Marcie.

"We do. It's over in the horse pasture along the Wichita River."

"Not much high ground over there and both of those rivers usually flood if we get much of a rain. Get caught between that and the Red and it'll wipe you out."

"That's what Chauncy said. But I wanna build south of the Wichita up on a little rise."

"Well, I reckon we can ride out that way for a look-see," Percy said. "Give us a good idea after all this rain."

"How big a house you think we should build?" Chauncy asked.

"Depends. How many kids you two plannin' to have?"

Marcie and Chauncy looked at each other. "Don't know," Chauncy said.

Percy got the feeling it wasn't a subject they'd spent much time talking about. "A couple of bedrooms, then, and a sleepin' loft," Percy said. "That sound about right?"

Chauncy shrugged and Marcie said, "Sounds good." She stood to check the biscuits, but they weren't ready so she returned to her seat. "How long does it take to build a house?"

"Four or five months, probably. We did it quicker than that when a monster twister roared through the ranch a few years ago. We had to replace every structure and I had to hire a bunch of extra help."

"Isn't there an old tale that a twister never strikes the same place twice?" Marcie asked.

"Well, I wouldn't put much stock in that," Percy said. "I know of several places on the ranch land that have been hit at least three times."

"Oh," Marcie said. "Maybe we ought to build over here with everybody else." She stood to check the biscuits, pulled them out of the oven, and carried the pan over to the table before retaking her seat.

Percy stuck his fork in a biscuit and put it on his plate. "Seth and Grace figure out what they're gonna do?" Percy asked.

"Not yet," Marcie said. "Seth still wants to be a lawyer, but I don't think they know where, yet."

"Makes sense," Percy said. He knew it would be dicey for Seth and Grace to choose a place too close to Fort Worth.

"Got any butter?" Chauncy asked around a mouthful of biscuit.

"Had some. Turned rancid," Percy said.

"You need a woman round here," Chauncy said.

Percy didn't bother to respond.

After breakfast, Percy offered to clean up and Marcie shooed him away. "Rain lets up, we'll ride out to look at the spot y'all want to build on," Percy said.

"Sounds good," Marcie said.

"Thanks for breakfast," Percy said.

Marcie grabbed the pan of leftover biscuits and carried it back to the stove. "You're welcome."

Percy paused by the front door long enough to buckle on his gun belt, slip on his slicker, and put on his Stetson before venturing outside. The rain had let up some, but the trail to the barn was a muddy mess. His boots were caked with red mud by the time he arrived, and he didn't care a lick. A good, hard rain cured a lot of ills. He didn't really have a specific task in mind and was enjoying the sound of the raindrops hitting his hat.

An hour after sunrise, the rain had tapered off and Percy was puttering around outside the barn when a rider came charging up, his horse blowing hard. It was Bobbie Townsend, a kid from town that Percy paid to bring out telegraph messages.

"Mr. Ridgeway," Townsend said, climbing off his mud-splattered horse, "I have a message for you."

A tingle of dread started at the base of Percy's neck and raced down his spine. If Bobbie was riding his horse that hard, it could only be bad news. He walked over and Townsend handed him the message. It was from his mother and had been sent from the train depot in El Paso. It read:

TRAIN DERAILED BY ROBBERS TWENTY
MILES EAST EL PASO. MINOR INJURIES.
EMMA, SIMON, AUTUMN, OTHERS
KIDNAPPED. ROBBERS IDENTITY
UNKNOWN. COME QUICK. BRING WAGON.

"Son of a bitch," Percy muttered. He spent a moment rereading the message then asked Townsend if he had a pencil. He did, and he handed it to Percy. Percy wrote a quick note telling his mother he'd be there as soon as he could, and he asked her to find out as much information as possible. He reached into a pocket and fished out a gold double eagle and handed it to Townsend.

Percy rattled off a list of things he wanted Townsend to do. "I want you to tell the railroad agent to hitch a flatcar and a stock car to this morning's train. Put your horse in the corral and pick out another one. I'll bring yours back to town when we come. See me before you leave. Might have some more messages for you."

Townsend slipped the twenty-dollar coin into his pocket and said, "Yes, sir."

Percy was a man of action. He strode over to the bunkhouse and pounded on the dinner bell until doors started opening. Eli was the first to arrive and Percy handed him the message. Leander was next, and he was short of breath from running.

"What's goin' on?" Leander asked.

Eli thought about trying to ease the blow of Leander's daughter being kidnapped but decided it would take too long. He handed him the message and the blood drained from Leander's face as he read it.

"You still have friends with the Rangers?" Percy asked Leander.

Leander nodded.

Percy handed the pencil to Leander and said, "Send them a telegraph."

Leander hurried back to his house to grab some paper as Isaac arrived. "What happened?"

Percy didn't know how to tell his brother-in-law that his daughter had been kidnapped a second time or that his grandson had also been captured. "Well, Isaac . . . I—" He thrust the message at Isaac and said, "Read this, but know we're going to get 'em all back. That I can promise you."

Isaac read the message and Percy saw his knees sag. It took Isaac a moment to recover and he looked up at Percy and said, "When we leavin'?"

"As soon as we can get the wagon hitched up. Go grab your guns and bring plenty of ammo."

Isaac nodded, turned, and hurried back to his house to retrieve his things.

Chauncy arrived and Percy handed him the message and said, "Home buildin's on hold."

Chauncy read it, handed it back, and said, "I'm goin'."

Percy studied his son for a moment. He hadn't considered taking Chauncy along, but he was a man now, capable of making his own decisions. "Okay," Percy said.

A half a dozen ranch hands came riding into the yard and several more came running out of the bunkhouse. Percy began barking orders as the message was passed around.

"Men, we don't have much time if we're goin' to make the morning train, so move your asses. Luis, you, Win, and Chauncy get the wagon out and dust off the cobwebs and load on more ammunition."

They turned and headed around the barn where the wagon was stored. There was no question about which wagon Percy was referring to because in a situation like this there was only one wagon that mattered.

"Moses, you and Jesse take a couple of hands and round up two mule teams and herd up some horses we can take with us. We're gonna run one team all the way to town and load the other onto the train."

Moses Wilcox said, "Where are we goin'?"

Percy gave Wilcox a hard stare. "Did you not read . . ." Percy stopped then said, "Forgot you can't read, Moses."

Percy relayed the contents of the message to Wilcox and then added, "I hope your trackin' skills ain't rusty."

"No, sirree," Wilcox said. "If they're out there, you can bet your ass I'm gonna find 'em."

"Good to hear," Percy said.

Moses and Jesse turned for their horses as Bobby Townsend came out of the barn with a fresh mount. Leander returned with a stack of messages and he passed them on to Townsend.

"Sorry I had to bring you bad news, Mr. Ridgeway," Townsend said as he climbed up in the saddle.

"Ain't your fault, Bobbie," Percy said. "Remember what you're gonna tell the railroad agent?"

"Yes, sir. Add on a flatcar and an extra stock car."

"That's right. And tell the agent if that train's gone when we get there, I'm goin' to shoot him right between the eyes."

"Yes, sir. What do you want me to do with the horse?"

"Tie him up at the train station. We'll take him with us," Percy said.

Townsend spurred the horse into motion as Percy, Eli, and Leander huddled up to strategize. "Who did you send the messages to?" Percy asked Leander.

"Every Ranger station south of Dallas," Leander said.

"It don't make no sense that a bunch of train robbers would take hostages," Percy said.

"It does if you look at it from a financial perspective," Eli said.

"You think they're gonna try and ransom them?" Percy asked.

Eli nodded. "I do."

"I ain't payin'," Leander said. "I'm gonna kill every one of them sonsabitches."

"I'm right there with ya, Leander. I think we got lucky that Emma's with 'em."

"Why?" Leander asked. "That one pistol she's packin' ain't gonna get the job done."

"I believe Percy was referring to Emma's mental toughness," Eli said. "She's lived as a captive before and she'll know how to keep a tight rein on her emotions. In fact, there's probably no one better to shepherd Autumn and Simon through what could be a grueling ordeal."

"I ain't laid eyes on the wagon for over a year," Percy said. "Let's go see how much work we're gonna have to do to get her ready."

The three men headed around the side of the barn where the wagon was stored. Chauncy and the other men already had the wagon out and, from a distance, everything looked to be in good order. Custom-built by the Peter Schuttler Wagon Works out of Chicago, the wagon was a rolling killing machine and had been an essential element of defense back when the Indians were raping and killing all across Texas. Outfitted with two weapons mounted on swivels, at the front was the six-barrel Gatling gun capable of firing over two hundred .45-70 caliber rounds a minute. There had been some modifications over the years, but the biggest improvements were the drum magazines that Percy had a machinist build. Each held two hundred rounds of ammunition and with six on hand, the operator could mow down a battalion of men before they knew what hit them.

And, if that wasn't enough firepower to get the job done, mounted at the back of the wagon was a twelve-pound mountain howitzer. Lighter and smaller than a traditional twelve-pounder, the still-massive gun could hit a target a half a mile away. But it wasn't the range that made the weapon so deadly, it was the ammunition the Ridgeways used. Like a giant shotgun only with a four-and-three-quarter-inch bore, the howitzer, when loaded with canister shot, unleashed hell on earth, expelling 148 .69 caliber steel balls in a single firing. Combined, the two weapons were as lethal as two hundred mounted men armed with repeating rifles. And to keep the deadly weapons in pristine condition while out in the elements, the company had built a folding cover that could be raised or lowered in seconds.

"How's it look?" Percy asked as they approached.

"Needs some cleanin'," Win said, "but we can do that on the way down."

"How are we on ammo?" Percy asked.

"I reckon if we ain't declaring war on Mexico, we're in good shape," Win said. "We got enough ammo to wipe out every town twixt here and El Paso."

"All right. Luis, Chauncy, and Win you're comin' with us to El Paso. We'll take Wilcox and Isaac, too. That'll leave Eli, Jesse, Mike Carter, Davy Edwards, and a few others to keep an eye on things. Now, go grab your personal gear and your weapons. We're leavin' here as soon as the team's harnessed."

CHAPTER
52

The sun was merciless on the eight captives who were being force-marched across the rugged terrain while being roped together, neck to neck. They had been walking since well before daylight and if any of the captives attempted to stop or was moving too slowly, they were whipped with a long bullwhip that was in the hands of one of their abductors who knew how to use it. Emma was sandwiched between Simon and Autumn and she was either urging her son on or gently pulling on the rope to keep Autumn moving.

Their five captors appeared to be a mix of half-breeds and whites, but they all had one thing in common—they were all heartless, vile men. The ringleader was a tall, gaunt man with long greasy hair, an unruly beard, and a mouthful of rotten teeth. He was the whip holder and the cruelest of the bunch. Emma called him Scarecrow, and she kept a close eye on him, vowing to kill him at the first opportunity. And she had the perfect tools for it after reclaiming her weapons before climbing out of the wrecked train car.

Although Scarecrow might be the ringleader, it was clear to Emma that another short, fat white man was the brains of the outfit. Much better groomed than the others, with short hair and a trimmed salt-and-pepper goatee, he was also much better outfitted than the rest of the ragtag group. Emma hadn't yet figured out how the man she nick-named Stubby fit in to the rest of the group, but something told her he wasn't a regular participant in whatever mayhem Scarecrow and his men might dream up.

Emma had no idea how long she had been unconscious after the train wreck, but her body was telling her she had taken a pounding. Her hair was caked with dried blood and it felt like she'd been kicked in the ribs by a horse. Simon and Autumn had plenty of scrapes and bruises and they'd been extremely lucky that no one in their car had been killed. The same couldn't be said for others. Emma had seen the bodies lying among the wreckage and she didn't know the final tally, having been led away by their kidnappers before a count could be made.

Although she was exhausted, sore, and now extremely thirsty, she was there of her own volition. Not one of the original selections by Scarecrow, Emma had inserted her-self into the group when one of his minions began stringing people together. There was no way those evil bastards were going to take her son and Autumn without her. She had no idea what was to come in the days ahead, but she knew for certain these men weren't in the same league as the Indians when it came to inflicting pain.

The one thing that had made the decision easier was the railroads. Now Percy and the others would be able to reach them within hours rather than the days and weeks it took them to track her through Comancheria. She glanced up at the sun to judge the time. She thought it close to midmorning and the one factor she was unsure about was how quickly Percy had been notified. If it had been early enough, he and the others could be loading on the train right now. That would put them in El Paso midmorning tomorrow. How far could they walk in a day and a half?

At this pace, not far, Emma thought. Which didn't make much sense. Emma would have thought the robbers would have ridden hard and fast for the border after derailing a train and killing a large number of people. But then a more sinister thought entered her mind. Did the railways keep passenger lists, something Stubby could have studied to pick his targets? Emma didn't know the answer, but as she trudged onward, she took a long look at the other five captives. There was one boy who was around Simon's age, two girls who appeared to be in their early teens, and two other women that Emma thought were somewhere close to her own age. Although the group varied in age, the other five captives appeared well groomed and well fed, or at least as far as Emma could tell given the current circumstances and considering everyone was still dressed in their nightclothes. When added to the fact that express train travel was expensive and, considering that no one had been molested yet by their abductors, Emma believed they were to be ransomed.

Let them think that, Emma thought. Even if Stubby somehow had access to the passenger lists and had picked the targets and, assuming ransom was his goal, he obviously hadn't done much research beyond the names on a list. If he had, he would have known his days were numbered once Percy, Leander, and the others rolled into El Paso. The only reward their captors would receive for their efforts would be a firestorm of lead bullets.

Of that, Emma had no doubt.

CHAPTER
53

Chauncy walked into the barn to grab his saddlebags before returning to the guesthouse. When he entered, Marcie was sitting at the small table in the kitchen, a cup of coffee in hand.

"What was all that racket about?"

Chauncy told her the contents of the telegraph and Marcie stood. "I'm going with you."

Chauncy shook his head and said, "We're gonna be ridin' hard."

"I'm not asking for your permission, Chauncy."

Rolling up an extra shirt to pack, he paused and looked at his wife. "Well, I reckon you don't need my permission, but I ought to have some say in it, ain't I?"

"Your opinion is always welcome."

"Okay, in my opinion you ought to stay here."

"Duly noted, but I'm going."

"Why?" Chauncy asked.

"You said there were injuries. Your grandma or the

others might need help. And I like Emma. I want to be there for her, too."

Chauncy finished rolling his shirt and stuffed it into a saddlebag. "Get dressed and pack a bag."

Marcie gave him a mock salute and said, "Yes, sir."

Chauncy smiled. She had some spunk, for sure. "You want me to saddle you a horse or you gonna ride in the wagon?"

"That wagon doesn't have a spring on it. I'll take a horse."

"Yes, ma'am," Chauncy said as he buckled on his gun rig. He grabbed three boxes of ammo for his pistols and stuffed them into his saddlebag before heading for the barn. Marcie was right about the springs. That wagon was like riding around on an iron-wheeled wagon. His father had told him the wagon makers had put springs on the first version, but they had all broken the first time they'd fired the mountain howitzer. So off came the springs, destroying any hopes for a comfortable ride.

Chauncy snagged two ropes as he walked through the barn and walked out to the large corral to pick out some horses. His father had already saddled his favorite horse, Mouse, and Chauncy chuckled. High-strung and well trained, the mare was a handful for anyone not named Percy. Around him, she was gentle as a kitten and she could cut, stop, and start faster than any horse Chauncy had ever seen.

They didn't keep a big herd of horses in the corral and Chauncy eyed them as they milled around, deciding on two of Mouse's offspring, both dappled-gray geldings. They were almost as quick as Mouse, but they had much better temperaments. He tossed ropes around their necks and led them back to the barn. Once he had them saddled, he led them outside and wrapped the reins around a hitching post.

His father was pacing the yard, waiting for the mules to show up. He glanced at Chauncy and said, "Why'd you saddle two horses?"

Chauncy didn't really want to tell him his wife was coming along although it was hard to explain two saddled horses. Two horses and one saddle wouldn't raise an eyebrow because cowpunchers always liked having an extra horse or two at hand. Chauncy shrugged and said, "Marcie's comin'."

Percy stopped pacing and looked at his son. "This ain't no vacation."

"She knows that. The message said there's injuries. She wants to be there to help."

Percy thought about it a moment and started pacing again. "Makes sense. Think we ought to get Grace to come along, too?"

"Not up to me," Chauncy said.

"I know it ain't. I'm askin' your opinion." Percy stopped pacing again and looked at Chauncy. "Probably ought to get Seth, too. He can stay in town and see to our needs while we're out searchin'."

"Want me to go roust them out?"

"Yep, and light a fire under their ass. We needed to be gone an hour ago."

Chauncy grabbed the message out of his father's hand and hurried to his grandmother's house, where Seth and Grace were staying. He banged on the back door and pushed it open. Both were sitting at the table, enjoying a leisurely breakfast. "Y'all not hear the dinner bell ringin'?"

"Sure, we heard it," Seth said. "Hard not to. I just figured Cookie was callin' in the hands for breakfast."

"They all had breakfast two hours ago," Chauncy said, somewhat irritated they didn't respond to what was obviously an emergency. He handed the message to Seth and he and Grace read it. "My pa wants y'all along to help," Chauncy said. "We don't got no idea who's hurt and who's not and Seth, you can ramrod things in town while we're out lookin'."

"Is Marcie goin'?" Grace asked as she and Seth stood.

"She is."

"How long until we leave?" Seth asked.

"Soon as the mules are hitched up."

"Okay, we'll be ready," Grace said. She gathered up the dirty dishes and dumped them into the washtub before hurrying to their bedroom.

Once she was out of earshot, Chauncy looked at Seth and said, "We ain't got no idea what we're up against. Best you bring your rifle and that scattergun of yours."

"I'll bring them."

"Don't forget extra ammo, too. You want me to saddle a couple of horses or you gonna ride the wagon to town?"

"Think I'll be able to find a horse to use while in El Paso?" Seth asked.

"Ain't got no idea."

"Saddle us two horses, then. Better to have them than not."

Chauncy exited the house as Seth hurried down the hall to gather up his things.

Wilcox and the crew finally returned, driving a dozen mules and a dozen horses in front of them. Everyone grabbed a rope and began roping the mules, leading them over to harness them. The wagon could function with a two-mule team, but it operated much better with four.

They harnessed the first team and strung a rope between

the other four mules that they were going to load onto the train. Those who hadn't saddled a horse, did so quickly. Bags were loaded onto the wagon and Luis climbed up on the driver's seat as everybody else mounted up. Once everyone was ready, Percy led out, setting a fast pace.

CHAPTER
54

El Paso was a bustling, pretty town framed by the Franklin Mountains, which soared high overhead as a backdrop. The Grand Central Hotel was the only one in town and, with the train wreck, it was full to the brim. Rachel had managed to snag a single room and they were sleeping wherever they could find a flat spot. In addition to a broken collarbone, Frances felt like she'd been caught in the middle of a stampede. Everyone was bruised and battered, but they were extremely lucky they hadn't been killed. Frances was the only member of the group to suffer a broken bone and there was still some concern on the doctor's part about internal injuries they may have suffered. The only way to know was for the doctor to cut them open for a look and nobody wanted any part of that.

The final tally of the dead stood at thirty-one, a combination of men, women, and children along with train's engineer and the fireman. Four men who had been riding in the express car were also dead although they died by gunfire at the hands of the train robbers. As of yet, there had been no word from the railroad about what their plans might be. Not that it mattered much to Frances and the rest of the group. They weren't leaving without Emma, Simon, and Autumn.

With her left arm in a sling, Frances ached every time she moved. Now in the hotel's dining room with Rachel, Abigail, and Clara, they were plowing through their breakfast so that someone else would be able to use their table when they finished. Surprised the proprietor hadn't run out of food yet, they were bracing for it. Since the accident, train travel in the area had screeched to a halt and that meant no supplies were being delivered to the town.

Frances took one last swallow of coffee and stood. "I'm going down the street to talk to the town marshal."

"Want one of us to go along?" Rachel asked.

"No, I want you three to mingle among the crowd and talk to the staff to gather as much information as possible. Those robbers didn't materialize out of thin air. Someone in this town knows who they were and where they might be going."

"Any word on what they took?" Clara asked.

"Nope," Frances answered. "Everybody I've talked to has been tight-lipped about it." Frances heard someone calling her name and she turned to see the man from the telegraph office wading through the crowd. Frances moved to intercept him, and he handed her the message. She read it as she walked back to the table then passed on the contents to the others. "Percy and the rest of the crew made the mornin' train out of Wichita Falls, though I don't know how much good it'll do them if they don't get the tracks down here cleared."

"I'm not worried," Rachel said. "Knowing Percy and

Leander, they'll get here if they have to commandeer the damn train."

"I sure hope you're right," Frances said. After the wreck, their luggage had been strewn across an open field and it taken them forever to find it all. Wagons had arrived from town to haul it all back, but there was far more luggage than available wagons and they didn't get their trunks back until this morning.

"Best get up and let someone else have the table," Frances said. "I'll be back in a bit." Turning, she threaded her way through the crowd and finally made it outside. She turned left and headed for the marshal's office and the jail down the street.

She didn't much care for Jim Taylor, the marshal, and she suspected he transitioned from lawman to outlaw and back to lawman whenever the mood struck him. Another knock against the man was the whiskey on his breath every time Frances talked to him. She could tolerate a lot of things, but drinking on the job was something she detested, especially for a man who was hired to protect the citizens of El Paso. When she arrived at his office, she opened the door and stepped inside.

The marshal was sitting behind his desk with his feet propped on top reading what looked like a wanted poster, a toothpick dangling from the corner of his mouth. When he glanced up to see who had entered, he dropped his feet, sat up in his chair, and smoothed the front of his shirt. "Mornin', Mrs. Ridgeway," Taylor said.

He waved toward a chair, but Frances opted to stand. "Busy, I see," Frances said.

"I am, ma'am." He fluttered the paper in his hand. "Goin' through these here wanted posters."

"Find anything?"

"Not yet, but I'm still lookin'."

"Marshal Taylor," Frances said, "I find it hard to believe that no one in this town knows the identity of the robbers."

"Got two deputies out shakin' the bushes now. Some say it mighta been Mexicans."

"I was there, Marshal. They spoke English."

"So? There's some beaners down south that talk English just fine."

"With a Southern accent?" Frances asked.

"Well, I don't rightly know, ma'am. Maybe."

"I think not, Mr. Taylor. Have you asked the Texas Rangers for help?"

"Railroad done did. Don't really know why 'cause we're gonna find them."

"It helps if you're actually out looking. As far as I can tell you haven't ventured much beyond your office or the saloon across the street. But that's all right. My son will be here sometime tomorrow, and he'll find them."

"You sound awful sure."

"Because I am. Can you at least tell me what was stolen from the express car?"

"I ain't at liberty to say."

"Of course you're not. To be frank, Marshal, you're about as useless as teats on a boar hog." Frances turned and walked out of the office. Standing on the boardwalk, she shaded her eyes with her hand and scanned the signs along the street, trying to determine the best place to gin up some reliable information. Her eyes eventually landed on the saloon and she dropped her hand and crossed the street. Nothing like a little booze to loosen a man's lips, she thought.

The place was empty when she entered, and the bartender was busy polishing glasses behind the bar. He looked up and said, "You lost, ma'am?"

"No, I'm not lost, sir." The floor under her feet was sticky and the rancid odor of spilled beer and body sweat that was baked into the woodwork filled her nostrils. "I'm looking for information," Frances said, stopping just short of the beat-up bar, which was pocked with bullet holes and scarred along the bottom from a thousand pairs of spurs.

The bartender tucked the rag under his apron string and said, "What kinda information you lookin' for?"

"I'm trying to find out who might have robbed the train."

"Sorry, can't help you, ma'am." He picked up another glass, tugged his rag free, and began polishing.

"Can't or won't?"

"Don't matter, either way since I don't know nothin' about it."

Frances reached into her pocket, pulled out a double eagle, and placed it on the bar. She'd been handing them out like candy, trying to drum up some information.

The bartender looked at the coin and licked his lips.

For good measure, Frances pulled another double eagle from her pocket and stacked it on top of the first. "There's more where those came from," Frances said.

A bead of perspiration welled up on his forehead as he looked all around the saloon as if people were hiding in the corners. Then his gaze returned to Frances. "Sorry, can't help you."

Frances dug out another coin and stacked it on top. "If my math is correct that's sixty dollars."

"I know what it is," the man snapped.

"How much you make a month in a saloon like this?"

"Don't matter. I can't help you if I don't know nothin'."

This time Frances pulled out two coins and she stacked them on top. "Anything you tell me stays with me. Besides, I don't even know your name."

The man looked around again and licked his lips. Frances didn't push and allowed him to take his time. Finally, his gaze returned to her. "Might look for a short, fat man by the name of Clyde Hightower."

"Where might I find this man?"

"I'm sorry, but I can't say no more."

"Come now, sir. People come in here, drink a little booze, and then start blabbing." This time, Frances pulled out a handful of double eagles and built a stack to match the first one.

The man wiped his forehead with the rag and looked hard at the two stacks of coins. "Can't spend a penny of that if I'm dead."

"I'm certainly not going to tell anyone about our little chat," Frances said.

"You might could find him in the Organ Mountains about twenty miles due north. If he's not there you're on your own."

"Have you heard about them takin' hostages before?" Frances asked.

"Don't think so, but I reckon there's a first time for everything. Be lucky if any of 'em get out alive."

"Oh, they'll be alive, all right." Frances patted the top of the bar and said, "Thank you, you've been very helpful."

"Don't think so. He and his gang'll kill anybody that comes after them."

"We'll see about that."

Frances turned to leave, and the man said, "Wait."

Frances turned back to look at the bartender.

"Use the back door, please."

"He's really got you spooked, huh?"

"Ain't just me. He'd just as soon kill ya as look at ya. He and his gang're deadlier than a den of rattlesnakes."

"Know how you kill a snake?" Frances asked. "You chop its head off." Frances exited into a filthy alley and held her breath as she stepped around the garbage, hurrying toward the next street. Once back on the boardwalk, she took a deep breath and pondered next steps. Wiring a message to Percy at Fort Worth made the most sense, but she didn't know if she could trust the local telegraph operator. If word spread around town that Frances had identified the robbers' ringleader and now knew their probable destination, it would put the bartender at risk and allow the kidnappers a chance to alter their plans.

Deciding to wait until she could talk to Percy directly, she turned and headed back toward the hotel.

CHAPTER
55

Concealed by the corner of a freight car, Grace Ferguson and Marcie Ridgeway stood next to each other, looking at a section of Hell's Half Acre that was across the street. This was the first time either had been back to Fort Worth and they were both thankful the train to El Paso would depart soon.

Grace looked at Marcie and said, "Miss any of it?"

"Hell, no. You?" Marcie asked.

"No. Did it seem that run-down when we were living there?"

"It did to me. You can almost smell the stink from here, all those people puking and pissing all over the place. Makes my stomach queasy just to think of it."

Grace tucked a flyaway strand of hair behind her ear. "I wouldn't mind seeing Josie again."

"Why?"

"She was nice to me."

"She had her moments, sure," Marcie said. "But I'm not ever settin' foot in that place again."

"Me, neither. We got pretty damn lucky, huh?" Grace asked.

"Chauncy can get cranky sometimes but even on his worst days it's a thousand times better than a day at Josie's place."

"I'm tired of lookin' at it and all the bad memories that place conjures up. Let's go."

The two turned and walked back to the train. They had both avoided going into the station, fearing whom they might bump into. And even out and walking around while waiting to board the next train, both had their heads on swivels trying to avoid an awkward encounter.

Grace walked over to Seth and put her arm around his waist.

Seth leaned in and whispered, "I saw you lookin'. Any regrets?"

Grace gave her head a vigorous shake and said, "Not for a second. How long until we board?"

"Should be anytime now."

Grace glanced back toward the depot and froze. The mayor of Fort Worth, a fat, balding man, was waddling out of the station. With a wife and six kids at home, the mayor had been a frequent visitor to The Belmont. Grace took a step to the right, trying to use Seth as a shield. Turning to look for Marcie, she saw her standing next to Chauncy, but she was looking the other way. She stared at the back of Marcie's head, willing her to turn around. The last thing she wanted to do was draw any undue attention by shouting or making any sudden movements.

Glancing back over her shoulder, she saw the mayor headed their way. Grace had to do something. She stepped away from Seth and, trying to keep her face hidden, walked over to Marcie. Grace sidled up next to her and whispered in her ear. "Don't look now, but the mayor's here."

She saw Marcie's shoulders tense.

"Is he coming this way?" Marcie whispered.

Grace stole another quick peek. "He's stopped now, but he's lookin' around."

"Maybe the fat bastard will drop dead of a heart attack," Marcie whispered. "How long until we board?"

"Seth said any—Uh-oh, he's on the move again."

Marcie glanced over her shoulder and saw the mayor waddling their way. Her eyes drifted down to Chauncy's pistol. She would like nothing more than to grab his pistol and send the mayor on his way to hell, but she knew that wasn't going to work.

"Wait," Grace said. "He's turning around."

"Let's get on the train," Marcie whispered.

"I don't know which coach is ours."

"It doesn't matter. We climb on and sit down at the first place we come to."

"Okay," Grace said. "I'm going to grab my bag."

Marcie nodded.

Grace casually made her way back to Seth, picked up her bag, and walked back to Marcie. "Ready?"

Marcie picked up her bag, and she and Grace walked down the loading platform and entered the train at the first door they came to. They dived onto a bench seat on the other side of the coach and slid down until only the tops of their heads were visible.

"Makes me sick to my stomach to even look at him," Marcie said.

"Me, too," Grace said. "Thank God, we got away from all that."

"Amen, sister."

CHAPTER
56

His face flushed red with anger, Percy was close to pulling his pistol and shooting the railroad ticket agent in the head. Because of the train wreck outside of El Paso, the train was running back and forth only between there and Sierra Blanca, a hundred miles and days of riding short of Percy's original destination. Although technically capable of traveling to the very point where the wreck had occurred, the agent was refusing Percy's demands to be dropped off closer to El Paso. The ticket agent's reasoning was that the Texas and Pacific Railway ended when their tracks merged with those of the Southern Pacific at Sierra Blanca. As far as Percy was concerned a railroad was a damn railroad, and whoever owned what was a bunch of bullshit.

"Sir, as I've said numerous times," the agent said, "you might convince the Southern Pacific folks to take you closer, but it's not anything I can do from here."

Percy lifted his hat from the counter and put it on. He gave the railroad man a hard look and said, "Thanks for nothin'.'" He turned, walked over to the telegraph office, and sent a heads-up message to the railroad depot in Sierra Blanca, then exited the building.

Leander was in charge of making sure their freight cars made it onto the train to Sierra Blanca and Percy wondered if that was going to turn into a fiasco, too. When he reached the loading platform a few moments later, he was pleasantly surprised to see the flatcar with the wagon and the stock car loaded with horses and mules already hooked on.

However, that pleasant feeling evaporated when he climbed the steps and walked inside the third-class passenger coach. Having just bought train tickets this morning, the only fares left were in this car and it was jammed with a bunch of people who appeared to be allergic to either water or soap. It was hotter than the hinges on the gates of hell and all of that heat was baking the mass of unwashed human bodies, creating a terrible stink. Percy dropped onto the bench seat next to Chauncy and took off his hat. "What did you find out about the dining car?" Percy asked.

"Accordin' to the conductor, it's a no-go for us."

Percy pulled a handkerchief from his back pocket and mopped his face. "What the hell are we supposed to eat?"

"He said there's a chance we might could order sandwiches or somethin'."

"That's big of 'im," Percy said. He leaned forward and looked at Marcie, who was on the other side of Chauncy. She looked miserable in the heavy dress, which was buttoned up to the bottom of her chin. "You doin' okay?"

"I will be if the train ever starts movin'."

"I hear ya," Percy said before leaning back in his seat. The only good thing was that all the people inside the car would be leaving the train at some point. Percy was hoping a good chunk of them would depart before they made Abilene, so they'd have more elbow room. And if most were gone by the time they got to Midland, they'd be able to stretch on the hard benches to get some shut-eye.

Finally, the train began to move, and the open windows didn't do much but stir the heat around. After a couple of stops to drop off or take on passengers, Percy quickly realized they were in for a long slog with each stop only a few miles from the last one. He pulled out the map the railroad had provided and began counting the stations. He stopped at twenty-five, refolded the map, and stuck it in his shirt pocket. An express train hadn't been one of their options and even though the going was slow, Percy had to admit it beat sitting a horse or riding in a wagon.

Once past Abilene, the country opened up with fewer stops, and they began to make up some time. The heat and the swaying and rocking were conducive for sleep and it wasn't long before heads were drooping to chests or lolling with the movement of the train. Percy fought it for as long as he could, but he too eventually succumbed.

When Percy awakened, the train was stopped again, and he stood to stretch his legs. He dug the makings out of his other shirt pocket and began rolling a cigarette. After licking the edge of the paper to seal it, he struck a match and lit up. He took a deep draw and looked out the window. Craning his neck to look up at the sign on the outside of the depot, he saw they were stopped in Sweetwater. He didn't know if the sign was true, but he could go for a long drink of cool, clear water. He walked back to his seat to grab his, Chauncy's, and Marcie's canteens and, before stepping off the train, told the others in his party they ought to refill while they could.

Someone had dug a well close to the depot and Percy turned the crank that drew a bucket up from below. The water didn't look or smell any different from that back home, and after a taste he didn't notice any difference. The water, however, was cool and refreshing. Percy dipped the accompanying ladle into the pail and dumped the water over his head. The relief was instantaneous, and a rash of goose bumps appeared on his arms. After unscrewing the lids, he poured out the old, stale water, and refilled the canteens.

A line had now formed at the well, the other passengers eager for some fresh water. Percy carried the canteens back inside and put on his cowboy hat before exiting again. His back ached from the hard bench seat and he twisted one way then the other, trying to loosen his aching muscles. It didn't help much, and Percy wasn't looking forward to the rest of the journey. By his count they still had many hours to go and he looked with envy at the passengers climbing down from the Pullman Palace car. He muttered a curse word or two, asked one of the conductors how long the stop would be, then made his way down the tracks to the dining car and climbed up.

One of the waiters gave him some lip about being there and Percy wanted to tell him that he'd buy the entire damn train just to fire his ass, but didn't. Instead, he ordered ham sandwiches for everyone in the group and took a seat at one of the tables to wait for them to be prepared. The leather chair was much more comfortable than the bench seat and Percy made a promise to himself to insist on a Pullman sleeping car for the return trip—whenever that might be. As of now, he didn't even know where to start the hunt for Emma, Simon, and Autumn.

While waiting, he quizzed several of the waiters about the train wreck down around El Paso and didn't learn much.

If someone knew who the robbers were, they weren't talking. He was hoping his mother had found out some information on her end so they could hit the ground running.

It wasn't long until one of the waiters returned with a stack of paper-wrapped sandwiches. Percy paid the man and exited the car. He walked down the tracks to the flatcar where Moses, Win, and Luis were working to clean and oil the guns. The wagon drew gawkers at every stop and Percy worked his way through the crowd and handed the sandwiches to his crew. He told the three about the well up by the depot and worked his way back through the crowd, heading back to their passenger coach. He passed out the rest of the sandwiches and took his, along with his canteen, back outside. Percy was unwrapping his sandwich and was about to take a bite, when he heard someone call his name. He turned to see his old friend Charlie Goodnight. He rewrapped the sandwich and shook hands with Goodnight.

"What're you doin' down this way, Charlie?"

"Been to Fort Worth to take care of some business and now I'm headed down to Midland to see about buyin' some more land."

"Ain't you got enough yet?" Percy asked. "How many acres you got already?"

Goodnight shrugged. "Somewhere north of a million, I reckon."

Percy whistled. "Well, I guess you and ol' fancy-pants John Adair are gettin' along just fine."

"It ain't easy, that I can tell you," Goodnight said.

"Y'all stringin' any of the devil's rope out your way?"

"We put up a couple of drift fences, but that's about it. Heard y'all been havin' some trouble with fence cutters."

"They's a menace, for sure. Don't know how it's goin' to end, but it could get ugly."

"A shootin' war?" Goodnight asked.

"Maybe," Percy said. "We ain't there yet, but we're gettin' closer every day. I know it sounds awful to talk about killin' someone over a wrecked fence, but fixin' 'em costs real money."

"I know it does. I hope y'all get it settled soon before it spreads out our way."

"We're tryin'."

"You're a long way from home."

Percy told him about the train wreck and subsequent kidnapping.

"Last time I saw your pa, y'all was lookin' for someone then, too. Ain't you got enough on your plate, runnin' that bunch of cattle of yours?"

"Gotta do what I gotta do," Percy said. "You know how it is. Any ideas about who mighta robbed the train?"

"None. That part of the country, the robbers and killers is thick as ticks." Goodnight nodded toward the back of the train. "That's got to be your wagon tied down to that flatcar."

"It is. Don't know how much good it'll do us with all the rough terrain down that way."

"I been all over the country and ain't never seen another wagon like it. You rake them with that Gatling gun and then lob a few shells from that howitzer and you'll put the fear of God in 'em."

"Gotta separate them from the hostages first. Ain't gonna be easy. You hear anything about what they might have stolen off the train? They derailed it and killed a bunch of people doin' it."

"I heard rumors," Goodnight said.

"Well?" Percy said.

Goodnight lowered his voice and said, "I heard they took eight thousand dollars in gold—"

"That don't make no sense," Percy said, cutting Goodnight off.

"You didn't let me finish. They also stole a half a million dollars in railroad bearer bonds. Know what that means, don't you?"

Percy was momentarily taken aback. "I do. They're untraceable and payable upon receipt to the man holdin' 'em."

"Yep."

"Why in the hell would they want to mess with a bunch of hostages, then? With that much money, the whole gang could live like kings for the rest of their days."

"Don't know, Percy," Goodnight said. "Greed's a powerful thing."

"Well, they ain't gonna be able to spend any of it anyway, 'cause I aim to kill 'em all."

"And I have no doubt you will."

One of the conductors stepped down and shouted, "All aboard!"

"Hey, listen Charlie, I want to thank you for takin' on my son-in-law and for lettin' 'em live at your place."

"Joe's a hell of a hand and Amanda's a sweetheart. We love havin' them and the kids around."

"Keep an eye on those young'uns for me. Sure will be glad when the railroad makes it out that way."

"You and me, both," Goodnight said. The two men shook hands and boarded the train. Percy retook his seat and unwrapped his sandwich again, wondering how the railroad had let five hundred thousand dollars in bearer bonds slip through their hands. Whoever had taken them, it was clear to Percy that at least one of the kidnappers had good sources and was a meticulous planner. And that soured his stomach a tad bit.

CHAPTER
57

With no trees anywhere in sight across the desolate landscape, shade was as scarce as water appeared to be and Emma's mouth felt like it was full of cotton. Since the train wreck had happened in the dead of night, all of the captives were shoeless, and the ground was rough and rocky, ripping their soles to shreds. And to add to her misery, Emma had slipped on a short-sleeved nightshirt because of the oppressive heat, and she could already feel her arms and neck beginning to burn. She did her best to force all of that from her mind and turned her focus to the two young charges in her care.

It was now late afternoon and they hadn't had a bite of food or a drink of water since they'd begun their trek well before daylight. Emma knew she could endure, and Simon appeared to be holding up, but Autumn concerned her. The chubby young boy tied on after Autumn was struggling mightily and every time he stumbled or fell, it pulled the rope tight around Autumn's neck. Her throat was red and raw, and Emma was doing her best to maintain some slack in the rope to give Autumn a break. Emma had thought about pulling her knife out to cut the boy loose but didn't, wanting to hold on to her ace in the hole as long as possible. The only advantage she had was the element of surprise and she needed to leverage that as much as possible. Her only option was to wait until dark before trying anything.

The five mounted men were well hydrated, having guzzled from their canteens throughout the day. That told Emma there was water ahead somewhere and they just needed to hold on until they found it. Their captors didn't spend much time talking among themselves and Emma hadn't gleaned any useful information. If they were planning to ransom them, they would need some way to communicate and she hadn't figured that part out yet. Off in the distance, she saw what looked like a small town, which might have a telegraph office although their current course would take them east of there by several miles. As far as Emma could tell, they were traveling almost due north and the only thing on the horizon in that direction was a group of funny-looking mountains about ten miles distant. If that was the final destination, Emma thought it would be well after dark before they arrived. At least darkness would bring relief from the unrelenting sun though it would also make travel more difficult, slowing their progress. Emma had to grudgingly admit she had no idea what their plans were, and all the speculation was burning energy she couldn't afford to lose.

However, she found it difficult to close her mind down and she continued to strategize. If they were going into the mountains, she liked her chances. If she could sneak the hostages away from camp and up to high ground, she might be able hold them off until help arrived. With that thought in mind, she stuck her hand into the pocket of her nightdress and ran her fingers over the precious few pistol cartridges she had recovered from the wrecked Pullman car. Slowly she counted them: *one, two, three, four, and five.* When added to the chambered rounds in the revolver, she would have ten opportunities to kill five well-armed men. She knew those weren't good odds, but she also knew it was a damn sight better than being weaponless. And if she could take out one or two with her knife, she would be able to grab their weapons and improve their odds dramatically.

To be sure, Emma did have a few doubts about her ability to kill a man with a knife without botching the job. Stabbing and killing Scar had been a kill-or-be-killed moment and Emma had acted on instinct. Trying to sneak up close enough for knife work on able-bodied men was another matter entirely. But if she waited until the captors went to sleep before going after the guard they would surely post, then she thought it just might work. Of course, best-laid plans and all of that and Emma knew she was going to need to improvise.

She had identified Scarecrow and Stubby and now she turned her attention to the other three men. All three were of the same height and build and the similarity of their facial features suggested Indian ancestry somewhere in their recent past. Emma thought them brothers, or if not brothers, maybe cousins or some other form of close kinship. Whatever the relationship among them, they were definitely attached to the same family tree. She named them Hickory, Dickory, and Dock after the old English nursery rhyme. She wasn't going to waste much time inventing more creative names because she knew their time on earth was limited. That clock had begun counting down the instant they had made the decision to take captives.

It was well after dark when the ground beneath their feet began to rise. The moon was up and it provided enough illumination for them to pick their way forward. Emma estimated they had climbed for an hour when Stubby called for a stop. The exhausted prisoners dropped where they stood as the men began to unsaddle their mounts. Much like an animal could smell water a long distance from its source, Emma's nostrils flared at the scent of damp ground and she knew water was nearby.

Not knowing if their captors were going to allow them a chance to drink, Emma watched the men for a few moments as they began setting up camp then she started crawling, gently tugging on the rope to get the others moving. Speaking in whispers and following her nose, Emma urged Simon and Autumn on as those behind them began crawling. Emma could see a glint of moonlight reflecting off a pool of water just ahead and her fellow captives must have seen it, too, because the rope grew taught as those around her began crawling faster. When they reached the water, everyone fanned out around the pool and dropped to their bellies, lapping up the water like a pack of wild dogs.

Without warning, a line of fire raced up Emma's back a millisecond before the end of the whip cracked next to her ear. Emma bit down on her tongue to keep from crying out and rolled over on her back. She could see Stubby' s silhouette as he recoiled his whip. "You think I didn't see what you was doin'?"

"You expect us to walk all day without water?" Emma asked, wanting to reach for her pistol to obliterate the sneer on his face with a couple of well-placed bullets. But she quickly tamped down her rage, knowing the time wasn't right.

"Ask next time, bitch. Now get up. All of you," Stubby said.

Once everyone was on their feet, Stubby marched them into a shallow canyon where the walls on three sides soared high overhead.

"Sit your asses down," Stubby ordered. "Next person to talk or move, dies."

Emma reached down and ran her fingers across the handle of her knife. Stubby would pay for that lash with his life.

Clyde Hightower, aka Stubby, took a seat on a rock and wiped his sweaty face with his sleeve. He didn't give a damn about the hostages and could care less if they lived or died. That entire scheme had been hatched inside the brain of Jim Gatewood, a tall, toothless man who didn't have a lick of sense. Hightower had gone along with the plan only to placate Gatewood and it was obvious the man had no clue about what to do with the hostages now that he had them.

Usually preferring to work alone, Hightower teamed up with this group of nitwits only when he needed some muscle to complete a job. Unable to read or write, the other four men had no concept of the bonds he had removed from the safe aboard the train. Yes, he would take his cut of the loot when they divvied it up, simply to keep up appearances, but his plan was to slip away at the first opportunity, a half a million dollars richer for his efforts.

The train robbery had taken months of meticulous planning and Gatewood's insistence on taking hostages at the last minute had threatened to blow Hightower's carefully conceived plan sky-high. But Hightower had adapted on the fly and he was quite pleased with the results. The one thing he hadn't planned for was the high body count although no one could predict the ending result when derailing a train. And in the eyes of the law, it didn't really matter if he'd killed one or a hundred. You could hang only once.

The only burr under his saddle now was his disrupted timeline. Hightower should have been well south of the border by now and here he was, only twenty miles from the scene of the crime and, more important, still in the United States. He should have cut and run when that numbskull Thompson was busy tying up the hostages. The only reason Hightower hadn't gone was because they hadn't yet divided up the take from the train and it would have created questions even in the feeble minds of his cohorts.

It wasn't all bad that he was still there. That pretty gal who now had a red welt on her back was a real looker— prime meat he was planning to get a taste of before departing. Hell, he wondered, why not take her with him? He wiped his face again as he pondered that question. She'd be good for at least a month or maybe longer and if she got to be too much of a burden, he could slit her throat, and no one would be the wiser. Sure, she might slow him down a little and if he'd been farther from the border, it might have been a concern. As it was, he could kill that idiot Thompson in his sleep, take his horse, ride hard for few hours, and still be in Mexico before anyone noticed they were gone. Or better yet, since he had suggested they picket the horses outside the canyon so they could graze, he could just take Thompson's horse and go. The more he thought about it, the more he liked it. And who knew, with a little food and water, he might could keep her around a lot longer. As far as he knew, no one had ever died from an occasional poke.

In the moonlight, Emma could read Stubby's face as if reading a book. His eyes narrowed when he looked her way and she knew exactly what was going on inside that diseased mind of his. It was the same way Scar had looked at her just before he had attacked. Emma didn't think the man was foolish enough to try anything now, but she knew it was coming. And she would be prepared.

Her thoughts were interrupted when Hickory handed her a cold corn tortilla. The prisoners stood and shuffled past a pot of cold beans. After spooning some beans onto their tortillas, the captives sat again, chewing their food in silence. Simon and Autumn snuggled up close to her and she shoved the last of her food into her mouth and wrapped her arms around them. The temperature had dropped since the sun went down and that was a welcome relief.

Simon looked up at his mother and whispered, "Is help comin'?"

Emma nodded and whispered, "Sometime tomorrow. You two just hang on a little longer." Emma turned to look at Autumn and said, "You holdin' up?"

"I wanna go home," Autumn whispered.

Emma gave her a squeeze and said, "Me, too. Soon, okay?"

Autumn nodded.

Emma turned and began sweeping rocks off the ground behind them. The terrain was hard and uneven and totally unfit for sleeping. When she had cleared all the rocks she could, they stretched out and the children snuggled up against her. Exhausted, it wasn't long before Emma heard the steady breathing of deep sleep coming from both of them. Slowly, and as gently as possible, Emma sat up and removed the rope from around her neck. If Stubby was planning a visit, she didn't want Simon and Autumn involved.

Sitting there, Emma took a moment to study the camp and saw that two guards had been posted. One was near the mouth of the canyon and the other was perched on an outcropping of rocks about ten feet above the floor of the ravine. That might be a problem, Emma thought. Even with the ground in deep shadow now, by the time the moon reached its apex, the floor of the canyon would be flooded with light and the second guard would be able to see everything that moved. She could only hope he fell asleep before Stubby made his move. Emma shifted her gaze to the area around her, picked out a spot away from the children, and crawled over.

She spent a few moments clearing the rocks then slipped the knife out of the sheath and stretched out, the handle gripped tightly in her right hand and the blade concealed under the folds of her nightdress. All she could do now was wait.

Thinking the hard, uneven ground and her aching body would combine to prevent her from drifting off to sleep, it wasn't long before her eyes grew heavy. Despite her best attempts, in a short while she was softly snoring.

Somctime later, Emma startled awake when someone clamped a hand over her mouth. Moving her right hand, she searched frantically for the knife as she opened her eyes to see Stubby staring down at her. He smiled, held up her knife, and whispered, "Looking for this?"

Emma groaned. She tried to open her mouth to bite his hand, but he was gripping her jaw so tightly she couldn't move it.

"I'm gonna keep my hand where it is till you stand up," he whispered. "You try to scream or run, I'll slit your throat. Got it?"

Emma nodded as she reached over to see if he had taken her pistol. When she felt the hard outline of the revolver's grip, her heart rate slowed. Stubby was in for a nasty surprise.

"Git up."

Emma sat up, tucked her knees under her, and pushed herself up. Stubby removed his hand and poked her arm with the tip of the knife. "Walk. We're leavin' the canyon."

Emma nodded and she began to walk. As they passed the man guarding the mouth of the canyon, Stubby said, "Goin' out for a little fun and games."

The guard chuckled and said, "Lucky bastard."

Laugh on, Emma thought. *This time tomorrow, your blood will have already soaked into this godforsaken ground.*

When they reached the area where the horses had been picketed, Emma saw that Mr. Efficient had already had a couple of them saddled. He pointed at the horse Scarecrow had been riding and mumbled something. Emma put her lacerated left foot in the stirrup and had to clamp her jaw shut to keep from screaming as she pulled herself up. Once she was seated, Stubby scooped up the reins of her horse and spurred his mount forward, leading Emma away from the canyon. He turned, looked at her, and smiled. When he turned back to the front, Emma snaked her hand up under her nightshirt and pulled out the pistol. Judging by the way he had looked at her, she had a hunch they wouldn't go too far before Stubby made his move. Emma was just hoping he'd wait long enough to put some distance between them and the camp so the others wouldn't hear the gunshot.

As they rode, Emma debated when to make her move. She wanted the first shot to be the kill shot and for that to happen she needed him close. At present, he was several feet in front of her and, although she was fairly confident she could kill him at that range, she knew there were risks involved when shooting from the back of a moving animal. A misstep or stutter could alter her aim and the last thing she needed was for him to get a hand on that pistol on her right hip.

The eastern horizon was glowing with the coming dawn when he stopped his horse and turned to look at her. He slowly licked his lips and said, "I reckon it's time for a little fun."

To alleviate any suspicion, Emma acted as if she were trembling and said, "P-p-please don't. You . . . you . . . can just . . . ride . . . ride . . . on."

Stubby laughed and climbed down from his horse. "I ain't gonna hurt you too bad. Now, get on down from there."

Emma needed him closer. "P-p-please . . . I . . . I . . . have . . . a . . . a . . . son . . . b-b-back . . . back . . . th-there."

Stubby stepped around his horse and grabbed her by the leg. "I said, get—"

His voice died in his throat when Emma jammed the pistol barrel against his forehead and pulled the trigger. His horse took off like a scalded cat and her horse jumped sideways and began to buck. Without the reins Emma had no way to control the horse, so she grabbed on to the saddle horn and rode it out. When the horse finally calmed, she stood in the stirrups, leaned forward, and grabbed the reins. Not knowing how things might turn out, Emma needed the other horse. She kicked her mount in the ribs and he went from standing to running in three strides.

The runaway hadn't gone far, and Emma grabbed the reins and rode back to the body. After dismounting, she unbuckled Stubby's gun belt, pulled it free, and climbed back on her horse. Now she needed to find a place where she could keep an eye on the camp.

CHAPTER
58

After rolling into Sierra Blanca before daybreak, the folks at the Southern Pacific Railroad had been very accommodating and it was now the middle of the afternoon and Percy and his crew were riding through the dusty streets of El Paso, Texas. Percy, mounted on Mouse, scanned the street, reading the signs and hoping to find a hotel that might be housing his family. Not expecting any trouble in town, Luis was the lone occupant in the war wagon and Chauncy, Marcie, Seth, Grace, Isaac, and Leander were mounted on their own horses. Moses Wilcox and Winfield Wilson were back at the wreck site unraveling the robbers' trail and would meet up with the rest of them somewhere along the line. A little farther up the street, Percy spotted a sign for the Grand Central Hotel and steered Mouse that way. It was the only hotel he'd seen and assumed it was the only one in town.

The women must have spotted them from inside because they rushed out as everyone dismounted. After hugs all around, Percy handed Chauncy some money and asked him and Luis to go stock up on supplies. They turned and headed across the street to the mercantile and Marcie hurried to catch up. Percy took his mother by the elbow and steered her gently down the boardwalk.

Percy looked at Frances's left arm in a sling and said, "How bad is it?"

"Broken collarbone. I'll live," Frances said.

"Anybody else in the family hurt?"

"Everyone is bruised and battered, but we're all alive. There's a bunch that aren't. Twenty-seven were killed in the train wreck and four more men were gunned down in the express car."

"Well, once I find 'em their robbin' and killin' days are over. How many men we talkin' about?"

"Five that I saw. A couple of white men and three that looked like they had a good dose of Indian blood."

"Don't really tell us much. I'm bettin' they made a bee-line for the border."

"That's what I thought, too, until I did a little askin' around. The ringleader's a short, fat man named Clyde Hightower. The man that told me that said Hightower might be holed up in the mountains about twenty miles north of here."

"You trust this guy?"

"I do. He was scared to death of this Hightower feller and his gang. Had to shell out two hundred dollars before he started talking."

"Well, I reckon we got a plan." Percy pulled out his pocket watch to check the time. "If we get movin' and ride hard, we might make it there before nightfall."

Frances took Percy's hand and looked him in the eyes. "Bring them home safe."

"We will." Percy leaned down and kissed his mother's

cheek. While still at eye level, he said, "Marcie and Grace came down here to help, so you let 'em."

"I'll find something for them to do."

"Good." He straightened up and he and Frances walked back to the others. Once the supplies were stowed away, Percy told the men where they were going, and they were riding out of town a few minutes later.

Two hours into the trip, they met up with Moses Wilcox and Winfield Wilson, who were trailing the robbers. Wilcox and Win rode on ahead and it wasn't long before the two trackers disappeared from sight. Other than dodging an occasional cactus, the traveling was easy, and they made good time.

At the four-hour mark, Percy and the crew caught up with Wilcox and Win, who had stopped. Percy nudged Mouse forward and he rode up next to Wilcox. "What's wrong?" Percy asked.

"Ain't no cover," Wilcox said. "Ain't no way to get close without 'em seeing us."

"Well, you got a plan or you wouldn't be sittin' here," Percy said.

"That I do." Wilcox pointed into the distance. "See that one little groupin' of mountains sittin' out there all by its lonesome?"

"I see it," Percy said.

"We get there, y'all cozy that wagon o' yours up in that little valley there. One man ain't gonna spook 'em none, so I'll ride on up and find out where they's at." Wilcox glanced up at the sky. "Be dark soon. Only cover we's gonna have."

"Makes sense," Percy said.

Wilcox clucked his tongue and spurred his horse forward. Percy and Win stayed where they were until the old tracker disappeared, then Percy waved everyone onward.

Thirty minutes later they veered right and rode a quarter of a mile up the treeless, grassless valley before Percy called a halt. Now all they could do was hunker down and wait.

With no wood within fifty miles, they made a cold camp and ate their supper of meat, vegetables, and fruit out of the tin cans they came in. Percy wished he had a cup coffee to wash it all down but settled for a drink from his canteen instead. Once he finished, he stretched out on the ground. After hours in those miserable train seats and more time in the saddle, his back was stiff and achy.

As he lay there, Percy ran a few scenarios through his head, trying to figure out how the night might play out once Wilcox returned with a scouting report. He knew now that bringing the war wagon along was overkill, but at that time they had no idea how many men they might be up against. Since they'd gone to all that trouble to bring it, he had every intention of using it. All of that firepower would create one hell of a diversion when they were ready to make their move.

Finding no relief for his back, Percy rolled over onto his side and put his hands beneath his head to act as a pillow. But it wasn't long before his hands went to sleep so he rolled over onto his back and stared up at the stars. Feeling around, he found a fist-sized rock and he slid it beneath his back to put some reverse pressure on his spine. He was getting too damn old to go traipsing around the country.

The moon had been up a couple of hours when Wilcox finally returned to camp. Percy, who had given up on finding any comfort from the hard, rocky ground, jumped down from the back of the wagon and called the others together. Weary from the journey, Wilcox groaned and cussed as he climbed down from his horse. Once on the ground, he placed his hands on his hips, arched his back, and muttered another string of curse words. Once he had limbered up some, he kneeled on the ground and pulled out his large bowie knife.

The moon was bright enough to read a newspaper if one held it at the proper angle and the men had no trouble seeing what Wilcox was drawing in the dirt.

"They's camped up in a canyon," Wilcox said, using the back of his knife blade to draw a horizontal U shape in the dirt. "Far as I can tell ain't but one way in, but you can see down where they's camped from this ridge right here." Wilcox drew a wavy line under his drawing of the canyon.

Percy squatted down next to Wilcox and said, "Why would they box themselves in?"

Wilcox shrugged. "Might be there's another way out. Can't really tell without ridin' down for a look-see."

"How many men did you see?"

"They's four of them, but you can't really tell 'cause the canyon's in shadow."

"Then how do you know there's only four?"

"Emma told me," Wilcox said. "Said they was five, but she done took care of one of 'em."

"Emma tell you this by using sign language or what?" Percy asked, confused.

"Nope, we talked," Wilcox said. He pointed at the wavy line in the dirt. "She's up on that there ridge, right now."

"I'll be damned," Percy muttered. "How may captives total?"

"Seven now that Emma got away."

"Did she say—never mind, I'll ask her myself.

"Guards?" Percy asked.

"Two." Wilcox drew an X near the mouth of the canyon.

"One here and another upon a ledge about here," Wilcox said, making another *X* about halfway down the lower leg of the U. Wilcox looked up at Percy. "You got a plan?"

"Not yet, but it ain't gonna take me and Leander long to make one."

Leander squatted down next to Percy and they passed Wilcox's knife back and forth as they hatched their plan. When they were in agreement, they detailed the plan for the rest of the men.

Everyone would climb the ridge so that they could see the layout of the camp. Once that was established, Chauncy and Emma would remain on the ridge with their rifles to take out the guard on the ledge and provide cover fire if the bad guys made a move for the captives. Moses, already exhausted, volunteered to handle the horses. Luis, Isaac, and Win were going to man the wagon, which would be parked near the mouth of the canyon. When Percy gave the signal, they would fire the howitzer and Gatling gun out into the desert and Percy and Leander would sweep into the canyon on foot, taking out the guard at the entrance and neutralizing the other two kidnappers, either by killing or capturing them.

"The one thing we can't do," Percy said, "is let them grab one of the captives." He looked up at Chauncy and said, "If you or Emma has a clear shot, take it."

"We will," Chauncy said. "How are you going to get the wagon close without spooking the guard?"

"We don't need it that close," Leander said. He turned to look at Luis. "Once you've shot your wad, hop onto the seat and drive the wagon across the mouth of the canyon."

"Sí, jefe," Luis said.

"Any other questions?" Leander asked.

When no one spoke up, Percy said, "Mount up. We'll let Wilcox tell us when to dismount."

An hour later and after a careful visual survey of the camp to pinpoint the remaining kidnappers' positions, everyone was ready. The wagon was parked about a hundred yards away and Percy and Leander were lurking around the entrance of the canyon. The guard posted just inside was dead to the world, his snores echoing softly off the surrounding hardscape. Wondering if they should rethink their strategy, Percy leaned in close to Leander and whispered, "Think we should hold off on the wagon guns?"

Leander shook his head and whispered, "We need it to mask our own gunfire. Either way they're gonna wake up, but when that howitzer fires, they're gonna think the wrath of God's rollin' down on 'em."

Percy nodded. He turned to the wagon and waved his arm and he and Leander plugged their ears with their fingers. Percy and Leander were moving before the shockwave arrived. They pulled their pistols and raced into the canyon. The first guard was in the process of getting up when Leander's bullet pierced his forehead and he was dead before he hit the ground.

The *rat-a-tat* of the Gatling gun was loud in the night and, with the canyon floor now bathed in moonlight, they could see a few of the frightened hostages screaming and pushing to their feet. Leander and Percy shouted for them to get down as they scanned for the last remaining outlaws. Percy motioned to the right with his pistol and he and Leander split up, working their way around the group of captives, their heads on swivels.

The Gatling gun finally fell silent and when they met

up on the other side, Percy said, "Where the hell did those other two go?"

The answer came a second later when a rifle round zinged off a giant boulder about sixty feet away. Percy and Leander turned to look up at the ridge and saw Chauncy standing, his rifle pointed at the giant rock and two fingers held high in the air. Percy waved to let him know he understood, then he and Leander squatted down to reduce their target profile and discussed options.

"Why don't you hustle the hostages out of here before someone gets hurt?" Percy asked.

Leander took his eyes off the boulder long enough to look at Percy. "And let you have all the fun? Together, we can wrap this up in about sixty seconds."

"You're more stubborn than a damn mule," Percy said. "Left or right?"

"It don't seem to matter which hand you shoot with so I'll take right."

"Cover me," Percy said. He stood and started running.

Trying to control the trajectory of the ricochets, Leander peppered both sides of the boulder with five well-placed shots. He ejected the spent shells and reloaded, waiting for Percy to give him the signal. Pain flared from an old bullet wound in Leander's right leg when he stood so he hobbled forward when Percy signaled.

Percy shifted his pistol to his left hand, held up three fingers on his right, and began counting down. When the last finger dropped, both men moved off in opposite directions, working their way around the massive rock. Four seconds later their pistols roared almost simultaneously, and the last two train robbers crumpled to the ground.

Both Leander and Percy ejected their spent shells and reloaded.

"What do you want to do with the bodies?" Leander asked.

Percy holstered his pistol and said, "Wolves and buzzards gotta eat, don't they?"

"Works for me," Leander said as he reseated his revolver.

The two men walked over to check on the hostages as Emma and Chauncy made their way down from the ridge. With the hostages hobbling around with their lacerated feet, Percy asked Luis to drive the wagon up the canyon to save them a few steps.

Leander scooped up his daughter and peppered her face with kisses. Autumn giggled and Leander thought it the sweetest sound he'd heard in a long while.

Once she reached level ground, Emma ignored the pain radiating up through the soles of her feet and hurried over to Simon, wrapping her arms around him.

Win, Wilcox, and Luis began opening the canned food and they passed it out to the hungry group. Although still battered and bruised from the train wreck and exhausted from their ordeal, the freed captives were in high spirits. Effusive with their thanks, the men were sheepish and somewhat embarrassed by all the praise. After all, they'd done only what needed doing.

Once everyone had eaten and the canteens refilled, the freed hostages began loading onto the wagon and Percy pulled Emma aside.

"Tell me about the guy you tangled with," Percy said.

"I nicknamed him Stubby," Emma said. "Believe me, he got exactly what he deserved."

Percy nodded and said, "No doubt. Which horse was his?"

Emma pointed at a bay gelding and said, "That one."

"I'm gonna take his saddlebags, okay?"

"Sure. What's in 'em?" Emma asked.

"If I find what I'm lookin' for, I'll show you when we're back on the train."

Percy walked over to Hightower's horse and unbuckled the saddlebag flaps for a peek. As he expected, the bearer bonds were inside, so he untied the bags and carried them over to Mouse and tied them on to his saddle. He'd need to do some thinking on the way back to El Paso. Having no intention of keeping them, the fact that they were untraceable meant the bonds would require delicate handling. And the last thing he wanted was for someone to find out he had them in his possession. If word got out that a half a million dollars in easy money was floating around, it would incite every crazy in the state of Texas. Preferring to arrive back home upright and walking, Percy realized he would need to leave El Paso as quickly as possible.

Once everyone was situated, Percy and Leander led them out of the canyon.

CHAPTER
59

When Percy and the crew rolled into El Paso around noon, people swarmed out of the hotel and the loved ones who had been taken were tearfully reunited with their families. After a lot of backslapping, hand shaking, and offers of drinks on the house, Percy finally separated from the crowd. With Hightower's saddlebags slung over his shoulder, he went looking for his mother, who had disappeared during the reunion. He found her seated in the hotel lobby and she stood from her chair to give him a hug.

"How hard were they to find?" Frances said, breaking the embrace and stepping back.

"With Wilcox and Win along, not too hard. Were you worried we wouldn't find 'em?"

"Of course not. I never once doubted you, now or ever. It's not in your nature to give up. And the robbers?"

"Their robbin' days are done."

"Good. Makes the world a better place." Having lived through all this before when Emma was abducted the first time, Frances looked around, lowered her voice, and said, "Were the captives abused?"

Percy knew exactly what she was asking. "No. That Hightower feller tried, but Emma put an end to him."

"She's tough as nails, that one. But I worry all the bad stuff she's been through is goin' to take a toll at some point."

"Bad stuff happens and the only thing you can do is deal with it and move on," Percy said. "I ain't too worried about Emma."

"I hope you're right."

"Are y'all goin' on to San Francisco when the wreck's cleared?"

"No. All we want to do is go home."

"I don't blame you there. I'm gonna ride over to the train station and see if I can make it happen."

"Want to leave your saddlebags with me?" Frances asked.

"Naw, I'll hang on to it."

Percy exited the hotel, climbed aboard Mouse, and rode to the train station. His first stop was the telegraph office. He spent a moment composing the message in his mind then stepped up to the man behind the counter. The telegraph operator was a graying, portly man with round, wire-rimmed spectacles perched on his nose.

"Need to send a message?" the telegraph operator asked.

Percy hesitated. If the operator blabbed, all hell would break lose. But, as far as he could see, he didn't have much choice. Percy stuck out his hand and said, "I'm Percy Ridgeway."

"Frank McFarland," the man said, shaking Percy's hand. "Nice to meet you, Mr. Ridgeway."

"Likewise," Percy said. He gave McFarland a long look and said, "Can I trust you, Mr. McFarland?"

"Well, that's not somethin' I get asked every day, but yes, you can trust me, Mr. Ridgeway. Would you like to send a message?"

"I would."

McFarland pulled a pencil from behind his ear and said, "Who do you want to send the message to?"

"Mr. Leland Stanford."

Hearing the name, McFarland's pencil stopped moving for a few seconds before he continued.

"Think you can find where to send it?" Percy asked.

"I'll find it," McFarland said. "Shouldn't be too hard since he owns a good chunk of the Southern Pacific Railroad."

Percy smiled.

"The message?" McFarland asked.

"Dear Mr. Stanford. Have something that will be of significant interest to you that I reacquired on your behalf near El Paso. Request private train, El Paso to Wichita Falls. Will meet your representative there. Attach my name and send it, please."

"Will do," McFarland said. "I'll bring you his response. You stayin' at the hotel?"

"I'll wait," Percy said.

"Might take a while," McFarland said.

"That's fine." Percy walked over to a chair in the lobby and took a seat. He assumed a railroad bigwig like Leland Stanford had dozens of telegraphers at his beck and call and he didn't think it would take long to get an answer. Exhausted after being up all night, Percy was really looking forward to his feather bed back home.

The ticking of a grandfather clock and the clatter of the telegraph keys filled the silence and it wasn't long before Percy found himself dozing off—a dangerous thing to do when toting around a half a million dollars. To ward it off, he stood, exited the office, and walked around the depot's loading platform.

He hadn't gone far when McFarland stuck his head out the door and called him back.

"Mr. Stanford's assistant wants to know how you'd like the train configured," McFarland said.

Percy was damn sure he wasn't riding back home in a third-class passenger coach, so he said, "A Pullman sleeper, a flatcar, and a couple of freight cars with plenty of forage for horses."

"Want a dining car, too?" McFarland asked.

Percy didn't want to appear greedy, but he was still pissed about the trip down and those greasy ham sandwiches. "Think he'll go for it?" Percy asked.

"Won't cost any extra to ask," McFarland said.

"Sure."

"Give me a moment to relay the information," McFarland said before ducking back inside.

Percy opened the door and followed McFarland. McFarland scooted behind the counter and began tapping on his little machine. How the entire thing worked was a mystery to Percy. He didn't know how the messages arrived at the right destination and he was a little worried that someone else had read his message to Stanford. Percy pointed at McFarland's machine and said, "Can anyone else read that?"

McFarland shook his head and continued tapping. Percy waited until he finished to ask again.

"The railroad uses a cipher code for messages like yours. By using a key, only the sender and receiver can decode the message."

Percy didn't understand all that cipher business. "So, no one else could read that message?"

"No. Your train will meet you in Belen in four hours."

"Where's Belen?" Percy asked.

McFarland pointed at the railroad tracks running off into the distance. "Thirteen miles that way."

"That'll work," Percy said. "Thank you."

McFarland handed Percy a piece of paper and said, "Mr. Stanford's assistant sent something along to help identify his representative when you two eventually meet."

Percy opened the note and read the words: *Give me the splendid, silent sun with all his beams full-dazzling.*

"A quote from Mr. Walt Whitman, I believe," McFarland said.

Percy refolded the note and tucked it in his shirt pocket. "Tried to read some of his stuff and didn't get far."

"He's different, that's for sure. Travel safely, Mr. Ridgeway."

The two men shook hands again and Percy took his leave. He thought everything was going great until he returned to the hotel. Eager to slip out of town unnoticed, he had forgotten about the mountain of luggage that now needed to be hauled to Belen. They'd be able to load a few onto the war wagon and Percy was okay with that as long as the guns remained functional. A lot could happen with thirteen miles to cover. That directive was met with resistance and more than one argument erupted because of it.

Leander finally ended the standoff by hiring a couple of wagons from a local livery. Once they were loaded and the hotel bill was paid, Percy made sure the howitzer was loaded and they set out. Percy hung toward the back to make sure no one was following, and Leander took the point. Win and Wilcox were ranging out ahead of the group, looking for any signs that might represent an impending threat. Before leaving town, Percy had shared the secret of the bonds with Leander and he now knew to be on the lookout for trouble. But the bearer bonds weren't Percy's only concern. Even if no one knew what he was carrying, it was fairly obvious from their clothing and equipment that they were people of means and, with all that luggage piled up in the wagons, he knew they were prime targets for any would-be robbers in the area. And, at present, the guns weren't even being manned, something Percy thought needed to change and quickly. Percy spurred Mouse into a trot and rode forward to ask Chauncy and Isaac to man the weapons, which they agreed to do. Luis slowed the wagon enough for them to get on and they tied their horses off at the back. That accomplished, Percy dropped back and asked the hired wagon drivers to close the gap.

"Why are you so nervous?" his mother asked. She, Rachel, and Autumn were riding in the first wagon and Emma, Abigail, Clara, and Simon occupied the second wagon.

Percy shrugged. "This is rough country full of rough people. Keep an eye out."

Percy dropped back farther then turned his horse and rode back over their trail for a quarter of a mile, his eyes scanning for movement or dust clouds in the distance. He didn't know what had him on edge but he'd learned over the years not to ignore it. No one was behind them and there were no other indications that anyone was following. Still, he couldn't shake the feeling. He turned Mouse around and trotted back to the group.

After riding for a while, Percy finally identified what was bothering him. The railroad tracks ran almost parallel with the Rio Grande and in some places the distance between the two could be measured in feet. If someone was hiding down the river bottom and decided to attack, they'd be on them in a matter of seconds. And their first targets would be Chauncy and Isaac, the two wagon gunners and that thought made Percy extremely uncomfortable. Not only were his son and his brother-in-law in the line of fire, if they went down or if the gun jammed or the howitzer misfired, there was a good chance they'd be overrun. Percy steered Mouse right for a closer look at the river.

With the lack of rainfall, the river was mostly dry with a small trickle of water running through the main channel. Nudging Mouse down the bank, Percy could see plenty of tracks though he didn't know if they'd been made in the last thirty minutes or the last thirty days. Percy pulled on the reins, bringing Mouse to a stop. Wilcox would know all of that and more and he debated calling him down for a look then decided it was best to leave Wilcox where he was. Not only was he an excellent tracker, he could also sniff out trouble well before it started and the numerous tracks on the road suggested they were traveling a frequently used thoroughfare.

Looking into the distance, Percy didn't see any obvious signs that a group of robbers were lying in wait. There was, however, plenty of cover in which to hide with a thick stand of trees running along both sides of the river's current course. Clucking his tongue, Percy put Mouse in motion. He rode along the sandy bottom a few more minutes and still didn't detect any signs of an imminent threat. Wondering if he was crazy, he was steering Mouse toward a game trail up the bank when he heard a horse snort. He whipped his head around to see a dozen riders breaking out of the trees.

Percy buried his spurs into Mouse's ribs and the big mare squatted for a half second then lunged forward, quickly gobbling up ground. Mouse hit the game trail at a full run, and she surged over the top and lengthened her stride even more on the flat ground. Percy pulled his pistol and snapped off three shots in the direction of the riders, more as a warning to the others than anything else. Percy looked ahead. He was three hundred yards away and closing quickly. The two hired wagons made sharp left turns, trying to put some distance between them and the war wagon. Percy hoped they kept going so that his mother and the rest of the family wouldn't bear witness to what was to come.

Percy glanced over his shoulder and was glad to see his lead had lengthened considerably. Turning back to the front, he could see Chauncy with a hand on the Gatling gun's crank and Isaac ready at the howitzer. Percy didn't know if the men chasing him were dumber than a stump or if they just hadn't done much scouting before deciding to attack. Either way they were in for a rude awakening. Using his knees, he steered Mouse a little more to the left and held that course until he was a hundred yards out then made a sweeping right-hand turn, bringing the men behind him broadside to the guns.

Not that Percy was hoping for a slaughter, which would have happened if he'd waited longer to make his turn. The spread of the cannon's canister shot at a hundred yards would still be lethal though more dispersed, meaning the survivability rates would be a bit higher. Percy glanced back and saw a couple of riders peeling away from the pack. Either they'd seen the weapons, or they had lost their nerve.

Percy streaked past the wagon at full gallop and was in the process of slowing Mouse when the cannon thundered. He wheeled the mare around as the Gatling gun started up, chasing those left alive back toward the river. Percy walked his horse back to the wagon and shouted, "Cease fire!"

Chauncy lifted his hand from the crank and the gun fell silent.

Not knowing if Luis would be able to hear him, Percy pointed at him, cocked his wrist down, and wiggled the first two fingers in a walking motion. With the smell of gunpowder and blood in the air, the mules were jittery, and it took Luis a couple of slaps with the reins to get them moving. Percy waved the other wagons forward and shouted for the drivers to maintain their current course. He didn't want the family to see all the severed limbs, both human and animal, or all the gore.

Leander rode up beside Percy and said, "I hope we never have to shoot that damn cannon again."

"I hear ya," Percy said. "How many men did you count chasin' me?"

"Thirteen."

"How many got away?"

"Four, maybe five. A round from the Gatlin' gun mighta caught the last one."

Percy nodded. He turned Mouse and let her set the pace as Leander fell in beside him. There was no joy in what they'd done, and Percy was kicking himself for drawing them in that close.

Leander looked over and said, "I know what you're thinkin'. You gotta remember they made their own choices.

And I can promise you those men weren't a bunch of choirboys."

Percy took in a deep breath, held it for a moment, and released it. "I know. It just turns my stomach to see somethin' like that."

"As it would for most people," Leander said. "Part of what makes us human."

Percy and Leander rode on in silence, each busy with their own thoughts. There were no other incidents along the way and Percy was glad to see the train already there when they rode up to the depot in Belen. After loading on all the trunks and bags with the help of two Pullman porters, Leander cut the rented wagons loose and the drivers headed back to El Paso, no doubt with a story to tell.

Using a block and tackle, they loaded on the wagon and secured it to the flatcar as Win and Luis took charge of the horses and mules. Once everything was loaded, Percy walked up to the locomotive to talk to the engineer. He climbed the steps up to the cab and introduced himself.

"Alonzo Briggs," the engineer said, shaking Percy's hand.

"Straight shot to Wichita Falls?" Percy asked.

Briggs nodded. "Other than a few stops to refill the tender we're full go all the way." He looked at Percy and scratched his head. "Mr. Ridgeway, I don't know who your friends are, but this here train's got the right of way all the way to Wichita Falls. Ain't never seen anything like it."

Percy chuckled. "Probably be the last time for both of us, too." Percy turned to leave, then stopped and turned back. "Alonzo?"

"Yes, Mr. Ridgeway?"

"The last train the ladies were on wrecked."

Briggs's eyes widened in surprise. "Well, it ain't gonna happen on my watch."

"Good to hear," Percy said. "We're ready when you are." He climbed down from the cab and made his way to the Pullman sleeper. Stepping aboard, he paused a moment to take it all in. He had traveled on a Pullman sleeper several times over the years, but the lavish interior of this one was over the top, with cut-glass chandeliers, walnut-paneled walls, and overstuffed armchairs.

"Little different than the trip down, huh?" Marcie asked.

"I'd say," Percy said, a note of wonderment in his voice. He walked over to where Chauncy was seated and squatted down beside him. "You okay, son?"

"Sure. Why wouldn't I be?"

"That's a hell of a thing you had to see."

Chauncy shrugged. "It's a cannon filled with canister shot. I kinda had an idea what was goin' to happen."

Percy wasn't all that surprised at Chauncy's reaction. He stood. "I'll talk to you later."

"Okay," Chauncy said.

Percy made his way across the car and took a seat next to his mother, who looked as tired as he felt. Percy took off his hat and put it and the saddlebags he'd been toting around on the floor. "Sorry you didn't get to see San Franny."

"The picture of it in my mind from all my reading is probably much better than the city anyway."

"You're probably right. A whole bunch of people all livin' in the same spot doesn't sound like much fun to me. How's the collarbone?"

"It aches some, but I'll live. Right now, I just want to go home and sleep in my own bed."

"Amen to that."

Frances turned to look at her son. "How did you know those men were going to attack?"

"I didn't know for sure. Just a feelin' I had. It has served me well over the years."

"Your father was the same way. He could smell trouble a mile away. Can I ask you to do something for me?"

"Sure," Percy said.

"Times are changin', Percy. I think it's time we did away with that awful wagon."

"How much of it did you see?"

"Enough to know I don't want to see anything like that ever again."

"As far as I'm concerned, it's going back in the barn never to be used again."

"Wouldn't it be better if you tore the damn thing apart?"

Percy shrugged. "I don't think either one of us can see the future. It's better to have it and not need it than to need it and not have it. And livin' where we do, next door to thousands of fickle Indians who might could stage an uprisin' at any time, I'd like to hang on to it a little longer."

"Good point. The wagon gets used only as a last resort."

"Agreed," Percy said.

"I know you're exhausted and so am I, but I'm dyin' to know how you pulled this private train outa your hat."

Percy leaned down and pulled Hightower's saddlebags onto his lap. After unbuckling the flap, he held the bag open for his mother to see.

"What are those?" Frances asked.

"Railroad bearer bonds. Know what those are?"

"Vaguely. I know they can't be traced. That what they took off the train?"

"Yep."

"How much are they worth?"

"A half a million dollars."

Frances was taken aback. "Oh Lordy. Now I understand why you was as jumpy as a cat cornered in a doghouse."

Percy chuckled. "Yeah. And I can't get rid of 'em fast enough."

The private train rolled into Wichita Falls eighteen hours after departing Belen, far faster than Percy could ever have imagined. Now midmorning, Percy put on his hat, picked up Hightower's saddlebags, tipped the Pullman porters handsomely, and stepped off the train. He had taken only a few steps when he was met by seven men, six of whom were heavily armed. A tall, thin man with a mustache and goatee stepped forward. He was carrying a handsome, beautifully stitched, leather bag, similar to a doctor's bag, which had probably cost a fortune.

"From the description I received, you must be Mr. Ridgeway."

"That's me," Percy said.

"My name is William Morrison and I'm here as an emissary for Mr. Leland Stanford."

The two men shook hands and Percy said, "Nice to meet you, Mr. Morrison."

Their conversation was momentarily interrupted when a locomotive arrived to pull the three freight cars off the main tracks so that Percy and his crew could unload them.

When they were clear, Morrison pulled a piece of paper from his coat pocket, handed it to Percy, and said, "A message from Mr. Stanford."

Percy unfolded the message and read it. Stanford praised Percy for being an honest man and for doing the right thing along with an offer of help anytime it was needed. Percy refolded the paper and stuck it in his back pocket. He looked at Morrison and said, "Not to be hardheaded but how do I know you are who you say you are?"

"I would have expected nothing less of you, Mr. Ridgeway," Morrison said. "I believe Mr. Stanford's assistant sent you something to help establish my identity."

Percy slipped the note out of his pocket and unfolded it. "He did."

Morrison mumbled something about rubbish and Whitman then said, "'Give me the splendid, silent sun with all his beams full-dazzling.'"

Percy slipped Hightower's saddlebag off his shoulder and handed it to Morrison, who immediately passed it on to one of the other men. Morrison lifted the handsome leather bag he was holding and said, "A token of gratitude from Mr. Stanford."

Percy held up his hands as if warding off something dangerous. "Use of the train was more than enough."

"Mr. Stanford was insistent. And he's not a man accustomed to hearing the word *no*. Take it, Mr. Ridgeway. You've earned it."

Reluctantly, Percy took the bag.

When Percy didn't make a move to open the bag, Morrison said, "Don't you want to know what's inside?"

"I wish you'd just take it back. I didn't bring those bonds back lookin' for a reward. And, like I said, that train was more than generous."

Morrison smiled. "Mr. Ridgeway, men like you are few and far between." He nodded at the bag in Percy's hand. "Please open it so that I might explain."

Percy lifted the flap and looked inside. What he saw were five smaller bags that were similar to the larger one, with the same elaborate stitching.

"For accounting purposes," Morrison said, "each bag contains ten thousand dollars in gold."

Percy was dumbfounded. He looked at Morrison and said, "That's way too much."

"Nonsense," Morrison said. "Did you enjoy Mr. Stanford's personal coach?"

"It's beautiful. How in the world did you get it there so fast?"

"Mr. Stanford has several coaches stationed around the country. The one you were on is stationed at Sierra Blanca most of the time."

Percy turned to look at the Pullman again then turned back. "How many of those does Mr. Stanford have?"

"Twenty or so at last count," Morrison said.

Percy turned back to look at Morrison. "Kinda makes you want to buy a railroad, huh?"

Morrison chuckled. "I don't think you or I want anything to do with the railroads right now. Half of them are bankrupt and the other are on the verge." He handed Percy a business card and said, "If you need anything, please don't hesitate to contact me."

"Thank you." Percy dropped the card inside the bag and stuck out his hand and the two men shook. "Please tell Mr. Stanford thank you."

"I will."

Morrison and his men loaded onto the same Pullman car the Ridgeway family had just vacated and Percy hadn't been expecting that. Not knowing how quickly the train would depart, he hurried toward the locomotive. When he reached it, he shouted up at Alonzo Briggs and waved for the engineer to come down.

Briggs climbed down the steps and walked over to

where Percy was standing. "I hope the trip was all right, Mr. Ridgeway."

"It was perfect." Percy dug down into his bag, pulled out one of the smaller ones filled with gold, and handed it to Briggs. "Share a little with your fireman."

Briggs looked confused. "What's this?"

"A gift of thanks."

Briggs tried to hand it back. "I get my wages from the railroad."

"I know you do. Think of it as a bonus for doin' a damn good job."

"You sure?" Briggs asked.

"I'm sure." Percy patted Briggs on the shoulder and walked around the nose of the steaming beast, headed for the freight cars. He hadn't gone far when he heard Briggs shout, "Lordy Jesus!"

Percy smiled and continued on. When he arrived, he saw that Mouse had already been unloaded and saddled.

"Everything all right?" Frances asked.

Percy looped the handle of the bag around his saddle horn and turned to face his mother. "Everything's just fine."

ACKNOWLEDGMENTS

The first round of thanks goes to you, the readers. Thank you for taking some time out of your busy lives to read.

Thanks to my terrific editor and good friend, Gary Goldstein.

A special shout-out to Doug Grad. Thanks for everything, Doug.

Thank you, Steven Zacharius. I'm eternally grateful to you and all the others who work at Kensington on my behalf, including Lou Malcangi, Elizabeth (Liz) May, James Akinaka, Crystal McCoy, Larissa Ackerman, and Vida Engstrand.

A special thanks to two people who have made me a much better writer—my production editor, Arthur Maisel, and my copy editor, Randie Lipkin.

Thanks to those who hold a special place in my heart: Kelsey, Andrew, Camdyn, and Graham Snider, Nickolas Washburn, and Karley Washburn. I love you all very, very much.

And lastly, to the woman who chose to share her life with me, Tonya. I love you forever and always.

CHAPTER
1

There was no hint of the approaching dawn when Cyrus Ridgeway pulled his rifle down from where it hung over the door and made his way outside, dropping wearily into one of the half-dozen rocking chairs that dotted the long front porch of their two-story home. He leaned the rifle against the house and sat back. Now at sixty-four, Cyrus had spent a majority of those years outside and on a horse and he didn't sleep well anymore. Too many aches and pains and something else—an ever-present worry that gnawed at Cyrus like a lingering toothache. And more than once he had cursed his ancestors for staking a claim to this land that, over the years, had absorbed a river of Ridgeway blood.

It's not that the ground under their feet wasn't fertile, because it was, the grass growing knee-high during the summer months and fattening the Ridgeways' ten thousand head of cattle. And it wasn't the climate, either. The area received adequate rainfall and most days were sunny and warm. No, what irked Cyrus was the location. Set hard against the Red River in northwest Texas, the Rocking R Ranch spanned for as far as the eye could see across more than forty thousand acres of relatively flat terrain. If it had been any other river it would have been acceptable. But not this river. And his contempt didn't have anything to do with the quality or quantity of water that flowed through her banks. In fact, it didn't have much to do with the river at all. No, his annoyance, disgust, and loathing stemmed from what was on the *other side* of the river—Indian Territory.

The Territory was home to a conglomeration of Indians, many of whom would rather slit your throat than look at you. And Cyrus thought he probably could have tolerated that if it was just the Indians he had to worry about. But it wasn't. There was more, much more, that kept him up at night. A lawless place, Indian Territory was also home to a large assortment of cattle rustlers, horse thieves, murderers, robbers, and would-be robbers, con men, swindlers, scoundrels, crooks, and many other nefarious no-gooders with evil on their minds. If Cyrus had a dollar for every stolen cow or horse, he would be rich—or rather—richer than he already was. His children and their families who lived on the ranch insisted the occasional losses should be chalked up to the cost of doing business. But that didn't sit well with Cyrus, who was a firm believer in protecting what was theirs, no matter the cost. And he'd gotten most of the stolen stock back over the years, with the thieves often paying a steep price for their transgressions when they found themselves at the end of a short rope that was tied to a tall tree.

Cyrus heard someone stirring around inside and listened to the footfalls, trying to decipher who was about to horn in on his quiet time. With a big family and four other homes on the place, it was difficult to know who was sleeping where on any given night. Most nights, a grandchild or two would slink up to his house after dark, well after Cyrus had already turned in. He didn't have to listen long to identify the footsteps as belonging to his wife, Frances. The door squealed when she opened it and stepped outside.

"What are you doing sitting out here in the dark, Cy?" she asked as she took a seat next to him.

"Can't sleep."

Frances reached out and put her hand on his back. "What's worrying that noggin of yours so early this morning?"

"Nothin' but the usual worries." Cyrus glanced in her direction. The moon glow was bright enough to see her profile and hints of her gray hair but not her individual features. And that was okay because Cyrus had them memorized by now, especially her blue eyes.

"That shoulder bothering you again?"

"Nah. Just can't sleep." Cyrus was a bear of a man at six-three with strong, powerful shoulders from a lifetime of hard work. He'd packed on a few extra pounds over the years and his once-dark hair was now mostly gray. With a full beard and mustache, he had started trimming it shorter after Frances teased him about looking like Santa Claus.

Frances removed her hand from his back and leaned back in her chair. "It's about time you let the boys carry some of the load."

"What about the girls, Franny? They not get a say in it?"

Cyrus and Frances had produced seven offspring, four of whom made it to adulthood—two sons, Percy and Elias, along with two daughters, Abigail and Rachel, the youngest. All now had families of their own and lived on the ranch.

"That'd probably be up to Percy. Shouldn't he get more say in who does what since he's the oldest?" Frances asked.

"Maybe," Cyrus said. "But I don't reckon any of it's writ in stone. And you're liable to stir up a passel of trouble if you ain't careful."

Frances clucked her tongue. "Decisions need to be made, Cy. We're not getting any younger." Tall at five-eight, her once-red hair was now gray and, lithe and lean as a teenager, her body was a bit stiffer but, remarkably, she still wore the same size dress as back then and still filled it out in all the right places.

"I ain't dead, yet," Cyrus said, a surly tone in his voice. "Besides, might be best to let the kids figure all that out when we're gone."

"Talk about stirring up trouble," Frances said. "I won't have my family ripped to pieces over this cattle ranch. We need a plan."

"What do you care? You'll likely be dead, too, fore it comes to that."

Frances sighed and pushed to her feet. "I'm going to put on some coffee."

Cyrus watched his wife's silhouette disappear into the house. His preference was to keep the ranch intact for the future generations, but Frances had mentioned a couple of times through the years that they should divvy it up and give it to the kids. "Over my dead body," Cyrus grumbled as he thought about it. Every time he pondered the situation, he ended up with a stomachache. The original Spanish land grant the ranch was founded upon had been in his family since Texas was still called Mexico, and Cyrus had added to their holdings over the years, buying up the farms and ranches of those who grew tired of fighting the Indians and the outlaws that drifted across the river. He'd worked too hard to make the ranch what it was and if the children wanted the land divided, they were going to have to wait until he was dead.

Cyrus wiped the sweat from his brow. August in this part of the country was hot, muggy, and miserable and those were the nighttime weather conditions. The same conditions existed during the day but were intensified about tenfold. The sun wasn't even up yet, and Cyrus was already damp with sweat. Thinking about the heat, a weariness crept into his bones. It didn't matter if it was scorching hot or finger-freezing cold, there was always work to be done—horses to be broken, cattle to be branded, corrals to be fixed, and on and on, all while keeping a watchful eye for marauding Indians, cattle rustlers, or others who might want what wasn't legally theirs. Sometimes Cyrus wished he had listened to Frances and moved to San Antonio when they were younger. And they might have if his two older brothers who were set to take over the ranch hadn't been slaughtered by a roving pack of Comanche savages while Cyrus and his new bride had been on a horse-buying trip to Saint Louis. Their deaths sealed Cyrus's fate because he was the last of the Ridgeway boys. But all that was years ago—

time that had slipped away, year after year, and, once Frances started having kids, leaving the ranch hadn't made any sense at all. Now here it was, 1873, and Cyrus knew his dead carcass would be buried up on the little knoll where they buried his brothers and all the children who had died way too early.

Frances returned a while later, handed her a husband a cup of coffee, and retook her seat just as the first rays of the sun stretched across the landscape. They sat in silence for a few moments as the orange orb peeked over the horizon. They had positioned the house so that they could watch the sunrise on the front porch and the sunset on the back porch. Hearing the clop of horses, Cyrus sat up and reached for the rifle he'd brought outside and then relaxed when the night riders rode past on their way to the bunkhouse.

"Good thing they weren't renegades," Frances said, "or they would have been on us before you could lever a shell into that rifle of yours."

"Hearin' ain't what it once was," Cyrus mumbled. "Maybe you ought to be the lookout since you still got all your faculties."

Frances chuckled. "Oh, Cy, you're doing just fine. Don't you think I'd have told you if trouble was headed our way?"

"Don't need my wife to tell me when there's trouble a-comin'. My damn eyes still work just fine." Cyrus turned to look at his wife. "We eatin' breakfast sometime today?"

Frances chuckled again. "Don't get all riled up, Cy. We all have our shortcomings." She stood and leaned over to kiss her husband on the cheek. "You'll always be my protector. What are you planning for the day?"

"Me and Percy and a few others are gonna track down them rustlers who stole them two steers yesterday afternoon."

"Aren't you getting a little old to be traipsing off after outlaws?"

"Like I said, I ain't dead yet. 'Sides, can't let them rustlers go unpunished or word would get out and we'd be robbed blind."

"And if you find them?"

Cyrus took a sip of his coffee then said, "Hang 'em, I reckon."

Connect with Us

Visit us online at
KensingtonBooks.com
to read more from your favorite authors, see books
by series, view reading group guides, and more.

Join us on social media

for sneak peeks, chances to win books and prize packs,
and to share your thoughts with other readers.

facebook.com/kensingtonpublishing
twitter.com/kensingtonbooks

Tell us what you think!

To share your thoughts, submit a review,
or sign up for our eNewsletters, please visit:
KensingtonBooks.com/TellUs.